ALSO BY NANCY CLARK

The Hills at Home

A Way from Home

Nancy Clark

A Way from Home

PANTHEON BOOKS, NEW YORK

All rights reserved. Published in the United States by Pantheon Books,
a division of Random House, Inc., New York, and in Canada by
Random House of Canada Limited, Toronto.

Pantheon Books and colophon are registered trademarks of
Random House, Inc.

Grateful acknowledgment is made to Random House, Inc., for permission to
reprint an excerpt from the poem "Law Like Love," copyright 1940 and
renewed 1968 by W. H. Auden, from *Collected Poems* by W. H. Auden.
Reprinted by permission of Random House, Inc.

Library of Congress Cataloging-in-Publication Data

Clark, Nancy, [date].
A way from home / Nancy Clark.
p.   cm.
ISBN 0-375-42328-1
1. Americans—Czech Republic—Fiction.   2. Prague (Czech Republic)—
Fiction.   3 . Americans—Libya—Fiction.   4. Libya—Fiction.   I. Title.

PS3603.L368W39 2005   813'.6—dc22   2004058731

www.pantheonbooks.com

Printed in the United States of America
First Edition
2 4 6 8 9 7 5 3 1

FOR MY SISTERS,
MARCIA AND BETH

Like love we don't know where or why,
Like love we can't compel or fly.
Like love we often weep,
Like love we seldom keep.

—From "Law Like Love," by W. H. Auden

Contents

A Way from Home

Summer, 1990

IN BETWEEN, UP IN THE AIR, *neither here nor there (yet), flying to Prague, Little Becky Lowe sat stuck in the middle seat, her parents settled on either side of her. Her mother had had to have the window seat; she had rendered herself insensible for the duration of the flight, downing her usual cocktail of gin and vermouth and a borrowed Valium at the departure gate just after the announcement bidding travelers with small children to begin boarding. Then, Becky had made the same old joke about herself being a simpering, whimpering child again, and, as she shook her pill from a twist of paper, Alden handed her the drink he ought not to have but had carried from the premises of the airport bar. Alden said the rules only applied to people who could not hold their liquor, and Little Becky used to think her father was referring to awful people who would have let their whiskey splash over their fingers and spill onto the gangway if not prevented.*

Her father always sat in the outside seat because it had long been established that Little Becky lolled; her foot strayed and her head rolled into the aisle and she was in danger of being clipped (and bloodied, once) by the service cart. Further, she made an unattractive nuisance of herself, impeding the other passengers as they negotiated their way back to the lavatory with that leaden tread of man in the air. In the past, on other flights, her brothers would have been sitting in the row behind, or the row in front. If in back, they would have kicked at her seat; if in front, they would have dangled things at her.

On this trip, however, her brothers had stayed behind in the States. Brooks and Rollins were enrolled for their final years of high school in an academy out west where a local uncle was going to keep an eye on them, and Glover had defied everyone and joined the army instead of going on to col

*lege as he was supposed to, although Alden and Becky had reconciled them-
selves to this, saying Glover was going to be learning plenty in the next few
years.*

*But you're coming with us, her parents had said. What a lucky girl you
are to have this opportunity to live in one of the world's great cities at this
most fascinating point in its long, rich history, they had said. Little Becky
had known enough not to ask if there was going to be a Banana Republic or
a Gap there, or a Tower Records or a Starbucks or a Tweeters or a Block-
buster or a Super CVS or a Saks. Her mother only mentioned museums and
concert halls and churches and architecture, so Little Becky was quite sure
there was no room left in Prague for anything good to be built.*

*Nor was the plane full, and it was never a positive sign when nobody else
wanted to visit a country; then again, at least she could have a bank of seats
to herself to stretch out on while she was being conveyed to such an un-
promising destination. Gently, she lifted her mother's languid hand, which
had come to rest upon her lap, and hefted her knapsack, incorrectly stowed
at her feet and packed with necessities: CDs and a Walkman and a bunch of
batteries and Sky Bars and L'Oreal hair conditioner and the light, strappy
sandals she had worn so successfully at her cousin's wedding a few weeks
earlier. She squeezed past her father, who did not try to stop her. He'd had
enough of her deep sighs and flailing elbows, and all he asked was to be left
in peace to read his book. Little Becky pitched down the aisle, dragged
along by the heavy knapsack, which she wore slung over a single shoulder.
She toppled into a row of seats as the plane shuddered through a cloudpack
and she figured here was as good as anywhere.*

*Presently, they came around with a flat, sealed dinner tray. She ate the
roll and the butter pat and picked the carrots from the salad and had a Sky
Bar for dessert. Then they darkened the cabin for the movie* My Left Foot,
*which Little Becky didn't think was going to do very much for her. The film
flickered onto the screen, running backward, this guy in a wheelchair rolling
around all backward, his frantic friends gesturing and running after him,
backward, until the movie itself seemed to run into a wall and shatter into
bits and pieces of scenery and actors. There was a smell of burning. A flight
attendant ran up the aisle and the screen fell blank.*

Little Becky had left her paperback in the pocket of her relinquished seat

(Paradise Lost, *on the summer reading list of the school she was going to be attending, and luckily she'd found the* Cliffs Notes). *Well, she wasn't about to return for it and risk being arbitrarily detained by her parents, so she was reduced to digging out her passport and musing over that for a while. The picture looked nothing like her, now. What a kid she had been. She wished she had thought to lose this passport so she could have been issued a new one with a more current and attractive representation of herself.*

"IN CASE OF DEATH OR ACCIDENT NOTIFY THE NEAREST AMERI- CAN DIPLOMATIC OR CONSULAR OFFICE AND THE INDIVIDUAL NAMED BELOW," she read. But no one had ever bothered to fill in the space below; her parents really were hopeless. Evidently, they couldn't care less whether she lay unclaimed (if dead) or unvisited (if gravely injured) in some funny foreign country.

She fished a pen from her knapsack (she'd brought three dozen black Bic Micro Metal pens in the event they didn't have Bics in Europe), and, steadying her passport against her knee, she wrote on the designated line: Bono Hewson. The guy from U2, *she added parenthetically. She filled in his home address and telephone number on the next line, which she happened to know; her brothers were computer geniuses and had found out the information through methods of their own and sold it to her for twenty-five dollars (well spent). Unfortunately, she would have to be dead before any- one phoned Bono on her behalf, but maybe he'd be inspired to write a song about her and whatever tragic circumstance had overwhelmed her. Not that Becky was a very promising name for songwriting purposes, because noth- ing rhymed with Becky, but that was the least of her problems, having to share a name with her mother (Rebecca, really) and being called Little Becky, at her age, to avoid confusion, although mistakes were always hap- pening anyway, on the telephone and such, trying to explain to telemarketers she was just the kid, not to mention sometimes opening one of Ma's letters, totally by accident, as if she wanted to know what her mother was up to.*

"WARNING: ALTERATION, ADDITION, OR MUTILATION OF EN- TRIES IS PROHIBITED." This was something else her passport asserted, just above the space where her name was printed; the juxtaposition of admo- nition and appellation immediately put the idea into her head that a pass- port could be and, in her case, should be altered. She had her knife from

dinner, a plastic serrated utensil that had fallen from the tray and wedged in the seat cushion. She fished around and found it and began to scrape at the R, at the E.

J-U-L-I-E, *she filled in the space she had cleared, writing in block letters to simulate the official script. She traced over the L-O-W-E to make the inks match, not that anyone ever looked very hard at kids and their documents when they were traveling. They told kids to sit on wooden benches and keep quiet as they made the parents open their luggage and explain themselves.*

She had always wanted to be named Julie (also, Sequoia and Tiffany and Eloise, but mostly Julie, and Julie possessed the further virtue of being a cinch to rhyme—truly, newly, coolly, etc.). And how very fortunate she had never actually bothered to sign her passport, so technically she was not really altering or adding to or mutilating her signature as she wrote a lavish Julie Lowe *across the bottom of the page.*

Her father came to fetch her as the plane prepared for its descent. Her mother, who had awakened in a rather smudged and sweet state, clung to Little Becky's hand as the engines growled and hitched and strained. "Dear Little Becky," Becky said, rather as if she were trying to place the girl.

"Actually," Little Becky said, "I wish you would call me Julie from now on. Look, I changed it on my passport, so it's practically official."

"Julie Lowe," Becky said. "Julie Lowe. How mellifluous the lee *and the* lo *sound together. All right. I must say, I understand your desire to reinvent yourself at the start of this new adventure. I'll try to remember, and remind me if I forget. That goes for you too, Alden. Remember who Julie would rather be, from now on."*

Alden said he'd been thinking of changing his name to Lookout B. Lowe.

"Ha-ha," Julie said. Hopeless.

One

Zabloudil jsem—I am lost (masc.)
Zabloudila jsem—I am lost (fem.)

"BECKY? WHERE ARE YOU? Well, don't move. Just stay where you are or we'll lose one another," Alden called out.

But Becky, wherever she had settled with an English magazine or her tapestry frame or the briefcase full of paperwork she had brought home for the weekend, would never hear him through the thick stone walls of the some-centuries-old castle in which they had been living for the past two years. Alden spoke aloud to keep his spirits up, or, as he scarcely admitted to himself, to keep the spirits at bay as he paced the Great Hall through the darkness the wan beam thrown by his flashlight only cleaved into blacker halves. So halved, the deepened gloom pressed twice as tenebrous on the left and on the right as Alden formed a sort of certainty that whatever lurked in the murk to his left lowered even more banefully than the second secret horror eeling through the utter inkiness to his right.

He really hadn't much good to say for Czech electricity. These power cuts happened too frequently and too mysteriously on perfect summer evenings when the air was so stilly composed that the ruffle-edged moths could not catch and heave themselves aloft on the least breath of air. This summer of 1992 in Prague was running so dry that the dependent wings of the wandering moths scritched across the parched earth and pavement. Alden had heard them as he lay upon his deck chair out in the lightless belvedere and slowly determined what the so-quiet creep and onward scrabble must be, aided by the brief flare and flame of a new and antique Cartier, or Cartier-style, lighter. He was sorry to say he had taken up smoking again. Tobacco was freely offered and enjoyed in this city and in this culture, although not within the culture and the keep of Castle Fortune, and so he smoked his Silk Cuts outside on a belvedere chaise as a conflux of grounded moths crept past him heading straight, he didn't doubt, for the dressing room wardrobe and his camel-hair blazer's slim and tender lapels.

"Rats." Svatopluk, Alden's right-hand man down at the Ministry of Finances outpost office, had offered this explanation for the power failures after Alden complained he had been prevented from toasting a too-hard bagel the night before. He had been given a globe-shaped jar of spreading honey by a supplicant speculator which may or may not have been intended as a bribe. If so, Alden was touched but not in the least suborned by the delicacy of the gesture. It was basswood honey, the supplicant said, which was said to taste of mint, but Alden, assessing a flavor conveyed by a sticky fingertip, privately thought, Bitter.

"Rats?" Alden had asked. "Do you mean those wretched rats you people keep running round inside revolving drums down at the generating station have all keeled over from fatal heart attacks?"

"Sir? No, no sir, no. Ha-ha, sir. I refer to the rodents gnawing on the cable wires, which taste of salt because of a galvanizing technique once in vogue. It is a problem. In fact, it is a scandal. No, our generators are, for the most part, coal powered," Alden had been patiently reminded by Svatopluk, to whom the task too often fell of reminding Mr. Lowe patiently or tactfully or preventively.

Ah yes, thought Alden, they burn that spongy, crumbling, pallid Bohemian coal they can't give away to the rest of the world free with magic beans, for he knew all about the fledgling Republic's production deficiencies and trade imbalances. Few in Prague knew, or needed to know, better than he about such matters. Alden had hardly had to invent the notion of rodent dynamos on his own. He wasn't sure he hadn't come across their like in some wretchedly reproduced précis of yet another hopeful, pleading prospectus.

And as for Svatopluk, what sort of a name was Svatopluk? Alden wondered. Was it the equivalent of having an assistant named Jethro or Clem, or Julian or Byron, or Bill or Bob? Ought he to speak of Svatopluk naturally or with a voice freighted with irony? Was a Svatopluk, in the language of the Ministry, to be listed among one's assets?

Furthermore, Alden minded these spontaneous blackouts because they caused him to misstep, as he misstepped now, off the edge of the thick-as-curbstone carpet laid down the span of the Long Gallery. He lurched and cracked himself against great carved objects. Very superior cupboards, Becky said they were, whose very superior contents had long since vanished along with the last Family in residence; to Paris and to Toronto, the Field Marshal and the porcelain had gotten away. Alden reminded himself that these obstacles could not possibly have been shoved out of position during the day to sabotage his blind progress. An army would have to be summoned to shift the towering chests and to lift the vast rugs. Any coin lost once and found now beneath the taken-up carpet would bear the image of one Habsburg or another turned to display a nonpareil profile to the least possessor of the merest haler. No, Alden's sense of displacement was existential.

He hoped Svatopluk wasn't Czech for Marmaduke.

Besides, Alden ventured less frequently into this part of the castle, crossing the Long Gallery toward the doors to the Pastels Room and the Music Chamber and the Southerly Conservatory, which constituted Becky's particular apartment. We must live in a castle as a castle is meant to be lived in, Becky had grandly pronounced at the start. They had all played at being grand in those early days. Becky was the Comtesse and Alden her Comte, and even Julie had consented to answer to Milady with fairly good grace since her folks had been so obliging about calling her Julie—when they weren't calling her Milady. Becky, after a considering stroll through their new domain while consulting an ancient floor plan printed on the heavy sheet of paper that the leasing agent had folded around the castle's several dozen tremendous and unmarked keys suspended from a chain, had assigned Alden the Great Hall and the Armaments Chamber and the library as his private suite of rooms. All the chilly, antlered places were to be his portion. Male and female, she created them, as Alden had tolerantly thought at the time but did not, of course, speak aloud. Julie, as maiden, was sent uncomplainingly to the Tower, where she could play her stereo as loudly as she had ever wished to until she annoyed even herself.

Becky had been so vital reinventing their world for them those early amazing weeks in Prague, when they had all been unfailingly charmed by every aspect of the My Bookhouse scenery on offer and by the magnificent accommodations and by the welcoming locals who were delighted in turn to greet such exotic yet reassuringly true-to-type Americans. Alden and Becky and Julie smiled with such beautiful teeth and took such long, confident strides with their long, confident legs. They glowed; their healthy skin, their cared-for hair, their precious metal watch faces and rings caught the sunlight and captured the eye. Every occasion, every new face, every attempt at conversation, seemed to call for generous outpourings of Alden's Scotch or an ice-cold Coca-Cola. The man who came to prod and prove the castle's several mysterious boilers became cordially drunk and had to return with his several supervisors and their several apprentices on another day. The Lowes had had no problem summoning workmen to puzzle over, on successive visits, the kitchen stove that shuddered and sparked but would not light; the pull-chain apparatus, which was meant to open and close a glass panel in the conservatory roof but had come crashing down when tugged; and the drains of every bathtub in every bathroom that, when the plugs were raised, caused the level of water standing in the tub to rise as a swampish and sedimented liquid swirled upward from the waste pipes. Even though they were raw newcomers to such a foreign land, the Lowes were quite sure this was not correct. These were not the antipodes, where the drains twirled wrong way round, and nowhere on earth did water flow upward.

But the Lowes had stood on their heads in order not to come across as conquerors, for they felt like conquerors, and how could they not be perceived as conquerors in Prague in the autumn of 1990? They handed round filled glasses as if to old friends as they presided with those wide-open smiles well fixed to the faces, and they listened to the elaborate explanations of why repairs could not easily or ever entirely successfully be effected. Alden and Becky nodded along, not really comprehending but coming to recognize the tone, or the tune, the strains of Czech bel can't -o, as Alden allowed. Technicians never said, You're all set, as they did in the States, those three little words that made his heart sing. Becky had failed to smile (her smiles favored other people, these days) at Alden's little joke. Besides, her bathtub now drained if a lever was jiggled, and her conservatory window could be pushed open and nudged shut by a telescoping pole and hook contraption, and the spark-spitting oven had been superseded by a gleaming La Cornue work of highly functional kitchen art that Alden was not allowed to use. He clattered and spattered the surfaces on the cook's day off, Becky said, and she had chosen the snow-white model, which particularly showed spills.

Alden had had no clue back then in the early days that Becky had begun as she meant to go on. Her pronouncements and crotchets, to which he had at first lightheartedly ascribed, as if to the evolving outlines of some new, diverting game being played out between them, had become, over time, codified into the strictures of a regime. The game had engaged him; the regime had removed, in turn, the die, the tiles, the recent run of aces from his hand. The particular moment when he ought to have spoken up had passed, recognized only too late among the shapes and shadows inhabiting the becloudments of subsequent developments. Alden believed President Havel, back when he was Provocateur and sometimes Prisoner Havel, had explained in a seminal essay how this sort of darkness could fall over an unvigilant people, how they allowed such a thing to happen to themselves, indeed, how they were enlisted to facilitate their oppressors in the act of their own suppression. This was the best established method, known to be so in the very bones of all the hard-line bosses of old. Perhaps Becky had been infected by the germ of the idea, which survived as a mutating virus being breathed in and out on the not very clean air of the frail and infant Republic they had been sent to nurture. Alden guessed Becky would recover presently, and he would reassure her then that he had understood what she was going through. But now was not the moment to remind Becky that he knew her better than she knew herself. She might become strongly motivated to surprise him, and at this point in their long marriage, he reckoned, all the good surprises had been sprung. Heights of passion, delights in children—those sorts of surprises, Alden wagered, were over.

Thus, Alden spent most of his evenings at home alone in the library chamber. He sat at a long central table. His legs pressed against one or another of the table's dozen legs, each table leg carved in the shape of the limbs of some manner of legendary beast, bescaled and hooved and muscular and woolly, the very beast which, for all Alden knew,

had roamed Central Europe back in the days when England contained
dragons and Ireland still had its snakes. Alden's inner imagination was
not well stocked with Central European mythic images. Last Christmas, the Prague street-corner Santa Clauses had struck him as clerical
and stern-looking beings, and Alden had asked Svatopluk not just to
explain the attenuated Father Christmases with their wispy beards and
poignantly underfilled sacks but also to direct him to some primary
source that would enlighten him and generally illuminate the native
scene. Svatopluk had considered, and then consulted a known authority
at Charles University who produced a fusty English translation of an
allegorical work by a seventeenth-century local divine, *The Labyrinth
of the World and the Paradise of the Heart*, by one Johan Comenius. Exactly, Alden had said to himself, as he studied the title. He instantly accepted its premise: the world *was* a place of twists and turns, and of
blocked and falling-open passageways, and, more often than not, of
finding oneself back at the beginning, retracing one's first too tentative
or too trusting steps—whereas the human heart remained the secret,
centered chamber where life and love were lodged and whose attendant sensations a seventeenth century might very well call paradisaical
and which modern man would less extravagantly characterize but be
no less thankful for. And reading further, pen in hand, Alden under-
lined and asterisked passages that struck him as sounding wise and true
down to this very day.

He had set his long library table with a sequence of workstations.
Feeling Mad Hatterish most evenings, he progressed from chair to
massive chair, first to read his papers, next relocating to write up his
notes, shifting himself to tap on his keyboard, and moving on then to
telephone, after which he got up and sat down again to fax contracts to
the as-yet-wide-awake West. He returned to his reading chair to study
documents faxed to him in reply or in query. His days never quite
seemed to end. They blurred one into the next, from the drifting-off
West to the arising East, for he was casting his net wide on the fledgling
Republic's behalf to entice investors into taking a chance on a hundred
dozen nascent privatization schemes. The Czechs had long manufactured very good steel and glass. Their small appliances enjoyed a fair
reputation in the Third World. They produced cement and textiles and

chemicals and potatoes and beets. In 1938, Czechoslovakia had boasted the fifteenth-best economy in the world. It had been, once upon a time, really a rather nice little country.

Late in the evenings, Alden at last looked up from his work, his tired eyes made more tired by the cold climb to the heights of the timbered, vaulted ceiling. His gaze fell back and was caught by the pronged horns of mounted game heads and arrested by the glossy glares of murdered stags, many of which had known the honor of being slaughtered by the Field Marshal himself. A great leather-bound volume was kept in a camphor-smelling drawer of a tambour-topped desk. The volume's thick, smooth pages recorded long-ago seasons' kills with comments and attributions that Alden had taught himself to read, after a fashion, after he mastered the specialist's vocabulary. Alden could speak the words for boars and points and covert and breechloader and bearer and hound. Svatopluk had let Alden know that Alden's efforts at small talk were sometimes held to be highly interesting by staff and client alike, which was not entirely a plus, or, in the specialist's vocabulary of the Ministry, an asset. The Czechs had yet to shed entirely their habits of cultivating protective coloration. They had no desire to stand out too conspicuously against the passing scene and so to draw the fire of whoever was allowed, at present, to possess the bullets and the guns; if not the Field Marshal nor any of his unnatural successors, then someone, somewhere, surely was sliding cartridges into cylinders and taking a look around.

Oh, buck up, Alden had wanted to tell them all, but he anticipated the confusion his use of this idiom would engender as his staff dove for the in-house English-language dictionary.

Now, Alden's failing flashlight dimmed, then died outright. He promptly wandered off course like a lost patrol overtaken by nightfall. His outrigger hand hit the hard surround of the Long Gallery's fireplace. He did not need to stoop as he swerved beneath the ogee arch of the mantel to step inside the massive fire chamber, which closed round him like a cave. Strands of a web skimmed and shredded across his cheek, feeling as if capillaries were letting go on the wrong side of his skin. The sour soot tang of last winter's and all the other winters' great log blazes caused his already narrow nares to pinch shut. The flaring detail of an andiron struck at his ankle bone; flaring details of andirons were always catching at his ankle bones whenever he slipped inside one of the castle's fireplaces for a private smoke. He lifted his lighter from his trouser pocket and shook an English Cut from the pack as he decided to return to the curiosity shop off Wenceslas Square where he had found the lighter to inquire after a similar gold-and-enamel cigarette case. The clasp and click of gold against gold felt right upon his fingertips, as if confirming his Midas touch. Some days he believed himself to be as allegorical as any figure encountered in *The Labyrinth of the World*, although Johan Comenius had anticipated no one quite like Alden in his chapter on alchemy. Comenius's alchemists had labored in vain, making the mistake of believing only gold could be golden. Alden tilted his head back and blew feathering smoke up the accommodating chimney stack. Yet man is born into trouble, as the sparks fly upward; this thought came to him from somewhere.

So, here he was. When he emerged from the fireplace he would stride in a direct line across open carpet straight to the paneled door of the Pastels Room, where Becky was most likely to have settled (for she sometimes referred to the Music Room as the Morning Room, Alden's clue that she seldom sat there in the evening). He would tap upon the door and enter simultaneously, the tap a concession to her professed sensibilities, the simultaneity of entrance an assertion on Alden's part of his opinion of certain sensibilities. When he had gained Becky's attention, when she looked up from her needlework or her magazine or one of the hopeful, pleading prospecti that fell into her lap as well as onto his own, and when she lowered the half-moon of her reading glasses and peered above the frames, aging herself ten years as she creased her forehead and doubled her chin at him, then Alden would say to her—well, he had yet to decide what he meant to say to her. She was seldom sympathetic to his invasions of the Pastels Room on the pretext of speaking firmly to the spectral prowler who had come out just after the power went off, perhaps one of the late Field Marshal's lingering nemeses, for surely he had reaped not a few affronted souls in his former line of work. Becky had advanced an alternative theory of her own as to why it was that Alden sometimes imagined himself not to be alone in the castle (and Alden had brooded over the syntax and the import of that sentence of Becky's). Perhaps, Becky said, Mrs. Cook (their cook) and Miss Mopsy (their cleaner) had installed stray relatives in the castle's attics. Those would be the luckless and unfortunate sort of relatives poor Mrs. Cook and Miss Mopsy could easily be assumed to be obliged to suffer; shiftless brothers or husbands or sons or nephews. Both women wore sloppy slippers on their aching feet during their working days, which suggested there was some other situation at home, at night, that kept them on their toes. Not that Becky begrudged either woman the unused attic space to lodge, in a pinch, one of these theoretical hangers-on—their surplus menfolk, a bad-penny former husband who had resurfaced to exploit an old and much regretted attachment. Evidently, Becky held strong and heretofore unrevealed views on such matters.

WHEN THE PASTELS ROOM FELL INTO DARKNESS, Becky sighed and lit the oil lamp that a thoughtful Miss Mopsy had ferreted from a storeroom and buffed up and filled with a luminous fluid that smelled of marigolds and tent canvas. Becky tossed aside the document she had been reading, a proposal to market a malleable and mucilaginous plastic material used to effect instant repairs to faux-leather handbags and automobile upholstery and office furniture. Alden had told her to make sure some wise guy wasn't just trying to repackage his leftover Semtex. Becky sighed again. Whenever Alden asked her about her clients, she braced herself for his inevitable smart remark.

She could not really read by the flicker of lamplight. Words, even the spill of technical words across the document face, stirred to trembly life upon the page. Hard PVC transmuted into softer TLC, and the letters of the compound alkenes segmented and reassembled themselves into the name of some palmy oasis calling to her from North Africa—none of which had anything to do with *U-Mend-It! Ltd.*'s bold mission statement to "patch the world planet one punctured dashboard at a time, patent pending." Although as Alden had also pointed out, the wasteful Western portion of the earth was less inclined to patch than to pitch, and besides, *U-Mend-It!* only came in black and white and brown. Becky had yet to break it to *U-Mend-It*'s creator that the Western world blossomed with all possible colors.

With an intake of breath, consciously reversing her series of sighs, perhaps to refuel herself so she could sigh some more, Becky turned to her needlepoint frame. She was stitching an Elizabeth Bradley pillow, the design of the broody Mother Hen and her Chicks, but Becky could not, in the half-light, distinguish among the tones of cream and yellow wools still to be worked into the old Mother Hen's tail feathers. Becky puzzled over the tangle of strands lying at the bottom of her sewing basket, organized once but now wriggled free of their label bands. She'd been at the thing for a hundred hours, she reckoned, and she was in an un-Penelope-like hurry to knot the last thread and flatten all the lumpy bits with a good steam pressing. Becky didn't even like the pattern of the pillow, a birthday gift from her sister-in-law in Kansas, who had scrawled across the accompanying card, This looks like you!

Becky tossed aside her tapestry frame. It slipped from the cushions of the tufted Pastels Room sofa onto the floor slates. The sofa was set back in an alcove where the walls were frescoed with the portraits of the last Family, executed (the portraits, not the Family—one felt one had to specify in this neck of the woods) sometime back in the thirties, judging by the women's crimped hair and the men's high shirt collars. The portraits betrayed either a family resemblance or the artist's inability to paint any mouth other than the mouth he could paint, a not very full and sidelong sort of mouth with a smile tucked into either corner. Or perhaps the artist had coaxed the same smile from each of his subjects by keeping up an amusing line of chat as he worked. He may have flirted with the wavy-haired women, and with the stiff-collared men as well. Becky was convinced Central Europeans could be sophisticated about such matters. She had been watching them closely these past two years and drawing her own conclusions, although she supposed her view of things was shaded by her own limitations at drawing from life.

For roundabout Prague, she could not always tell or be told. She had to interpret for herself, not knowing words enough to ask, or the words of any answer beyond a standard for getting by in a concert ticket queue or recognizing on a menu a dish she had liked well enough before. Initially, she made do with a *Blue Guide*, seeking out the museums and churches listed in the index. She noted central ironwork canopies and age-darkened icons and traces of medieval fortifications overwhelmed by Prague's progress. She wandered the paths of well-ordered gardens and sat upon elegant benches angled toward views that, after six or so weeks of earnest tourism, she realized she was failing to see even as she disposed herself to look. Spires, cathedrals, the great and small squares, the Moldau of Smetana flowing below the arches of the ancient bridges all receded into the background and people emerged from the buildings and byways, strolling or bustling past, faces and figures coming into the picture and stepping between Becky and her appraisal of the scenery, as if to insist, Consider us, now.

First, Becky noticed intact family groups gathered on Cathedral steps or lazing in the greenness of a park or spilling from a car carrying pastries in a box and disappearing into an undistinguished apartment block. Yes, or no, Becky decided after every appraisal. The happiest families were the most vulnerable, she knew. They lacked antibodies against the troubles borne on ill winds. A bad blow could carry them off before they knew what had hit them. But the frowning families, Becky believed, would swallow yet another of the usual bitter pills and they would survive.

And then, on another day, as if opting to visit a shopping arcade instead of standing before yet another worthy's neglected tomb, Becky had turned from what had become a study of families and she allowed herself to notice the couples. The city afforded at every aspect snug cafés and quiet corners. The housing stock was strained; lovers could not always linger in private, but Prague ceded them space and a measure of grace to inhabit. This was later in the Lowes' first autumn in Prague, but not urgently so. Lovers still sat outside at sidewalk tables, tilted toward a subsiding sun and sipping at something warm or warming and richly colored in a steep-sided glass. They engaged in intense conversations. They were a handsome-looking people, with emphatic cheekbones and dark, emotional eyes. They wore black coats and cloaks and red scarves, or white ones, wound round their throats. They canted forward. Their hands swept back the other's shiny backswept hair, as falling locks obscured their beloved's face. Becky understood they were all conducting complicated and necessarily secret or some-how unsanctioned love affairs in which these conversations played as vital a part as any physical intimacies. There was so much to say. There came a point at which there was too much to say in a tumble of words and words and words.

That symbiotic self-absorption of entranced couples . . . No one un-derstands me but you . . . No one understands you but me . . . never begging the obvious question: Why are we so impossible to get along with? But then, lovers thought not in terms of their prior difficulties but of their present distinction. Becky, sitting in a café corner with her own glass of local pilsner, which she had learned to take in small mouthfuls, could not in these alien cases designate a predictor of suc-cess or nonsuccess for an affair. For example, what tribal divides were being defied? Becky could not appreciate nuances of dress. That pair over there, *her* suit was career correct but was *he* wearing a graduate student's or a laborer's loose and shabby shirt? Becky could not detect a telling accent within the prevailing accent, a too-rough or too-rustic voice answering the standard version. Were Czech men known to be faithful? Were Czech women homebodies or, with those great watch-ful eyes of theirs, potential queens of tragedy? Nor could Becky say how these lovers would define their success as a couple, and if she had to prescribe for them in her theoretical musings, Becky wasn't sure what she would wish for them: safe and fond marriages, or ever more romances conducted in the open air amid the calendar-page scenery, dreaming away all their now-free afternoons? Becky, who had under-taken her tour in the hopeful spirit of a pilgrim traveler (either to or from a vital point on the map, Becky still wavered on that point), had to own at last that she had come full circle. She was back where she had started from, asking and not answering the same question, and now, as then, it seemed, was utterly in the dark.

Well, she had too much to do and no way of accomplishing any of it that evening. Her work from work, the needlepoint project that she was keen to see the last of, a difficult letter tucked two days earlier be-neath her desk blotter and yet to be acknowledged, all would have to wait until daylight to be dealt with. She reached and doused the irresolute flame of the unsatisfactory oil lamp. The flickerings queased her stomach after another one of Mrs. Cook's dinners. Alden said he wished they had thought to call her Mrs. Take-Out and left a sheaf of menus availably by the telephone.

Becky was ever leery of tipping over a lamp or a candle and starting a fire here—and indeed, there was a barrel of sand and a long-handled ax kept in an old porter's cupboard just inside the Great Hall door, so she may not have been far wrong in her assessment of Castle Fortune as a tinderbox biding its time until a shuttered room quietly flashed ablaze. Becky knew you were supposed to fling sand (somehow) at a smoldering Empire ormolu *lit-en-bateau* (say), but she didn't know what good an ax was. Fleeing from a fire down the castle's twisting stairs and corridors could be perilous enough; fleeing the fire while wielding an ax would be lunatic.

She leaned back among the cushions heaped upon the Pastels Room's long, tufted sofa. She decided she would fall asleep here, tonight, still in her loosened clothes and with her face unwashed and uncreamed just this once. She simply could not rise to accomplish the long blind trek to their bedroom, nor could she endure the seven-minute wait for hottish water to spurt from her bathroom sink's wheezing taps, then, to perform certain rituals of tooth and skin care, and finally to listen to Alden's every usual question.

Bed? he would ask as she turned down the covers.

Tired? he would ask as she yawned.

Hot? he would ask as she kicked away blankets.

Well dear? came his occasional query after sex.

And tomorrow morning, before Alden could ask her why she hadn't come to bed last night, before he could ask and establish a tone of concern or aggrievement, she would mention with a yawn that she had fallen asleep while waiting up until Julie came in, safely home from her nightly prowl of Prague's corners and cafés. And I'm fully intending, Becky would bristle and assert, to *speak* to that girl.

ALDEN TRAVERSED THE VAST RUG. He seized the cut-crystal sphere of the Pastels Room's paneled, painted door, and the sphere sagged

into his hand, a dead weight. To refit the knob (this had happened before) was a two-person undertaking, Alden knew. Becky would have to
stand on the other side of the door and hold the opposing knob firmly
in place as the outer knob was threaded back onto its stripped spindle.
Were Alden to hazard a solo repair he might very well knock the shaft
through to the other side, and the interior crystal knob would fall to the
stone floor and shatter spectacularly. Castle Fortune was not infrequently the site of spectacular shatterings—decorations detaching from
heights hitting hardness—one might almost formulate an equation to
quantify the phenomenon. Becky, if within the Pastels Room, would be
trapped there. The only other method of egress would be by a long
drop from a high window that Alden was pretty sure could not be, was
never meant to be, opened.

But Alden balked at knocking upon the door. He laid an ear against
the jamb and detected no interior rustlings. Nevertheless, the silence
that met him seemed a familiar one, much as a household's usual tap
water, while not having a taste, can still be said to have a nontaste all
its own, and Becky, particularly a Becky fallen silent, would not take
kindly to being disturbed by his account of the mismanaged doorknob
and at being asked to play her passive part as he fumbled in the dark ef-
fecting one more repair until the next time. No, Alden really couldn't
deal with Becky tonight. She would sigh at him. She would sigh and
sigh and sigh at him.

He decided, then, to do nothing. He knelt and felt about the floor and
placed the crystal sphere upon an edge of thick carpet where not entirely
implausibly it might be presumed to have flown when Becky's careless
approach to the doorknob from *her* side of the door had launched it.
For Becky had lately developed a rough touch, a tendency to slam and
to wrestle and to thump. A near disaster with the door might serve as a
lesson to her. Tomorrow, Alden would ask Josef to find someone to fix
the knob for good, to bolt, weld, magnetize, splice, strap (he would
consult his phrase book) the thing into permanent place. Just this once,
Alden would let Becky take the fall, but he would also make certain
that it would not happen again. Alden supposed this was playing fair
enough. This would be *his* game that they were playing here tonight.

He reflected, as he had reflected before, that he should only be grateful the castle did not harbor real dungeons, just excellent apses for wine storage and certain vaulted, subterranean chambers still cluttered with the junk of the socialist youth organization last headquartered here: their hardworn sports equipment, the bright banners and sashes they wore on their frequent marches in parades, and their picture-book manuals describing in simple words even Alden could understand the unlikeliest of pleasures one might experience while living under the least benign of systems.

Two

Rovně—Straight Ahead

ALDEN SAT IN THE BACK OF THE LONG BLACK CAR, cooling his heels on another dull-aired morning in Prague. He clicked open and then clicked shut his briefcase. He glanced toward the castle's less massive west-side door, their "everyday" exit and entrance (the Great Portal was reserved for Occasions). He clicked open his briefcase. He had forgotten he had meant to ascertain that he had not left behind the contract from RAM Corp. in some corner of his library office setup. Yes, it lay atop a shuffle of other contracts and reports that would, in their own time, rise to the surface of his briefcase like a maple tree's roots tipping from the lawn toward the sun, and with, Alden reckoned, as many knots and gnarls and toe-catchers attached to watch out for. Czech law was rather mutable at present. An *i* dotted just yesterday might on the morrow be regarded as a flyspeck upon the page by the light of latest legislative developments and EC dictates. Alden approved of this fluent state of affairs despite any short-term inconvenience RAM Corp.'s attorneys might suffer, huddled in the Hotel Inter Continental Praha for a second weekend, negotiating to have their shirts laundered and making expensive calls home. Alden, stuck in the Republic, privy to the longer view, was pleased to stand witness at the birth of certain investment and security regulations because, ultimately, when *his* time came he meant to be in on the kill. And *that* was going to be like shooting farm-raised trout in a barrel, further aided by a map of the barrel.

Josef, their chauffeur, sat hunched with his burly uniform-jacketed arms slung round the steering wheel, head bowed and reading between the spokes a contrarian newspaper folded over his thick uniformtrousered legs. Alden had long since learned that Josef would respond to any cheerful word with the same grunt of dissent he had accorded his previous Boss, an apparatchik of the old order who, Alden understood, was at present undertaking to purchase a privatized malt cereal factory on the strength of his proven ability of being good with the People and perhaps for his great experience with malt products as well. Josef, obliquely quizzed about his former employer, had scowled and observed that a Boss was a Boss. *Is* a Boss, of course, Alden had added, and Josef had shot him one of his better-knowing looks. The Czechs liked to look upon Americans as children, for, they said, Americans had never known real suffering. Alden protested—at least the Czechs had not had to live through the Slough of Despond that had been the Carter administration. Oh, the looks of incomprehension that were leveled at Alden. But Alden might have argued further that it was children who were subject to arbitrary rules, children who were restricted and confined, children who were not free to come and go as they pleased and to express dissenting views and to sign binding legal contracts. Children were told and taken charge of, for their own good. It's the Czechs who were the children, Alden countered silently. They were unhappy, unkindly brought-up children who were going to require years of talk therapy and a series of bad marriages and the consolations of self-indulgent addictions before they sorted themselves out, if ever. If I too am a child, thought Alden, I am glad I am a well-loved and happy and fully functioning child.

Becky was running late this morning and Julie was impossibly lagging. He had warned Julie, cupping his hands and calling up the Tower's twisting stairs, that she would be left behind if she didn't get a move on, which was hardly a motivating caution. Julie was only hitching a ride into town to attend a half day of summer school classes after which she would drift across the river and prowl the outdoor market stalls searching for counterfeit-label T-shirts and small startling objects to dangle from the several holes in her ears. Alden trusted that Julie's at-large quests were quite harmless. He tended to believe she was guarded from harm by a shield of sheer orneriness. She was too intractable to be misled anywhere, and he was counting on any would-be seducer to reel away feeling flayed from any encounter with his prickly daughter.

"What?" she had hollered from the heights of her Tower. "What? *What?*"

When Alden had left Becky she was still sitting at her dressing table wearing a black lace slip and her slippers, twisting columns of lipstick up and down their shiny tubes, not caring for any of the colors. She had mentioned she was meeting with her aesthetician-sister clients that morning and she did not wish to be critically eyed as if she'd just fallen off the Tammy Faye Bakker truck. *Ach, ach, ach,* the sisters would say.

"I'll go out and appease Josef," Alden had told her, as if Josef were a summoned taxi driver left to idle with his meter running, Becky thought but did not say because she was lining her lips, very carefully tracing just outside the lines as lately she had been instructed to do. She had been told she wanted a fuller mouth, and while in the past she would have laughed and replied, Why should I want that? now she was willing to try.

Besides, Josef did not care to hear of the dilatoriness of women in the morning. Becky maintained Josef wasn't in the least interested in any aspect of womankind. Poor Miss Mopsy, looking over the household and spying only Josef, had set her cap at him. ("You mean she set her hair net at him," Alden had said.) Miss Mopsy had boiled Josef's feather pillow on a sunny drying day, and she reported that she had dusted his porcelain collection and put everything back exactly, across a trembly shelf up in his stable quarters, all to no avail. Midmorning, midafternoon, and in-between staff cake-and-coffee breaks around the kitchen table were fraught now, where they had been only strained before. Trust the Czechs to be sensitive to gradations of angst, Alden said.

They had tried to dismiss Josef, though not on the strength of Miss Mopsy's miff. She scrubbed harder after she was spurned. Stains on the floor had acquired a face and a name, one felt. No, Alden and Becky would just rather have driven themselves about the town and country. Alden, or Becky, or even Julie (who had a driver's license now, achieved on a flying visit to Colorado and her uncle's ranch; she could drive a springless livestock truck, a doorless 4x4, and a Lincoln Continental)—whoever was at the wheel would have been more amenable than Josef to discharging a passenger at the address requested instead of arriving at an approximate vicinity via a route that avoided one-way streets, any notorious series of uncoordinated red lights, interfering police presences, entangling intersections, cobblestone surfaces, tram lines, bicyclists, narrow bridges crossing deep water, and public works projects involving detours and dustiness and a man waving a red rag flag—Josef avoided them all. But he had come as a perquisite with Alden's new responsibilities, and men in Alden's position could not drive themselves because men occupying positions below Alden's also did not drive themselves. In the old days there had been 105 percent employment in Czechoslovakia, aided by such dictates as who might and who might not be observed chauffeuring himself.

We are losing skills, Becky allowed—navigational, traffic fighting, funny foreign petrol purchasing, parallel parking in fourteenth-century lanes, working out at a high speed what a sudden traffic sign had been attempting to advise them in Czech. There was no need to check the oil or to ask for oil (somehow) or to line up (somewhere) to apply for registration and assorted permissions to display upon the windscreen and above the rear bumper. Alden and Becky could both drink, as well, on their evenings out when, Alden privately allowed, it was sometimes a help to return to the castle in matching elevated moods. The Designated Driver phenomenon was another of those concepts that had yet to catch on in Europe, so he didn't need to abstain. Then again, he had no wish to veer off the road and run over any village chickens; fairly or foully, he would be enthusiastically sued as an American with deep pockets and excellent insurance; one felt the Czechs would seize upon the complications of a lawsuit.

The Czechs asked, Does the Designated Driver wear a badge or a sash of office? Must he sit for an examination? What other powers does he enjoy?

A Designated Driver can also be a woman, Becky said, and it's just an informal arrangement among friends because of strict laws and penalties.

Ah, we have those too. Arrangements. Between friends. Because of strict laws and penalties. We find we must, even now, even under this regime, the Czechs sympathetically observed.

Those cross-cultural exchanges: So much was expressed to so little effect.

Movement caught Alden's eye; the small side door of the castle swung slowly open. Becky emerged and turned and retreated into interior shadows. She stepped outside a second time, firmly guiding Julie by a hand bolted into the small of the girl's back. Julie pitched and wobbled at her mother's side, raised on the balls of her feet, having reverted to her childhood walk of unwillingness. She was wearing the Paisley Room's curtain as a sarong skirt this morning, knotted over a scarlet leotard.

Those exaggeratedly long castle-life distances to be covered—the path across the lawn from the castle to the driveway stretched and curved elegantly and unnecessarily, winding round an inscribed obelisk that had lost its point. Becky, flushed and furious, propelled Julie through the car door that Josef, clambering from the driver's seat, had pulled open at the last possible moment. He considered the door-tending aspect of his service to be servile, and the human form, angling and telescoping into a backseat, was seldom a pretty sight.

"Tell her, Alden," Becky commanded. She had daubed Chloe on her pulse points. The scent welled. Julie exuded a thick and hottish patchouli smell. The passenger compartment dulcified as nature never intended, not even in a rose garden, and Josef struck at some venting switch on the dashboard. An interior wind began to whistle.

"I'm telling you, Julie. Whatever your mother says. Consider yourself twice told," Alden said.

"I have told her she may have no more late school nights if she can't get up for school in the morning," Becky said.

Julie, flinching her hip bone away from a brass-covered corner of Becky's not very gently managed briefcase (Becky was rummaging for a folder marked USDA asap) did not bother to react to her parents' latest fiat. They did not expect her to obey. They were just putting themselves on the record and on the side of the angels as veteran parents and also veteran politicians will do. Julie brushed her bittersweet orange and straw-textured hair across her forehead, above a kohl-lined eye, covering a pale cheek made paler by rice powder, catching strands in the corner of her almost-black mouth. She tucked more orange hair behind a studded ear so that its arc of ornamentation could be observed: the long hoop strung with beads; a gold star; a copper crescent moon; a brilliant cut ruby; a microchip that had come from a decommissioned ICBM guidance system, her big brother Glover in the army said when he sent it to her. Julie's ear was pierced from the lobe up through the cartilage and the pinna, which was what that scrolly part of the ear was called. All this body work she'd had done was educational, at least as educational as summer school, where she was prepping in math and several sciences, for US College Boards loomed. Even here the system was still in sway. And her parents were making her take Czech, as well, to be polite to the Culture, although she was also learning plenty enough local, and localized, words from her boyfriends, another beneficial offshoot of unsanctioned behavior and staying out late on a summer school night, *really* learning Czech.

"You and Dad went to that concert last night," Julie said. "You were out late."

"Your father and I are not children and your father and I did not receive Fs in chemistry," Becky said.

"Well, you would now. Chemistry is not like when you were in school. It's much, much harder because of all the discoveries." Julie smirked, thinking of all that had been found out since her parents' day.

"And don't chew on your hair. It can't be good for you, that awful drugstore dye you used. I'm telling you, these people don't have an FDA. You'll discolor your tongue, whatever color your tongue is these days. Speaking of chemistry," Becky said.

Interested, Julie extended her tongue and attempted to see.

"At least you haven't pierced that yet," Becky said and then could have bitten her own tongue. Julie might decide a gauntlet had been flung.

But her new boyfriend had made Julie promise not to sink a stud precisely there. Her boyfriend had informed her men didn't like running into foreign objects. The touch and taste of a warm, wet steel plug came as a distraction. Her boyfriend explained everything so patiently and Julie was pleased to comply; when a reason was given, she was notably reasonable in turn.

Nevertheless, no harm could come of provoking her mother. Julie warned, "Maybe I'll get a big tattoo. But I'll have to think what of. Something really appropriate since I'll probably have it forever."

Becky, however, rather doubted Julie would submit to either procedure, tongue stud or tattoo. Julie could hardly bear to have her toe-
nails cut. She must have been very motivated when she sat for her
piercings—motivated or drunk. Becky sighed. But she still didn't believe Julie would run into very serious trouble at large, at night, in
Prague. Prague's rebellious youth could not hold a candle to Prague's
rebellious elders. Prague's rebellious youth, still a drumbeat behind the
rest of the world, only adapted crazes that other nations' youth had indulged in and survived and moved on from. She patted Julie's knee as
Julie flinched away from her. My disco-punk retro-mod hippie-chick
girl, Becky thought. How quaint.

They had reached the city proper. The streets were clogged with
morning traffic. Josef stopped and started. He consulted his contrarian
paper through the spokes of the steering wheel. His passengers lurched
as he braked and jerked as he accelerated. Their hands shot forward to
catch themselves; their hands clutched upholstery to restrain themselves. Old buildings, ugly new buildings, slid by. The air was already
unfresh, hot and fumy with diesel exhaust. The alder trees dipped,
greyly enduring, alongside the river. Boxy trams clamored. People on
foot surged and crossed the road anywhere. Alden never understood
how cities managed to coordinate all their moving parts. He did not
know why they simply did not break down finally and for good, con-
gealed in a mass like hornets caught in a honeypot.

Josef charted a roundabout course. Julie was to be dropped off first
at her school, which was not on the way to, but situated on the way
from, her parents' offices if the route was logical, as theirs was not.
Josef waited by the curb as Becky and Alden watched Julie pass through
the glass door of the American-style alternative school they had found
for her. Her brash hair jounced up a stairway. Josef waited a further
two minutes. Julie might attempt to double back and make a break for
one of her more congenial haunts. But the startling figure did not reappear. Josef drove slowly to the corner as Alden watched through the
rear window. Julie seemed to have decided to sit tight for today, unless
she was planning to be very canny and wait a full fifteen minutes before
bolting, though during those fifteen minutes she was likely to be taken
into custody by one of her teachers, who knew all about the girl's

habits and kept an eye out and engaged her on the pretext of teaching her something.

"See you at six," Alden told Josef as Josef nosed into a spot near Knights of the Cross Square to drop them off. They would walk across the Charles Bridge, which was closed to traffic, although Josef could have driven them over the Mán esův most to reach their office but chose not to.

"No, at seven, I think," Becky said. She had so much more on her plate than Alden, she believed, although Alden knew she simply could not delegate. Few women could unless they needed something heavy to be retrieved from a spidery storeroom.

"Seven," Alden informed Josef, who grunted and slammed the passenger door shut, as if in the elapsing seconds between the rescinded order and the next one he had formed a dozen plans and arrangements for the evening and the switch from six to seven o'clock ruined everything.

As they strolled off, Becky remarked generally that she was growing very weary of manifestations of personality. Alden observed that personalities had been discouraged by the old order so that only now were people tentatively, and not always successfully, trying on new ones. He leaned and caught Becky's face with a kiss, and Becky's mouth, fuller and redder now, brushed the air with the sound of a kiss, just missing Alden's cheek as if she had not yet become used to the size and shape of her newly drawn-on lips. They parted by a news kiosk whose proprietor had come to look for them as a signpost along his working day and who sometimes imagined who they might be. They were handsome and affluent people who, nevertheless, did not seem particularly happy as, by his lights, they ought to have been. He faulted them for this failure—a failure of joy, he supposed.

FRANCA BROUGHT ALDEN HIS MAIL and excellent coffee, which she poured from a slender porcelain pot set upon a linen cloth–covered tray. The tray itself was ordinary tin beneath the cloth. It was the officially issued tray, and thus far it had not occurred to Franca to petition for a nicer one; she only wished, to no effect, that a worthier tray would appear one day. Someone ought to have *known*. She lifted tongs and dropped cubed sugar into a pretty cup. She tilted a dollop of a too-yellow and too-viscous cream from a pitcher. She stirred with a bendable plastic rod. She couldn't think what had become of the office spoon. As Alden sat at his desk and sipped the hot, not particularly desired offering, Franca awaited orders, watching Alden drink and flicking dust from the wispy projections of a potted plant she had placed upon his desk in the early days of her employment.

She had already opened and ordered his mail according to her worked-out sense of what would be most interesting to Alden, although none of it could be called riveting: droning confirmations of long-since-decided and -settled issues; queries after matters so trivial and arcane that no answer or any answer at all would suffice. There were pages of unreal figures attesting to the doubtful assets of formerly state-run enterprises. However, as of January 1, accounting practices were going to have to meet standards set in conformity to EC regulations. The literal day of reckoning was going to come as a shock to the Republic's calculator brigade, although from what Alden knew of the EC, those new mandates would only replace clouds with mists.

"Oh yes," Alden remembered. "Franca—"

"Yes, Mr. Lowe?" she asked eagerly. She loved him with all her heart. She prayed he hadn't guessed; then again, what if he should guess? She had trembled for months on the brink of this possibility.

"They faxed me the contract from RAM Corp. We're going to need four copies, if you wouldn't mind," Alden said. The coffee, the plant polishing, her obsession with trays—she seemed more maid than secretary.

"Yes, Mr. Lowe, at once. I mean, as at once as I can be," Franca vowed as she accepted the document from Alden and clutched the pages to her breast until she was struck by Mr. Lowe's being struck by her evident high feelings for RAM Corp's offprints. Then, she dandled the folder in the crook of her arm, on the jut of her hip, rather like an old-hat baby.

"Of course," Alden said, understandingly.

The office staff had access to a copy machine, an elderly Xerox knockoff that smelled like an overworked sewing machine and, indeed, routinely perforated documents. But they were lucky to have any copier at all, even this one, near exhausted by after-hours samizdat production in its former life in former times. Franca did not know that she should despise the misfiring machine and refuse to approach it in its unventilated little hole at the far end of a lonely sloping corridor tethered to the only appropriate socket. Instead, after a hard half hour of wrangling, Franca only knew the exhilaration of having at last produced passable documents, and often she had to fill in by hand a final swallowed line of print. Alden appreciated that his junior staff was poised, for this brief moment, at a charming stage of development. He was reminded of his own boys, and of little Julie, when they were three or four years old, when they were no longer mewling and helpless, when they could walk but not run off, and talk but not answer back. They had been so proud when they colored inside the lines, and when they had labored to raise great snow fortresses as high as their snowsuit knees. Alden found them all, his staff, so touchingly dauntless and, if only for this little while, entirely workable in his hands.

He decided to call a staff meeting. Alden had not conducted one of his inspirational sessions with his people lately, and they seemed always to appreciate his words. If not quite according him the mantle of wisdom, they at least acknowledged his superior experience, for he had long lived in their futures. He could show them, not by laying down Tarot cards but by fanning out business cards, just how their world was going to be. He could tell them who they were going to be, as well. If he had known he was going to schedule this chat, he would have tossed the latest J. Crew and Pottery Barn catalogs that had arrived at the castle into his briefcase so they might wander in their minds' eyes through airily overfurnished rooms while decked out in difficult-to-keep-pressed casual wear.

Summoned, Tilla shut down her electric typewriter. She remembered to stick an edge of scrap paper between the page and the machine to catch the imprint of the S key, which sometimes flung itself at the platen as if in a last-ditch effort to be heard from when the Off switch was struck. Jaroslav and Michal drew a telephone conference to its conclusion. Svatopluk snapped shut a ledger, rubbed his forehead, and stood reluctantly. The office was hopping; deadlines pressed. The Stock

Exchange was supposed to be up and running by the end of the year, and everyone was bracing for the enactment of the new tax laws. The pace of the auctions of small, state-owned retail shops had slowed; questions had arisen over restitution issues, but Alden said to forge ahead and let those questions clutter some other office's desktops at some future date. Certain banks were declaring negative net worths while others reported profits of 1,000 percent, which ought not to be allowed but was, these days. And of course, the nation was soon to split asunder, which was thought to be best for all concerned. The Slovaks had a poor attitude, three-quarters of them believing that changes were going to end in greater social injustice—although, Alden pointed out, the injustices would not be greater, just different, and now the unlucky ones would be self-selected, which was unfortunate but a fact of life. Human beings, when truly free, arranged themselves in this manner. Nevertheless, any divorce, however desired, however velvet, always left both parties feeling at a bit of a loss, even if you were the party who got to keep the cement and petrochemical factories, Alden had observed one day, in another one of his moods.

"Are we in for the rallying talk?" Michal inquired of Jaroslav as they wandered into the meeting room. The air of the closed-off room dealt them a fusty slap as they entered. "Open a window," Michal said, and he lifted the sash himself, supporting it with an upstanding edition of the floating office reference *Dictionary of Finance and Investment Terms*. Michal had been a talented postgraduate student in economics who had spent a dozen years stoking a furnace. "Hot in here," he complained now. He had been ousted from his university position after he had signed Charter 77 and only with effort had he found work as a night janitor, out of sight and mind, in the university's cellars. His present colleagues, too young to have had to take a stand in 1977, admired him and asserted that they would have acted as he had—or perhaps not. For what had Charter 77 achieved for Michal but common labor and an irretrievable past, and hadn't the world turned out all right in the end, and not because of a straggling set of signatures endorsing yet another Manifesto? A Manifesto had been the problem in the first place.

"They are like jazz riffs, Alden's solo talks to us," said Michal, who lived for his LPs. "Jazz is the only authentic American art form," he quoted from the back of an album sleeve.

"Not their cinema as well?" asked Jaroslav.

"I think the French can first claim cinema as an art," Tilla said.

"American technology?" suggested Jaroslav. "Surely we must admire that."

"It is not an art," Michal said. "A technical competence is not an art."

"That's just a knack for ingenuity," shrugged Tilla.

Franca hurried into the meeting, clutching collated documents. She borrowed Michal's automatic pencil and briskly numbered the papers and then changed her mind. She made four three and three four, assessing gradations of unclarity. Mr. Lowe must be spared unclarity. He had to remove his reading glasses to rub his poor, sore eyes when reading bad copies, and he would gaze up at her blurrily as if through a veil of tears. She found this gratifying even as she realized it was not very nice of her.

"What are we discussing?" she asked. If they were talking about Mr. Lowe, she would be able to speak his name naturally.

"We are discussing the artlessness of Americans," Svatopluk said.

They all smiled then; even Franca smiled, because Mr. Lowe *was* such an innocent. After all these months he still had not *guessed*. They took their places around the meeting room table, sliding about on folding chairs, seeking a more solid interface between floorboards and chair legs. Alden, still riding his late train of thought, decided they were like exceptionally pleasant children as he took his seat at the head of the table, lowering himself into a sturdier chair than the others', with armrests and a crocheted cushion and which bore the crest of a disbanded cultural organization. The Czechs had not gone haywire effacing their recent past. This was mentally healthy of them, Alden thought: to be able to live with now what they had been then. Besides, the cultural organization had never been hated, but only held to be slightly ridiculous. Its members had been keen on promoting the Boii, an original Celtic tribe overwhelmed by Germanic people in the first century AD. The Boii enthusiasts had worn kilts in the forest and presided over excavations. Alden knew he could never have been an archaeologist; he could never distinguish between stone tools worked by man and stone shards grooved by water and wear, even when they were laid before him and labeled in a museum case. Nor would he have cared to crouch in the rough forest beside a hole in the ground, clad in a rough kilt held together with inauthentic but necessary safety pins and a skinny rope sash.

He had his staff's attention. They attended to him best when he sat and said nothing. Silences, in their experience, had often been construed as ominous: the silences of official permissions that never came, of a neighbor who vanished, of a telephone line going dead. Alden did not mean to exploit their sensibilities, but he frequently found himself doing so. He could not anticipate every area where some old hangover might yet cause headaches, or heartaches.

"Do not be afraid," Alden began, "of prosperity." He had spoken impressively. The practicing Roman Catholics among the staff felt their fingers tense, preparing to sketch the sign of the cross.

"I have been reading from an estimable old book recommended to me as providing insight into your national character," Alden said. Franca and Tilla inclined their heads, very interested in the Czech national character. They enjoyed being told what they were like by an outsider; they accepted the flattering aspects and argued against the criticisms. Jaroslav and Michal exchanged a glance, and Svatopluk folded his arms across his chest like a Cossack until his posture struck even himself as defensive, or, perhaps, aggressive.

"A fascinating work," Alden said, "by one of your seventeenth-century divines who imagined himself embarked upon a Bunyanesque quest in search of a suitably righteous life's work to earn his mortal keep, and then, of course, even his holy thoughts turned to the great question of love. Work and love, that's what it's all about, even Freud said so. He was a crank, of course, your Johan Comenius—well, Freud too—but Comenius was a divine crank as cranks go. You people exiled him early on. I don't know why, was it over one of your Hussite flaps? Try as I might, the fine points of your history blur a bit for me, forgive me. But then fate almost carried Comenius off to the New World, for they actually considered appointing him president of Harvard; he boasted considerable pedagogical credentials, apparently. I like to think the gang in Cambridge would have been a mite surprised by whom they'd hired on when their new wonder boy stepped off the boat with his black robes aswirl and wearing one of those Old World ear-flapped scholar's helmets and a bilious expression because I don't think he was much of a sailor. He describes a perilous sea voyage and ship-wreck allegorically but compellingly in *The Labyrinth*. His wife and children had long since died of the plague. I can't imagine how he felt about that, I mean, I truly can't, because I think they took that sort of thing more in stride in those days. I'm sure they all possessed a far more certain hope of meeting in heaven, which would have taken the sting off somewhat. I suspect heaven was easier to imagine in those days before TV and the movies began to imagine all the big concepts for us; the instinct has atrophied. I myself seldom dream these days; it's done for me during my waking hours."

Franca breathed in sharply. Michal leaned back. He softly snapped his fingers below the tabletop and winked at Tilla.

Alden slid a small notebook from his suit-coat pocket and rustled through its pages. "I jotted down this passage from *The Labyrinth* I was particularly struck by, which resonates down to this very day to explain a great deal about you people. I believe you are still befuddled by certain systemic, certain cultural dogma, such as this." He read aloud, *". . . and I saw everywhere (especially among dealers in the same commodities) much envy and ill-will. If one had more work and had made more sales than another, his neighbors instantly looked daggers at him and gnashed their teeth at him and whenever they could injured his business. This resulted in quarrels, ill-will, and abusive language. Some out of sheer despair threw their tools away and lapsed into idleness and voluntary mendicancy out of spite for others."*

"In translation, much is lost, or acquired," Svatopluk supposed.

"I read Klíma and Kundera and Hrabal. I have never read Comenius except excerpts at school when we banged our heads on our desk at having to read Comenius," Franca said. "Please, Mr. Lowe, I can lend you copies of our modern writers, or read them to you to explain words, at your convenience after work, in a café. If you wish to read about us, to read about real life now, as we are today."

"In school we also read Jan Neruda," Tilla recalled, "and your

Robert Frost sometimes too. I liked him even though he was American. We had to memorize him in simple English. *'From what I've tasted of desire / I hold with those who favor fire.'* I remember that one, about the ending of the world which we were all certain of, and we believed Mr. Frost had information encoded in that poem. We had seen a picture of him, in our textbook, with Kennedy, at an official function. It made us think he was in a position to know things."

" *'Sob on the long cooling winding saxophone, Go to it, O jazzman,'* " Michal retrieved a bit of verse he had come across on the back of another album sleeve.

"That should be pronounced with a long I. It's *winding* saxophones. Although your version works for me, too," Alden said.

"Winding, winding, long I, winding," Michal repeated to fix the pronunciation into the appropriate groove of his brain.

"At any rate," said Alden, as he turned to another notebook page, "bearing the previous passage in mind, listen to this fact: US steelworkers, on average, produce 497.6 tons of steel per employee, per year. A Slovakian steelworker puts out 266.7 tons per worker."

"Poor American workers," observed Tilla. "So bowed down and demanded of by a relentless and soulless corporate culture."

"Slovakians," said Svatopluk. "What do you expect?"

"There were years, you know, when the Bosses imposed hay quotas on the factory workers because of hay shortages for livestock. Meadows were assigned," Michal said. "Our Slovakian steelworkers may have been diverted from their true work."

"Well, your Bosses," Alden said. "The motivation of your Bosses left much to be desired. No one had any incentive to achieve. Your economic egalitarianism kick didn't inspire anyone to make more than the minimum effort, and so you never produced anything but an equality of *want* as you all looked over your shoulders to make sure no one was getting *more*. What you people have got to learn, what you have got to believe, what you have to engrave on your hearts, is this: Every financial transaction is not a zero-sum game. When one person gains, another person does not lose. Do not look daggers at your high-achieving neighbors. You must strive to emulate them."

"Are you sure of that?" questioned Franca. She had, in her life, been shown many pictures of pies. Those pies had been sliced in ten, twelve, or twenty slices, and there had only ever been just so much pie to go around. They had been challenged in schoolroom classes to find a way to make the pie go further. Franca, a diligent student and keen, as well, to advance the fortunes of her society, had tried very hard, for the benefit of all, to come up with more. She had, she recalled, one day suddenly shot an exultant arm into the air. She had said, We might also slice the pie horizontally through the middle, and there will be twice as many pieces. Her classmates had held their breaths; they could not decide if they wanted her to be right or wrong. She thought she was so smart; nevertheless, perhaps she had found a way to procure for them Nike sneakers and Sony televisions. But their teacher, Herr Black (Franca would never forget his name nor his fierceness at that moment), had thundered back at her, There will only ever be the same volume of pie, and who, Queen Franca, will you decree to receive the upper crust, and who will be left with the bottom? How well Franca had learned the lesson that provocative questions were posed not to seek solutions to problems but to endorse the historic inevitability of all such dilemmas.

"But there really wasn't enough hay," Jaroslav reminded Alden.

"Because some pie-in-the-sky economic plan had been laid down from above ten years earlier deciding for you how much hay there should be in order to make Column A add up to Column B. In a free market, there would have been sufficient hay," Alden said.

"What? Can a free market make the weather rain on the fields?" asked Jaroslav. "Do you buy better weather from Mexico and tow it north to America with NASA jets?"

"No, we can't do that yet," Alden allowed. "But in a free market, a farmer would have stockpiled hay after assessing long-range forecasts. In the West there is great competition among forecasters to come up with the most accurate long-range picture, and they're not afraid to say what their clients don't want to hear. Besides, they can always peddle their bad news elsewhere, to other, rival interests. That's the beauty of the system. So, let's assume we're talking about a dairy farmer. Armed with a long-range forecast, he would have known to leave more fields in hay. He would have gone out beforehand and bought additional hay to stockpile. He would have raised the price of his milk during lean times, and milk consumption would have fallen correspondingly, so even with less milk being produced because there was less hay, there would still be enough milk to go around, fair and square even during a period of drought and shortages. A free market adjusts and regulates itself."

"You pay more for less? That is good? Why is that good?" asked Jaroslav.

"It is good to ensure the supply, to discourage hoarding, and to avert panics," Alden said. "Besides, far more typically in this kind of economy there is an abundance of a product and you pay less for it. And abundances are self-generating because a free market goes into overdrive to produce more and more of what the public wants. The price of high-consumer items will fall. Look at what's happened with camcorders. They're cheaper all the time even as their quality improves, as competitive interests strive to win your dollars."

"Dollars," muttered Svatopluk. Alden was talking about how dollars behaved, not koruna, which were prettier and frailer than dollars. He wished his nation's currency were more serious looking and did not feel the necessity to assert itself in the world through design values alone.

"And then there's enough to go around for everyone," Tilla supposed.

Franca sat up straighter in her chair. Why had she not realized this in her long-ago schoolroom? Why had she not raised her arm in the air and declared that one could always run out to fetch another pie? Why had she not seen that she could have taken herself off to the kitchen and baked a pie of her very own and of a variety she preferred—cherry, in season, or gooseberry from a jar?

"And where will it ever end?" wondered Michal, who knew all this capitalist cant. He had reflected upon these theories during his years in exile among the steam pipes and hissing valves. He had formulated his own answer to his own query, of course, and it was one in which he passed less easily over the inevitable existence of those to whom even ever so slightly more expensive milk would be out of reach. Let them drink Coke, he supposed Alden would say. Even now, there was paperwork on his desk detailing how Coke distributorships would flourish in the Republic.

Alden said, "When the sun sears itself out in a supernova, that's when the world will end in a flash of fire *and* ice, and personally, I think NASA will be on top of that little problem, too. In the meanwhile, here in this office, we'll all just aim to please, and believe me, we won't run out of willing targets."

Jaroslav laughed and clutched the vicinity of his heart. "You've got me, pardner," he drawled, in his best Western voice.

BECKY'S BRIGHT-WALLED OFFICE SUITE was poised above the Nerudastrasse, a charming set of old and upper rooms in one of the more ancient structures lining the road as it rose toward Prague Castle. One million among ten million Czechs had registered as entrepreneurs, a tenfold increase since the right of a citizen to create his own business had lately been recognized. The Czechs were very keen to succeed. As Becky presided over her small agency, she felt the power of a force undammed. Even here, even in her backwater, residual waves pulsed and lapped up her charmingly proportioned stairwell.

Becky's area of interest made up a subcategory within a side category. She advised the female owners of very small businesses whose products or services primarily addressed meeting the needs or wants of other women. These lady entrepreneurs, who had frequently ventured in from the far countryside on the first, slow train of the morning that picked up milk and vegetables and flowers at leafy junctions along the way, had at first been directed and misdirected to various other unhelpful outer offices. They were handed high-numbered tickets and told to wait their turn as they worried the ticket over and over in their hands— number 61, not 19. They were required to fill in forms they knew were not the right ones. ESTIMATE ADVERSE ENVIRONMENTAL IMPACT . . . Sometimes the jam spills onto the tabletop when I am filling the jars. The expressions of the bureaucrats, as faceless as in the old days, remained as masklike. But a few of these women, whom Becky liked to think of as the lucky ones, were sent along to see her.

Becky's ladies hurried up the Nerudastrasse clutching and consulting another high-numbered ticket, which they matched at last to the ceramic number affixed to a pretty plaque beside a painted doorway.

On the first visit, which often occurred late in their day, the ladies were too spent to admire the wares on display in the window of the fine-linens shop that inhabited the first floor of the premises. But on ensuing visits, they began to notice and to pause and eventually to enter and to ask to have something unfolded for inspection, and when their ships came in, or had hoved into view, they made a first purchase, of a drawn-thread table scarf or scented drawer-liner paper or a lacy camisole. Show me, Becky would ask, at the telltale rustle and rosy glimpse of a Rosalina's shopping bag. How lovely, she would declare. The fact of this first purchase was her measure of success with a client. So, your bottom line rests upon frilly knickers, Alden had said as Becky tried to explain her yardstick.

That morning, Maria, Becky's assistant, was already in the office and at her desk, thoughtfully studying a glossy magazine—a permitted pastime here, indeed one that was encouraged. Maria was monitoring popular Western trends, all the better to serve and advise their clients. Torn paper slips marked nearly every page. Maria had noticed, this morning, that fashion layouts and advertising copy were employing babies as props and accessories. Babies were being held and babies were being floated and babies were crawling at the feet of long-legged, high-heeled women.

"And how might that affect us?" asked Becky as Maria presented her evidence of infants as accessories. "How big and blank babies' heads are," Becky said. She had forgotten this. "They look like empty balloon captions. All the time they're thinking, Feed Me, Pick Me Up, Boo Hoo."

"We have the applicant who proposes manufacturing dress-up buntings for the little babies," Maria reminded Becky. "In velvets and satins and such, which she procures in small pieces as remnants from a maker of formal wear located in her district."

"But these are awfully naked little babies in the photos," Becky said. "What am I looking at?" She consulted the magazine's cover. "Oh, well, this is *Vogue*, which is all about skin these days. Even the models aren't wearing much, for all this is a fashion magazine. I think the babies are featured for their soft and perfect baby skin because the models are considered over the hill when they turn fourteen."

"Yes," sighed Maria, "when they grow their woman hips the models are out. Although breasts are acceptable. They even purchase larger ones, but no one buys larger hips."

"I wasn't really taken with the formal baby bunting idea," Becky said. "Babies are such slopping-over creatures and dry cleaning is expensive here and, frankly, not always very reliable."

"The swaddlings are for special days, for church and festivals," Maria said.

"Babies have no instinct for occasion. They're hopeless," Becky said. "Or if they have an instinct it's for shrilling into high gear at the worst possible moment. What's the birthrate in the Republic, anyway? I know it's low. People are getting pets instead of having children. I want you to write back to that woman, Maria. Ask her if she'd consider designing deluxe pet clothes. The remnants would be the right size. We're talking bitsy dogs, silly pampered city dogs. The styles can't be all that different. You don't need legs or sleeves, and just include extra cutaways for tails and openings to accommodate Nature. People are beginning to have disposable income to waste on this sort of thing."

"Disposable income? Like plastic spoons for yogurt lunches?" wondered Maria as she made a note to count all the little children and all the little dogs in the street to determine which there was more of, although Mrs. Lowe was always right about this sort of thing.

"You know, money to burn, money burning a hole in your pocket, mad money, glad money," Becky said. She had settled in at her desk. She sorted through her briefcase contents. She flipped the pages of her daybook. "And speaking of dreams of baby-soft skin, the sisters have an appointment with us today," she said. "The sisters," so renowned in the office they needed no names.

"Yes, I am anticipating them," Maria said.

For Maria had dressed very carefully that day, Becky saw, no doubt in the sisters' honor. Maria was being very *Dallas* at present. The American television series had aired in translation over the winter and Maria had developed a taste for bourbon-based drinks. She sewed broad shoulder pads into her business suits and lashings of fringe swung from her sleeves and hemlines. Even in the winter, even when there was ice, she would only wear those sling-back stiletto-heeled pumps that were referred to as Catch Me, Thrill Me shoes. A proclaiming American corporate wife, encountered at Smetana Hall, had trumpeted the term while noisily deploring the naive locals' ill-advised absorption in the dreadful melodrama. You seem to know more about it than I, Becky had told her at the time, turning away. That evening's program of Brahms had left her feeling too tender to take her place among brash Americans.

"The sisters will be tycoon women," Maria foretold. "Can women be called tycoons? Or is there another American word for them?"

"No, there's no special term for high-achieving women that I am aware of," Becky said. "I don't suppose there has been a need for one, until lately." She considered. "You may be a Lady Macbeth if you're ambitious for your husband's sake."

"I should not want to be *her*," Maria declared, and her emphasis caused Becky to wonder, then, whom Maria *would* wish to be. Becky had her suspicions that Maria was biding her time until she identified the most promising new venture to pass through their office door and then would propose herself as a partner.

"The sisters' skin food is an excellent formulation," Maria said.

"You hardly need it, at your young age." Becky smiled.

"Oh, but one must practice conservation from the very beginning," Maria said. "My mother says. My mother says she wishes she had known before what she has come to know too late. She says she would have gone to Vienna in 1957. She had her chances, but she thought to herself, no, life here will improve, here I was born and here I will stay."

"Regret is a near-universal condition," Becky allowed. "Perhaps someone will come to us asking for help marketing a functioning time-travel machine. I suppose certain years would become as crowded as Venice or St. Croix. We could advertise, 'Visit the Resort Year of 1926,' or 'Drop In on 1969 Again,' just to see . . .'"

"Wasn't that the Summer of Love?" Maria asked. "I have read about the Summer of Love in history books. 'Make Love Not War.' "

"Was that 1969? Well, it was one of those summers we used to have then. When summers were longer and hotter and brighter," Becky said.

The morning passed. They were busy on the telephones and with the mail, completing what Becky referred to as their routine house-keeping chores. Maria brought back sandwiches from the good bakery on the corner at two o'clock and they shared a bottle of wine.

The sisters, who lived together in a Prague tower block, were policemen's early widows. Nothing heroic had carried off either husband; strong drink had killed one and an embolism finished off the other, as if the idea of an early death had been lodged in his brain. Eva and Agnes were uncompromisingly plain women, long faced and dark dressed and spare from wear and care. They most resembled woodcut crones from a nursery primer, and Becky reexperienced a childhood inability to decide which witch was the fiercer and which would be the more inveiglingly treacherous and thus the more menacing to a lost little girl. But, in fact, neither sister ever demonstrated any personal malice or ill-temper. The only enmity they expressed—and this they expressed routinely—was against a forehead wrinkle or an under-eye pouch or sagging jowls or a crepey neck. They may have felt too strongly about the lack, or the loss, of good looks. They may have trusted too unquestioningly in the sovereignty of physical beauty. They may have believed that had they been more favored, their husbands would have held on to life with surer grips, and the lift shaft of their jerry-built tower block would not stink of boiling root vegetables and drains and they would not have had to endure, greyly and un-valiantly existing for forty years beneath the thumb of a shabby little regime. Perhaps the sisters were not witches, after all, Becky reflected. Perhaps they were would-be fairy godmothers who had at last been released from a stronger conjurer's blacker spell.

The sisters' long, grey-threaded hair grew back from the same cowled hairline and was coiled into an S and a pinwheel-shaped bun against the nape of the neck. Becky imagined one sister pulling and tugging the other's hair into the configuration she would have pre-ferred on herself. But Eva and Agnes never disagreed. Stepping slightly forward, Eva spoke for both of them as Agnes nodded her assent to all that Eva said. They worked out their strategies at home, beforehand, as they tinkered in their kitchen laboratory, hatching their further plans as a timed experiment crepitated to a desired consistency in an iron pot

and then was decanted into cleaned-up jam jars, for which they perenni-
ally scouted in the more genteel-appearing rubbish bins of their high-
rise block. They knew, by now, where to look for them.

The sisters arrived midafternoon. Becky supposed the time was
approaching to take them out to a celebratory business dinner in a
restaurant they would adjudge neither too humble nor too grand for
the occasion. (How those analytic sisters measured things!) Maria might
know where to book, at some place serving excellent food in an atmosphere that had seen better days, with blackened frescoes and tarnished
and substantial knives and forks almost too blunted to slice and spear
with. There would be elderly waiters who really ought not to lift heavy
trays nor be trusted to flambé *palačinky* tableside.

Eva and Agnes carried string bags holding the recent fruits of their
research, several jars containing dollops of a magnesia-cream mask.
The lids were labeled in careful block-print English and a scrawl of
Czech. Becky always asked to sniff, first. The sisters' earliest efforts
had smelled of horseradish and vinegar—like a Moravian stockpot,
Maria had said, bleating into a tissue and daubing tears from her eyes
after a first whiff from a prototype jar. Becky had had to ground the
sisters in olfactory reality, and they had proved willing to learn. They
acknowledged that there was the science of science and the science of
lady things, verities of scents and colors and appellations and the inclu-
sion of softly flexing application wands of which they did not know.
Now, Agnes untwisted a jar top and with long, worn fingers directed
fragrance Becky's way. A vanilla-rose aroma lightly advanced. Home
Rose, Becky privately dubbed the scent, for she was reminded of home
(wherever that was, these days) and of the fresh pinkness of petals.

"Mmmmm," said Becky as everyone smiled.

"Try," Eva urged her.

"I too," Maria said. "On me."

Eva began to pat and rub areas of Maria's willingly offered face,
demonstrating the proper circular motion of application, and the short
upward strokes that facilitated absorption.

Agnes bid Becky to sit beside the office window and turned her
toward the sunny day. Delving in a string bag, Agnes withdrew her
magnifying glass swaddled in a flannel sheath. The magnifying glass

was an impressive instrument, which Becky supposed was a relic of the constable husband. She speculated that the pellucid lens had been trained upon its share of telltale and implicated slivers and specks and had, over time, acquired a specific sensitivity for spotting and highlighting the very worst of a matter. The lens's extreme clarity certainly was not clouded by sentiment.

Agnes's huge eye peered at Becky's skin, inspecting its surface centimeter by centimeter. Becky, who knew the drill, did not move or attempt to speak. Whenever she blinked, however necessarily, Agnes gusted a licorice-pastille sigh and the huge eye essayed a saccade back to a starting point and began again, detecting. At present, Becky was becoming aware of a sensation above her cheekbone. Her fingers itched to scratch there. She sat. The huge eye bore at her. The feeling above her cheekbone quickened. Nerves leapt. A point of pain declared itself. Becky flinched. Agnes exclaimed, *Tchah!*

"I believe I was being burned. A directed ray of sun focused by the lens was burning me," Becky said. "See. Burn. Hurt," she explained to Agnes.

Agnes delved into the string bag for a tube of salve. She daubed a cool cream onto Becky's cheek. "No red," she said firmly, as if the admonition were part of the treatment. Becky's hand strayed toward her face. "No touch," commanded Agnes.

Eva looked on and addressed Maria in Czech.

"They used to burn away warts with sunlight, like that. Eva says she can just remember," Maria reported.

"Those were the days," Becky remarked.

"They should think of writing a book of old wisdoms," Maria said. "Also, mole may be burned off, they say."

"They mustn't do that. Suspicious moles must be biopsied. Tell them not to do that," said Becky.

"They can cure baldness with rum and childlessness with bull's blood and if you cannot always remember little details of facts, make an infusion of mulberries and inhale the steam. That is for mental stimulation," Maria said. "Also paprika is best for staunching wounds."

"Indeed," said Becky. "Well, let's just stick to complexion formulations for now." She hoped the sisters weren't about to become carried away with cronish creativity and cure-alls just when she was about to put them through their paces before certain buyers from a certain New York department-store chain. "Tell them to stick to the subject. Eyes on the prize," Becky told Maria as she returned to her desk. She selected papers from her briefcase.

Agnes, having tenderly stowed her magnifying glass, began to catechize Becky.

"You use the grains?" Agnes asked.

"Yes," Becky said.

"You use the splashing tonic?"

"Yes."

"Every night?"

"Every night? Well, almost every."

"You use this cream. Today and next today and after again. Use, please."

"Yes, I shall."

"Good. Use all. They make—change."

"A change. An improvement. Yes, I honestly think so too. I'm very pleased with the results of your products," Becky said.

"Better," confirmed Agnes.

"Eva thinks you look like a different person," Maria told Becky. "She thinks you look like Catherine Deneuve. Before, you looked like Catherine Deneuve's mother. She also notices, as I have, that you have lost much weight since they first met you."

"Yes, yes, I believe I have," Becky said. "I find I walk more with a chauffeur. He makes such a fuss about driving us where we need to go it's simpler to just hoof it. And our cook is not a very good cook, you know. We only eat enough to be polite." Becky consulted her notes. Eva and Agnes sat facing her across the desk. Maria perched on a corner of the desk, braced by a befringed arm.

"There's still so much to decide. We have to design the jarrage," Becky said. She was fond of that word, jarrage. She had noticed the cosmetics trade was susceptible to extra syllables that sounded elegant, or scientific, or perhaps suggested a fusion of the two.

"And we have to come up with a company name. I propose something along the lines of 'Prague-Matics,' because European locations carry great credibility in skin-care circles. And the 'Matics' references the several different products that must be used together to—well, frankly, to milk the consumer of as many of her consecutive skin-care dollars as we can. Then again, your ingredients are also very practical, or pragmatic. Believe me, this works in English. And I think the jarrage should be practical as well. I see something along the lines of a plain tin or enameled shaker container to sift out the cleansing grains. Plain, but with an elegant profile. Nothing froufrou because good skin isn't froufrou. It's a basic necessity. That's your corporate mission statement, I've just decided. Good skin is a basic necessity."

Froufrou?

The sisters declared themselves not to be on the side of the froufrou, after Maria explained the word to them after Becky explained it to her.

Becky decided not to mention Alden's proposed advertising slogan, *Beauty Is Youth and Youth Is Beauty*, which was just Alden being Alden. Besides, Alden had failed to notice that women were allowed to be older here. Becky had watched women her own age and beyond out enjoying themselves in the cafés, having conversations with keenly attentive men which were obviously not about the children or the plumbing or the checkbook.

"First, though, we have one more hurdle," Becky said. "We have to satisfy the US FDA that your ingredients pass muster. They have to be satisfied."

"What is US FDA?" asked Eva.

Becky explained. Agnes scowled. She toed her string bag closer to her ankles.

"And I take it we're all against animal testing?" asked Becky.

The mystified sisters were enlightened by Maria. Eva scowled.

"We are all very against," Maria said. "Eva and Agnes own a darling pug whom they pet and pamper ridiculously." An adored pet—how wise Becky was.

"I think we're safe on the ingredients front, anyway," Becky said. "The cleanser consists of powdered milk, powdered horseradish, and powdered alum, and the toner is just water and lavender water and glycerin, and the new mask cream is a combination of . . ."

"Primarily powdered magnesium and rose water," Maria translated, "and proper application and don't speak or smile while the mask is in place and drink fresh springwater every day and don't sleep on your face at night, it is forbidden."

"You can practically eat the stuff. And the moisturizer is just petrolatum and lanolin and oil of almond and an inert substance. Well, I'm no chemist, but I shouldn't look for trouble from an inert substance, would you?" Becky said. "So our next step is to document the formulae through an independent lab's analysis, which Eva and Agnes must authorize and agree to pay for upon receipt of said analysis. Make sure the ladies understand this, please, Maria. You have to spend money to make money. Can that be expressed idiomatically in Czech?"

Agnes and Eva listened to Maria. They swayed as they understood, then stiffened with resolve and nodded, together. Becky envisioned their life's savings kept in a stocking drawer enfolded in tissue, wrapped in brown paper, hidden in an old shortbread tin knotted inside a lingerie bag tucked beneath a boned corset of the sort traditionally relied upon for its proven qualities of containment and defense.

"And then we must go to the bank with our business plan and our purchase orders in hand, and tell them we have a factory standing by—I am inquiring about factory space—and the bank will give them all the money they need to get started. Tell them, Maria," Becky said. "Tell them that's what banks are for."

"No," uttered Agnes, who had never heard such a thing in all her days.

"Yes," Becky said. "Believe me, banks live to lend money."

"They're terribly authentic, aren't they?" Becky remarked to Maria after the sisters had been seen off clutching more forms and documents to puzzle over and to fill in with their most honest answers. "I noticed Eva particularly speaking to you at the end. Has she some other concern?"

Maria hesitated. She concentrated on untangling some wayward hem fringe, and then she said, "Eva was saying that she knows her concoctions are very, very good, but in her opinion it is also something else, or someone else, who is making you look so entirely new. Someone else? I asked her. Do you mean a romance? I suddenly asked her, because even Eva was sparkling a bit at the idea of a romance."

"And what did you tell her?" asked Becky.

"I reminded Eva that Mrs. Lowe is a respectable married woman and did not come to us from the Wild West city of *Dallas*," Maria said primly.

AN ASSORTMENT OF INTERNATIONAL YOUTH took up space in the third-floor classroom as a ceiling fan juddered so noisily that Herr Wolfe, standing at the head of the room beside the pale green chalkboard, seemed to be reciting *kap-tunk, kap-tunk* as he—what did one do to verbs?—conjugated the Czech for To be. Nouns were always declined, Julie recalled. She'd be happy to decline all the funny nouns Herr Wolfe had on offer round here. She smiled generally upon her fellow students as she thought up this thought. She toyed with an earring, and another earring, and the earring after that.

Just pronounce everything as if you're buzzed, was her recommendation. They all slurred their words here; that was the secret of speaking Czech. The students at the International Youth High School were all very good at learning the local secrets, Julie had observed; they knew whether you had to pay before or after you ate at the cafés, and the legal or getting-away-with-it drinking age, except the waiters automatically brought everybody a beer at the crowded pub places whether asked to or not. Cigarettes and bus tickets were on sale at *Tabuis-Trafiks*, like people were supposed to smoke on the trams here. Well, fine. International Youth itself could be defined and understood by nationality. Only the Americans and the English had any musical taste. American youth ruled, but they had to be kind of cool and not too obvious about how American clothes and American movies and American music and American stuff were better than anybody else's in the world. The other youth could say so while the American youth just sort of shrugged it off, as if it didn't matter that it mattered. The English kids were like deputies or sidekicks to the Americans, almost as clued in about what was what. But French youth came off as awfully old—not adult, just old. They liked to lip-sync to CDs after they'd dressed themselves up like the performer, in Madonna's bustier or with Prince's stenciled-on goatee. German youth came on too strong and liked to argue. Everybody felt kind of sorry for the Czech youth; whatever they tried to have like other kids had they could only ever afford one piece, like just the jacket instead of the whole outfit, or the single instead of the album. Their parents were not very rich at all. But everyone got along with each other pretty well. They were Youth together, International Youth allied in opposition to All Adults.

Herr Wolfe kept on reciting *kap-tunk, kap-tunk.* Julie knew not to stare at him too hard for he would think she was paying attention. He would think she was interested and he would call on her to recite with every hope. Not to know the answer, Julie didn't mind that, but leading Herr Wolfe on seemed unkind. Poor man, he was flogging such a useless language. Everybody spoke English, at least anyone you might want to talk to. There were other ancient leftover people her mother could jumble at in German. Her mother had studied German so she could sing the words of Schubert and suchlike with proper expression and emotion, but her mother was a tremendously conscientious person, or she used to be before she got all tied up in her new career.

Kap-fluffle-tunk, kap-fluffle-tunk. The ceiling fan had snagged the end of a fluttering length of flypaper suspended too close. All of the International Youth had been willing this to happen. The fan tugged the flypaper free and it flailed from blade to blade, and then the blades began to shred the ribbon, dispersing fly bits all over the heads of the International Youth. Several of the Italian kids fled the room, exclaiming strenuously.

But Julie was satisfied here—no, not *here* being rained fly on, but here in Prague, living in a castle with a distracted set of parents, free to come and go as she pleased, being given pretty much whatever she wanted without even having to ask very hard. Her brothers were far distant and out of her way at last. At last she was cool in school. At last she was in love, and not hopelessly so; the guy loved her back. Indeed, she was successfully in love for the third time since coming to Prague, which made the exercise seem reassuringly undesperate. Demonstrably, the rule here was not just one to a customer, so she did not have to hold on hard to a boyfriend as if for the very life of her.

Herr Wolfe was wandering up and down the classroom aisles now, his too-white, too-gentle hand extended (Julie noticed this sort of detail, a man's hand, these days). Some of the International Youth, the Japanese and the Canadians, *those* countries, were flourishing note-book pages at him, but most were averting their heads and muttering extenuating native versions of why their homework assignment was not available. The dog ate my homework—everybody loved Julie's classic American excuse whenever she trotted it out. Herr Wolfe's hand withdrew courteously at the nonperformers' utterances. He never re-vealed his feelings. Herr Wolfe would have been an ambassador, Julie's father said, if only he hadn't signed something or other at some time or other objecting to the old government and so been punished for that. They forced him to become a humble schoolmaster, teaching, at times, the English and German and Russian and French he ought, by rights, to have been speaking in an embassy as an ambassador, complimenting other cultures with his knowledge of their languages. But now Herr Wolfe was too bowed by his travails to reclaim his true place in the world. The tide had turned too late for him. Poor Herr Wolfe, her fa-ther said. Freedom's just another word for nothing left to lose. Oh shut up, will you, Alden, her mother had said.

Today, most amazingly, Julie also had a piece of paper to give to Herr Wolfe. Her cohorts nudged one another, and Neville drew down the corners of his eyes and bucked his teeth. Julie smiled, not un-pleased with herself as Herr Wolfe's pace quickened past Wesley from Denmark, who had curled into a shrimp shape, pinkening. Herr Wolfe reached over Wesley's head and, taking the piece of paper, noted with pleasure a block of neat word processing accomplished with a fresh ink cassette.

"Děkuji," he said, very nicely.

"Neni Zač," Julie answered very carefully, suffering a slight pang of remorse, which she suppressed.

AT SIX MARIA PREPARED to leave the office. Those magazines from abroad, the sisters' latest cosmetic samples, her synthetic silk blouse (she had changed into a bustier; she was meeting a new man after work) were secured inside the briefcase Becky had given her on her re-cent birthday. The actresses of *Dallas* carried great shiny briefcases as they strode, sashayed—stormed (as was their wont)—onto all those high-rise office sets which, oddly, looked like nothing so much as twenty-sixth-century spaceships' flight decks, as Alden had once observed (and the Dallas-scape beyond also appearing like no place on earth). Maria had been making do with an old watercolorist's wooden box, shellacked a glossy black and from which she had prised partitioning slats and the leather loops that held brushes and blocks of gum arabic in place. Becky had thought the makeshift item a charming simulation, but she understood how Maria yearned for the real thing, wrought in calfskin by Louis Vuitton, initialed in gold script, with a combination lock of tumblers set to spring open at the sequential numbers of her birth date. The briefcase had cost far more than Maria ·would have been capable of guessing or of believing, if told, but at present Maria was less concerned with ascertaining how much such objects cost than with learning how to go about procuring them. She longed, as well, for a pocket-size device into which one might enter the day's appointments and engagements and which emitted a discreet tone as each allotted hour approached.

"Good night. I hope he's nice," Becky said to Maria, who had outlined her evening's plans as she slipped from blouse into bustier, requiring Becky to cinch the lattice of lacing tighter than Becky had thought wise.

"Nice?" inquired Maria, quirking an eyebrow.

"What am I saying? I mean, I hope he's handsome but not conventionally handsome—that's suspect—and that he's a rising star in his chosen field of endeavor, and a bit of a bastard to boot but only as a defensive measure because he's so secretly sensitive underneath as only you, Maria, are woman enough to perceive and to understand and to unlock, with just the right combination of guile and guilelessness, the fortress that is his heart," Becky said. Maria chattered unguardedly about her romances, for on *Dallas* everyone brought their personal lives into the office. Indeed, secretaries were always being cautioned by their bosses not to interrupt them with business matters as passionate affairs blossomed and then imploded behind closed conference room doors while Saudi Arabian princes were left to languish in the reception area after coming all that way from the desert in their robes.

"Now you are making fun of me," said Maria. "But perhaps you are also trying to tell me for my own good that I should be content to settle for Mr. Nice?"

"Do you know, I think that's the last thing I should tell you," Becky said.

"Tell me the first thing then, please," Maria challenged her.

"*You* look very *nice,*" said Becky, having the last word after all as Maria, laughing at the very idea (because she could only agree), flew down the office stairs and became a bright speck upon the busy end of the working-day scene on the Nerudastrasse.

Becky watched from the upper window overhanging the crooked sidewalk to make certain that Maria was well away, and then she returned to her desk and unlatched her own briefcase and lifted out a folder. Sifting through some fodder, she extracted a letter, which had for a week now required a reply. It had been shoved into her skirt pocket, pushed beneath her desk blotter at home for several days, and then folded into the novel she was reading. She had come across the letter again at the turn of a page.

With All My Will, but Much Against My Heart told the tale of a middle-aged woman named Meredith-Grace. A ripe and bowing rose bled petals across the book's dust jacket, and within, the emotional plight of its heroine was signaled by her many baking failures. The author had noticed that knead and need were homonymns—as were symbol and cymbal, Becky reflected, also woe and whoa, and awful and offal. Her mind had wandered as she read. There was a husbandly husband, often heard from, and a dishy Rector given to quoting Coventry Patmore in place of Scripture, while an impending Apple Festival inspired double-edged talk of tarts among the villagers. You do the math, Becky thought, as she willed Meredith-Grace to get on with it, or at the very least to realize that she needed to knead her leaden piecrusts less and with a lighter touch. (Adding a drop or two of vinegar wouldn't hurt, either.) When William's lost, latest letter reappeared at the turn of a page, Becky's eye slipped from one narrative line to the other and she and William had become just two more people in another story, and one that Becky was equally as keen to get on with.

When she reread William's letter at such a remove, viewing William

and herself and their situation as if none of it were quite real and therefore none of it really mattered, she allowed herself to admit that William's letter was very wonderful indeed. She had not read William's
words with her usual critical eye, neither rolling nor narrowing her
eyes at his expressions of love and longing for her, and now, uncapping
her pen and squaring a sheet of writing paper upon her desk blotter,
she found she did not want to reply to him with her usual bland and im-
personal descriptions of meals and the weather in the streets and other
aspects of the local scene. Sometimes she cribbed entire paragraphs
from the Blue Guide, or filled further sheets of paper with the latest
twist in the drama of the castle drains. She could never quite identify
the nature of the satisfaction she derived from producing such quelling
replies to William's protestations. She suspected there might well be
more than a tinge of malice involved, whether aimed at him or herself,
she could not have said. And was she mocking him or herself when she
informed William, "By far the best means of touring the city is on foot,
though visitors should be warned that the comparatively short distances are made up for by the numerous Hills to be negotiated"?

But then, he ought to be grateful that anyone at all among his old
friends was willing to write to him however tiresomely and nonrespon-
sively after news of his espionage activities had come to light and he
had hied off to Libya, where Western authorities could not touch him.
Just how much harm he had actually done, no one was certain. There
had been some tut-tutting coverage in the press but the nature of the
information William had traded in had not been of a kind to cause
much in the way of a popular outcry. The scandal was just not sexy
enough, as Alden said, and of course, neither was William.

Becky's pen began to move of its own accord, forming words across
the page, the words coming in a rush as if they had been locked for far
too long inside the barrel of the pen. The words tumbled out in someone else's script and idiom, neither neat nor careful, now swirling and
urgent. Dear William, Becky wrote, Dearest William. William, My
Dear One, Dear, Dear William, My Dear.

Three

Večer—In the Evening

THEY WERE, IT SEEMED, ABOUT TO THROW a very large party on rather short notice.

Alden's actor cousin was coming to Prague. Arthur Hill had been cast in a big new production of a remake of the old French film *Children of Paradise*. He had been signed on, according to a press release, to re-create the Jean-Louis Barrault role of Baptiste, the mime who enchanted audiences even as his own great heart was breaking. At present, Prague could more successfully play nineteenth-century Paris than could Paris herself, for Prague's beautiful clocks had been summarily stopped and art directors did not quite yet have to design their shots around ATM machines and Golden Arches and glass-and-steel eruptions shouldering above ancient tiled rooftops.

Arthur had explained all of this when he telephoned on a thin-sizzling line from Montana, where he had a place now—or perhaps Montana *was* his place. Alden had not quite caught the claims of acreage and proud possession as his younger cousin relayed them. Alden had been privately marveling that someone related to him was about to strut across the silver cineplex screen projected twelve feet high for all the world to see, openly emoting and remembering his lines. Alden was sure he himself could not do both at once; he recited woodenly, and felt, he felt, inarticulately; his words were inadequate and his gestures were dumb at those times when a stronger performance was called for.

"But who else is going to be in this movie?" Alden asked, or objected.

Arthur, who in his career to date had only ever shone in an offishly odd sitcom and once again when he became known as the guy in the

car-rental commercial who had to get to the hillbilly wedding in Lost
Stick, Tennessee, happily named Names whom Alden attempted to
picture on memory's reel. He was, however, no cineast. The last movie
he and Becky had actively gone to was *The Crying Game*, which had
not left much of an impression. Between all the glottal, permanent-
head-cold British accents and a distracting scroll of Czech subtitles,
Alden had failed to grasp either thread of the story (evidently, some
woman was not what she appeared to be), and furthermore, he had
been waiting for Michael Caine to appear to steal the movie in a fi-
nessed scene or two, for Michael Caine, whom Alden recalled always
liking in whatever he did, seemed to have a part in all those earnest English efforts which he subsidized with star turns in those godawful
blockbusters where things exploded and people were blown up.

"And who is Michael Caine going to play in your movie?" Alden
asked Arthur.

"What? What have you heard?" asked Arthur, sitting up halfway
around the world.

After ringing off, Alden went in search of Becky. He had news, and
news which even Becky in her most decidedly dissenting of tempers
could not fail to receive with at least a flicker of interest, which Alden
would fan. He was looking forward, they would both look forward together, to the movie folk coming to town. He and Becky would angle
to be extras in the big, international motion picture; they would play
two among many in the crowd scenes: aristocrats presiding at court,
ruffians lurking in an alleyway. They could play powdered, they could
play muddied. Although he wondered whether the locals wouldn't
have the advantage of historical authenticity over Becky and himself.
The Czechs had submitted to less cosmetic dentistry, and they would
wear the unstylish costume clothes less self-consciously. Alden began
to worry he and Becky would not make the cut, for his heart was quite
set upon playing the Courtly Gentleman or even the Courteous Beggar
if that was all they offered him.

He found Becky in the kitchen dooryard. She had been rummaging
for their Saturday-night supper—half a loaf, a wedge of cheese, a can
of soup were lined up on the stovetop—and then she had lost interest.

Alden told her Arthur's news.

"Oh dear, did Arthur really say that, about acting Baptiste as laughing on the outside and crying on the inside?" Becky asked. "But Baptiste is a very romantic character. Can Arthur be romantic? Arthur? Your cousin Arthur? I can't picture those pipe-cleaner arms of his wrapping round anyone in a big cinematic clinch."

"My dear, he's family," Alden objected. "Don't you feel you married into a highly romantic line?" he asked, leadingly. Perhaps this chat would wind its way round to a rapprochement; if Becky was putting this much thought into the subject of men's embraces, he regarded that as a hopeful sign. Mrs. Cook was away, Julie had gone out earlier, and Josef had announced his intention of becoming very drunk, that evening, in his stable quarters, no reason offered as Josef's narrowed eyes defied the Boss to object. Much later tonight, Josef would roam the belvedere and launch empty bottles from its height. But with any luck Alden and Becky would not be aware of anyone or anything else by then.

"I don't like to think of them desecrating the memory of the original film. It was such a good movie. Remember when you and I saw it? Oh that was years ago in some revival house in New York," she recalled. Alden had turned to her and said, *I* would never have let *you* get away as Baptiste had Garance. They had leaned back and rather complacently watched the credits to see who had been whom, playing the supporting roles.

"Did we? No, I don't think I ever saw it," Alden said.

"Wasn't that you?" asked Becky. "That wasn't you? Surely, that was you."

"Nothing Arthur said rang a bell," Alden said. "Who or what is a funambule? Arthur kept going on about that."

"I saw it with someone. Because I know I discussed it afterward. It's one of those earnest-discussion-afterward movies."

"That must have been one of your other beaus, dear. But we'll catch the new version and talk about that one. Arthur said they're contemplating a happier ending. I take it the last time out things ended badly," Alden said.

"It was terribly romantic. A *look* passed between Baptiste and Garance," Becky said.

"Satisfied with a look, were they? French people?" asked Alden.

To which Becky only replied, Oh, Alden, as she turned away from him. She had stepped outside to see if the tomato plants she had found in the marketplace and brought home had done anything. Miss Mopsy had promised to water the seedlings and to move them round the walled dooryard to catch the sun in passage across the slates.

"Drat," Becky said, kneeling by a terra-cotta pot. "Those weren't tomatoes I bought. They seem to be some sort of pepper. I wonder if they're hot ones. They have those hot peppers here that I don't like."

Alden knelt beside her and prodded the side of one green globe as if he could tell by touch. "It feels cool enough," he said.

"Don't touch your eyes now. If it is a hot pepper you'll make your eyes burn," Becky said.

There was an antique well in the kitchen dooryard, edged with a low-set ring of eroding bricks and covered, at some lost time, with planks that had long since split and fallen away. A frog, who used a broken board as a sort of ramp, dwelling neither in nor out of the well, said, "MCWZD, MCWZD" (Alden said), and the last of the carp slopped to the surface in pursuit of a substanceless, skimming bug, and subsided. The just-disturbed water breathed up a sulphur smell. Alden rinsed his fingers off in the murk.

"Now you'll get typhus," Becky remarked.

"They could film nineteenth-century Paris right here," Alden said. "Although we might have to smarten up a bit, for the scene where that Baptiste fellow takes out the garbage or has to tinker with the lawn mower—talk about the kind of ending no one has the courage to shoot."

"Oh, Alden," Becky said again.

"Oh, Becky. Let's go out to dinner," Alden offered. "Instead of sitting here in this fetid gloom being gloomy and eating that local soup which I *wish* tasted of the tin so it would at least taste like something. And I'm leery of that pepper."

"Josef is blotto and where do you suppose the car keys are? In his unlovely pocket, that's where. He keeps them from us, haven't you noticed? And we don't have reservations anywhere decent, and besides, I'm tired of being overcharged because they think all foreigners are stupid tourists. They do that here, it's so unattractive," Becky said. "I have to send Maria out every day to buy our lunch."

"Let's have a party at the castle, then," Alden suddenly decided.

"When? Tonight? Asking whom? No, of course not," Becky said. "A party," she added quellingly.

"Not now. But let's plan a party. We'll invite all of Arthur's movie colleagues when they get here, and everyone else we know. We'll string fairy lights along the trees of the Avenue and set alight flaming torchieres across the belvedere."

"There's rather more to a party than providing actors and illumination," Becky said.

"Hire a band, hire a caterer, hire a bartender, hire a ringmaster. Let's fling a 'fin de siècle, wake up with a handgun and a heap of baccarat chits on the pillowcase and blowing out the barn boards, night to remember' party," Alden said. "We haven't done that lately."

"Oh, all right," sighed Becky. "If that's what you think you want, I suppose I can throw something together."

BECKY HAD A CLIENT WHO CATERED, and a lady vintner and a lady brewer client, and a client whose son worked as an electrician for the Ministry of Culture and who lit all the museum exhibitions and cathedral spires and international music festivals, spotlighting the lovely parts and leaving the rest cloaked in shadows. Another client ran a secretarial bureau, and she issued the invitations to all of those included on the several long lists written in several longhands (Becky's, Alden's, Julie's). On her own initiative, Kathinka addressed envelopes to those whom the Lowes had overlooked. Prague society was not so large, in her opinion, that you could not not ask everyone after a certain point. Besides, she had her own social and business agenda to advance, and she was coming to the party, of course; Mr. Lowe, dropping by with the lists, had appended her name to his muster roll when he had said, We'll see you there, and she had shaken her head and looked wistful.

Arthur, who had arrived in the Republic on cue, delivered all the film folk, who were intrigued by the promise of a warm reception at an actual castle tucked away in this authentic Old World corner. Some among them believed Arthur's local cousin to be a bona fide nobleman, and Arthur himself might have been cast without enduring too many hours in the makeup chair as the palely conflicted last son of some crumbling dynasty.

On the day of the party, the dance band arrived in the late afternoon to set up in the Great Hall, and Alden, long since pronounced tone-deaf by Becky, left them to their odd blurts and running scales. He wandered off to plant a steadying foot on the bottom ladder rung for the electrician, whose backside disappeared up a tree and was swallowed by the foliage. The weather had cooperated, continuing as warm and what passed for fair in the damaged atmosphere that hung low enough above the city to make one want to reach up and winnow away the haze like the neighbors' barbecue smoke drifting over a fence. Alden turned toward the castle. Viewing it from this distance (the electrician was wiring the last of the trees lining the carriageway), Alden decided that his domain looked entirely plausible. That's the word that came to him, plausible. For the last few weeks, caught up in the preparations, Becky had not had time to be silent and cold and remote. They had had several conversations about the relative merits of smoked salmon and sablefish. Alden had said they could serve both and Becky had agreed, both, and so he began to hope.

He descried, then, the figure of Josef stalking across the stable yard, headed for the residence. One of Josef's hands projected forward. Cylindrical objects dangled by their tails, caught between his stiffened fingers. Alerted by Josef's predatory attitude, Alden abandoned his post at the ladder bottom and took off across the grounds. He pelted over tough grass and across gravel walks and the courtyard cobblestones. He tripped up the shallowly shelving marble steps and burst through the great door of the Great Hall, propped open by an aslant sixteenth-century pike because the caterers were beginning to arrive and unload trays of foodstuff and crates of bottles and sheaves of flowers from the backs of panel ruchs.

Josef was setting alight sausage-shaped firecrackers, clamping them in his fist until the fizzling tails had well nigh consumed themselves, when, rounding off, he flung them up and away toward the Great Hall's high, vaulted rafters where some swallows had been peaceably roosting. Detonations shortly retorted and reverberated. Birds swooped, they soared, they plunged. The musicians cried out and covered their ears and ducked away from flying firecrackers and plummeting birds. The percussionist sheltered his drum set with his body. Josef's laugh exclaimed amidst all the trouble he had caused. Josef's rusty laugh, never declared before, needled the turbulent chamber like iron filings until he was arrested by Alden, who caught his arm and snatched the last firecracker from him. A musician uttered hard words in Czech; Fool or Idiot, he must have accused, and Josef, suddenly sullen again, muttered, "I try. To help." He kicked away one among many shuddering, fallen swallows in demonstration. It skidded into a pile of its twitching fellows.

Alden sought out Becky at her dressing table.

"And what am I supposed to do?" Becky asked. She leaned toward the mirror and slowly smoothed a pearl-size clot of cream into her brow, which she willed not to crease, not now, not even for this.

Alden shook his head. Agony was agony. The panicked birds were broken and dying. He had reeled from the Hall. He could not go back there until Becky had made the place right again. He slumped onto the end of a silk-covered chaise, as wretched now as he had been ebullient just an hour earlier when he taught the several hired-on bartenders how to mix a perfect manhattan.

"I can't," Alden said. "I can't bear to look."

"Oh Lord," Becky relented. She watched the unhappy Alden, obliquely pictured in a panel of her dressing-table mirror. She knew all about his soft heart and her capable hands, the component aspects of the entity labeled Us. Alden shifted, sliding about on the chaise. The posture of dejection was not easy to maintain on silky cushions. He ought to have fallen upon a heap of sackcloth, although she would have criticized him for that piteous choice as well, were the choice there to be made in their elegant bedchamber. Becky admitted as much, for as hard as she was on Alden these days, neither did she spare herself from her newly disparaging eye. Her constant unkindness to him did not reflect well upon herself even though she was uncommonly pleased with the face she saw gazing back from her looking glass. She sighed and picked up a tube and expelled a worm of rose glycerin onto her palm. Rubbing and wringing her hands over and over, she made an effort.

"I don't want to see, either," Becky said. She had learned, over the past two years, that she did not always have to be the one to brave the fray, bearing a broom and offering the apologies. "Ring for Miss Mopsy and tell her to sweep out the Hall and, mind you, tip her tremendously. And give the musicians beer and tip them tremendously too. Then, first thing Monday morning, you must firmly tell whoever is in charge of him down at the Ministry that Josef is a psychopath. They probably already know that anyway. They just hoped we'd think he was being foreign, the resident local color. Tell them we insist upon returning him, and in the meanwhile, tell Josef he's fired. Tell him to stay out of sight and to keep out of everyone's way tonight. No, wait, I'll tell him. You'll be too soft on him. He'll know he's been told when I tell him. Besides, I shall enjoy telling him."

"Yes, yes, all right," said Alden, rising. "I'll go ask Miss Mopsy and dispense the largesse where needed." He scooped more currency from his stud box, where he kept a pile of Czech money; he was collecting a bill in every denomination and meant to have them framed someday.

"And don't let this ruin the party for you," Becky said.

"No, no, I shan't, dear," Alden assured her. "We'll soldier on together."

"Because this shindig of yours was costing us a fortune even before the necessity for massive bribery arose, although I'm going to write off a goodly portion as a business expense. Networking is such a nebulous concept, it should float," Becky said. She dismissed Alden, then. She turned farther away from him as he worked out just how, physiologically, his wife could contrive to show him the back of her back. She flexed her shoulder blades against the thin stuff of her dressing gown, as close as she could come to raising hackles at him as she pushed to and fro impatiently among the clutter of bottles and jars and boxes scattered across her dressing-table top. She was scheduled to lie still for an hour now, with the sisters' prescribed compress of flaxseeds covering her eyes, a fixed and defenseless position and one in which it would be unendurable to her to be rocked to the pitch of soft mattress should Alden lie down beside her to rest before the party and to continue this conversation or perhaps to pick up the pieces of some other one which they had also let drop.

AN HOUR ON, BECKY ROSE AND DRESSED in a long black gown that seemed such a limp, discarded thing on the hanger and became something else altogether when put on. Becky remembered how she had formerly selected dresses based upon the attractiveness of their appearance on the hanger. The neat and pleasant prospect of a new dress set swinging against the back of a closet door prior to the beginning of an evening out had assured her that she too was likely to look quite as nice. She would place the pumps she had decided to wear on the floor below the hem, and approximately position a necklace, a bracelet, some earrings (clipped to the shoulders of the dress) just to see. She'd suspend a handbag from the closet doorknob, which would swing as she opened and closed her closet door in pursuit of second thoughts about the pumps, or a scarf, although she'd never been one of those people who was good with scarves.

On most of those evenings out, Becky acknowledged now, she might just as well have sent off her dress and the assembled accessories draped over Alden's arm, perhaps with a small cassette player tucked inside the handbag turned on to emit at intervals soft murmurs of assent or gentle query. No matter what was being said to her, soft murmurs of assent and gentle queries had been all the conversation required of Becky, which, as she allowed now, had often let her off one hook even as she had been content to peg herself to another.

Becky sat before her dressing-table mirror and began to rummage, again, among pots and tubes, a little logjam of rolling-about tubes, a tottering ziggurat of pots. She smoothed on foundation with fingertips that trembled slightly, although she hadn't thought she was nervous about the party; nor did she believe she was pleasurably anticipating the night to come. She could not think what condition lay wedged between wishing and not wishing for a moment to arrive—some suspended state, a frozen one? Perhaps her hands shook with the coldness of that circumstance.

Those had been highly constructed dresses she had formerly worn;

she had been well contained within them. Padding and darts and shirring and tucks and panels and stiffening underslips had shaped her according to a type to which Becky and all of her kind who shopped at the nice shops were persuaded to aspire. Their breasts and waists were acknowledged as small rises and slight indentations, their hips were skimmed over by forgiving flares of fabric. Their legs began below their knees. They displayed wrists, but no tapering lengths of arm. Some pretty detail of ruffle or ruche at the neck framed faces that had been painted on for the evening. Still, Becky had not really minded observing such strictures even if she had occasionally wondered whether she might not look better were she to make a better effort. She had never quite gotten round to exploring the possibility, because she had been so busy with the children then, and Alden was spending twelve hours a day at the office, and even though she had help, as she used to say to Alden, she often regarded them as Help! Besides, she may have learned that she was already doing the best she could and that she wasn't such an undiscovered gem after all, who needed only to be prised from the ore.

She stood, or, rather, she uncoiled, as her sudden rising movement appeared to her as glimpsed in the dressing-table mirror, as if her shadow self were just emerging from some tight, private corner, released and springing into being again. Her hands brushed downward to arrange her gown, but her gown had arranged itself, falling, caught, falling, caught, from her shoulders to her shoes. She was, she knew then, in the mood for a party after all, and her immediate task, that of tracking down Josef and thoroughly firing him, struck her oddly but energetically as just the kickoff she required. She would banish Josef and celebrate by consuming a first slick, cold martini. Alden claimed he had trained the local bartenders to mix all the retro vermouthy cocktails that the grown-ups (who had seemed so grown-up, then) used to drink during the Eisenhower administration. We'll see about that, Becky said.

Josef lived above the stables. He had taken up residence before they had arrived. An initial demur and her subsequent dislike of him had kept Becky from visiting his quarters with a vase of flowers or a plate of Toll House cookies. He had moved in early so he could meet his new employers at the airport with the car, already knowing the way to and from the castle. He had arrived very late that first day, but the courteous Lowes, biding their time on a hard plastic bench and regretting that the bar had closed for the night, had feigned not to notice that his initial step was such a wrong one. Poor fellow, they thought. He'd only recently ceased being an oppressed person. They had stood and stretched and strained after luggage and then followed Josef into the night on the strength of his thumb jutting *Let's go.* Becky had asked him if he was comfortable in his room, if he was all set, and his muttered yes had settled the question for good. His spare arrangements were already in place. A barrel had been pulled from beneath the spill of a downspout to receive his empty beer bottles. A laundry line, steeply slung from gable to gatepost, sagged with his grey washing, which he must have transported, soiled, from his previous address, there was so much of it. He had to have left his previous post in a hurry, Becky realized now, which proved he could be dislodged with a swift boot.

Josef possessed few, if any, mechanical skills. He turned up the radio when the undercarriage developed a rattle after he backed over a basalt pillar marker on the wrong road to Most. He listened to a squawking, revisionist Slovakian radio station until the affronted chatter subsided from the ether at dusk. Then he turned to the military marching-band channel. Alden had handed him a tin of Turtle Wax one day and told him to use it, but Josef failed to follow some necessary step of the application process. Wax still adhered to the car's body as a scaly paste, impervious to a hose, or the rain, although the substance had cracked in the cold last winter and was blistering into beads beneath this summer's sun. The beads could be gouged free with a thumbnail, and picking away at the wax at least gave the Lowes something to do as they waited for Josef to emerge from a tabak or a tavern, after some errand of his own.

But now Josef had really stepped over the line as he had so far barely managed not to do in the courteous American household he had been sent to serve. Becky plucked up the hem of her skirt as she strode across the stable-yard cobblestones. Alden's fairy lights had been strung from gables to gateposts, and a remote switch, just struck, set the lights asparkle. Becky tsked. She had hoped to catch Josef off guard, and here was the stable yard blazing like a gulag perimeter. Still, she determined, she would count upon Josef to begrudge the canopy of lights the favor of his attention. On the wrong road to Most, he had kept his eyes fixed straight ahead as Becky, a great one for saying Oh look! during their early days in the Republic, tried to include him in the outing, which was how he had come to flatten the basalt marker, refusing as usual to look when she had told him, this time, to look *out*.

She entered the stable through a pulled-apart door. She avoided the bulk of the car and a spill of oil beside which a mound of sand seemed to be wicking up the oil, although a heap of oily sand seemed a worse sort of mess to leave lying about than a slick of oil. She climbed a stone stairway leading to a large loft that was just dimly illuminated through low-set windows by the garlands of exterior lights. Josef lay in a far corner of the room, sprawled just as he'd flung himself across the broad, ornately carved bed which, Becky now realized, he must have wrestled over from the castle during his initial solitary and unmonitored occupancy. He had also helped himself to a marble-topped table, a pair of gilt-wood fauteuils, a mahogany and marquetry bombe chest, and a gilt-wood chair upon which he had placed a Minton Parian figure of Iseult the Fair. Becky knew who she must be because a companion Tristan stood alone upon the Music Room mantelpiece and an inventory list mentioned there had been a pair. There were scattered books and magazines. Becky could just make out a magazine title, and a photograph on an open page. Oh. Oh dear. It was pornographic. Josef's glance followed Becky's glance and he saw that she saw.

He did not rise from his bed. Certain shirt buttons and trouser fastenings had been undone and his boot laces left unknotted and astraggle. Sudden movement did not recommend itself. He made no fumble toward restoring decency. Becky, who had viewed his grey laundry sagging on the clothesline, did not recoil from further grey glimpses of it upon the man. One could not have said who was more satisfied by the spectacle of Josef, caught as he was—at his worst, in Becky's opinion, or, at his best, as Josef thought, believing that his true self was the better self if only because it was true.

The truth. Josef had to smile at the very idea. He was sure Mrs. Lowe professed a great regard for the truth, but only as she arranged matters to conform to her own views. She was the typical Boss, even now, even as she was about to become his Boss No Longer (for he knew what was coming). She would continue to assume like any Boss that her version prevailed and that people would listen to her and nod along with her as she insisted, and never remember because they never knew that they did not have to sit still and receive the big lie once the Bosses were overthrown. The people could not not believe in the Bosses, because they had never been in possession of an even bigger truth, as he was.

Josef heaved himself onto his side and propped himself more comfortably upon an elbow. His eyes traveled to the ormolu chest, and Becky, alert to his every movement—she was carefully keeping the gilt-wood chair between Josef and herself, planning to fling it at him should he lunge at her—also glanced at the chest, although aside from its unauthorized presence in Josef's quarters, she did not know what else the chest was meant to reveal, or, perhaps, conceal. She felt she was being invited to investigate and to discover more pornography, or further evidence of Josef's thefts. Not now, however. On Monday morning she would tell the Ministry to send over some sort of official disposal squad to oversee the ultimate expulsion of Josef and his effects and to ensure the recovery of the castle's pilfered furnishings.

Josef's smirk became more profound. A noise rumbled in his throat which prompted Becky to speak before the rumble could assemble into a specific provocation, like a swallowed bee spat into the air and furiously darting at her ear.

"I want you out of here," she said.

Oh, but Mrs. Lowe was looking very beautiful tonight. Frankly, Josef had not heretofore understood her appeal. To him, she had always appeared as parts, in the rearview mirror, through the windscreen, between the front-seat headrests. Those parts had never added up to much, her mouth issuing uncongenial orders, her hands signaling Slow down, Stop smoking, Stop here, her legs hurrying at him whenever he fetched her, pulling up before a slightly misheard street address. She wore mannish suits; she hefted a briefcase; she frowned habitually. She was frowning at him now, but with alive and atremble lips. She was

wearing a sinuous dress. She was caught in the grip of strong emotions. Josef approved of strong emotions in a woman, of strong, negative emotions. He had always been able to work with those.

"Out," agreed Josef. "So, I am out." He shrugged. "Out there," he
remarked as if he didn't really mind—indeed as if, on the whole, he
was going to be rather glad to find himself out and about in the world
again. He regarded Becky. In his experience, a cool reply only made a
woman's anger flash further forward to repel such coldness. He waited
for the suddenly very beautiful Mrs. Lowe to perform. He was keen to
see. He liked to watch women take heaving breaths and work their
mouths round words of outrage.

But he was mistaken. For Becky struggled, instead, within the grip
of a strong, comical emotion. She had just been struck by the huddled
arrangement of Josef's select pieces of stolen furniture, crowded into
one dark corner of the spacious loft, and she had decided that Josef
must have imagined that protective walls had been raised around himself and his treasures. But he had built himself such a mean little chamber and Becky could imagine him carefully not bumping into his
invisible walls. She guessed he had designated a place for a door upon
which, she gathered, she ought to have pretended to knock, stamping a
heel against the floorboard as a sound effect. She tried to frown, then
gave up the fight and let herself laugh. She supposed she and Josef had
both been utilizing strange new powers of X-ray vision, as they confronted one another through lath and plaster and paint.

She spied the car keys then, flung down upon the marble-topped
table. She advanced through solid wall (and this was how she caught
Josef by surprise) and swept them up and clutched them in her hand
(her elegant dress was pocketless). Several great rings gleamed across
her fingers, and although the stones, the clear and the colored ones, did
not glint blindingly in the low light filtering through the low windows,
Josef blinked, dazzled by the idea of their worth, of which he was no
longer allowed to be ignorant. The Republic's papers, even his own no
longer entirely reliable rag, ran instructional articles these days advising the populace how to make the most of the new consumer economy,
telling them what they must all set about to acquire in order to become
successful capitalists, and how much it was going to cost them all now

that everyone was about to be rich. Josef had been forewarned that women were going to become very expensive within the new order of things, not that he would ever buy a woman a magnificent jeweled ring, but he felt himself slipping even lower against a recalibrated standard, albeit one to which the women he knew knew they had no hope of holding him. Perhaps it was the women who must slip ever lower on his scale, willing to accept less and less, when, according to the papers, they were due more and more.

Not like this one, this Mrs. Lowe who had seized her fair share and then far more. She made a tchucking sound at him and she snatched the very pretty porcelain lady he liked so much. He had moved her from her shelf to sit upon the gilt-wood chair, companionably. He had turned her to face him. She had followed his movements about his room with her eyes as he had heard great works of art were able to do. She had attended to him when he ventured some remark aloud, alone, yet not so alone, in his chamber.

As if she knew of all this, Mrs. Lowe laughed again, appraising all the incongruities between the Fair Iseult and Josef. She held the figure carelessly, as if the precious piece had become less precious after time spent in his possession. Mrs. Lowe's laugh, her attitude, her actions were far more expressive than any words of which they shared too few in common to serve at present. But Josef and the Lowes had, all along, been communicating by gesture and by mien, so the established idiom was eloquent enough for Josef to catch every meaning, and after Mrs. Lowe left him, turning and walking briskly away on high tip-tapping heels, Josef subsided onto his back and began to plot his reply, in kind.

THE FAIRY LIGHTS BLINKED ON, powered by a portable generator hidden and humming away in a gardener's hovel tucked out of view in a fold of the parkland. Cars arrived, a first few, then many more caught up in the procession rolling down the luminous Avenue. Julie, who had absented herself for the day lest she be required of in some uncongenial capacity—compelled to layer puff pastries with custard, to straighten her outposts of disorder in the Tower's stacked stories, to be polite to her parents' friends—showed up at last with her own gang of friends. She admired, like a guest herself, the transformed castle. The Great Hall, scoured of all evidence of the recent outrage, nevertheless presented after a quick, rough scrubbing a buffeted, brightened aspect, like eyes lately widened at a horror. But if a certain residuum of dread was communicated, the glow of all good feelings rendered that lingering sense into piquancy. Tongues told sharper tattle; the one sex pursued the other with more purpose. Alden, shouldering through what had swiftly become a crush, was sensitive to all varieties of mood tonight, and he understood that such edginess only guaranteed the success of the evening. But he wondered, now, too late in the day to do anything about it, whether they ought to have locked off the many spare bedchambers on some prior evening, determining which great unlabeled key suspended from the wardresslike clanking chain of castle keys secured which better-left-unpassed-through doors.

"BUT YOU'RE NOT PHOEBE." Alden had so accused the young woman newly met and hanging on to Arthur's arm as he and Becky received their guests in the Great Hall. Becky had pinched Alden hard on a buttock to stay further comment. Nevertheless, she was as startled as he that Arthur's old girlfriend, whom they had known and liked and believed to be the one, had, by all evidence, been left behind somewhere along the way.

However, the other young woman, this not-Phoebe person, acknowledged the greeting by snuggling against Arthur's side, burrowing into his accommodating concavity as if she had made a nest there. She rewarded Alden with a bright smile for getting it right on his first try. No, she was decidedly not the old girlfriend, and she waited a beat for a further flashbulb to pop and for these people to realize who, instead, she most decidedly was. There was often this little lapse between the brain recognizing and the tongue untangling; she had that effect upon the public.

"But I know who you are," Becky said. "I read, in some silly magazine, you're that little actress, Holly Holladay, and *you're* going to play Garance in the film?" Now Alden placed a warning hand upon Becky's sleeve (deciding not to push his luck with a mindful buttock pinch of his own).

Arthur stepped forward to hug Becky. The clinging Holly was also involved in the embrace. Her body felt, at once, both sharp and cushioned, and Becky wondered whether this range of surface tensions was something that men particularly liked. Alden would have submitted to an all-around embosoming as well, and he advanced with both arms outstretched, but Arthur only seized his hand and shook it.

"So, how does it feel to be rich and famous?" Alden asked.

"Oh, pretty good," Arthur said. "It sure beats working." His practiced answer; he had remained a regular guy.

"You look very well," Becky said. "Happy?" she hazarded.

"Sure. You too?" Arthur asked. He was gazing up into the rafters, across the thronging Hall, toward the grand staircase. He noted the tapestries, the lanterns, the statuary, the carvings, the flambeaus. "Hey," he said. "Some castle."

"We like it," Alden said. "Don't we, dear?"

"Everyone should try living in a castle," Becky said.

"Or in Malibu," Holly said.

"Or in a castle in Malibu," Alden suggested.

"Don't be giving Holly any ideas," Arthur said, which made Alden and then Becky laugh, joined by Arthur as well when he heard what he'd just said. Holly, who had been born bored, noticed everyone was having fun except her, and she undertook to sidle away, bearing Arthur with her across the flagstone floor toward the vibrations of the band and the surging sea of dancers that parted and then closed upon them.

"Arthur has gone as soft as a grape," Alden said. "What was that girl wearing?"

A tulle net skirt, a T-shirt from Daytona Beach, black high-tops, and a fez.

"DADDY!" JULIE HAILED AND CAPTURED ALDEN. She was happy to claim her parent and her place at this moment. Her friends, the International Youth, clustered round her, this knot of young people tying up the floor. Tonight they were dressed in dark, scarred leather and heavy, hard-edged ornaments and were sworn to hang together; perhaps the many chains they also wore accomplished this. They had intercepted several servers bearing cocktails and mushroom vol-au-vents on trays. They knew they liked the hot, puffy vol-au-vents and they were deciding about the manhattans. They despised the noise the dance band was making in their ears. Nevertheless, some among Julie's crowd spotted a local Czech actor whom they actually recognized out on the floor dancing, close dancing, cling-to-your-partner dancing, that sort of dancing, to some lightly crooned lyrics and thrumming instruments. The actor was not a leading man. In *Children of Paradise* he was only going to play a tavern keeper. But still.

Her friends shifted their feet and regarded Julie's father. He wore immaculate evening dress. (They did not think "immaculate" but sensed as much about the fit and the cut.) His hair and his eyes were grey but he looked as if he could still kick a football and sprint down the field and knock a defender cleanly out by the goal, not that they cared about football, but still. Alden bore two wine flutes. He sipped at intervals from one and then the other, keeping the content level even between glass and glass. He was making the best of having lost Becky, who had sent him after their drinks and then vanished from the spot she had been sworn not to stray from until his return.

"Daddy," echoed all the International Youth. They mocked, they thought. Alden quite ignored them, and the International Youth felt, for all their bravado, neglected by a glamorous parent whom they would, just then, have given anything to impress.

"Honey," Alden greeted Julie. "So glad you made it."

Julie peered at her father and saw he was not being snide. He gestured helplessly. He would embrace her but his hands were occupied. Oh, very well. He extended his arms carefully and Julie stepped between them.

"Daddy," she protested. How could she not have come? She smiled and clutched his elbow.

"Oh," she suddenly remembered. "Where's Arthur? Did he really come? My cousin Arthur," she told their friends. "From the movies. Like I told you about, Arthur. The actor."

Yes, yes, the friends knew all about Arthur. Their older cousins were only law students or computer operators or taking a year off before university.

"Arthur has arrived. I know he'll be delighted to see you," Alden said.

"Ah." Julie wheeled round on the IY to see how they were taking all this.

Alden excused himself. He had spied newly arrived faces from the Ministry uncertainly consulting one another. Michal had removed his shoes and was carrying them, and a twine-cinched stack of albums as well. Jaroslav was wondering if he too should remove his shoes while Mrs. Jaroslav, who wished to mingle with people not from her husband's office, regarded Michal and Michal's best-occasion wingtips and his copy of *Mingus Alive* as pure impedimenta. But then Mr. Lowe appeared and exclaimed how particularly charming she looked tonight, shimmering in shantung, and he at once detached her from Jaroslav as if conjugal pairs were not permitted at this gathering and steered her toward a venture capitalist who also kept bees and with whom, he was certain, she would have everything in common after a drink or two. Money and honey, Alden assured Mrs. Jaroslav; everyone liked money and honey.

ALDEN DISTRACTEDLY ACCEPTED Franca's offering of flowers, which, having been thrust upon him by his out-of-breath secretary, who could not summon the words of presentation she had practiced, only caused him to wonder what he was to make of the stiff paper funnel afflicted by a drip from its tapered end and the handing over of which had seemed urgent. He failed to acknowledge the exuberant existence within the paper cone of the snapdragons and baby's breath that Franca had selected stem by inspected stem from successive flower vendors along the riverbank where she had wandered, alone but well companioned by her thoughts of the future and, alternatively, by thoughts of a revised past which contained more favorable implications for an improved present. It scarcely mattered; dream time could be any time and all time. Alden and the bouquet had been borne away from her by a

scrum of stout, high-colored men in evening clothes to strategize over
their next big business moves. Franca followed Alden's progress, his
silver head gliding above the animated press of his guests as he crossed
the vaulted and raftered Great Hall. At the last, he turned and waved
high the sheaf of flowers in Franca's direction, which Franca decided
was notice enough to serve. The gift to him of green growing things
satisfied her that a seed had been sown.

Franca had Alden almost all to herself during her working week, a
situation she knew was better suited to her true purpose of quietly
loving him. This evening, here at last in the famous castle, she would
devote herself to finding out all that she could about the particulars
of Alden's existence when he was apart from her. Heretofore, she had
only been able to collect shards of that other life; how his steamy bathroom air must smell of lime soap and his astringent aftershave; how
there must be a bristling bush just outside his front door, for, on many
mornings first thing at the office, she was obliged to pick burrs from
his jacket sleeve. Wait, sir, wait, she said to him, you have those burrs
again, and Alden froze as if they were children playing Statues, his
arms held out, offering her both arms. He never recalled that the burrs
only ever clung to his right sleeve. The bristling bush stood to the right
of the path outside his door; Franca knew that, even if he could never
remember. She plucked swiftly as if to minimize the sting felt by
his sleeve, grasping the burrs firmly between two fingertips and her
thumbs, pricking her fingertips and her thumb and then licking the
bright beads of blood from her hand. She had not picked up those few
shards of Alden's other life without paying a price.

This evening, Franca had resolved to locate Mrs. Lowe before com-
mencing her prowl of discovery about the castle. She would rather see
Mrs. Lowe before Mrs. Lowe saw her. Franca braced herself for her
dealings with Alden's wife whenever that formidable lady invaded the
Ministry office on infrequent, impromptu sallies. Becky perched upon
an edge of Alden's desk, picking up and putting down out of order
the documents spread across his blotter, all the while talking over
Alden's head to Franca, who had pursued the swiftly striding Mrs.
Lowe from reception to the inner office, repeating the offer of coffee
which office etiquette dictated be made to anyone of any standing (al-

though Alden seemed to think that the tired and discouraged farmers from the countryside who sometimes still arrived searching for the rural development agency, which had long since relocated to Bratislava, particularly qualified for a steaming cup from a fresh pot as well as a sympathetic if unuseful hearing by whichever junior member of the LLP staff had contrived least well to look most busy at that moment).

Upon the occasions of his wife's visits, Alden leaned against a file cabinet, arms folded and massaging his biceps with his thumbs. Becky presided from the desktop. She chattered away at Franca, who, rather than withdraw after the coffee offer was waved away, hovered on, irresistibly drawn into the performance.

Poor Franca, Becky sighed—who had to run after Alden all day long, forcing him to return his phone calls and show up on time for appointments. None knew better than Becky how much tap dancing around it took to keep Alden on his toes.

No, but no, Franca would say. Mr. Lowe is a considerate boss. She dared declare no more than that on his behalf.

Oh, come on, Becky said. How many times a day do you have to find his fountain pen for him shut inside his Week-at-a-Glance planner?

Franca finds my pen for me constantly, Alden said. Franca is unfailingly patient.

Well, don't be too patient, dear, Becky advised Franca, and she turned to Alden, then, to take up whatever matter had brought her there, as Franca retired to her cubicle to muse upon the true nature of the Lowes' marriage.

Who are all these people? Franca wondered now, examining and dismissing faces as she made her way through the crowd of party guests. She declined an offered drink, and also shook her head at the drink offered in its stead, and she could not be tempted by savory tidbits arrayed across trays. She did not wish to dull her senses or, perhaps, to leave behind some fairy-tale trail of pastry crumbs by which she might be followed as she delved and poked about the castle. She made her way toward the door that stood in opposition to the one through which Alden had disappeared, borne away by that scrum of burly businessmen. She studied and rejected more faces. Several actors and politicians met her great dark eyes and primed themselves to be recognized and approached by the lovely young woman who was so earnestly searching for someone. But Franca glided past the actors and the politicians as the actors and politicians, not entirely unused to the occasional rebuff in their respective lines of work, tried not to mind. Franca veered away from Tilla and her husband, who was a moodsome man, long out of work, whatever work he used to have, performing a mid-level bureaucratic function utterly peculiar to the old ways of doing business. Alden had once proposed turning Pavel into an exhibit in the Human Misery and Futility Theme Park that Alden claimed to be designing in his spare time. Alden was always saying things he ought not to say to Franca, who always laughed as she ought not to have laughed.

Franca's sharp turn away from Tilla and Pavel brought her, like a caroming pinball, smack into Becky, who was chatting with Maria in a little bandbox salon. Maria coolly nodded at Franca, who was, after all, just Alden's ordinary little secretary whereas she, Maria, functioned as right-hand Girl Friday to Becky.

"Franca dear," said Becky. "Everybody's here tonight," she remarked, as if Franca had only gained admittance on a general ticket.

"Yes," Franca said. "I believe so."

"I think someone has spiked the guest list," Becky said.

"Yes," Franca again agreed, because Becky seemed so certain. Spiked? S-P-I-K-E-D? She would consult her English dictionary at the first opportunity.

"I really should find out who asked all these extra people so I can scold them," Becky said. "Or do I mean to thank them?"

"I will ask," Franca offered. "I will ask around," she said, gesturing castlewide.

"You do that, dear," Becky said. "Thank you."

"At once," promised Franca. How well the encounter had gone. She had won permission to look everywhere in the castle, no matter that she was not sure what, or whom, she had undertaken to find for Becky.

Maria assessed the cut and fit of Franca's dress as she departed. Maria wondered where someone like her shopped; tussah silk, the fabric moved well on the body.

"Aren't you having fun?" Becky asked as Maria frowned. "You put so much effort into helping me make this party come off, you of all people should get the benefit."

Maria shrugged. The caterer and the captain of the waiters and the barman had all come to her bearing their problems as if she were still on duty to be consulted about mishaps in the kitchen and with the staff. She had tilted an unrisen soufflé into a sink; she had informed an inebriated waiter he was not very professional, and he had asked what had given her the impression he was a professional; she had told the barman not to serve the waiters—he was incorrect in his belief that this was a democratically American custom.

"No more troubleshooting for me tonight," Becky declared. "We'll just let the evening degenerate from here on. In the meanwhile, you look far too pretty to be on your own. We must find someone nice for you—oh, I don't mean nice, you know what I mean. We've had this conversation before."

"Someone feasible," Maria suggested.

"Oh, I know who would be perfect for you. Why haven't I thought of this before? Yes, now my heart is quite set on getting you together with Svatopluk. You've met him, from Alden's office. I saw him earlier. He's wearing a tartan waistcoat, but don't hold that against him," Becky said.

"He is very serious," Maria said. "That has always been my impression."

"You ought to like that. You'll have something to work with there. All you have to do is to persuade him to become very serious about *you*," Becky said.

FRANCA WAS NOT UNFAMILIAR with the ways of castles. She had been admitted to more than a few noblemen's residences upon the tendering of a ticket, and a mile from her grandfather's farm outside of Klatovy, a half-hour's walk across the fields, stood an ancient Rýzmberk fortress of topless archways and broken walls where perdurable nature presided now, throwing down flower carpets and flinging up vine tapestries, with tumbled stone tables and chairs and a high, hard bed over which the sun spread itself like a cloth of gold. Franca had scaled the sculpted pile of a stairway that curved and soared to nowhere. Then, she had turned and descended, which was the more dignified progress she had always thought, facing those gathered below and gazing up at her as she returned to them from on high. She and her country cousins had feasted on the tart berries thriving wild among the bindweed, and they called out to one another, using their royal titles which had been bestowed according to order of birth. The senior cousins reigned arbitrarily and the little ones hid in the great scooped-out chimneys to discuss the insoluble problem; however old they grew, they would never become oldest. Franca supposed she and her cousins had not been very good young Socialists, but nobody she knew had ever played commissars and cosmonauts. They had wanted to be kings and queens and the princess's snow-white, dance-stepping pony. They had played very happily in the Rýzmberks' forgotten castle even though the wild berries grew very sour there, and the sun-covered bed was hard, and the stairs led nowhere but up and then down again. There were bitterer tastes and worse beds to lie upon, and a hundred futile exercises to pace through every day in real life back in the real city, and all of that occurred without the benefit of the embrace of a beautiful facade, one that wear and time and wars had altered but could not make any less beautiful, only differently, more deeply, and more lastingly beautiful, Franca had always believed.

She wandered down the Long Gallery back into the Great Hall, rejoining the jostling, merrymaking crowd. She noticed a small, private door screened by the band's amplifier stack. The band was resting at the moment and some woman was playing the cimbalom, raptly, amateurishly, raising the notes of a hoary old dumka which, nevertheless, sounded sweeter to Franca's ear than the real musicians' rote rendering of the latest always-asked-for song from America. This summer everyone wanted to hear "Unforgettable." The native tune carried Franca through the narrow door, and frisked and then faded as she moved along a stone-walled corridor lined with bundled and stacked pamphlets and furled and propped banners. This was the cast-off clutter of the bygone youth organization last in residence here, and Franca extracted from this view of these remains a hopeful thought about the inevitable passing of all such regrettable institutions.

She arrived at a wooden stairway, a steep one that rose toward darkness and the dim outline of a door. She made her way up, a hand on one wall to steady herself. At the top, the door yielded to the wrench of a knob and the thumping of a foot against the panel, the sudden release propelling her into an upper hallway along which more doors beckoned.

MICHAL HAD FOUND THE HI-FI SET in its library corner. He had known there was an estimable old hi-fi at the castle, for Alden had mentioned being saddled with an old record player, a real behemoth, a real white elephant, Alden had said. Michal had only eventually understood what he was talking about, and then he had begun to plan for the day when he could convey his most treasured albums to the castle and place each precious disc upon the venerable turntable. LPs and instrument, they had been made for each other, like B. B. King and his Lucille. Entering the library, Alden saw that Michal had tugged a deep armchair into position facing the hi-fi. He slumped in the chair, his stocking feet extended, his arms melded into the chair arms, his hands dangling. His mouth hung just open and his eyes were closed. His ears stood out from his head, primed. Everyone who passed through the library knew not to pass between Michal and his music. Even the International Youth who had whirled into the library had whirled away from Michal.

They were, at present, taking running starts and flinging themselves flat out on their stomachs down the long, gleaming central table. Where was Julie? Alden would have liked a quiet word with her about her friends. Their randomly flailing chains and bolted-on body piercings weren't doing the wood any good.

One of the barreling boys, a kid from the Netherlands known as Weed, slithered too fast and too far and came to grief against a knobby chair back. He folded himself, groaning, into the chair, his damaged head lolling as a warning on the tabletop, much as his ancestors had once displayed the enemy's severed head upon a stake. International Youth also seated themselves around the table, as if contemplation of Weed's interesting agony was the next item on their agenda. They were cool customers, these kids, Alden allowed. He wondered whether they would be nicer children if they lived among their own kind, whether they minded what few manners they possessed when they were at home: where they had a family name to uphold, good graces to get into in order to achieve entrance to a university or a professional guild, and grandparents who would grab them by their absurd horns of hair and drag them off to be barbered. Then again, Alden was arrested by a thought: What if your grandparents were themselves bohemians? He slid into a place at the International Youth table, next to the Czech kid. Alden could always pick out the Czech kids; they were dark but not glossy.

All of the IY regarded Alden. Weed propped his skull the better to gaze blurrily upon the glamorous and heretofore dismissive parent whose impeccably tied tie had twirled askew and whose haughty manner had thawed like the ice cubes in an old-fashioned, diluting what had begun the evening as a stronger presence.

"Kid," Alden addressed the Czech kid. He paused and winnowed the vicinity of his ear with a bothered hand, brushing away a spatter of jazz notes come floating over from Michal's corner.

"Kid," Alden began again. "I want to ask you this. I want to know the answer to this. How does one, I mean to say, how do *you*, as a restless and rebellious young person, set about kicking over the traces when your grandparents are *themselves* bohemians? How do you react to that? What's left to reject, or to embrace? Do you *not* read Ginsberg and Kerouac? Do you *not* stay awake until dawn throwing paint at tremendous canvases with more will than skill? And why do you wear black leather and chains? Because I should think you'd rub against the old folks' bohemian grain far more effectively if you showed up dressed in well-pressed chinos and a polo shirt. Now, in Julie's case, in my own daughter's case, I appreciate and understand the reasons underlying her estrangement from her mother's and my complete orthodoxy. We make it easy for her. Just wear a linen blazer after Labor Day in our circle and you'll evoke gratifying gasps all around. But my next question is this: Does Julie's rejection of her mother and me run any deeper than merely dressing for our distress? What is she trying to accomplish? As our own American bohemian, if I may so characterize him, as our own iconoclast, Henry David Thoreau, once memorably warned, 'Beware of all enterprises that require new clothes,' which I myself shall amend in your present company to this: 'Beware all enterprises that require a pierced nose.' "

The International Youth had stolen away. They slumped and ducked beneath the long table and scrambled for the shadows at the far end of the library chamber and escaped through the tall portal to seek more movie stars and more food and more drink before Mr. Lowe scoffed all the Scotch, if he hadn't already done so.

BECKY WAS TO BE GLIMPSED ALWAYS at the center of one cluster or another of her party guests. She laughed and flung her hair; she had achieved wonderful hair that night, which rearranged itself after each toss as if caught and dressed by phantom hands. She held up her empty glasses, which were, at once, supplanted by full ones, as if other spirits hovered to attend her. She caressed a bare shoulder or a tailored back in parting, ever so gently moving her guests on as she executed her next cordial encounter. She had not expected to be enjoying herself tonight, nor was she, but she was deriving satisfaction from the success of her performance, one by which she was not not letting Alden down so much as showing him up, she supposed. At some later hour, should Alden attempt to coax the admission from her of having had fun despite having foretold her own coming martyrdom, she would inform him that he must not know her very well if he thought that.

Seized by the consciousness of herself as virtuosa, she approached the bandleader and whispered in his ear. Yes, the boys knew "Bewitched, Bothered, and Bewildered." Becky summoned a high stool from somewhere (wafted to her, that spectral staff again). She sat, perched for all to see, and she crossed her legs, a foot outstretched, rudderlike; the stool was tipsy, or maybe it was her. The foot seemed about to lose its shoe. Several men in the vicinity stood on alert to be the one to recover and refit Becky's silver sandal, should it fall.

Julie, to her amazement, did not die of embarrassment on the spot at her mother's exhibition. She had looked over when the band went quiet for a moment, hoping they would stay quiet—she had such a clarinet headache—and she beheld her mother clambering onto a high chair and flashing her legs. A microphone materialized in Becky's hand, and Julie thought, Oh horror.

She listened and watched, sheltering behind a spandrel column, pressed into the shadows where no one could observe her witnessing this. She held herself fast against the cold stone, which slowly began to warm beneath her as if leaching the fire flush of complete mortification from her skin until she could only shiver. Because she knew the song, although she didn't see how, a song like that. The words came to her a beat before her mother sang them, and not just because the phrases and the rhymes slipped so inevitably into place.

Burned a lot / But I learned a lot.

Julie wondered, then, whether her mother had not privately crooned show-tune lullabies to her baby daughter. That figured. She had been exposed to this stuff long before she had any speech or language; when her modes of expression had alternated between crying and not crying, her mother had had no idea she was filling Julie's head with bitter lyrics, with sounds and syllables that, years and years later, she would only just begin to understand.

Alden was just sorry to hear he had missed the show.

ALDEN HAD SOUGHT FRESHER AIR out on the belvedere. He rather feared he may have grinned too hard at that pretty actress girl, that Holly, earlier and he wished that Becky had chucked him under his chin and shut his mouth for him. He never minded when she recalibrated his response to a pretty girl.

He strolled between alit flambeaus that further warmed what breeze there was. Lights sparked across the parkland and figures moved along and away from the gravel paths. He heard laughter and the sounds of splashing about in the ornamental pond. Cars continued to sweep down the Avenue and pull into the stable yard, which was as crammed with vehicles as if some excitable boy had tumbled his toy collection from its wooden box. A boy's considering hand would be necessary to unsort the scramble. Parking was to have been Josef's department, and

Alden imagined the disgraced chauffeur crouched below his stable quarters' window ledge malignly watching and willing the worst, which probably would not happen after all, for the Czechs were proving to be competent untanglers of the tangles they had made. They were all well able to follow a thread, and they all seemed to have caught hold of one thread or another, to which they clung with conviction. Soon, however, they were going to have to be persuaded to recommit their single threads to the deliberate and elegant new web of Alden's devising, the delicate filament of each personal thread traceable by the glint of dew and sun caught along its length as the filaments assembled into a net that would cradle within its entwining strands more treasure than any single thread could lasso and tether alone. Alden stood upon the belvedere and leaned over a parapet to catch what breeze there was as he mused upon this new parable with which he might further inspire his staff come Monday morning as they gathered once again to advance the young Republic's fortunes in the world. There was a lot to be said for mutual funds.

He was overtaken then, by two women whom he could not quite place. They startled him, stepping purposefully from the shadows, stark, scowling women in black bygone dresses, their hair skimmed back and piled high on long skulls so they towered and tipped like a pair of pantomime duchesses. A nod to the occasion was evidenced by the silk shawls they wore tightly wound round their shoulders, the rich fabrics imprinted with bright swirling patterns. The women displayed their shawls like flags of safe passage, whatever flags were worth these days of ever more shifting loyalties and borders.

"Ladies, you haven't any drinks. Let me fetch a waiter," said Alden, as he had been saying all evening to people he could not quite place. The hired-on waiters, all young and all artists or actors or writers or those performance artist types who took it upon themselves to write and to act and to create art all at once, were catering only to the film folk, either kowtowing as fans or hobnobbing as colleagues—Alden didn't really care what motivated the waitstaff. He wished Becky would speak to them.

"We have had," said Eva. Agnes held out three fingers. She seemed to think some drinks ration had been met or even exceeded, and she begged no favors here or anywhere else.

"Oh well," said Alden. "Good."

The women regarded him aggressively. Advancing upon him from either flank, they backed him against the stone parapet at the point where the drop from the wall fell particularly steeply into a wilderness of corn cockles. Alden knew who the women were now: Becky's weird cosmetic widows whom he had met once at Becky's office in the early days, when dropping by to say hello had not yet been viewed as an effort to give advice where none was needed, and he remembered Becky had recently mentioned that the sisters had secured a contract to supply a line of skin-care products to a department-store chain in the States.

"Congratulations on your success," Alden said. "Becky told me."

"Yes," said Eva. "*You* are happy. It is for *you* to be happy."

"Certainly," Alden agreed. "I'm one happy fella. Or as happy as anyone can reasonably be," he amended, lest the gods were listening and reckoned he was due for a corrective blow.

"Tchah," Agnes marveled at his easy admission. She and Eva consulted, thinking the same silent thoughts. Meanings flickered across their faces. Formula-minded, they looked first for a conspiracy as catalyst.

"Your wife," said Eva, "has sent us to you."

Agnes pointed with one stern finger, retracing their trajectory from Becky's side to Alden's. The moving finger sketched the detours the sisters had taken, a false turn and the ascent and descent of a grand flight of stairs, and indicated their impeded trek across the crowd-filled Great Hall, through a violently swinging door, along a haunted, stone-walled passageway, emerging out onto this belvedere where they shrank beneath the circling sweep and fall of whistling bats. The accusing finger soared and dipped and settled, at last, upon Alden.

Alden could only furrow his brow and ask, "Becky?"

The sisters stiffened. Had he another wife? Of course they meant Mrs. Lowe. But they had witnessed sights here this evening for which their ungentle but virtue-ridden history had not prepared them. Western decadence, in two words, was everywhere on view: rocking music, writhing dancers, public embracing and unending kisses, and the spontaneous removal of encumbering garments by dancing lovers. And there was so much on display for the eating and the drinking that the guests piled on more and more without first consuming what already sat upon their plates. Filled plates had been set upon tabletops and forgotten. Emptied glasses cluttered every surface.

"Your *wife* said you would be able to help us," said Eva. "She says the new tax system we have here now is all your doing."

"Well, not entirely. In fact, hardly at all," Alden demurred. "I may have made a few suggestions when asked for my input. Becky is just being kind to say I am responsible for the Republic's rather elegant little scheme."

"Do not shelter behind a skirt," commanded Eva.

Agnes held up a stern hand to forbid him further from sheltering there.

"I take it you have a question about your taxes," Alden guessed. "You have some concern? Some issue? A problem? A misunderstanding? An objection?"

"Objection," spoke Eva.

"And your objection is?" asked Alden.

"Objection," repeated Eva. "Objection," she said.

"You have a general objection, a philosophical objection, perhaps." Alden nodded. "Well, I daresay you've been caught by surprise. The situation is this: There has been a lapse between people such as yourself who are realizing the first fruits of entrepreneurship and private enterprise, and the necessary implementation of a tax code. In the old days, as you know, when the state owned everything, it just shifted money wherever money was needed. It was everybody's money and nobody's money. But the other shoe has dropped. *You* are prosperous, so *you* now enjoy the privilege of paying taxes. Have you received a notice? What was it, a quarterly bill based upon expected earnings? And did you paint matters a trifle rosy for the bankers when you applied for your start-up loan? Institutions talk to one another, you know; they're very chatty, very indiscreet. And now you're crunching real numbers and a due date looms? You will have to write a check? That can be a shock. But look on the bright side. If you weren't coining it, they wouldn't be taxing it."

"Tchah," said Eva through her teeth.

Agnes pulled her brilliant shawl more tightly round her gaunt shoulders and swayed.

"Help us," directed Eva.

"I don't know, off the top of my head. What can you do? Go offshore?" Alden suggested. "Since you spoke of sheltering, you ladies might want to avail yourself of a nice little safe harbor. I always recommend somewhere in the Caribbean. That way you can visit your funds and write off the trip."

"Tchah," said Eva, but less forcefully. In all their hard lives, neither she nor Agnes had ever imagined their ship would come in, nor that, when it did come in, they could board the vessel and sail away on a pleasure cruise.

"Yes, I'm pretty sure you ladies can shelter offshore since you conduct business internationally. But you're going to have to get a legal adviser to keep it all on the up and up."

"Spend for a lawyer?" questioned Eva.

"You have to spend money to keep money," Alden counseled the sisters.

They received this fresh wisdom with an exchange of unhappy glances. They had heard something of the sort, a variation of this apparent verity, somewhere else not so very long ago. Eva queried Agnes with a lift of her brow, and Agnes closed her eyes to contain and concentrate her thoughts. She retrieved the intelligence she sought and she blinked and gloomed at Alden. You have to spend money to make money and to keep money you must spend.

Alden bore being gloomed at rather well these days, for the Czech physiognomy arranged itself along certain fault (or faultfinding) lines naturally. He had, in the past, come close to suggesting that foreign trade delegations be coached in producing pleasant facial expressions before venturing forth to meet with the world's banks and boardrooms, but he was not convinced these people could ever really be happy, not with their long faces and their long history. Even those Czechs who, leavened by the American presence, were whooping it up at the party tonight would regard their hangovers and their remorse of tomorrow morning as a just and inevitable levy. So, the sisters ought not to balk at having to make out the occasional check payable to the Republic's Treasury, and a second check to Kovac, Kolar, and Kolodny. They could wail and bemoan themselves up a treat once they were rich, Alden decided, and he answered their gloom with a grin.

"HERR WOLFE, YOU STARTLED ME. And you don't have a drink, let me get you a drink." Julie, not unamused, heard herself sounding just like her parents as she happened upon her teacher in a small leather-walled room for which the Lowes had found little use. The leather was oxblood red and always damp and the room itself just a narrow cleft between the Dining Hall and the Armaments Chamber.

Julie further felt herself to have been distinctly ambushed. Herr Wolfe had sprung at her from a collapsing divan upon which he had been pointedly loitering. Julie recognized his technique, which might have been her own social form back in another lifetime before she reinvented herself and became so good at braving parties and all; but Herr Wolfe's lonely watch, the eager pounce, she knew them. Now, he held on to her arm and pressed but he remained heavyhearted for all his success at having captured Julie at last.

"No, I have a drink. I have sufficient drink," he said. He had set his glass upon the floor, where it tangled with a sweep of divan fringe. A bullion twist coiled inside the glass.

"But let me fetch you a drink without, you know, all fringe in it," Julie said. She cast about helplessly. All those waiters her parents had hired, where had they vanished to? And she had detached herself from the International Youth; they'd gone floating off to gawp at the actors. They had goggled at Arthur, who said he was used to being goggled at, which was cool of Arthur but uncool of the IY, who could not always be entirely counted upon not to let her down (they still eagerly stabbed the ABBA buttons on jukeboxes), so Julie had been looking for someone else to round off her night. She'd been looking for him in the quieter corners of the castle, where, she had every hope, he would also contrive to be found by her.

"It does not matter," Herr Wolfe said.

"Yes, it does," Julie said. "You really shouldn't have to drink around fringe."

"No, I mean, the *drink* does not matter, " Herr Wolfe said significantly, and then Julie knew what all of this had to be about.

"Oh, well, look," she said. "You know."

Herr Wolfe shook his head.

"Czech is a very, very hard language and no one except you people talk it," she complained. "Are you going to tell my parents?"

"No," Herr Wolfe said.

"Really? No? That's great. Hey, would you like to be in my cousin's movie? He said he can get us all in, just, like, in the background, but still," Julie offered, then.

Herr Wolfe thought not.

"So, okay?" Julie hazarded. "Because I'm very, very sorry and I've been feeling just awfully sorry and all. I won't do it again. I have learned my lesson." She had had to cut his class for the last few weeks. She had been inconvenienced by all the avoidance maneuvers necessary to take until the fuss, if fuss there was going to be, blew over. She had invited Herr Wolfe to the castle tonight as a sort of peace offering, or payoff, or perhaps to let him see just what he was up against if, indeed, anything was up. That was three bases covered, and, anyway, she'd been thinking she was home free by now. She had begun to hope Herr Wolfe had lost the assignment through that sad unpatched hole in the bottom of his old satchel.

"It is not so much the incident of scholastic plagiarism," Herr Wolfe said, "which is grave enough. I need not say how grave. But to plagiarize such a great poet as our own Neruda. We have named avenues after him. Haven't you even noticed? Still, my distress is not that you should have thought I would be too stupid not to notice what you were attempting to get away with. No, it is my sorrow at my failure as your teacher that you are, and that you remain, so stupid."

"Hey," said Julie. "Hey."

"I have taken my time deciding what your penance must be, and I have devised one which you will come to see in the fullness of time as a benefit. I shall insist that you learn our language and that you will learn to love our language and all the poets, the great and the good celebrators of our language, so that their voices will become the voice murmuring in your inner ear. That is my pledge to you, that you will learn, and to attain that end you must have intensive private tuition every day. Every afternoon for two hours. You must tell your parents you require them. I am sure they will deny you nothing," Herr Wolfe said, not unbitterly.

"It wasn't a fair assignment, to have us write a poem, in summer school," Julie argued. "I mean, a whole poem? Nobody else even tried. At least I made an effort. I mean, I went to the library and looked up a poem, you know, I saw it was poem-shaped and I even figured out it was something about a mother so I knew it was an appropriate poem, a very nice poem. Right? I know I should have come up with something on my own, something baby-lame like *The Cat in the Hat*, only that doesn't really work in Czech. I went all the way to the library and asked them for Czech poetry," and she had been directed to a falling-apart anthology that no one had checked out since 1964. She had had to slide her eyes over a hundred poems to find one the right size, smoothing out the onionskin and sticking a blank sheet beneath the page because the next poem showed through the skimpy paper, in order to copy the lines. "I should think looking up a poem counts. Be fair. It was a way unfair assignment."

Herr Wolfe thought not. "You must do the honorable thing, however difficult it is for all of us," he said, and sighed.

Julie raised unconvinced eyebrows at the extraordinary mention of honor, which she was quite certain she had never heard spoken of in real-life conversation. She really tried to think, then, of when and where but couldn't, only in big historical thee-and-thou plays. She had not known an average person could speak of honor and keep his regular face on straight, but she was under enough pressure to make the attempt. She said, "I think it would be more honorable to tell my parents what I've done and then they can deal with me in their own way and see that I'd only be wasting your time and their money. I really think they should know what I've done. I'm hopeless. No one has ever taught me anything." Footsteps creaked into the little room. She turned and exclaimed, "Tell him, Mr. Palacky, how I'm always such a general disappointment to my parents."

"Miss Lowe," said Svatopluk, bowing slightly to Julie, to Herr Wolfe. "I know nothing of such matters. I am not qualified to speak. I only know your presence is required in the Great Hall." His eyes flickered over the tousled divan, the red leather walls, the bedraggled drink, and Herr Wolfe's pale hand pressed against Julie's tensed arm.

"Oh, I'm so sorry. My presence is required," Julie told Herr Wolfe, kindly. Her costume, her dress that evening, featured a skirt long and full enough to swirl as she spun on her high heels and exited. Svatopluk followed her with a concerned, custodial air, one hand gripped below but not touching her elbow, remotely guiding her. A backward glance at Herr Wolfe suggested that he watch himself.

Herr Wolfe, like many men who have had a great gift refused, decided after all to forage for a fresher drink. The dunked bullion tassel had discolored, and a swallow confirmed that a tarnished taste disflavored his rusty nail. He had recognized a long-ago classmate earlier in the evening, glimpsed among the thronging partygoers, and as Herr Wolfe rejoined the fray, a slight, sidling figure muttering Excuse me, Excuse me, he searched every face for the one he had known at university. Had the world been fairer, as fair to him as Julie wanted the world to be fair to her, Herr Wolfe might have become Jan's esteemed colleague in the upper reaches of government service. Herr Wolfe had tracked his classmate's trajectory over the years, an easy enough exercise, for Jan's star shone conspicuously—being of a particularly gaseous composition, Herr Wolfe had often thought. And Jan had known when the time came to leap, just before the government fell. He had caught favorable currents, up in the star stratosphere he inhabited, and been wafted down to land on his feet, squarely within the new order.

The humble teacher had not felt equal to hailing his long-ago friend earlier in the evening, and even less did he desire a reunion now, with fresh proof of his latest failure surely as evident as a brand spelling out the word across his stooped shoulders. But not to confront Jan now would not be brave, and Herr Wolfe had always had that, the knowledge that he could be brave.

He seldom went out, even these days when, he was always being told, there was so much more worth going out for in the evening. He still stayed home and he read and he thought and he wrote down his further thoughts about justice and goodness and freedom and equality, as he had always done although he read and thought and wrote with more urgency than before for he knew the right people, after this transitional, flirtatious period, were soon to be slotted into the right positions, and the times were about to become right and ripe and receptive to his plan. Of course, he had a plan and a program. He believed in plans and programs and declarations. He had sacrificed his own future by signing such a declaration, ill-timedly, as he had been well aware; nevertheless, the cold war had finally succumbed to a relentless series of such very small drafts as his.

But what a crowd he was encountering here tonight. He began to wonder whether he ought to have ventured out on those other evenings. So this was what had been hatching after hours while he soldiered on according to his own lights. Foreigners had taken over the castle. The old villains were prospering in new guises, in new suits. Every word he heard was English, every concept commercial, every conversation a shouted one. Youth had defied him, and the old friend of his youth, whom he cornered at last beside a table resonant with clanking bottles, claimed not to know Herr Wolfe, and the work of reminding him, of leading Jan back to the point where their ways had converged, was not easy. And then Jan told him that true virtue lay with those who had fought the state from within, and not with those who had been content to carp at the system from without.

FRANCA PROWLED THE UPPER ROOMS. Several times, opening doors, she disturbed indistinct figures moving upon dim and moundlike beds. Limbs disengaged and hands fumbled and delved and pitched pillows toward the sudden invasion of light and a questing silhouette. Franca withdrew, intent upon her further search for a more compelling scene, which, presently, she found, happening at last upon the marital chamber of the Lowes.

A lamp had been left burning as insurance against a late and mud-dled return and collisions with the furniture, the gleaming and carved and inlaid tables and chests and armoires set all over with vases and bowls and urns. There were heavy framed mirrors on the walls, gravely gazing one into another, and thickly covered canvases of forest scenes inhabited by wonderful beasts and beings that hung from long, dark cords. They had the look of pictures that had always been there and always would be, as forever fixed as the views through a window. Sleek electronics had been discreetly, recently installed: a cube of television set, a wafer of CD player, a telephone capable of sending and receiving messages all on its own; a red light, a green light, a white light were pulsing even now on its matte black cradle. There were many scattered books, most of which were travel guides to local and less-local places: Prague, Prague, Prague (the Lowes seemed to feel there was a great deal they needed to find out about Prague), Vienna, Munich. The titles promised to lead susceptible wanderers to the most romantic corners of these destinations, which gave Franca pause. She would have said she traveled—or, at any rate, hoped to travel someday—in pursuit of edification, spectacle, and better shopping. Love and such, romance, if you will, had always been happened upon wherever love had happened to be. Still, she did not suppose any of the Prague guides would dispatch the hopeful pilgrim to her own flat or to the Ministry office.

Franca lowered herself into one of the plump armchairs. A pair of ornamental scissors, crocodile shaped, all shearing jaws, the haunches for handles, had been left plunged between the cushions. So this was where Becky sat and sewed prettily of an evening. She and Alden sat here together, relaxing together, picking up and putting down their books and their magazines, lazing before the warm flicker of the fire in their fireplace, or the hotter flicker of an episode of *Dallas*, as further ideas occurred to them concerning their upcoming trip to *Vienna, A Lover's Getaway*, although why they should ever wish to get away from this wonderful bedroom, Franca could not begin to guess. If this were her bedroom, she would never leave. She would never sleep. She would lie back among the pillows and then not be able to close her eyes for fear it would all disappear. She would have to buy a satin eye mask to blinker herself. She wondered if Becky found it necessary to wear a mask to bed.

Franca regarded, then, from across the room the immense and imperial bed, canopied and overlaid with openwork and lashings of strong
brocades. She was not at all sure she liked the looks of this, such an
eventful venue, this voluptuous bed so well endowed with every ac-
commodation for him and for her; a tumble of pillows heaped, a swell
of extra blankets, with a pair of tulipwood parquetry tables placed on
either side and supporting two Anglepoise reading lamps, two cut-
glass carafes for fresh water, and two silver boxes from which a froth of
tissues flourished. Yes, down to those details was their life ordered,
anticipating every sniffle and thirst and spill in the night. And while
Franca knew in her bones it was the estimable Becky who had arranged
all this, Alden had to have been complicit. Together, they had constructed this edifice of possessions and indulgences to wall themselves
in, and, as effectively, to wall everyone else out. Franca suddenly knew
how very happy Alden and Becky had to be, in private in this beautiful
room among all their beautiful things. How very happy they really
must be in ways she could not begin to understand with her own slight
experience of domestic beauty and ease. Perhaps those public displays
of acidity between Alden and Becky had been staged to vary the per-
fected pitch of their one-note harmony, sounding the odd sour note
during those discordant intervals to counter (so they could reencounter
anew) so much sweetness. Oh, take away Alden and Becky's props and
they might fly apart, but which of them would ever opt to kick over the
traces? Why ever would they do that, and for whom? What did the
likes of Franca have to offer Alden in exchange? She lived in a two-
room flat behind a flimsy door beyond a noisy landing where any attempt to make her two rooms nice only ever came to that, just another
attempt. The spume of her steam radiator had killed her African violet.
Her snow-white curtains had become mottled and grey in the afflicted
air of her district, but until this moment, Franca had been able to imagine Alden in her flat, seated, facing her across a late supper table. She
had fine-tuned this someday supper menu a hundred times as more and
more items appeared on her local grocery's shelves, green seedless
grapes from Chile now available, and the Ritz Crackers by Nabisco
which came in such a bright box, but she saw now how disastrously
wrong all that would have been and nothing beautiful could have or

would have come of any of it, Alden uncertainly perched on the less unsteady of her two wooden chairs as the neighbors battled on the landing and the radiator hissed and the cracker appetizers failed to live up to their name, whatever she put on the Ritz.

How ill-equipped she was to move through this new territory in which she found herself. There was a need for some seeker who had been there and back to write a guidebook to lead Franca and her kind safely through the complexities and perils encountered along the road to love in a consumer society. The landscape was so different now: the castles were repeopled, the shops restocked. It was not at all like before, when your entire world was reflected in a pair of shining eyes, and all your earthly share could be carried from a wife's to a lover's flat in a valise and a satchel and an orange crate.

Franca rose then, and drifted toward a different door from the one by which she had entered. She passed through a dressing room into another corridor that reminded her of a study in perspective stretching toward a diminishing point. She moved on, walking over a patterned carpet of green and gold arabesques which tended in a direction and led her to the steep edge of a great staircase. Voices and laughter and music welled from below as if calling to her. Her steadying hand slid along the polished stone of the banister. Her hip struck, with every other step she took, the carved outflarings of an as-polished stone baluster. Her heels, very high ones that evening, clicked against the stone treads. At least, she assumed her high heels clicked, for she could not hear them doing so above the surge of party clatter, and this nullification of personal affect—she stamped, she stamped again to confirm—fostered a not-unwelcome sense that she was, just now, not quite real; as if, she told herself, she was undergoing a metamorphosis on this entirely significant evening. She had come to a standstill upon the staircase, certain that if she moved at this moment she would shed shreds of her dissolving and reassembling self, matter (no matter) trailing away like a chiffon scarf so substanceless around the throat that one did not notice its uncoiling. Seconds passed. A moment. Her heart began to beat more slowly and more heavily. A shiver seized and stiffened her frame. She willed not a single molecule that had once hoped to love Alden Lowe to remain unaltered. She did not wish a single cell of her being to shelter any memories of how she had mused upon and dreamed of him and had invented long conversations, taking her own part and his replies, murmured to her in fluent, ardent Czech. She would not remember how she had drunk alone, and had felt so wretched after she drank alone, the successive bottles of wine she had laid down with every hope they would be shared.

Those wretched times, she would never revisit them, she resolved. She would no longer be that forlorn creature. She was now someone else. She glanced at the hand, her hand, still gripping the polished stone banister. The flesh of the thumb, *her* thumb, plumped out as it pressed down. She pressed harder; the nail whitened to the quick and her knuckle joint twinged and Franca supposed she had safely passed from one condition to the next. This was all so very strange to her. She had no idea what the rules were to be, but she told herself she would watch and listen and pick up cues and clues. Receptivity seemed a signal quality of her state, and she knew hers was far too interesting a situation not to be experimented with at large. She resumed her descent of the grand staircase and she rejoined the world.

THE ACTORS AND THE POLITICIANS whom Franca had rebuffed earlier in the evening sought to court her again when she returned to their midst. They saw the change in her. Her resolutely searching look had been supplanted by a more questioning gaze. Her steps were tentative. She advanced, then retreated from a cluster of couples slowly dancing beneath the Great Hall's vaulted ceiling. She plucked a drink from a hovering tray as it swerved toward her and darted away, and she turned from all the eyes now turned upon her to see, what next? She contemplated an age-stained tapestry unfurled across a stone block wall. She fell, naturally, into a considering posture, the one women and men adopt in galleries and at exhibitions, standing about in wary proximity to one another, seeming to be, but not at all, randomly spaced, like the uncaptured pieces in a drawn-out game of chess. Neither pawn nor queen, Franca was the castle now. She tilted her head, crossed her arms, and held her wineglass up by her ear. Her gown was seen to its best advantage from the back. It was cut very low. Her shoulders and the line of her spine were pretty. She was aware of this.

She wished she had not snatched so impulsively from the hovering drinks tray. She would have preferred any tipple to this local wine, an untraveled vintage undesired elsewhere. And what was she supposed to be looking at? She was positioned too close to the tapestry's wide field to take in the subject. She picked out stitches. She identified a stitch called Flame, which, worked by the tens of thousands, formed furious flames of a red that, surely, had once been redder. She noted, in the border, the small detail of a flower, some sort of meadow cinque-foil which was about to be crushed beneath a hoof, a horse's hoof, the hoof of a white horse being spurred forward by a banner-bearing knight.

"Are you a student of such things?" a deep voice asked her over her graceful shoulder.

"Of what such things?" Franca asked. "I cannot really see from here what I am seeing."

"Of Templars and Mahometans, of Jerusalem burning, of lost causes," she was told.

"Oh no. No. I am not at all drawn to lost causes," Franca heard herself declare.

"Nor am I. I fail to appreciate the romance of such hopeless quests. This wall hanging is nineteenth century, of course, seven hundred years after the fact still insisting the Crusades were a glorious adventure."

"Still insisting," Franca echoed.

"And now is not the time to look backward, decidedly not, not at this juncture of our history."

"No," supposed Franca.

"We must now all look forward with resolve and ally ourselves only with winning causes," the deep voice declaimed.

Who *is* this man? Franca wondered. She turned to face him. He was tall, and he had a wide brow like a vizsla. She knew who he was, a member of the new Parliament who seemed to be incorporating elements of his campaign speech to woo her. At least, she hoped he was attempting to pick her up. Perhaps he was only after her future vote, and he had mistaken her for a denizen of his well-to-do district. But perhaps he embraced national ambition. Or perhaps he only embraced ambition.

She nodded and drank her unwanted wine and gazed above and beyond the parliamentarian's haircut as he held forth. He was speaking now of the universe. (Did he aspire to a position in the EC?) His gesturing hand rounded the contours of the globe, or possibly those of a ripe, heavy breast. Well, hers were small and rather pointed. Franca wished the local wine would hurry up and go to her head instead of refluxively swilling round in her esophagus.

He asked her (because she had smiled—at herself, but he could not know that) whether she wished to stroll with him about the grounds. She was so very pale, he said. "You are as pale as lace," he said, sounding concerned and intrigued.

To be likened to lace. Franca had never before been likened to lace. She felt, then, like something that ought to be taken tenderly outside to be exposed to the moonlight and the breezes and the dew.

Abroad in the populated and fairy-lit night, they had skirted the castle lawn, circled the ornamental pond, toiled up and canted down an abrupt little hill, crunched along a gravel walk, wondered at a statue of some god giving chase and a girl turning into a tree, and they had taken cover beneath the branches and boles and among the shadows and rustlings of a grove. In here, he said, just touching her shoulder and glancing all around. He was a public man in search of a private corner, Franca understood this, and she pressed on after him. But she fell behind as she slithered and pitched on her too-high heels and the woods closed in all around her. In such a hurry, he assumed (no doubt as a function of his profession) that Franca followed where he led. She thought to cry out to him, but she could only recall the sobriquet the opposition press had given him, which was not at all a kind one. What was his given name? She opted not to shout, Help!, for help struck her as too strong a request to make under the circumstances, as formally dressed partygoers sipped champagne cocktails on the lawn only meters away. Besides, to raise such an alarm, and then to be rescued in a distressed and disheveled state, to disclose that a rising politician had enticed her into the thicket and mislaid her there, the innocent explanation might not be believed. She half suspected the budding Republic would relish a Western-style sex scandal as evidence of how they had all come of age. She listened then, for *him* to call for her. He had, however, never asked her name. Perhaps he had not asked because he had sensed her identity was, at present, such a tentative one. His lace remark had been an astute one—he had seen right through her. Nevertheless, he might at least inquire, My dear?, or even, if he must, just Miss? Then again, he may have been drunk enough to believe she had turned into a Wych elm like the girl in the statue and concluded there wasn't any point in appealing to every tree in the forest.

And after all, she was not seriously lost. This was not a serious wilderness; rather, it served as a decorative element in the landscape, a woodcut miniature of a woods. She need only take a deep, deliberative breath and proceed in a straight line, instead of charging this way and that, to make her way out toward the soft twinkle of fairy lights and the strains of high laughter and a fresh view of the castle which sat just a bit longer off and skewed to present a different profile as she emerged at a point not far from where she'd gone in.

As Franca walked back toward the castle, she decided she was glad she had shaken off her admirer, that they had not, after all, kissed and clutched at one another in the woods. She was not even a member of his political party, which was why his direct hit of a nickname had sprung so readily to her mind. How reckless she had been, and while she firmly intended to renounce Alden conclusively and forthwith this very evening, she had no wish to hurt Alden by hurting herself. No, she had no desire at all to hurt Alden. What she really wanted, she realized, was to relinquish him in some exemplary way that he would never recognize nor appreciate, of course, but somehow her noble act would resonate and he would be touched, from a distance, by its clear, sweet chord.

As she passed by the stables, Franca ducked into the yard to make repairs. She threaded a route among the angled tangle of guests' cars, and, where the light was best, below a gently aswing string of lights, she consulted the rearview mirror of a fine Mercedes coupe. She raked her hair with her fingers. She had gained a crown of twigs in the woods and she brushed a smudge from her cheek. As she crouched to slip off a shoe—she had acquired a pebble beneath her heel—she felt the spider scuttle of raveling silk race over her knee and zigzag down her calf. Tchah, a disaster. The ladder had occurred just where the skirt of her gown was split to show the length of her slender leg. Truly, wicked forces were abroad tonight. She retreated to a darker corner, where she shimmied up her gown. She hooked her thumbs over the waistband of her pantyhose and shimmied again, removing them. Tchah, tchah, such an unlovely object, a pair of wrecked pantyhose, a useless clutch of sag and droop which, nevertheless, had just been stretched as taut and smooth as a second skin over her shapely limbs. It made one think, if one permitted oneself to think, of all manner of mortal frailties suggested by this phenomenon, of aging and of failing and of dying at last, alone and unloved in a stable yard.

Where was a rubbish bin? She was in need of a rubbish bin. She did not want either of the Lowes, neither the fastidious Alden nor the sibylline Becky (who would know whose they were) to happen upon the crumpled hose crammed behind a drainpipe Sunday morning on their way to the American church where they would kneel upon soft cushions and with their private, affronted prayers inform their God that the Czechs were a dissolute race and agree that He had been correct not to have particularly smiled upon them for the last thousand years. Franca, not often given to sighs, sighed and looked about for a receptacle.

She pushed through an ajar door and entered the stable where, she reckoned, there ought to be some sort of barrel, here in what she supposed were the working quarters of the castle, where the Lowes dispatched all their empty champagne magnums and the crumpled packing materials that had cushioned high consumer items shipped to them from the States. She stepped around the rising fender of the Lowes' immense vehicle, the one that always came and carried Alden away to the best restaurants and embassy receptions and to all those subscription concerts his wife professed to adore. Franca could not see very well in here. Fairy light only seeped through grimy windowpanes. She stepped against something that toppled soundlessly—a paper sack from Tesco spilled polishing rags across the oil-slick floor, squares of chamois, flannel, cotton shirting (Franca could feel). She righted and restuffed the bag, into which her stockings managed to vanish and by the time they reappeared everyone would think they had belonged to Becky, for Franca had purchased a pair as fine as any Becky would possess.

Later, during the long hours she devoted to considering and reconsidering the events of the night of the party at Castle Fortune, Franca could never account to herself why she had begun to climb the creaking stairs that rose to the stable loft. She had found herself already ascending them when the protest of a tread had snapped her out of the abstracted state she had retreated to after the evening's string of disappointments.

She had not, at first, noticed Josef. At first, she had surveyed the vaulted vastness of the loft space, and, while on her earlier castle wanderings she had not begrudged the vanished nobility their grand interior vistas, she wondered now whether the barn really needed to be six times the size of an ordinary family's house. What had they kept up here in the loft, those lost aristocrats? Ah, Franca knew. Here they had stored their golden hoards of hay. She smiled then, despite everything (despite that string of the evening's disappointments that twisted and tightened like a strand of false, imperfect pearls round and round her throat). Because Alden must have been correct, after all, about the consequence of hay in the great world, even though the office staff had been gibing him ever since his talk to them, his hay and pie and the price of milk jazz riff lecture. Hay, the other staff had taken to greeting each other in English. Hey, they spoke with every permutation of voice and tone, in every situation. But perhaps Franca would begin to utter Hays of her own and so mock the mockers with what she had found out.

Josef had not stirred from his bed since the scene with Becky. He had rolled over and reached for the bottle wedged between the mattress and the wall, and he listened to the arrivals of the guests, to the subsiding rumble of motors, the slams of doors, the eager chatter. He had not risen from his bed to crouch before an eye-shaped window to see for himself the Bosses' highfalutin friends, the foreign invaders, the toadying locals, the actresses from the movies. No, not even at the promise of movie actresses did Josef arise. Besides, the best and most beautiful of the women would roll up the Avenue in night-black limousines and be left before the Great Portal. The best and most beautiful ones would never walk round from the stable yard in their silver sandals as breezes snatched at the careful arrangements of their hair and gowns. Josef knew, in his professional capacity, all about the nuances of arrivals, and of exits.

And I've been kicked out of better places than this, he assured himself, although a review of his life history failed to confirm when and where that better place had ever been realized for him. More to the point, memory, when consulted, referred him back to all those occasions of past stark departures as he overturned dresser drawers and kicked away the resident cat he had come to despise and need no longer placate with chicken bones lest it savage the legs of his other pair of pants, left hanging from a door hook. On those occasions, flinging boots, his cap, a kava jar full of halers into his valise, Josef had muttered, The next place can't be any worse, which he understood only now, with a revelatory jolt of awful clarity, had been one of those reckless assertions that sent his attending demon to rummage among the foulest corners of his kit just to show it was not for the likes of Josef to say how very bad bad could be. Yes, in the old days someone had always been lingering and listening and laying down yet another law. But these days, under this new regime, everyone was expected to go into business for himself. Even I can be an entrepreneur, Josef reminded himself. If he wanted to, if he bestirred himself, he too could call the shots. He had, after all, acquired the means. He required, next, he supposed, an opportunity. He propped himself upon folded pillows and sat up, somewhat, holding on to the vaguest idea that this posture signaled his willingness to receive his chance. He fastened his trouser fly. He smoothed an eyebrow. He heard, then, light footsteps tapping up his stairway.

A woman appeared. She gazed generally, wonderingly, about the loft. She smiled, although not at him. Her hand rose to her throat and fell. She squared lovely shoulders which could not stay squared, they were so softly curving. Josef knew her. She was the Boss's secretary. He'd seen her before. He'd seen her around. He'd seen her often.

"Oh, hello," Franca said to the man who lay across a grand bed presiding (the bed, not the man) in the farther corner. She recognized him; he was the Lowes' driver. But what was his name? Late in the working day, Alden would look down from his office window and say, At last, Mr. Toad has come to take me for my wild ride, as he snapped his brief-case shut and reached for his topcoat.

"Are you hiding from the party for a quiet moment? I myself am," Franca said as she approached Josef. "What lovely furniture you have. What a lovely room," she told him. "Excuse me, I am just catching a breath. And exploring," she added.

Josef motioned. He fanned a hand her way. He guessed there was sufficient oxygen in his chamber.

"When do you suppose they stopped keeping horses and started keeping motorcars in the stables?" Franca asked. "What became of the princess's white pony?"

Josef did not know, but he did not find her question as idiotic as most questions put to him. If he had to say, he'd wager that the horses and the motors had coexisted for some while in the twenties, a little earlier, a little later, perhaps, as the groom and the chauffeur had vied, waiting for the call for a carriage or for a car to come down from the castle. But the chauffeur had prevailed in the end, so that was all right. Josef smirked at the thought of the vanquished groom, and, fumbling his bottle from his tangled bedclothes, he offered Franca a swig based on the strength of her sensible question and fine shoulders. He approved of her all the more when she thanked him nicely but declined as she gauged there was not enough left in the bottle to benefit both of them.

"I just need to sit for a minute, if I may," Franca said. "Is it all right to sit upon this beautiful chair? Yes?"

Yes, there where his stolen Iseult had lately perched, let her sit there. Let him look at her.

"But I'm not having a very good time, actually," Franca confessed. "I'd intended to, tonight. I'd been so looking forward, but somehow it hasn't been what I'd thought."

Not for the likes of us, at a party like this. Josef nodded, not for the Boss's little secretary and her hopes for the evening, and don't think he didn't know what her hopes for the evening had been. He had seen the girl, he had come to watch for the girl as she followed the Boss, or as, very cleverly, she anticipated where the Boss would be and arrived there before him. Josef had spotted her all over Prague, tarrying outside restaurants where the Boss was dining, happening to pass by hotels where he had business meetings, sitting alone at a café table across the road from the door of the concert hall from which he was soon to emerge at the end of a performance. Josef had seen her time and time again as he arrived in his tardy way, taking some roundabout route to drop off or to fetch the Boss, the foolish girl feigning indifference to a rainstorm or interest in a shop window, and waiting as successive trams passed her by, always waiting for the next one, then the one after that.

"I have American cigarettes," Franca said. "I bought some so I could produce my own, when Americans offered me Marlboros in that way Americans have, expecting you to jump for them. They give you one for now and two for later, such largesse. It warms their hearts, I think, as if we are all urchins in World War Two movies, but I think Hershey's chocolate tastes like wax. I planned the evening down to that detail. 'Cigarette, Franca? No, no thank you, I have brought my own Kent 100s, do try one, they're delicious.'" She delved inside a sparkly little clutch purse. "I offer you one now, sir, in the pure spirit of brotherhood, like American Indians sharing the peace pipe." She chucked the pack into Josef's lap.

"She doesn't let him smoke in the castle," Josef remarked, lighting up.

"She has waived the rules tonight," Franca said.

"Then tomorrow she will give him room spray and a sweep broom," Josef said. He raised a finger and depressed an aerosol nozzle. "Ssss," he said. He aimed his finger at himself. "Ssss," Josef said. "She would like to spray him away too, I think."

"No, that can't be true," Franca protested. "How could that be true? I am sure you are wrong," Franca told him.

Why not? Josef thought. Why not tell the girl? Why not expose Madam Boss as the hypocrite that she was? Why not let a local girl grab Alden and his wealth which he had plundered from the Czech working people. Why not seize this opportunity and tell the girl what he knew, for a price, for there had to be something in this for him, money enough to get him to Berlin. He would hand over the documentary evidence for a price and he would go to Berlin and the girl could run with the information, do with it as she would and so do herself a great good and bring every harm down upon Becky's head. She was foolish, this Franca, but not stupid. (Her surveillance techniques were quite good; he had been impressed by them for months now.) She would know how to proceed, once he had shown her the way.

"She has a lover," Josef said, streamering smoke from his nostrils, then swigging a dousing gulp from his bottle.

"What?" asked Franca. The formidable Becky had a lover? Who would presume? Who would dare? Who would attempt? Who would approach such a lacquered edifice of slippery silks and charmeuses? If such a man existed, his grasp must be strong.

"She has a lover who sends her letters. Such letters. I have read them," Josef said.

"In English letters?" Franca asked. "How do you know the kind of letters they are? Do you read English?"

"I can read enough. And I can tell from the way she is with the letters, what they are. She hides them. They are too dangerous to keep but she will not destroy them. She reads them again and again. She watches for the next letter and she snatches it from all the other letters in the stack, even letters from her sons, she ignores them. Then she denies she has received a letter. Into her pocket, under a cushion, thrust between the pages of a book when the Boss comes into the room." Josef knew these people. He had been lingering and listening and he knew them.

"How very wicked . . ." Franca observed.

"Yes," Josef said.

". . . of you to read private letters," Franca said.

"But she is very wicked," Josef objected.

"Yes, well, perhaps, but that's her business," Franca said.

"And the Boss's too. What about him?" Josef asked. "Ought he not to know?"

"The truth will come out," Franca said.

Josef uttered a raspy note of disgust.

"And when the truth comes out . . ." Franca began.

"How? How do you think the truth comes out?" Josef asked.

"It just does. It will emerge, in time," Franca said.

"No. Truth is told. Haven't you learned that?" Josef asked. "Haven't you seen how the truth tellers are rewarded these days? Why not be the one to tell it? Why not be there with him when he learns it, because he will be, he will be . . ."

"Ruined," Franca said. "Alden will be shattered." And she did not see how he could ever put himself back together again. There would be too many pieces. Franca could see the splinters of fine furniture and the tatters of stock certificates and the whirlwind of his oldest, dearest memories blurring and tearing apart, the debris rising in a cloud and then plunging back to earth to crush a bowed, ruined Alden.

"I have the proof," Josef said. "All the proof you need."

"What do you have?" Franca asked warily.

"I made copies," Josef said. "I take the letters and make copies and put them back, under her cushions."

"Copies?" Franca withheld a brief snort of laughter. "You've made copies for Alden? And now you're going to go to him with these copies of these secret love letters?"

"This information is better coming from you. He's fond of you," Josef said.

"How do you know that?" Franca questioned him. "Why do you say that? Has he said something?"

"You are better for him than her," Josef said.

"I should not have thought you were so very concerned about your employer's well-being. You are a very—caring man?" Franca ventured.

Josef shrugged. He could not claim caringness.

"You are a moral man?" Franca asked.

Josef declined the characterization. He tapped another cigarette from Franca's American pack.

"Or perhaps you are more of an enterprising man?" Franca asked.

"Yes," said Josef. "That is what I am."

"How enterprising are you?" Franca asked. "Specifically?"

Josef mentioned a sum that was four months' pay for Franca.

"All right," she said slowly. "But I don't have it on me, of course. I don't carry so much money, but I can get it. I have it. First, though, I want to see what I'll be buying."

Josef stiffened and tried, very hard, to think.

"I have to see whether the letters are worth the price, and at that price, they'll have to be very good letters," Franca said. "That's how commerce operates these days. We are a consumer society now, a consumer society of informed consumers. With choices. It took me three hours to buy these shoes. The shop bought me coffee, as such a valued consumer of their shoes who also had the option of walking out their door and down the street to another shop that sells shoes and serves coffee." Franca raised and arched a foot. She pulled up her long skirt so he could see the shoe she had bought.

Josef gazed at her smooth, bare leg. God, he hated stockings on women; how he resented stockings on a woman. They would let him stroke their thighs, but don't tear our stockings, they'd say. Oh no. He rose, trailing bedding and fumbling at his buttons. He approached the little bombé chest and pulled out the lower drawer. He tossed magazines onto the floor—Franca averted her eyes from them—and he extracted, last, a folder which he passed to her extended hand. Her skirt slid back down her shin.

"What poor copies," Franca said, opening the folder. "What make of machine did you use?"

Josef told her; just the old model they had down at the Union Hall.

"I too use the same model. It's such a problem making duplicate duplicates, isn't it, unscrewing the front plate, probing with a pencil point to adjust the multiple-copies counter," Franca observed, tilting the first letter toward better light.

Josef stared at her, then shrugged. What was she talking about?

"These are all, then?" Franca asked. "Every copy. Just the one?"

"Yes," Josef said. "Yes, all." It occurred to him that this should be remedied. He ought to have made more copies to keep for future use, speaking of commerce and of opportunities, and opportunities for further commerce.

"All right," Franca said. "Just let me read. Don't look at me while I read such wicked letters. You fluster me, watching me, and I must concentrate my mind."

Josef retreated to the edge of his bed. He kneaded a twist of top sheet and regarded Franca obliquely. Her eyes narrowed. She sighed. She traced a line of curlicuing script with a considering finger. She frowned.

"He 'craves her benison,' " she said. "What is 'benison'? What is 'crave'? They are not improper, I am sure."

Josef lay back upon his folded pillows. His sciatic nerve twinged, a chauffeur's curse. He reached and extracted the bottle from beneath his hip.

"A lot of this English is in French, phrases and such," Franca observed. "*Que m'importe que tu sois sage? Sois belle! et sois triste!* Oh my. Who can this man be?" She rustled several pages forward.

Josef turned to lie upon his less-afflicted hip. He cradled his bottle, effected a careful sideways swallow, and closed, just for a moment, his eyes.

Franca jumped to her feet. She clasped the folder of letters to her breast and bolted across the loft space. She scorched down the stairs and raced through the stable and across the stable yard. She made for the castle wall, running full out over the lawns, skidding onto the path, scattering gravel. She startled a strolling couple, who came apart as she hurtled between them and then reunited as she passed.

MARIA, DANCING WITH AN AMERICAN ACTOR, whirled from his grasp, and she was supplanted as his partner by another pretty girl who was also wearing a beautiful gown, all before the pulsing West Gallery had turned itself round right again and Maria could find her way back to the actor's magnificent arms in which she had felt herself most persuasively enfolded up until the moment he let her go. Matters in the West Gallery had devolved into a sort of disco-disant. A Charles University professor of ancient civilizations had come to the castle toting an eight-track cassette player and a strobe-light machine strapped to those portable luggage wheels the airlines don't like to send along their conveyor belts.

Maria recovered her breath, which exertion and affront had snatched away in equal measure, and she regarded the scene from which she had been expelled. I am like a butterfly sent fluttering from an anthill, she salved the slight to herself by privately contending. Yes, just look at them all. She was a far finer dancer than any of those churning Americans. Her footwork, her posturing, she had the moves down right. Step as if you are avoiding gum upon the sidewalk . . . Gesture as if you are pointing to the blessed angels up in heaven. Maria and her grammar-school set had gotten their hands on the *Popular-You Guide to Disco-Ballroom* back in the days when such a Western artefact, from Belgium, was crystal rare and entirely compelling. The schoolgirls had learned the lady's steps, as depicted on the page by a sharp triangle poised above a pinprick of heel (such glamour), and each intricate step taken had seemed, back in those days, to be a step taken onward toward—what? What was it they yearned for? They had hoped to be present at a night very like this one, Maria supposed, and to seem to all eyes to belong there.

But the Americans did not take their dancing very seriously. They mocked the dance and then mocked themselves for dancing it, and they had mocked the late era's anthem "I Will Survive" as proclaimed by Miss Glorious Gaynor over the eight-track speakers when Maria had been cast spinning away from the prancing actor and, in refutation of Miss Gaynor's words, been replaced in his embrace by the next pretty girl waiting in line. There were far too many pretty girls swaying and laughing and at their best here in the castle this evening, and Maria recalled how Becky had spoken of the concept of disposability in a high consumer culture, of mass appeal and overproduction and the planned obsolescence of objects that only yesterday you had desired with all your heart until your heart was tugged another way by the next big thing.

Maria rued that she had not vetted the guest list with a more self-interested eye when Becky had asked her to cross off anyone who wouldn't do. Becky had not been sure whose presence would cast a pall—Anabaptists, Hanoverian princes? Maria had had to revise her employer's idea of who was socially unacceptable these days, and Becky had said, Oh dear, now I shall have to be conspicuously kind to the Gypsies in the street and I so don't want to be, and a further discussion had followed during which Becky had explained what liberal guilt was and how inconvenient it could be. Distracted from her study of the guest list, Maria had not thought through the subject of editing out rivals, but next time, should a next time be necessary, Maria vowed, the Lowes would invite only the bachelor elite of Prague and herself.

She remembered to smile as she retreated from the dance floor, and to smile as if she knew better, not as if she had been having fun. She wandered on, passing through a great, sagging door, and she found herself in the unfrequented and underlit Armaments Chamber. Why not gloom here for a while before facing the rest of the evening, she decided. She wondered why party-givers didn't schedule intermissions as they did at the theater. Then again, theater intervals were themselves very like parties, with the drinking and the mingling and the eyeing and the sizing up, and she supposed at a party the arc of a dozen unfolding dramas would necessitate a dozen different entr'actes, none of which, in any case, could be anticipated and planned for. They could not engrave upon the invitations a stage direction such as this: *Maria, having made a fool of herself upon the dance floor, retires for the present to think her own thoughts and to retrench. Her lipstick has been smudged, not by kisses, but by the rims of glasses of champagne which she has pressed to her mouth in lieu of those unattainable kisses.*

The caterers had been heaving emptied trays into a corner of the Armaments Chamber all night long. The salvers had accumulated into a mound that, currently, one of the castle rats was scaling, snuffling and shredding flavor-soaked serviettes. He was the least of rats, and a civil one who kept to the deepest shadows so he could be no more than glimpsed. He scrabbled across the platter surfaces. His little rat hooves scuff-scuffed until Maria had to pluck a cannonball from a squat pyramid of cannonballs and roll it across the stone slab floor toward the darkest corner, eliciting a shrill little cry, and then silence.

Pah, protested Maria. I can't have killed it. The cannonball had not struck her as a very formidable projectile as she had so easily lifted and bowled it. Indeed, she would not be at all surprised to learn that such cannonballs had only ever struck the side of a targeted fortress and bounced off and back onto the person who had fired them. Nor were the ancient sword blades sharp to the finger, and the tips of all the antique arrows were as blunt against her palm as a boy's forsaken toys. This was rather fun; in this private castle, in this private museum, she could touch the exhibits. She examined a spiked sphere attached to a chain that looked like a garden ornament for training ivy round; the chain would be sunk into cement to deter the thieving Gypsies. She did not see how it could ever have been easy to finish off an enemy back in olden times wielding such slow, dull, inscrutable weaponry. Your victim must have been required to cooperate, to some degree, by making himself available to repeated hacks and blows, which can't have been good for anyone involved; imagine the things that could have been said on both sides, all the while. Maria shivered fastidiously. Were she bent upon conquest, she would lay siege to a fortress. She would poison the well and catapult a plague-infected blanket over the ramparts and withdraw to a fresh-aired hilltop to await further developments, far removed from the wailing and the moans. But, in truth, she had never desired someone else's kingdom. She had only ever wanted a nice, safe, comfortable home of her own.

As for knights in shining armor, there was a reconstructed specimen listing against a niche in the wall. What had Becky called him, that time in the early days when Maria had dined with the Lowes and they had explored more rooms than they could count, and they had come upon the Armaments Chamber? Becky, on that occasion, had referred to the knight as the empty suit, and Alden had kept saying, The Czech's in the mail, and he had laughed so he must have meant it to be a joke of some kind. She had intended to do research so she might understand what had been so funny, but she had forgotten until now.

"Are you a student of such things?" a deep voice asked her from behind her back. A well-tended hand, a well-cut sleeve, extended above and beyond her shoulder and sweepingly indicated the collection.

"No, no. I think I am quite the innocent after all," Maria, startled from her musings, heard herself own.

"Warfare is not for the fairer sex to know of," the deep voice assured her. "And may you never need to know, as far as it lies within my power, to spare you such knowledge," he further vowed.

His power? Who was he? Maria turned to see what the well-tended hand and the several centimeters of snowy shirt cuff might further signify. She puzzled at the face through the gloom (although less a gloom than a romantic twilight, as Maria was prepared, perhaps, to reconsider) and familiar-seeming features assembled beneath a wave of dark hair cresting above a wide brow, his own as-quizzical eyes as frankly regarding her. His expressive mouth now expressed, "May this past remain another country." He delivered this sentiment as a sort of civic prayer. Who was he to be offering up civic prayers on her behalf?

Oh—he looked like his picture in the newspaper. By this dim light, he appeared as achromatic as his file photo, in shades of shadow and grey. He sounded as he sounded on her television, for the Armaments Chamber gave off the same jangling reverberation as her old East German–made console set produced. He was a member of Parliament who was said to play politics Western-style, which meant he appealed directly to the people, but only to certain people. He was building a constituency among the rising class even as they were advancing him, in an act of mutual self-creation and elevation. He figured to most as a lightning rod, as either a brilliant or a destructive force. Maria recalled all this in a flash.

"I could never follow all the details of clashes and battles at school," she said, and she fluttered helpless hands at a starburst of spears arrayed against a wall.

The politician tutted consolingly. Of course not.

"Those sorts of historical matters were not very interesting to me," Maria continued. "What I always wanted to know was, what did people wear, and what did they have to eat for breakfast, and how did they spend a quiet evening at home in the seventeenth century? I wanted to know, did people wear wool or cotton next to their skin? And what *about* their skin? What sort of products did they use? Because that's what it's now my business to know about because of the way *real* history has turned out. These days, I identify trends and I advise and consult with developing small enterprises and service-oriented industries here in the Republic, and internationally, as well."

He—his name was Albrecht, as anyone au courant would know—took her arm as if in pledge and Maria allowed him, as if in trust, to tuck her elbow against his ribcage, where it seemed to fit.

"Although I am not a fancier of old skin," Albrecht mentioned, and stroked her forearm with his energetic thumb.

"My research has shown me that no one is," Maria informed him briskly, and she turned again, bearing Albrecht around as well, to contemplate the knight atilt in his niche.

"Do you understand why a woman should bitterly refer to a suit of armor as an empty suit?" she asked.

Albrecht did not know. "That seems self-evident," he said.

"Then do you understand why this English phrase, " 'The Czech's in the mail,' should be considered a particularly humorous saying?" she asked.

"No," he said. "Upon consideration, I do not."

They shared a smile over their common inability to find anything funny about the saying.

As if of one mind, they drifted arm in arm from the Armaments Chamber and, without discussion, steered from the raucous voices and music spilling from a further room. In a castle one, or two, could always wander on and beyond.

"You are as pale as linen," Albrecht noticed now beneath the brighter glow of a lantern which swung on an iron chain from the ceiling above a carpeted hallway.

"Am I?" asked Maria, and she touched her cheek as if paleness could be verified beneath the press of a fingertip. Pale would feel cool, and smooth.

To be likened to linen. How had he known of her love for linen? How had he known that every morning before she scaled the office stairs, she gazed for a moment into Rosalina's shop window as she looked forward to the day when she would sleep upon a bed made up in Rosalina's finest Irish linen sheets and pillowslips and coverlets? Although before that day arrived, she would need to buy a bigger and better bed, but first she would have to be able to find and to afford a bigger and better apartment—on Golden Lane, perhaps, beneath the citadel—to contain the bigger and better bed that would be a worthy enough vessel to receive and support the finest Irish linens. Maria rehearsed her plans every morning as she stood with her nose not quite pressed (she was too proud for that) against Rosalina's wonderful window. The sequence of imagined events had taken on the repetitive cadence of a fairy-tale slate of necessary tasks to be completed before a spell could be broken, and an enchantment set into motion. Maria believed everyone privately held on to some symbol which came weighted with a meaning all out of proportion to any reason or reality attributable to a mere symbol. Half their clients had also fastened onto their own treasures, folded within scented tissues on Rosalina's shelves, and even Becky must have invested every secret hope in those praiseful and pleading letters from some man in Africa which she so imperfectly hid, slipped among the pages of a contract, or left forgotten in an English-language novel she lent Maria. And Albrecht himself, Maria suddenly knew, as certain of his emblematic object as she was of her own, had come here tonight to the castle intent upon finding a wife. He had come in quest of a consort equal to him and his ambitions. Of course she would be beautiful and she would be set apart so he would recognize her and he would know what to say to her to elicit the reply he sought.

"Shall we seek the air? Shall we wander the grounds?" Albrecht asked her. His grasp on her arm tightened.

"I would rather wander upstairs," Maria said. "I have been to this castle before and there are such lovely quiet chambers, above."

BECKY WAS SUMMONED TO THE KITCHEN, where Holly Holladay had been carried after she was happened upon in the Conservatory curled beneath the *Punica granatum* in an unwakeable state. She had not roused at the sound of her special name, anxiously spoken, and she had not responded to a courteous slap by the bravest of her several discoverers. Becky wondered at the instinct that had caused Holly's rescuers to convey her to the kitchen. Did the tiled walls, the glaring overhead lights, the availability of sharp knives and hot water represent a clinic to them? Had they all been born at home on the kitchen table, like Kafka? Holly had been laid atop the long scrubbed wooden table, the caterer's clutter swept aside. The cleaning supplies beneath the sink had been rifled through and a take-charge individual was waving an uncapped bottle of ammonia beneath Holly's flaccid nostrils. Onlookers clustered and suggested. Is there a doctor present? someone asked, and the only doctor, a professor of semiotics, was pushed forward, and, wishing very much to help, suggested reconciling the patient with an external reference point. Just how to accomplish this was debated. Pavel, Tilla's morose husband, had first come across the body, and it was just his luck not to have encountered it in motion. Tilla, roped in by the affinal tie, thought to fetch the capable Mrs. Lowe, lately observed at solitary ease eating red grapes in an elegant salon. Tilla had not sought Alden—not discounting him in a crisis, but feeling he would be shocked and saddened by the turn of events, and when she'd last seen him, dancing up a storm with Mrs. Jaroslav, he had seemed so happy. They had been remembering together how to rhumba.

"Has anyone called for an ambulance?" Becky asked. How did one call an ambulance here? She ought to have found out before agreeing to Alden's fin de siècle bacchanal. Well, he'd warned her. "You did? Oh, thank you, Tilla. I don't suppose you requested the no-siren option, considering the neighborhood? No? Oh well."

Becky peered over shoulders then, to see for herself. Must Holly always be the center of attention? The tulle net of her skirt refused to lie decently flat across her legs, such a spectacle. Even her hair suffered from whatever ailed her. Strands turned belly up and shone a fish-scale green.

"Are you sure you want to bring her around?" Becky asked the man who was wielding the ammonia bottle. "Perhaps it would be kinder to let her drift along in dreamland." This drew consenting murmurs all around. What a nice way to describe a coma.

They all stood about admiring the copper pots and the formidable stove and discussing the theater until the ambulance shrilled up the Avenue.

The driver had sounded the alarm with unnecessary glee, in Becky's opinion, and the siren sound, first detected from a distance, then drawing nearer, and coming *here*, had had the effect of clashing a soup ladle against a pot lid to scatter crows from a cornfield. Many partygoers took off on the heels and peals of the ambulance, anxious to get away before real trouble broke out, while others flurried and then alighted again, but less confidently so. The bartenders and waitstaff, having made calculations that just enough drink and food remained to be reasonably divided among the rucksacks and satchels they had all brought with them, folded away aprons and loosened bow ties and lit cigarettes and sagged against the nearest reliable objects to resume conversations among themselves. The candles, the flambeaus, had burned to nubs and spindles and wearily flickered with tarnished emphasis over empty glasses uncollected upon broad windowsills and the parapets. The dance band had disbanded. They had loaded their instruments into their panel van and then could not leave the stable yard. A tinny little car blocked the passageway. A scrum of men was assembled to pick up and put down the vehicle, left rocking atop an abrupt knoll where it remained until happened upon by its owner, who could not quite remember parking there. He directed his passengers, his wife and her friend, to sit as heavily as they could manage upon the trunk to seesaw the front end up and the back end down, rear tires just catching the turf as the motor was gunned and the car shot backward and made what had come to seem to the occupants as their escape.

Becky stood before the Great Portal, which had been flung open with the hope that everyone would get the idea. She spoke good-bye and good-bye, and she smiled and smiled. She had no idea where Alden could be, and everyone asked her, Where's Alden, we have to thank him, too, so much.

As the saying-good-night business abated, Becky began to feel as if she were waiting for satisfied customers who no longer thronged, and so she declared herself out of business. She crossed the Great Hall and glanced down the Long Gallery and through the French doors out to the belvedere, where the very last of the guests seemed determined to watch for the stripes and streaks of dawn to consolidate into true morning just beyond the fixed point of the Tower. After which, Becky didn't doubt, they would repair to the kitchen, confident of finding pastries and honey and tea on offer there. Perhaps they had mistaken the castle for a luxury hotel. Or it may have happened, under the influence of strong song and drink, that they had reverted to olden ways and re-nationalized the property in an impromptu putsch and they were, at present, making themselves thoroughly at home in the name of the People. God, people. Becky ached only for bed and solitude and she could think of no further reason not to seek both.

She charted a way up the Grand Staircase, stepping over wineglasses and side plates and ad hoc ashtrays. Her feet tangled with a pale wisp of scarf, which she snatched up and tossed over the banister as she would have liked to snatch up and toss the wineglasses and side plates and saucer bottoms spilling filter tips and ash. But, she supposed, Miss Mopsy would be up and about at half past seven, banging and crashing away at the party debris on her behalf, and Becky could only imagine what Mrs. Cook would have to say if confronted in her kitchen by in- dividuals dressed in crumpled evening wear requesting, with yawns and petulance, their breakfast. How convenient to have such a loyal staff—not that they were loyal to her, Becky understood, but they could be entirely relied upon to stand by guns of their own. It was rather like relying on mercenaries, and Becky was not averse to relying on merce- naries as long as she knew with whom she was dealing.

Becky closed her bedroom door firmly behind herself and leaned against its solid weight, which did not need her added support to debar any astray dawdlers who may have followed her here (why anyone should want to pursue her, she did not know, but she was just so used to being required of). Becky allowed herself to make a gesture of exclu- sion, spinning and flinging herself at the door in a rather stagey man- ner, her hands and the side of her face flattened against its panels.

The figure of Franca stepped from the shadows, in which she had sought concealment of a sort, if only from the sight of herself presum- ing to return to the Lowes' marital chamber to await Becky's eventual return there. The grand grouping of mirrors from wall to wall, which had not acknowledged her on her earlier visit, had received Franca a second time with steady gazes, sharing from surface to surface what Franca could only fear were their views of her. But she could account for her presence. She had come to speak to Becky in quiet and in pri- vate, here where they would be neither disturbed nor overheard. No, no one would interrupt them—for, Franca happened to know, Alden would not be coming up to bed that night.

She had left him in the library, where he had passed out on the long leather sofa, fallen into a full-length swoon, an arm flung one way, a leg crooked another, his head thrown back and curved over a bolster cush- ion. He looked as if he had fallen from a height but achieved a soft landing. To make certain of him, Franca had touched his foot, his knee, his chest, his brow. He had not awakened as she carefully sat beside him, her hip touching his hip, there was no room for their hips not to touch. She leaned across him. He was breathing, he was detectably breathing, but she determined he would breathe more easily were his neck not so strainedly arched over the hard cushion, and so she eased his chin down onto his chest. His mouth sagged open and he rasped and snorted as if he had swallowed a moth. His evening clothes no longer seemed to fit him, which was a pity, they had fit him so well, earlier in the evening.

She had gathered up the handful of letters she let drop onto the floor just below the insensible Alden. She ruffled them and fanned the air and tapped the sheets of paper into order against the sofa back. She had ruffled and tapped them again. This had been a test; she had allowed herself to conduct this test. She owed it to him, and to herself. Because if he *should* love her, if he were ever possibly going to love her, he would open his eyes and sit up and say, Franca, thank God it's you. What's that you have there? And he would pluck the sheath of letters from her grasp before she could protest and prevent him. She had given the Fates every chance to take matters out of her hands. She fanned the air with the momentous letters as if the Fates might be coaxed and enlivened like coals, but the Fates remained cold to her appeal.

Franca had arisen at last. She had heard a siren, running footsteps, voices. Alden just stirred and then resettled at the slight give and release of the sofa cushion. He muttered some contented syllable as she left him. She wondered if she would ever love him less than she loved him now, and she could not decide whether to endure or to waver in her devotion would be the sadder course to take. She grieved, at the moment, for some future time when she would look back at herself and fail to honor her present sorrow. But sorrow also seemed something she could bank upon; it would accrue and perhaps it could be redeemed, someday. She was convinced this great loss was all she would ever have to call her own.

She had shivered at the fineness and the finality of what she intended to do, as she entered the splendid bedchamber. She turned, then, from the sight of herself caught in all the mirrors on the wall, for the face of a bewildered child had stared back at her, as if only the earliest innocence, or ignorance, could account for her decision. That this effect was mere affect, of dim light, of speckled glass, of local wine tossed too quickly over her palate, Franca was perfectly aware. Nevertheless, she was not certain that one of the apparitions in one of the mirrors might not begin to weep.

The rustle of paper in her hand reminded her that she had sufficient diverting reading material with which to while away her wait for Becky's return. She settled into a soft chair and selected one letter from among the many. She tilted the page toward the aglow lamp and she read, until she wearied of reading, a tribute to Becky's eyes—the jeweled truth revealed therein, her gazes meant to be stern but gentled by the goodness of her great heart. Tchah. Franca skimmed ahead to a description of a visit to the Roman ruins at a place called Sabratha, sited above the sea among a stand of cyprus where he, Becky's beloved, had wandered among gold-hued columns and the remains of an amphitheater. He had picked up and pocketed uncataloged artefacts among the weeds and stones, a tessera, a bead. So, this man was a thief.

He was in love with the past, the man confessed. He had been very alone on his travels, well pleased the spot was so unfrequented, only regretting that Becky was not there with him so they could be alone together. He was only living for the day when he and Becky would wander Sabratha's ways. He wrote,

> *When I do come, she will speak not, she will stand,*
> > *Either hand*
> *On my shoulder, give her eyes the first embrace*
> > *Of my face,*
> *Ere we rush, ere we extinguish sight and speech,*
> > *Each on each.*

Oh, that was good, that was really rather good, Franca had to allow. She was always in favor of the practical utility of poetry in real-life situations. She wondered where Becky's suitor had come across those lines, yearning for the occasion of love among the ruins.

BECKY RECOVERED FROM HER STARTLEMENT. The intruder in her bedroom was only Franca, only a misplaced little Franca. Becky stepped away from the door against which she had pressed herself. With any luck, Franca, who was rubbing her great dark eyes, had not noticed her odd entrance. Perhaps Franca had drifted into the bedroom to take a nap, for she had struck Becky as someone who, when overwhelmed, would shut down entirely, much as the girl's native city was also a place of overloaded circuits and spontaneous suspensions of systems. At the moment, Franca was standing in for all of Prague, and Becky was thoroughly weary of Prague with its intrigues and insufficiencies. She longed above all else for a hot bath even as she despaired of simply achieving one, the castle's geysers and drains being what they were, and also contrivances of the city's strange inner workings.

But Franca was asking Becky, "Are you being pursued?" She joined Becky by the door. She leaned against the carved jamb and listened through the paneled wood. A thought came to her. "Is *he* here? Tonight?" she asked. She raised a forbidding hand, the one clutching a disorder of papers.

"Everybody was here tonight," Becky complained. She retreated to her dressing table and its familiar clutter of jars and tubes necessary for the application and removal of her public face. She postponed the latter exercise as she twisted off bracelets and rings and threw them at an available porcelain dish. Franca had never heard such a careless and expensive sound.

"And I was not being pursued, although I'll admit to having made my getaway," Becky said. She reached behind her head to fiddle with the clasp of her necklace. "Have you lost your ride home?" she asked. "I'm sure if you hurry you'll catch up with some obliging straggler, I shouldn't doubt, if you hurry."

The circlet of garnets unjoined and an end flailed. The dark gems did not flash. Instead, they took in the lamp glow and held it and Franca was not sure that stones such as these did not grow when exposed to the light. She knew so little of such matters. Nevertheless, she too was in possession of something of value.

"As luck would have it, I dismissed the chauffeur earlier this evening, so he's not available to drive you home," Becky said. "But you might call a taxi. Feel free to use the telephone located in that sort of porter's alcove beside the Great Portal," she suggested. But by now, Becky knew in her bones—and the knowledge made her bones ache— that Franca had sought her out to speak to her. Those closely written-over pages and pages Franca held in her hand rattled and thrust with a life of their own. Oh, these people were still so dossier driven, even the young ones, who seemed not to understand one should just set a match to the archives and move on.

Franca resolved to take it on faith that one of Becky's stern glances had ever "been gentled by the goodness of her heart," although Becky's cold stare was leveled at the bundle of copied letters. She might not have directed such scorn at a human being. Franca hoped not, for Alden's sake, or he would not, she thought wildly, have any skin left.

"I'd recommission the chauffeur temporarily but he'll be royally drunk by now. Really, I ought to have anticipated and named a designated driver," Becky said, and she laughed socially even though the party had ended and she had slipped off her sandals and it hardly seemed fair to have to continue to make an insincere effort in the sanctuary of her bedroom, where such insincere effort should not have to be necessary even if lately that had been too much the case between Alden and herself. Becky liked Franca even less for reminding her of all those replies politely phrased, and those embraces endured. And now the obstinate girl expected her to read her dossier or documents or whatever it was she had compiled. Unless, perhaps, Franca had just caught some entrepreneurial bee in her bonnet, in which case she should go through channels and schedule an appointment during regular business hours like everyone else. Unless Franca's little idea could be dismissed outright tonight and that would be that.

"All right. Give me," Becky said, and she reached with scant patience. Franca stepped forward, and, as ordered, surrendered her evidence, although had she not been so ordered she might, even at this last moment, have lost courage and simply gone away.

"I can't read this," Becky said after a glance at pale, blurred copy print and a block of handwriting uncentered on the page. "My glasses." She indicated she had no glasses.

"On your dressing-table top." Franca spotted a pair of horn-rimmed half-moon spectacles, a house pair, as Alden called them, of a compromise magnification, too weak for his vision but which made Becky feel as if she were peering at a forest through German binoculars and every twiglet loomed like a log.

"I don't like these glasses," Becky said, as she slid them up and down her nose. "These aren't the right glasses," she said as she looked down upon a page. "These are the wrong glasses," she said, as she recognized the handwriting and the words which, so enhanced, came back to her at a shout. Franca read Becky's face as Becky read the letter.

"How did you come by these?" Becky demanded of Franca, even as she owned to herself that the originals of the letters had not been well concealed. Alden could have happened upon them at any time, anywhere, had he delved under cushions, had he lifted her desk blotter, had he cared to seek out what it was that had come between them. But who had been paying attention? Becky wondered.

"Does that matter?" asked Franca, because in truth her every thought and deed of the past two years had led to this moment. Her prominent part in the story, her undue interest in the state of the Lowes' marriage, her possession of the letters, all figured in a way she would rather not recount at this late, last point.

But Becky summed up succinctly, with sudden revelation. "Josef," she said.

"Yes, yes. He was boasting and displaying and I grabbed them," Franca said.

"Boasting? To whom? Not to everyone?" Becky asked.

"Only to me," Franca assured her.

"Boasting only to you? To impress you? Oh, watch out for that one. He's a devil," Becky warned.

"No, he wanted to sell to me, not to ravish me. But I tricked him and

I took them from him and I ran from him and he was too drunk to run after me. I hope he may also be too drunk to remember it was me," Franca said. It occurred to her that she had best be careful when she left Becky and walked through the deserted castle and across the empty grounds. She frowned at Becky, who had brought this trouble upon them all. Well, the time had come for Becky to sit still and be instructed in the program of necessary reforms to which she must dedicate herself from this night forward. The face of a fierce child stared back at Franca from the dark surface of a gilded mirror, knowing best now.

Becky seemed to have forgotten Franca. She had found an accommodating angle of spectacle lens and she was reading and rearranging th.ᵉ letters, putting them down in some sort of order upon her dressing table, inventorying them or judging them or, perhaps, enjoying them.

"And now, do you wish to sell them to me?" she looked up and asked Franca. She seemed almost amused, or if not quite amused, she had assumed that American attitude Franca could never quite understand. She had watched Americans shopping at the farmers' market, too rich to have to bother to bargain and growing impatient with the game as played by the locals, nevertheless appreciating, until the exercise became just too tiresome, that this was an "experience." They photographed one another holding tomatoes and carrots standing next to the stall keeper, towering over the stall keeper.

"No," said Franca. "I do not wish to sell your own letters to you. I give them back to you. Freely."

"But I can only assume you must want something," Becky said.

"No," Franca said.

"No?" Becky very much doubted that.

"Well, yes," Franca said. "There is something."

"Quite," said Becky. She brushed aside one of the letters in question and she fingered the glinting coil of a discarded bracelet, sliding it toward Franca. The gemstones pulsed like some object found beneath a rotting log and toward which one irresistibly inclines to determine whether it seeths with life or with putrescence.

"What I want," said Franca, "all I want is for you to stop permitting such letters to come and to stop answering such letters and to stop keeping such letters and to stop desiring such letters and also, as well, to stop being so unkind to Mr. Lowe and so impatient with him. Oh, just please, Mrs. Lowe, please just stop."

"Stop," repeated Becky. "So, I am to stop. But they're such appealing letters. I trust you've read them, or read enough to get the gist, read enough to know not to like what you've read," she said. "Well, thank you for all your efforts on my behalf," she said. She regathered the letters and tapped them into a bundle, which she slipped inside a dressing-table drawer. She pushed at the drawer front negligently, leaving it ajar.

Franca stared at the telltale flash of white paper. "I am warning you," she said. "Alden must not know of this. His happiness lies with you," she bitterly conceded.

"Possibly," Becky reluctantly allowed, as she considered the great and constant question of Alden's happiness. How clever, or how caring, of Franca to have discerned that and to cite now Alden's happiness as that essential element of his temperament which must always be nurtured and for which Becky had, somehow, assumed every responsibility. Or to whom the burden had been handed off in a swift, smooth maneuver when her fuller attention had been engaged elsewhere. The transaction had occurred on her wedding day, Becky was sure, while she was searching for one face in particular among those gathered in the meadow, when she had let her train trail through a patch of mud she had been cautioned against by her several attendants. Then, she had cried, I must go away and change, and they had all insisted, No, no, you cannot leave now, and in the confusion of detaining arms and figures clad in pastel satin standing between herself and the garden gate, the switch must have been made.

"No, not as a possibility. Definitely so. You are Alden's happiness," Franca declared, forcing that which she was compelled to relinquish upon Becky, who seemed so reluctant to take it back. Franca's position felt at once false and true, for she sensed she was acting truly in the face of a falsity and so she was consoled by a further, faint idea that in this instance her own small part must stand out as very, very good. And though by tradition and imposition, her people had never been much for religion or God or what have you, she believed she saw how the Church thrived on such sacrifices as hers, providing a place on Sunday morning for those who had no place to go on Saturday night. She was not automatically disposed to reject this consolation. She entertained a vision of herself as a Vision; her image, glimpsed in the room's many looking glasses, now shone back at her pale and finely drawn.

"But I really can't claim to have made Alden very happy lately," Becky said. "I've been so hard on him, lately. This whole horrible party arose from his desire to cheer me up, actually. He can't be content unless I profess to be, that's always been our dynamic. He cracks one of his jokes and I laugh, whether or not—well, you've been exposed to his jokes, haven't you, Franca? But you have no idea how utterly downcast Alden can become. He can be floored by the least little setback. Four years ago, when he was eased out of his old firm, on the most favorable of terms, mind you, he could have marched across the street to the next firm along, who would have snapped him up in a heartbeat. Oh, all right, after a remark or two and the raising of an eyebrow, but that's all. Instead, he fell into a funk for fifteen months. He uprooted our entire family while he embarked on his great middle-age quest for the meaning of life. It was an impossible time for all of us, how impossible I am only now admitting to myself. I have only lately and at last wiped the terrible complicit grin from my face." She snatched a froth of Kleenex from a silver cube and she swiped at her bright, painted mouth. She held out the stained, torn tissue, which Franca, instantly obedient to the commanding gesture, received from her.

JULIE AND SVATOPLUK HAD, HOURS BEFORE, climbed the Tower staircase, which rose high and steep and winding and railless. Julie, who had inhabited this space for months, darted up careless as a chamois traversing a mountain pass as Svatopluk proceeded with all due caution, his tense shoulder hugging the on-and-on curve of hewn stone and rough plaster wall, his feet unsurely scuffing over each wedge-shaped and slanting tread, feeling how each tread was angled and pitched unlike the last. They climbed, at their separate paces, in darkness even though there was a light, as Julie's voice, receding, fading, informed him. There was a switch at the base of the stairs but there was no switch at the top, which had been very stupid planning on someone's part, or maybe they used to have a castle servant whose job it had been just to stand there, at the switch.

Julie, still chattering on about the party, halted to wait for Svatopluk to catch up when she seriously required an answer from him. Did he, as a guy, think Holly Holladay was so hot as all that? she wanted to know. Because hadn't he noticed Holly's hands were really fat? If you really studied them, her fingers looked like all big toes. Julie sat upon a window ledge swinging restless legs, flurrying her long skirt, as Svatopluk, stolidly taking step after step, approached. He only realized his sight had been dimly restored as he avoided being kicked backward, heels over head, to his likely death; moonlight, starlight, penetrated the windowpanes just where Julie had perched, palely illuminating her, describing in shadows and smudges the outlines of the intense figure of which, he realized, he had become very fond. That she held the power, perhaps, to injure him with her heedless impetuosity made her seem less trifling. He had not believed she could ever really matter to him, but his heart seemed to be beating harder now, and not solely from exertion or his sudden fright.

"Oh no," Svatopluk spoke aloud, which Julie took to be his response to her question about Holly.

"Actually," Julie said, "this is the wrong kind of window for a castle, you know." This was the first time she had invited him into her Tower, and she fell as automatically as her parents did into a tour-guide patter. "In a real castle, in a real tower, the windows are narrow slits set at a slant for the arrow shooters."

"Archers," supplied Svatopluk.

"Yes, yes, I know, archers. I said arrow shooters for your benefit. I speak excellent English, only bad Czech. Anyway, archers could aim shots out of the narrow, sideways window slits, but the enemy couldn't shoot in, unless it were a very lucky shot, if this were a real tower. So, I am completely undefended up here if anyone changes their mind about the Revolution and all us Americans being over here trying to help make you become . . ." She hesitated. Did she mean to say happy and civilized and rich? Would Svatopluk mind that she had noticed he was not happy and civilized and rich?

When arrived at, Julie's quarters were a glorious mess, for which Julie, rightly, did not apologize, nor did she effortlessly run about whisking up shoes and clothing and books and belongings and all the boxes those belongings had come in, and Svatopluk regarded the display as a treasure heap, with every idea he had ever heard about American teenagers' lifestyles altogether verified.

Much later in the evening, Julie was to wonder, "Do you think there's still the party?"

"I don't know. Why? Do you want to go back down to it?" Svatopluk asked, and he yawned into her shoulder. He placed a reminiscent hand lightly upon the blade of her hipbone. Julie arched beneath this suggestion of restraint, then subsided into the caress that he intended. "Get up and get dressed? Have to talk with those other people?"

The way he spoke of other people—Julie felt sorry for all those other people, but not very. "No, I don't want any more of that party," she said. "They're just going to go on and on until there aren't any more you can even pretend are clean glasses left, and outside, some car'll keep honking for somebody who's still inside to come out, who's the only person who can't hear the horn honking."

"Did you huddle beneath your childhood blanket, Little Julie, and listen through the wall to the grown-ups at play?" asked Svatopluk. He needed now to know everything about her. He wished he had known her always. He vowed, starting tonight, to know her forever.

"Oh, we had very thick walls, and anyway, they let us stay up for parties, my brothers and me. My brothers could mix drinks between them. When they were very little, when they stood behind the sideboard, the bottles and shakers and glasses looked like they were levitating on their own. I'm too young to remember, I'm the youngest, but everybody says. My party trick was to try on the ladies' coats—well, the fur ones, anyway. I loved animals. And I used to tie all the scarves together; the scarves always slid out of coat sleeves and got all mixed up anyways. I used to hang my scarf rope out the coat bedroom window, not to the ground though, even though I used to lean way out. My idea was to escape down my scarf rope but we lived on the fifth floor when we lived in New York," Julie said. "My parents probably should have been arrested," she added, without rancor. "*I* got in trouble for all the un-un-undoable knots, because the scarves were always Hermès or Gucci, you know, they had to be *signed* Hermès or Gucci. That's how I learned to read, not 'See Spot run,' but designer labels. I was a consumer prodigy, actually."

Svatopluk held her as if to keep her from falling from the long-ago New York window. He listened through her skin through his own skin as she breathed in and out.

"I think surviving such indifferent parenting exposes you to so much stuff you're immunized for life," Julie said. "Or maybe it's having such indulgent parents that makes you go so soft that if you fall, you just sort of bounce." She was not usually given to introspection, nor was she at all accustomed to being attended to as she spoke her thoughts aloud. She had never been persuaded, anyway, that the past could support very much in the way of revisiting. Her days were used and used up, and she viewed each succeeding day as a blank slate, just as her diary presented her with a series of blank pages upon which to write what she would, as she would: a self-imposed discipline for which, nevertheless, she sometimes resented her higher and prior-deciding self, scrawling her entries in a hand scarcely decipherable even to her own accustomed eye. Small wonder she came away with such variant readings when she did consult the official record.

"It's the second instance which explains you to me," said Svatopluk.

"Really?" Julie asked. She began to strike the mattress with her hand, with her foot. Her arm, his arm, her leg, his leg rebounded. "Am I like this? Like this? A real carnival ride?" she asked.

"Not the bounce part, the soft part," said Svatopluk as he caught and kissed her hand and stilled her foot with his foot. "I see the way you draw yourself in such hard, harsh colors and lines, your lips and your eyes, with your sharp, pointed piercings. You make yourself so fierce, so wild, in your appearance, like an animal displaying hackles and teeth, like a bird ruffling and puffling its feathers. Just as I have read in my guidebook to the American Western states where I shall visit someday, this advisory to foreign tourists should they encounter a grizzly bear on a backcountry trail. One must stand one's ground and tent one's coat up above one's head and wave one's arms from side to side so one appears twice as tall and twice as wide to the bear than one in fact is. So I understand why, Julie, you put on your bold display, because you are, in fact, so small and so soft in the world."

"But I'm not from out west, though I've been there a whole lot, at my uncle's. You've been reading the wrong *Fodor's,*" Julie said. "Because in New York, you're not supposed to look too rich, like wearing a leather coat and talking in your school voice on the subway. Except when you have to look rich for your friends so they'll still be your friends. Then you take a cab when you go see them. It's very complicated, but maybe you'll understand someday if your country ever progresses beyond being happy for finally having a Benetton and maybe a Gap. Mostly, though, the way you want to look is to fit in, but to fit in better than anyone else you're fitting in with. Besides, when we lived in New York, I had all those brothers around and they were big, believe me. Really, Svatopluk, if you want to go to Colorado to mess with the bears, you'd better have a shotgun or hire some local guy who has a shotgun to go with you. I'm not sure foreigners are allowed to carry guns. I shouldn't think so; they wouldn't have enough insurance to pay for damages if they shot someone."

"And will your brothers come gunning for me?" asked Svatopluk. "Will they hunt me down and dispatch me, as your seducer?"

Julie burrowed into his side and she swiped his mouth to snatch away that last word, so funny, so old-fashioned, so inaccurate, as if she had had to be wooed and convinced by Svatopluk. Because the first time she ever set eyes upon him she had vowed to make him notice her. She had come upon him in her father's office, seated at his desk in his shirtsleeves before an open window with the breeze fingering his dark hair as if seeking to tease him away from his so-serious perusal of a sheet of figures—mostly zeroes, whether the good kind denoting billions or the other sort signifying nothing, Julie had been interested enough in Svatopluk to be interested in his list of numbers. She had longed to tease him away from his desk, to flutter his dark hair as if she were a new breeze blowing, to make him turn to her with as concentrated a gaze as he had trained upon his businesswork. She had taken to stopping by the Ministry outpost office on pretexts, the devisings of which had stretched her imagination. She had expended further mental effort constructing conversational openings. She and Svatopluk had discussed the weather very thoroughly. Luckily enough, the weather in Prague had changed from that first September through May, so she had been able to vary her remarks. Nevertheless, discussions of the heat, the cold, the rain, the snow, the return of heat, of rain, of leaves and blossoms, had never advanced beyond metaphor. By May, nothing had bloomed between them, until the day when, forgetting herself so far as to behave naturally, Julie had complained that the return of fine weather had caused the doors of the city's beer halls to be propped open, allowing a fug of tobacco smoke and old beer cat pee puddle stinks to waft in visible clouds across the sidewalks. Julie had leaned across Svatopluk's desk and winnowed, a ring-jammed and purple-scarlet-nailed hand waving in front of his face. Like, did Prague really need to have a million beer halls? Julie had wanted to know. Because in normal countries normal people felt like having an Orange Julius sometimes.

She had sighed extravagantly and sat upon a corner of his desk as if exhausted by her ordeals. She had picked up and put down, with her vivid hands, his important papers, which, she and Svatopluk realized, he did not mind although he would have minded had anyone else disturbed his arrangements. They had shared a first, amazed glance, swiftly retracted. Svatopluk had stated then, he was sure Orange Julies must be very delicious, but every man, woman, and child in Czecho-slovakia consumed a pint of beer a day. Beer had been brewed in his country since the twelfth century, and Czech brews were rivaled by none in the world. To drink beer was almost a national religion, the true Church having left such a bitter historical aftertaste. But there were, in fact, only eight thousand registered beer halls in Prague, which was a far cry from the million establishments Julie had estimated.

Weird, Julie had pronounced to herself, less at the wave of infor-mation than from her sudden insight into Svatopluk's enthusiasm for explaining matters. She had subsequently abandoned stating the un-answerably obvious (hot, cold, rainy) and had reverted to the child-hood gambit of eternally asking Why? which proved easy enough in Prague, where nothing made sense anyway. Office conversations had begun to flow as Julie delicately diverted the stream. And so, all of this

(Svatopluk, her, here, tonight) was her doing, achieved after a further yearlong effort to convince him she was not just a silly child. She further demonstrated her maturity by not boasting of her strategizing, at this moment. She did, however, weave her fingers through his thick head of hair and give it a tug, as if she were about to shear a sheep.

"Well," asked Svatopluk. "What is to be my punishment? Tell me, what would your big brothers do to me?"

Julie considered. "They wouldn't kill you. They wouldn't kill anybody, anyway, except by accident. Glover's in the army, but they just send him to school all the time, he's really smart, and Brooks and Rollins just fool with computers all day. I know, that's how they'd do it. They'd go on their computer and make it like you'd never gone to school, never passed your exams, never got your degree, never had a job, never lived at any address, never had a bank account or a credit card or a driver's license or a passport. They'd make it so you'd never been born. You would not exist, so they wouldn't have to kill you."

"I should find a way to exist," declared Svatopluk. "I would find proof. I would make proof. I shall carve my name and your name here, somewhere in the castle, somewhere in the Tower, in a secret corner only you and I would know. Up there," he decided, "up there among the rafters."

"Oh, that's just being romantic," Julie said. "And don't think something won't come along and gnaw away whatever you wrote. We've got rats all over the castle. But you know what would work? You know what does survive? Sometimes you can write your name and the guy's name on a windowpane with your big sharp diamond ring and a hundred years later people will still come along and wonder, Who did they think they were?"

Four

C'e Nebbia—It Is Foggy

"JULIE, DO YOU KNOW WHERE YOUR MOTHER IS?"

"Huh?"

"I said—Julie, please don't walk away while I'm speaking to you. I asked you, do you know where your mother has gone?"

"Huh? No."

"Your mother didn't say?"

"Huh? No. She just left a note."

"Your mother left a note?"

"I guess a note. In an envelope for you it says on the envelope."

"Please don't walk away while I'm talking to you. Where is this envelope? Because your mother and I are supposed to be at the theater in forty-five minutes and she should be home now unless our plans have changed unbeknownst to me. Perhaps I am meant to meet her there."

"It's on the table where she put it."

"On which table?"

"By the door."

"By which door?"

"By the big door."

"By which big door?"

"By the way big door. Because Mum had all these big suitcases with her. And she took the car."

"Your mother took the car?"

"I *said* she *took* the *car* with *suitcases.*"

They had bought a snub-nosed Peugeot alleged to have been lightly preused by OIEC officials who had journeyed to Prague and then gone away. Josef, too, had gone away a few evenings after the party, when se-

curity officers showed up at Castle Fortune, acting on whose authority
no one was sure, for by then Josef had been complained of to many
agencies. The men who came for Josef looked disconcertingly, or perhaps reassuringly, old guard as they escorted him across the courtyard
and down the Avenue between the soldier-straight lindens, ultimately,
Alden had said, to be mercifully released back into the wild. They
sold the limousine, which they'd never liked anyway, to a Turkish
gentleman from EFTA whom Alden had come to know. The Turkish
gentleman had tested the horn and turned on the emergency blinkers'
gratifying display—they pulsed, not on and off, but bright and brighter.
The proud new owner refitted the scuffled floor mats with woven carpet squares before driving off, well pleased. Home to his lovely wives,
Alden had said, blandly smiling and waving to Mr. Fez across the stable
yard and down the Avenue between the lindens which now seemed as
sensuously asway as Mr. Fez's troupe of belly-dancing wives waiting for
him at home. Funny how the trees knew, Alden called after Becky as
she walked away from him. They bought the Peugeot to tide them over
until they ordered something better in the spring and then the Poor Joe
was going to end its days as transport for the International Youth, as
the IY's absurdly overloaded, careening-about-town clown car. That
had been Alden's stated plan; Becky, however, had her own ideas.

"Perhaps your mother says in her note where she's taking the car.
But you said she had suitcases."

"I don't know anything about it."

"To tell you the truth, I wasn't really up for Ibsen tonight, although
perhaps it's really better to be down for Ibsen," Alden said. "Unless
you're too far down, and then there might be an unseemly scramble for
the Gabler family gun at the end."

DOES IT MATTER WHAT BECKY'S LAST LETTER to Alden said? She had
attempted many versions, some advancing no further than the saluta-
tion, *Dear Alden,* which sat so long upon the page that any impetus to
continue was lost as her pen tapped to no avail. *Dear Alden,* she wrote
again in a rush, as if she were attacking a balky zipper, startling it into
releasing its gritted teeth. Then, she had written a confession so tender

and so regretful that what she said could not possibly be true, for if all she professed to feel for Alden were really so she would not be poised on the brink of leaving him. She had paused for the longest while to give any tender feelings every honest chance to rise (if they had been suppressed), to regather (if they had become scattered). A clock tocked. Some flitting hymenopteran razzled her. A round tear, not at first known as her own, dropped onto the page and dissolved a word. But it was not a significant word. Becky swiped at her eyes and peered. It was just an indefinite article obliterated, when perhaps she had hoped there would be some revelatory message to behold beneath a washed-away text. Just at the last, as she had, perhaps, come near to praying to be prevented she had, instead, been mocked.

Becky sat at the little writing table in the Pastels Room. Alden was away on an overnight trip, having left late in the afternoon for Bratislava. Julie could be counted upon to be out that evening as well. Almost always away before, she was never home now, ever since the party a few weeks ago. Becky was certain something (something else) had happened at that party, but she had not asked. She had contrived not to examine any of the evidence as Julie slumped at the breakfast table, wearing one of *his* shirts as a dress (he was very tall, whoever he was), tightly belted with one of *his* neckties. Julie veered from smug to sad in the single act of stirring her coffee, remembering him, missing him, and her spoon began to clank against the side of her mug when she arrived at the sad part of her musings, of having had to say good night, the night before. Alden, raising the barrier of yesterday's *Financial Times* from London, only registered that the shirt and the tie were not his own. Their last breakfast that last September morning, their last breakfast as a family, with its sighs and rustlings and clanks, had been a study in triple counterpoint. *Non nobis Domine,* Becky had reflected then.

She picked up her pen. She had set it down to swat at the rattling insect. She tried again. *Dear Alden, I am going on a trip. I shall be taking the car. I am going south. My plans are unformed but you will hear from me when I know better.* When I know better—Becky wasn't sure she cared for the sound of that, for in what sense was she allowing that she might come to know better? . . . *when I know better what my plans are going to be,* she amended.

All this letter writing. Letters had precipitated the crisis in the first place. William's letters, the originals and the palely whispering copies, she had stuffed inside a large envelope, licked it shut, and slipped it beneath the lining paper of her stocking drawer, where the packet bulged like a scoffed-up toad swelling the smooth coil of a snake. But Alden never raided her bureau drawers as she did his for his warm socks and big handkerchiefs, and Becky did not really fear further discovery. The crucial disclosure had already been made when Becky had been revealed to herself, when she had been subjected to what she had come to think of as The Judgment of Franca. All Becky asked now was to manage any subsequent exposure, which seemed inevitable now that her mask had slipped. She only asked for time to assume the new pose she would choose to present to the world. That one mask was to replace another, she acknowledged, but she would paint the new image with a more practiced hand. She would give herself a more determined set to her jaw, a sterner mouth, skin less alive to the burn of all-suffusing blushes. Only her eyes resisted revision. They remained the eyes that had, so long ago, first gazed upon William, and since that day nothing had ever really changed, nor had anything ever been the same.

She could think of nothing more to say to Alden. She would, she decided, provide him with a running account as developments warranted, issuing necessarily compressed updates on the backs of postcards, the fronts of which she must remember to vet thoroughly lest they convey further accidental meaning. She would avoid religious depictions of saints and martyrs, and she would eschew the classical scene: no male, no female nudes, standing alone as avatar or entwined as lovers. Cityscapes viewed from a vantage point would have to serve, provided they were not cities where she and Alden had once believed themselves to be particularly happy at another time, on another trip, traveling through Italy. Then again, the selection and sending of postcards might not seem so very urgent when the time came. She recalled the message-in-a-bottle sensation that always overtook her when she stood before an Italian letterbox and pulled or pushed (confusing, *tirare, springere*) at a flap.

———

HOURS LATER, HOURS INTO HER JOURNEY, it seemed to Becky that she was just coming to as she became aware of her hands gripping a leather-wrapped steering wheel, of her palms sweating into the leather and of the leather sweating into her palms. The crumbs of a hurried sandwich speckled the blue linen lap of her skirt. The torn-into loaf and a lolling bottle of water sat on the passenger seat. Plums rolled about on the dashboard. Her foot pressed too hard upon the gas pedal. She eased up and was overtaken by cars, all of them German-made and powerful and pricey, and for a dazzled moment (she was driving into the afternoon sun) Becky wondered whether she had not just blinked herself awake from the most real of dreams about living in Prague, about leaving Alden. For she suddenly felt she was driving over a smooth, fast bypass rounding the outskirts of a gilded American suburb where all the cars would, of course, be sleek and German models. But the profiles she glanced through tinted, rolled-shut windows were unmistakably the profiles of foreign coins. She was not home but here, approaching Munich (signs said), which she meant to shoot past just as she meant to shoot past all the other place-names, Innsbruck, Bolzano, past Florence and on beyond Rome. One could travel forever and never really arrive anywhere. The featureless road obliterated miles and geography; the flat fields, the overripened fields, the reaped fields, those meticulously regrown forests, the different houses, the different barns, the different cows, the different churches, the castles which were not so very different from the one that had so recently been her own.

She stopped for the first night at a hotel—or motel, motor hotel, what were they attempting?—just off the autobahn, not wishing to stray from the road she had kept to so far. The place resembled a ski chalet, a Texaco station, a barracks. There was a detached little all-sorts emporium alongside where Becky stopped first to buy a bottle of Riesling and another of brandy and a four-pack of Twix and an emergency sewing kit, as it claimed to be in seven languages. She bought an eyeglass repair kit and a (further) emergency rain poncho, and she hesitated over a flashlight, a collapsible shovel, and some chains, imagining ever more emergencies and rejecting them in her case, or, at any rate, refusing to admit them. She checked in to the motel, filling out documents accurately with a legible hand. Should inquiries ever come

to be made, she would not make Alden spend too much on some private detective's hourly rates.

She was sent outside, back to her car, which she drove to an assigned
parking spot, grateful no one else had parked there. She hadn't the will
to return to the front desk to ask, What now? What next? What am I to
do? She carried her smallest handgrip and her recent shopping up an
external staircase and walked the length of an interior hallway, exitless
as a laboratory maze, and she emerged onto a long balcony overlook-
ing the highway, cantilevered like a grandstand just above the southerly
breakdown lane. The rooms were fronted with sliding glass doors. She
averted her eyes from immodest displays within occupied rooms and
located her own door at last, which glided open too easily at the inser-
tion of the least of keys. She knocked, for some reason, before she entered, and inquired, *Bitte?*

There was a bed crowded in a corner with its coverlet mis-tucked as
if just snatched up and over some wanton act. A photograph of the
Augsburg town hall, festooned for a festival, sat framed upon a wall.
There was a Formica-topped desk. Four square, spaced indentations in
the carpet pile told where a chair had stood, and Becky experienced a
sensation, not so set as a certainty, that the chair had lately been flung
with passion from the balcony onto a lane of the autobahn to quell—
she noticed it now and would not not notice it henceforth—the ceaseless rumble and drum of ever-ongoing traffic just below. She tossed her
handgrip and her shopping bags onto the bed and regarded the unsatisfactory glass door. She pulled open the door of the clothes cupboard
and wrenched the rod free from flimsy fixtures as hangers, the only
three provided, clattered to the floor. The clothes rod fit in the sliders'
running track as if measured and cut to length, and Becky, who was
looking for signs everywhere, besides the signs for Munich, Bolzano,
and Rome, welcomed this as an indication that the universe did not
wish her to be murdered in her bed, not tonight, not here in this dreadful place. The universe had provided her with a suitable stick. She drew
beige cloth curtains that met in the middle but pulled shy of the edges
of the glass door, but any voyeur would really have to work to see anything from that angle.

Becky spent minutes, the better part of an hour, fussing over her purchases. There was a wafer of beeswax in the sewing kit to coat the thread; there was a lozenge of magnifying lens in the eyeglass repair kit to assist the unaided eye. She slid the poncho from its plastic wrappings and rolled and stuffed it, per printed instructions, into one of its own pockets. The paperback she had brought to see her through the journey, a copy of *The Devastating Boys,* found by chance on a table at the English church's jumble sale, she placed upon the shelf above the bed beside her travel clock, which she set to an early hour that she knew she'd be up by on her own, waking to the start of inner alarm and first light and loud lorries.

Presently, she went to shower in a stall so small she had to step from its confines in order to bend to pick up the soap when she dropped it. She dripped onto the bathroom tiles where pooling water activated a dried and stuck-on cleaning compound that frothed hotly against the soles of her feet. She plunged herself beneath the shower spray and registered only after a beat that the water was now running ice cold.

She gave up and retreated to the bed. She watched German TV in the dark, clicking from a comedy to a concert to a drama to a discussion. She clicked back to the concert, from Bayreuth. She ate the last of her loaf and some of the plums and raisins from a box and one of the Twix. She drank half the wine and made a dent in the brandy, reading for a while by a low-wattage bulb until she fell asleep, stirring only in mild bewilderment to switch off the burning bulb and the droning television. In the morning she brewed coffee in the contraption provided and she reattached the clothes rod to its fixtures, which should stay put, she reckoned, until someone tried to hang up a coat there, but she'd be long gone by then. She pondered this, her most unaccustomed position of nonanswerableness, as she found her way back onto the highway. So far, this had all been too easy. She supposed she ought to be telling herself to give some voice to a hostage thought or two which might be held against her success in the days to come.

That second day her only bother occurred at the borders. She was fated to be sandwiched between great exhaust-effusing trucks during the last slow crawl to the crossing points, knowing that their drivers might not be entirely aware of her presence, for she herself had to ask, Am I really here? Rain was turned on for each crossing. Wet-slickered sleeves seeped over her documents, which she had at the ready to be promptly produced as she leaned over her steering wheel, peering forward the next few meters into the territory ahead. Her posture and the dates of accruing passport stamps verified she was making time. She was a woman in a hurry who allowed herself an exasperated intake of breath as those wet-slickered sleeves reached through her car window, when the car's interior seemed to have been invaded by alien beings who enjoyed no standing there in her overheated (against the rain, the mountain air) demesne where luggage mounded in the backseat and fruits flourished on the dashboard. She wanted to demand documents of them, she felt such an independent entity. The dashboard fruits were pronounced to be forbidden—arbitrarily forbidden, Becky suspected, as she gathered and scornfully relinquished plums and Jaffa oranges to fumbling hands.

"Where is your husband today, madam?" she was asked. Surely, they were not allowed to ask her that in this day and age? But the Austrians and the Italians wanted to know, in turn responding to an independent woman from their separate senses of affront. The Austrian officials summoned a husband's authority over his wife. The Italian functionary invoked notions of a husband's devoted care. In either case, these were states to which Becky ought to submit herself instead of driving off alone, into the weather, into the world.

"I have left him in Prague," Becky stated. So, she had something to declare after all.

"But you are meeting him? He will join you?" The Austrian barked his question. The Italian inquired gently and with every hope.

"No," Becky answered, and she reached for a spiral-bound notebook. Uncapping a pen, she made a private entry on a turned-to page. She had to keep track of her mileage; the Peugeot's gas gauge gave overly optimistic assessments of unexpended fuel capacity. Nevertheless, Becky might have been a border-crossing critic rating the courteousness of the officers and the neatness of the foundation plantings and the treatment of those undergrown and intensely wary dark brown people dressed in wrinkled cotton tunics with knots and squares and scarves on their heads who had been directed to stand to one side, out of everyone's way, to await further considerations of their cases. She wondered where all those poor people were going, and she realized, then, they were bound the same way as she. She recapped her pen. The guards waved her through as they pondered that last look on Becky's face and as she, who had been so keen to travel onward, stole backward glances in her side mirror after the prevented ones, who fell back smaller and smaller upon a widening field of vision and then were lost to sight.

She had gained Italy at last. She sped through the first, inauthentic part with its Alps and redheads and *das Rotwild* on the menus. Then, the air relaxed into southern winds. The land unfolded and rolled, presenting impeccable studies in perspective of farmhouses and distant towns and upright, individual trees all wrought in mezzotints of approaching evening and awakening memory. It was late September. Italy was hot and being harvested.

All the men noticed her now. As they overtook her in their working trucks and family cars and shiny, humming subcompacts, they craned and peered at her. Becky returned their gazes with one of inquiry. Was her tailpipe dragging? Was a tire wobbling? Oh. Although she was no longer young, she was fair and female and on her own and they were Italian men. She had always been rather an item in Italy. She had tasted here what it might have been like to be famous; those starts of pleased recognition by strangers, the occasional approach to make small talk *("Bellissima")* or a greater request *("Mi sposi")*. She knew she ought to have minded being turned into a mere object, even if one of such high admiration, but she allowed she'd have felt distinctly let down had she not been paid these attentions. Although Alden used to tell her she was just imagining things.

They all look at me too, he said.

That's only because you're with me, Becky said.

And how very lucky I am, said Alden.

WILLIAM HAD BEEN THERE AS WELL, IN ITALY. He had arranged to spend a few days of their first foreign vacation with them. He greeted them at the prearranged piazza. He was newly based in Europe in those days and had arrived early. He had already viewed the Correggios and he recommended them as if it were his place to say so. He had taken the liberty of requesting Campari and soda all around, and of selecting a table with a view of an otherwise overlooked Romanesque facade rather than the famous fountain all the tourists were gawping at with uninformed pleasure.

In 1971, William had turned up bearded, as preter-neatly bearded as any Meissenware gallant. Alden had lately grown sideburns, which came in pale and not very lush. William, on his holiday, wore a new pair of flared denim jeans that revealed the beginnings of a paunch. Alden's trousers were unremarkable, cuffed and unpleated chinos, but he had packed several flowered shirts with solid-colored tab collars, unthinkable attire in the States but he decided he dared be gay in Italy. One could still use the word *gay* like that in 1971. Becky wore sleeveless linen shifts, with her hair upswept and a great deal of eyeliner, very like Julie Christie, who was not just then in high fashion but never really went out of style, so that was all right. That summer, the Canadian student types were pinning maple leaves to their flannel shirts and impressing decals onto their knapsacks so they wouldn't be mistaken for Americans by the Red Brigade or the Baader-Meinhof Gang and be particularly targeted in airport atrocities. Alden had wondered, Where was a Quebecois Separatist when you really wanted one?

They had been so young then, although they professed to have become very old as they rendezvoused in the piazza. Alden had had to be nudged not to stare at William's polished goatee. William had, a few months before, turned thirty (as Becky and Alden would in a year or two), the era's designated age of damnation, or, as Alden said, Don't trust anyone who even looks as if they intend to survive past thirty. They had all come up with examples of people they knew who were bucking to make young and ravaged corpses.

"To the old married couple," William had raised a glass. His hand trembled a bit. How many other Campari and sodas had he ordered while he waited for Becky and Alden to make their way from their romantic hotel (below the Janiculum, antique filled, a trifle funky; they did not yet have very much money) to this, inconvenient for them, piazza?

"Two years this summer," Alden said.

"Indeed." William was well aware.

"I recommend it," Alden said. "Marriage," he clarified. "To someone as like Becky as you can find."

William gloomed at the unappreciated Romanesque facade, as if he could see right through its stolid front to its pain (old and alone in an alien world), and Becky found herself telling the story (it was Alden's story) about the American tourist who had driven from one end of Italy to the other trying to find the town of Pedaggio, which he was convinced must be an extraordinarily special place because the signs for Pedaggio were posted everywhere—the promise of Pedaggio indicated to the north, then Pedaggio had slipped to the south, Pedaggio upcoming, Pedaggio passed by, yet everyone he asked pointed and said, *Sì, sì, Pedaggio!* Well, this American never found Pedaggio. Becky supposed he went mad or perhaps he just went home but he should have gone for his English/Italian phrase book because *pedaggio* is the Italian word for toll, she explained. He was forever driving on toll roads and one would think that it would have sunk in, after the fifteenth or twentieth time he paid. Then again, no Pedaggio could have equaled the Pedaggio of his dreams. She hoped he never found out his mistake, kinder really not to know.

Alden and William had laughed at her. No one could worry over a simple story like Becky, but she didn't mind. She hoped they'd be all right, the three of them, as long as they could laugh at one another, any two of them laughing at any one of them. William, though, particularly endeavored to enlist Becky against Alden, and Becky had known better than to join in too freely when Alden jested William.

William had brought a hundred-year-old guidebook to Rome. Becky and Alden were committed to looking the everywhere-at-once that their expert, Georgina Masson, demanded of her followers. They set out on their city walks consulting their separate authorities and found that the masterworks, the busts, the friezes, the fallen columns, the altars, the arches, the temples, the tombs, had not, on the whole, been moved from where earlier impulses, man's hand or Earth's gravity, had set them down. Certain events subsequent to 1866 were acknowledged by changes in place-names (the Via XX Settembre and Piazza della Republica—William could be at a disadvantage when telling a cabdriver where to take him). The trees in the Borghese Gardens which had, so regrettably, been cut down during the Siege of 1849 seemed to have grown back; William's Mr. Murray would have been happy to know that. Every place William suggested for lunch seemed to have been closed since the Risorgimento, but finding food in Italy is never a problem. Alden and William would send Becky into the most bustling trattoria on the piazza to charm a waiter into giving them a prime table with a view of the inevitable fountain, and to allow the fountain a view of Becky.

"During the summer, this piazza was inundated twice a week for the amusement of the people, recalling the ancient *Naumachia* of which this was formerly the site," William read from his book.

"No, my wife cannot go out with you this evening. She is going back to our hotel with me," Alden told the waiter.

"*Carciofe* are artichokes," Becky looked up from the menu and remembered. "Who was it who told me not to miss the artichokes here? Was that your sister, Alden? I'd better order some. She'll quiz me."

"Prince Piombo's eldest son shall be known as the Duke of Sora," William read further.

"Prince Piombo's eldest son is probably the night porter at your hotel," Alden said. "And he's calling you sir."

"I fear you're right. Nothing is as it was, or should be, yet how I wish it were. I prefer the past. I would live in the past, if I could, and this guidebook is as close as I can come to time traveling," William said. "Just for a little while this summer, I'll pretend."

Becky had turned very pink. Too much holiday sun; she ought to buy a hat at one of those hat places, Alden had been urging her.

"Well, load up on IBM stock when you're back there in yesterday-land," Alden said. "Or rescue J. P. Morgan from a runaway carriage even if you have to spook the horses yourself and then present yourself availably."

"Always the commercial instinct. However, I may not be the only time traveler. Listen to this." William read, " 'For tea, groceries in general, wine, porter et cetera, Mr. *Lowe* who has for many years been established at 76, Piazza Spagna is one of the most respectable tradesmen in Rome and can be strongly recommended to English and American families.' "

"For heaven's sake," Becky said. "At least Mr. Lowe was respectable. I wonder how he ended up so far away from home."

"I'll bet he married a local girl," Alden said, "and events just ran away with him, but then, that's the story of, that's the glory of love."

On their last evening in Italy together when saying good-bye (he was flying out absurdly early in the morning), William announced he had resolved to look ahead to the future, after all, and to that end, he said, they must make a solemn pact to meet again in Rome next year, and every year to come, to replenish their souls (at least those of them who possessed one—he smiled at Becky), and to eat their fill of *pollo all zingara* at George's. William was prepared to extract a pledge from them. He had bought a bottle of Benedictine brandy from the monks, his bearded and round-bellied fellow bachelors. He asked the waiter to bring three empty glasses; they knew him well enough at this café, by then. With some ceremony, William positioned the glasses and he poured and gestured for Alden and for Becky to take one. Alden reached. Becky hesitated.

"I probably shouldn't," she said.

"What? Shouldn't what?" asked William. He was jolly, despite having just proposed a solemn pact.

"I ought not to drink," Becky said.

"We've been drinking all holiday. Why stop now? Stop tomorrow. Be sensible tomorrow," William said, and he smiled at her as he smiled at no one else, so happily, yet so uncertainly. He knew, at heart, he had no reason to be happy, but the sensation visited him so infrequently he had, he acknowledged, never developed defenses against its onrush.

"Becky's right. She probably ought not to drink," Alden said. "Nor should I, at least, not to your proposal. Because next summer we might not be able to get away. (We have to tell him, Becky, don't make that pleading face, darling.) The thing is, William, we're starting a family."

"Hoping to," said Becky. "We don't know, but we have reason to hope, and so we've decided, no more alcohol for me just to be safe. I'm very sorry, William. I mean, after all your trouble, seeking out the monks and all." She met his eye, to prove to herself she could still meet his eye.

"Don't be sorry," Alden said. "William and I will do justice to his fine brandy. He'll just have to give us a different toast, that's all. We'll order Becky a blood orange juice."

And William had come up with something else to say, which had been below his general standard but he had never before been asked to rise to this particular occasion. A child, a child? Why would anyone bring a child into a world like this one, a world packed with danger and evil, a world in which one should only seek to accrue as much pleasure and fine living as one could for as long as one could. Yet here were these two, who surely knew better, providing their own offering to the blighted future, relinquishing whatever chance they had had for a civilized life (while civilization lasted) in New York. William did not, on that warm Roman night, advance beyond thoughts of Alden and Becky's betrayal of historical inevitability and common sense as Alden nattered on, describing their perfect child. He would have Becky's hair and Becky's tranquillity and Becky's facility with small and balky mechanical objects, and perhaps Alden's natural immunity to jellyfish stings as well as sharing his beating-all-comers-at-squash chromosome, although Becky said she hoped any *girl* of theirs would show a little mercy to a lesser squash opponent, however differently Gloria Steinem might counsel in that magazine of hers she'd just started. How did one pronounce that newly coined word—*Miz*?

William reserved his further contemplation of Becky's betrayal for other, wintry nights back at his post, locked away in a grey northern city of shrilling sirens and chronic insufficiencies.

Alden and Becky saw William on his regular trips home to the States, over the years. They had sublet his apartment in the city by then, and a valued and practical friendship was carefully tended. William and Becky corresponded about routine maintenance, details of redecoration, the radiators. They mentioned, as well, what they were reading and the movies they'd seen, and concerts and plays and lectures and readings they had attended. They wrote, Guess who I've just run into, and reported the gossip. Becky, as a matter of course, employed the pronoun We—we went, we laughed, we bought—and William would look away from the page, losing his half smile and his place. From time to time William let slip a *we* in his account—we toured, we didn't care for, nevertheless, we continued on. And then it was Becky's turn to wonder.

By 1986, they had all prospered. That summer, Becky's brother, who had taken over the big place out west, asked if he could have the children (four of them, by then) for a monthlong visit. He had some idea of unplugging them from their video games and putting them up on quarter horses. There was always fence to mend on the ranch, he said. Rosemary was looking forward to doting on the sullen little sister and teaching her to bake macaroons by the half batch, prettily tinted rose pink and palest yellow. Such a missionary impulse on Hap and Rosemary's part. Becky, who had always suspected the Hottentots had regarded the Methodists with a mix of resentment and amusement, knew she had guessed right. Becky pitied the horses. She did not share Rosemary's faith in the redemptive value of baking lessons. She had borne four ornery and independent and unimpressible kids. They took after Alden's family, but the side of the family Alden himself was quite unlike. Nevertheless, he knew their ways and he had learned his lessons hard and early.

Let's take advantage, Alden said. Let's get away ourselves. Let's go to Italy again, just the two of us.

Alden scheduled a few days of meetings in Milan and then he was to be free. William, apprised of the summer's plans (the apartment's floors were going to be refinished while everyone was away), wrote that he needed to be in Rome around the same time, perhaps they could meet? Arrangements were made to get together, just the three of them as they had been in the past.

"Just as well you've got William to pal around with," Alden said. The Milan business had not gone particularly well and he had to hang around the hotel in Rome waiting by a telephone. Cables were incoming and outgoing and somebody Swiss was flying in from London. Alden wished he had sent a minion to the Milanese meetings. His presence had caused certain interests in Europe to think they were more important than they were and they refused to be unconvinced.

"William's business doesn't seem very pressing," Becky said. "Yesterday afternoon he was off doing something mysterious but he wouldn't say what. He was so cagey. I think he was just covering up a case of Roman tummy, which I have stuff for. But I daren't presume to prescribe for him."

"Slip an antacid into his Campari and soda while he's not looking. I'll create a diversion. I'll say, oh look, there's Federico Fellini, with Anita Ekberg and her bosoms."

Becky supposed she ought to shop when in Rome. The boutiques and galleries were richer now and so was she. She wanted to attend a concert or two. There were open-air performances at the Baths of Caracalla, or perhaps she could find an early music concert in a plain and ancient church, a beautifully austere occasion in which music and meaningfulness might merge and some of William's old-fashioned time-travel tourism might kick in for her. Museumgoing was so iffy. So many places were closed for cleaning, closed for renovations, closed by arcane labor disputes, closed because of the crowds that would surge, were the museum ever opened. One could no longer clamber all over the Colosseum, scrambling up to the top tier, and sit, eating pastries and batting away the bees, up where the riffraff had sat during the Empire and where there could be read, if one knew where to look, a very rude graffito cut into the stone. Mostly, Becky was content to sit up on the roof garden of their hotel, gazing out over the Pincio as she made up her mind about a handbag she had liked at Romani, but not loved. She supposed she was better off feeling calm about a handbag than excited; one saw more clearly through the undazzled eye.

William was stout now, and clean shaven, and these days he bought all his clothes and shoes and shaving soaps and eyeglasses in Europe. He offered Becky his arm, a courtesy which had long since become routine with him, emblematic, perhaps, of the limits of what he had to offer to any woman. Becky wore poly-silk separates, having packed nine pieces which made up fourteen different outfits, combined in shades of cream and sage. They won respectful glances. They were a noticeable pair, an interesting couple in their courtesy, their reserve, their measured manner with each other. He carried her shopping bags, all from the most elegant establishments. She held his hat, his walking stick, the shopping bags, when he paused to photograph a ruin. Sometimes, another man joined them, late and apologizing for being late as he attempted to catch up on luncheon and drinks, on dinner and drinks.

That both men loved the woman and did not like one another, any observer could see.

Nothing could please William anymore. He deprecated the proportions of San Pietro in Vincolo; he declared he could no longer look at any Raphael Madonna, that all he saw were the simpering babies. The Church, the clergy, the pilgrims, earned his contempt. There were additives in the wine. The vegetables were grown in African soil. The cheese makers catered to ignorant foreign tastes. The Romans had lost their chic. They wore T-shirts and jeans, just as Americans did.

"No American can wear jeans and a T-shirt like *that*," Becky told him as a young man strolled past them on the Via Veneto. "He's a walking Bernini."

Only Becky could calm William. He found fault everywhere, so Becky was obliged to placate him over and over again. She appealed to him. She turned her thoughts and concerns upon him. She made inquiries on his behalf.

"These artichokes came from Umbria last night in a truck. The proprietor says so," Becky told William. "His own brother grew them and I told him my brother has a farm too. Well, a ranch. A farm of the American West with cows, I think I said."

Becky said, "Try standing off to one side. It's the tour buses out in front you don't like, not San Pietro in Vincolo itself. I think we're meant to first apprehend the facade by approaching it obliquely, even humbly, as of old when the surrounding streets were narrow and crowded."

Becky said, "Raphael's Holy Infants aren't simpering. They look as if they're colicky, and he must have painted them as they were. The babies were all farmed out to tubercular wet nurses in those days. It's a wonder they survived at all."

Becky said, "I rather admire people who persist in believing in the Church. Belief can be very difficult, very inconvenient. Have you read the Sermon on the Mount lately? I find that I often fail to do as Jesus said, and frankly, there are times that I don't even want to make the attempt. It's very wrong of me, but I cannot pretend otherwise."

Becky loved the found theater of the Italian wedding, the burst from a shadowy cathedral interior of a brilliantly billowing bride in full sail, propelling the slim slip of her groom alongside her as the gull cries of waving, flapping family and friends proclaimed, There they go, launched.

"Look over there," she told William, who looked, then looked away.

"A man who is tired of Rome is tired of life," she told him.

"Yes, as you say," said William.

"I'm serious. I mean it," said Becky. "I really think it's fair to say you can regard Italy as a yardstick. You can follow the progress of human history up and down its length and you can assess your own state of mind and being when you're here by discovering which Italy most tugs at you at that moment."

"Explain," said William.

"Are you drawn to Florence? Do you respond to the scale and order and refinement and beauty of the Quattrocento? Have you arrived at that same serene and assured place within yourself? Or do you seek *la dolce vita*, riding on Vespas and splashing in fountains and striving to see and be seen in your leather pants and your lacy shirt? I should hope we're all long past that Italy. Then there's Catholic Italy, lighting candles and drifting through cloisters and praying along what seems a direct line to heaven on some desperate day. That's the 'searching soul in torment' version of Italy. And there's pagan Italy, all in ruins now but they're such vital ruins and you find yourself thinking what a great party that must have been before everyone took on jobs and got married and had kids, when it was still possible that the handsome stranger you happened upon in a sacred grove really was the god he seemed to be, as he took you in his arms and kissed you."

"Is that the 'middle-aged rue and regret' version of Italy?" asked William. "Shall we hire a car tomorrow and drive down to ramble round Pompeii together? I can stand it if you can."

"No, tomorrow I'm visiting Keats's grave. I've ordered flowers from the hotel, which I shall lay upon the ivy there. And I shall probably recite some bits of his which I know by heart as I'm doing so, so fair warning, William. I'll be seeking the 'where but to think is to be full of sorrow and leaden-eyed despairs' version of Italy. You can come too, if *you* can stand it."

———

BECKY DROVE ON, SCARCELY GLANCING to her left or to the right, Italy having become little more to her than a one-way thoroughfare interspersed with bewildering service plazas where she alone among motorists was capable of selecting a single straggling line at the petrol pumps and sticking to it. At the end of the second day of her journey, she stopped outside Verona (a Marriott, immaculate), and the next night found her on the far side of Rome (midprice albergo, damp carpeting, hovering Hoovering proprietor). Then, she came to a halt at the toe of the cavalier's boot. She stayed at a city hotel with a shuddering lift. A Ferrara Torrone had been placed beneath her pillow and she had had to turn on her bedside lamp to see what her shelving hand had touched as she reached for sleep.

She made the short crossing to Messina on the morning of her fourth day out of Prague. She drove onward along the north shore of Sicily upon a generally good road although it came and went, in places. She suffered local traffic, threading through the town squares of fishing villages where she alone among motorists committed to a single lane. She sped, where she could, alongside the sea, through the empty countryside so many people had left, or had come from once. The land was sere here, the earth ancient and crumbling away at this rim. The spectrum's richest colors had been used up elsewhere, on other skies and other fields. *Opuntia pyrus* spiked from the shifting dust kicked up by creation's further efforts. Remanent stones were heaped, or had fallen. Italy was finished for her; that's what Becky was being told, this last time.

THE BOAT TO AFRICA SAILED FROM TRAPANI. Becky stood on deck at the bow, her hip, a hand, holding steady to the rail as she was rocked, rocked. The day had come up foggy, night's smooth blackness turning to clotted grey and then translating into this swirling whiteness. Becky, lying awake waiting for morning, minded least the very dark which could be vanquished by switching on a lamp. (She had read for a while.) But lamplight, a flashlight, a searchlight, only showed there was depth to the blankness of the fog, proving that it was not a membrane but a mass; not a soft wall to be broken through but an entire world of shadows and shapes and missteps and fleeting glimpses of the way out which were lost the moment one stepped forward.

Becky had not, at the last, been permitted to take her car onto the ferry. Her documents were not in order, she was told.

"Well, they're *Czech*," she confided, and she shrugged in Italian, words and gesture. She did not doubt her credentials were wrong. Indeed, she would have been amazed had they been correct. She shuffled through the packet of papers crammed into the glove compartment and extracted a certificate printed on thick stock and embossed with a splendid crest depicting an eagle trailing banners in its talons. "Is this anything?" she asked.

She had been obliged to back down the foggy ferry ramp. She had crunched the front bumper of the next car in line. She waved off the remonstrations of a skull-headed German as the mists swallowed her. She knew, and it had galled her to know, that she would have been allowed to drive her car on board had the ranking officer not been a woman and a hard one at that. Italian females above the age of twenty ought not to wear trousers. Had she been dealing with a male official, Becky would have regarded him with a sweet yet perplexed smile, searching his eyes, his moving lips, until he told her something she chose to understand *("Procedete, signora")*, which would have left everyone pleased, no harm done, no German bumpers nudged, no occasion having arisen for giving offense, for Becky had, at the last, muttered at the female officer. *Vacca,* Becky had called her, which she now hoped didn't mean what she'd meant it to. She had become calm again as she asked herself whether she would not be better off not taking the car to North Africa. She wasn't even sure which side of the road they drove on over there, both perhaps, nor was she certain their Stop signs would still be bright red octagons or done in some other design of blue mosaic tiles and broken bits of mirror. She reminded herself that all the taxi drivers in New York had learned to drive in the Muslim Third World.

She scraped along a bollard at pier's edge and she halted. She had just spied the sketchy outline of a gangplank through a gap in the haziness winnowed away by the swing of a crane loading containers. She hauled her bags from the trunk and hailed several porters, who trundled her luggage off in the right direction. She drove slowly on and shoved her car nose first into an alleyway between two corrugated-iron warehouses. She locked the doors against casual mischief, flung the keys overhand toward the water, and walked back to board the last boat of the season bound for Africa.

PRESENTLY, BECKY RETREATED FROM THE DECK. She had hoped for a final view of Europe, but that was to be denied her, or perhaps she was being spared. A change in the rumble of the ferry's engines and a sightless sensation of gathering speed informed her when the harbor and the channel had been cleared and they were truly underway. Becky braced herself against the wrench of this final leave-taking, but she was more aware of a need for coffee and some sort of sweet roll and possibly a blood orange, if one was to be had. The stillness in the muffled air, her near solitude on deck, had led her to hope that only a handful of other passengers had come on board. However, as she passed through a heavy swinging door into an interior corridor she found it swarming with people. They were, at a glance, the very, or very like, the people she had left behind at the custom posts. They must have slipped onto the boat quietly. Becky stepped around them, she stepped over them. They had spread blankets and strewn their bundles and arranged themselves across the floor. There were so many darting little ones. Becky caught a child who had smacked into her knee and tumbled. Its mother, or grandmother (who could tell, with these women?), snatched the child from Becky, half fearfully, half indignantly. Perhaps Becky ought not to have touched it; then again, its elders ought to have kept better charge of it, if that was the case. Becky found herself hoping she hadn't contracted some skin disease from the, frankly, not very well-maintained child. Sometimes these taboos and prohibitions rose from sensible precautions to the mutual benefit of the Faithful and—what was Becky, the Faithless?

She made her way in silence, for silences fell as she made her way down the passage. On another voyage, she would have nodded hello to everyone encountered and felt obliged to speak of a particularly lovely coastline drifting past or to share misinformed gossip about the supposed owners of a great private yacht riding the waves with such arrogant ease.

The café was a crush, as well, every table taken by more and, presumably, more well-heeled North Africans. They were all male and young in here, and they wore Levi's and Georgetown University T-shirts and Adidas running shoes and they carried plastic satchels from electronics stores. They were tuning brand-new boom boxes to stations just coming in from the approaching shore, catching the first muse from home, tinkling, syncopated songs sung with throbbing voices describing assorted plaintive emotional states.

"Over here, honey," an American voice hailed Becky.

Roger and Veevee Luther, who wore berets and binoculars and had been easy to spot, were heading to Tunisia to visit a new resort of sorts, a seaside-desert-themed full-service facility with Moorish architecture and international cuisine and every assurance that the locals would not stone the Swedish tourists sunning on the beach in their mono-kinis. Roger and Veevee were travel agents from northern Virginia—which, they hastened to say, was not as exciting as it sounded; witness the present moment. They sure weren't going to book any of their clients on the boat from Sicily; they'd never hear the end of it.

"This is not very nice," Becky agreed. "Then again, it's fair to say, most ferries are usually rather last-resort choices, except, of course, the ones to places like Edgartown, although nowadays more and more people are taking their private planes to the Vineyard so even *that* ferry is full of people eyeing other people thinking, So you don't have your own little jet either."

"Are you in the business too? I ask, since you know so much about transportation," Veevee said.

"No, I'm just on a trip," Becky said, but she was not able to be very forthcoming when Roger and Veevee inquired after her further plans with professional curiosity about the tastes of an affluent, off-season, single middle-aged female mid-adventure traveler, an emerging category; articles in the trade magazines were describing strategies for dining alone and debating the fairness of the single supplement.

So Roger and Veevee mentioned hotels where they asked Becky to mention them, and they recommended routes and restaurants and sites of particular interest and advised her how not to be taken advantage of by local guides and local urchins and local rug merchants and brass sellers and dealers in antiquities and never, never to touch ivory items, no provenance was innocent even if they swore the elephant had died of natural causes during the Punic War, and Roger was about to warn Becky against disappearing into curtained recesses to try on embroidered caftans in the bazaars because she might never be heard from again, when Veevee nudged him and sent him off to forage for food. All the waiters seemed to think they were the customers in this café, if Becky knew what she meant.

Roger returned with mint tea, and some squat figs.

"And don't eat any fresh fruit where you're going unless you've peeled it yourself," Veevee said. "Although I must say, the really good establishments have a horror of guests coming down with diarrhea and word getting round. Some of them even ask you, at checkout. They're not being fresh, so tell them."

After a while, Roger and Veevee excused themselves to track down the retro-hippie contingent they had spotted in the second-class saloon, whom they wished to quiz on behalf of their more budget-restricted clients about cheap but survivable accommodations in Africa and other ins and outs of "going native." Becky decided to seek a quieter spot, if there was one to be had anywhere on the ship. The café boom boxes were all spilling over with the top of the Tunisian pop charts, the stations from home found and firmly fixed on their dials. She wondered if she would ever get used to such noise, either to be able to listen to or to cease to hear it.

Wandering down a passageway, she came upon an ajar door marked *Privato* and decided to read the sign as a promise of what she'd find within rather than as a warning against entry by the uncredentialed. She stepped into a well-furnished lounge, a set-aside for VIPs, with bowl-size ashtrays, magazines, and silver serving trays stashed behind a locked glassfront cabinet crammed with Dewars whiskey and Boodles gin. She pulled the passageway door shut behind her. This door also locked. She sat in a low-legged armchair positioned in front of a picture window washed, still, with fog. In size and in shape and in its whiteness, the window reminded Becky of a screen in an art-house

cinema's third and smallest screening room, the venue where they presented the films whose subtitles required footnotes and the whispered
asides of the guy who had sat through two showings and who could
say whether the Minotaur sequence had been real or only a dream. Or
only something in a movie.

IT HAD SEEMED SAFE ENOUGH TO AGREE to catch a showing of
Children of Paradise at the revival house theater in her neighborhood.
Someone else was supposed to have gone with them: Becky's friend
from work at the Wild Flower Society, Eleanor Della, who was really
William's friend, first. Eleanor had been the link. She knew William
through her brother David; the two had been at school together. David,
for his part, had been prepared to be very fond of Becky, and when she
was around him, Becky had had to be careful lest she mislead him in
all innocence. Eleanor had already warned Becky against displaying
her—the only phrase for it was, her natural warmth. Pressed to identify
those signals Becky was unaware she was giving out but which might
be misconstrued as being warm ones, Eleanor could only ask, Must you
gaze? Must you listen? Must you always remember to ask David how
his novel is coming along?

"But I am sincerely very interested," Becky said.

As a stranger in New York, and almost alone in the world, Becky
had marveled at having acquired such a circle of friends. David's novel
was going to be about a circle of friends in New York, circa 1968, none
of whom, it seemed, could fall in love with the right person, just as in
A Midsummer Night's Dream, only different, of course, although there
were going to be ass and mind-altering drugs in David's book as well.

"Forgive me for making you wait. Becky?" William at last appeared
on the corner where Becky had been standing for ten minutes. She had
been eight minutes early, William two minutes late. Becky debited from
his account four minutes. He ought to have been two minutes early, and
were she more confident, she'd have showed up right on time.

"But where is Eleanor?" Becky asked instead of saying hello.

"She broke her heel in the grate outside her building."

"No! Did she fall? Was she hurt?"

"No. Eleanor just listed to one side and hobbled away, complaining at me over her shoulder that she couldn't come to a second decision about shoes twice on the same evening." William seemed quite amused.

"Oh." Becky wondered if she would ever become worldly enough to miss a movie because she had too many shoes to choose from.

The next morning at work, Eleanor wanted to know, "Did you have fun last night? I figured you couldn't come to any harm alone with William."

Becky looked up from her desk with a mild smile. "The movie was terribly sad. I'm afraid I cried, not necessarily *at* the movie. It was more as if *with* the movie. You know that kind of crying?"

Oh yes, Eleanor knew. She asked, "And what did William do about your tears?"

"He pointed out that the policeman in the pickpocketing scene was equipped with the wrong small arms for the period and he gave me his handkerchief, only I discovered I had a Kleenex so I gave him back his handkerchief, completely unused, but he jammed it into his jacket's side pocket instead of rearraying it in his breast pocket," Becky said.

"Well," Eleanor considered. "I don't know what that means. Did he say anything about me? You were supposed to draw him out on the subject of me." Eleanor was always ready to discuss personal matters in the office. No one senior (for they knew themselves to be very junior) oversaw them day to day, and nothing that crossed their desks ever proved urgent.

The Wild Flower Society was a private charity that provided used or surplus string instruments to schoolchildren. The organization's logo was that of a bright-faced daisy growing up through a sidewalk crack, and urban children benefited from the project. Becky's task was to write to manufacturers, to orchestras and chamber ensembles, to schools of music and university music departments describing the mission of the Wild Flower Society and asking for "whatever help you may be willing or able to give to this worthy cause." She wrote as well to churches and to Elks and Rotary Clubs and Shriners, proposing they organize local drives to collect unwanted violins and cellos and viols— Check the Attic! Look in Junior's Closet! People were inclined to want to help urban children, post-Watts.

In those days, Becky was also studying voice under private tuition. She sang with a cathedral choir and she tried out for grander choruses and she attended all the concerts and recitals the city had to offer. She practiced, she listened, she auditioned, she performed. She was not, however, definitely set on hot pursuit of a big career, whether or not one was achievable in her case. Madam Tantamount, her voice teacher, did not doubt Becky's ability, but she questioned her commitment. A Life in the Arts, Madam Tantamount informed Becky, required cohabitation with, alternately, an invalid and a monster. Whether barely breathing or roaring forward at full throttle, A Life in the Arts was a creation forever demanding specialized feed and care of one kind or another. But for Becky, everything real depended upon Alden and whatever was going to happen next after he returned and after they were married. Becky was not persuaded she wanted anything more than Alden and a happy home of their own for Alden and herself where there would be scant room for an overweening talent, particularly if she and Alden were to have children. She did not want to expose young children to a monster, or an invalid.

I ran into Sgt. Pepper today, Alden wrote. *Not the real one.*

In 1968, in New York, in her circle, no one quite knew what to make of the fact of Becky possessing a fiancé in uniform, in the army, in Vietnam. Becky seldom volunteered this information because people could be so unthinking in their remarks and she was obliged to be embarrassed for them. People would have been much nicer had she owned to a fiancé serving time in prison for throwing animal blood at Clark M. Clifford.

But Alden had walked into the fire deliberately, forgoing further student deferments and alternative service, for, as he said, they'd just send somebody else in his place and the only person to benefit from that would be himself. He regretted there had been no middle ground for him to seize, where, he allowed, he would always prefer to make his stand, although he wasn't sure that that wasn't where he had ended up after all (and whether he'd taken the low road or the high road there, he could not say), because from where he crouched, at present, people seemed to be drawing a bead on him from all sides.

But Alden's letters from Saigon were usually upbeat. He dined out rather often, and took in the scenery and the culture (which they possessed there), and he was carrying on delicate negotiations to purchase a very old Chinese vase, not from a shop but from an agent who came to Alden with his wares. Sometimes, Alden was tapped to escort a junketing congressman to view sites considered acceptable for congressmen to see; his colonel had served with an uncle of Alden's in a different war, which, as Alden wrote, didn't hurt. He accepted the arbitrariness of military rules and the randomness of combat damage. His strategy was to obey orders and, when not under orders, to obey impulses. Reason didn't seem to enter into anything here, where he was. Otherwise, Alden interviewed selected detainees and attempted to determine whether they were telling him the truth when they swore they didn't know who had blown up the bridge or fired the rocket. This was excellent training for fatherhood, Alden wrote to Becky, having stern talks with fierce little people wearing pajamas.

Becky had not asked him, What about me? What am I to do while you are away? It seemed that if Alden was to be brave, then she must be good. She planned her trousseau. She embroidered guest towels and pillow slips. She labored at her music. She wrote to Elks and Lions on behalf of needy children. She wrote to Alden every Friday during the last hour of her working week when Eleanor locked the outer door and began to change into her night-on-the-town attire of white fishnet stockings, a bright and short Marimekko dress, and her gold-digger boots. She lifted from a file drawer her special mirror, illuminated from within by three lighting options labeled DAYTIME, OFFICE, and EVENING, by which she applied a fresh coat of makeup. OFFICE wattage made Eleanor appear yellow and blemished, so she never agreed to meet anyone at Wild Flowers. EVENING light called for a heavy hand with her white liquid eyeliner and cake mascara. She layered pale lipstick with puffs of ivory face powder to make her mouth disappear; all eyes turned to look at the girls who were all eyes in those days. She kept a teasing comb, its teeth clogged with broken tufts, in the petty cash box. She amplified her hair and smoothed long strands over the tangled pouf and hissed White Rain, saturating her arrangements. A cloud of alcohol and acetone hung in the air.

"Can you see the top of my stockings when I go like this?" asked Eleanor, raising her arms.

"Yes. Don't go like that."

"How about this?" Eleanor sat and crossed her legs.

"Especially not that."

"What are you telling Alden?" Eleanor would ask then, content just to sit, carefully, and to let her EVENING persona "set."

"I am describing potential china patterns, reminding him to keep in mind what my mother's flatware pattern looks like, so they'll be compatible." Becky's parents had died when she was nineteen and they were fifty, after brief, startling hospitalizations. She possessed now, in lieu of parents, reassuringly middle-aged belongings: a covered turkey roaster, the *Encyclopaedia Britannica,* and a cattle ranch in Colorado. The old foreman was running the place for Becky and her brother until Hap was through school. Then, they were going to decide.

"And have you mentioned William?" Eleanor asked. Late-Friday-afternoon talks often turned, as Becky thought of them, hair salonish. That little White Rain cloud caused an atmosphere.

"Yes, I've mentioned William," Becky said. She read, " 'He is a friend of the Dellas' who is awaiting the results of the Foreign Service exam and reading Talleyrand, at present. We saw a very sad French film. He held up a long envelope in front of the screen to block out the subtitles, not, I believe, sheerly out of ostentation that his French was so good; rather, he was truly pained by the poor quality of the translation. I wonder his arm didn't drop off. I said, Somebody ought to invent a subtitle-blocking device moviegoers can wear, you know, like that thing Dylan hooks over his ears to hold his harmonica to his lips when he does "Blowin' in the Wind." William was taken with the idea. He wants to call the device the *Lingua Blanca* and he is going to consult a patent attorney.' "

"I knew you'd be safe with William," Eleanor said.

Becky and William had become friends on a subsequent Sunday spent sketching designs on coffee-shop place mats until coming to agree by the end of a long afternoon that the concept would enjoy only limited appeal, and they further decided that commercial enterprises were really rather sordid and one-note, anyway, profitability being their single standard of success. Art, diplomacy, charity offered the rewards Becky and William sought, those of personal satisfaction and the knowledge they were doing good in the world.

They both lived in limbo at this time, Becky waiting for Alden and William waiting for his examination results and then for his assignment, for the results proved to be as highly favorable as forecast by all. He had to gain proficiency in another language, a minor one no one faulted him for not yet knowing. He and Becky then shared the common goal of learning to give voice to strange new sounds and expressions. Their respective teachers lived close by one another in an émigré neighborhood where there existed, in those days, a concentration of book- and icon-filled rooms and walkup flats crowded with shawl-covered tables and coffee mills and undervalued abilities. Madam Tantamount declared she had found herself back where she had begun, surrounded by penny-poor students, Free Love, Thomas Mann, and sandals. His professor, William reported, had not regained his bearings since 1939. There were various lessons on offer up and down the length of Sixteenth Street, and in the winter of 1968–69, Becky and William were prepared to be enlightened by their elders' sad examples. Becky and William shared the common purpose of making their stays in this limbo as brief as possible, and in their minds, escape—and subsequent avoidance—would be easy enough, the location was so easy to mark on the map.

All this time, Becky had been wearing a ring on her left hand, a very large and brilliant diamond set in a crown of platinum, which had been Alden's great-great-grandmother's on his father's side and which would have gone to Alden's mother but for the fact that Granny Lowe had lasted and lasted and the ring remained on her bent and frozen finger. The ring had been resized, made larger for a modern hand, but Becky had lost weight and the heavy ring grew loose and slipped and tugged round toward her palm, where Becky let it remain. All around her, other people were getting engaged with Cracker Jack emeralds and braided hoops of their beloved's hair, which they didn't have to worry about leaving by the kitchen sink and losing down the drain, when sentiment might have been offended but not an almost Immortal. Further, when she and William were out and about together and the enormous

ring was too much in evidence, William was often congratulated on being a very lucky man and Becky was told she was a very lucky girl, and
they were told how right they were for one another, anyone could tell
how truly in love they were. Then Becky had to explain, and everyone
felt sorry for William, and for Alden as well, although no one felt sorry
for Becky, who one way or another was going to land on her feet with
two such suitors, the accepted one and the would-be one. But Becky
could not not wear the ring, which she had sworn never to remove except when she was scrubbing a roasting pan or kneading bread, and at
night, before she went to bed, because the high-set stone left an imprint
on her cheek as she fell asleep with her face resting upon her folded
hands. William knew nothing of that, of course. He only knew he
hated all rings, and circles and round things, any closed entity, complete in itself, which allowed no entry.

"I have eyes in my head," Eleanor Della told Becky. "Do you know
what you're doing? Are you sure about Alden? Maybe this has something to do with losing your parents so young. Maybe you're really in
love with Alden's family. Why are you laughing, Becky? Have I said
something funny?"

Then Alden came home quietly, as was the way in those days. He
showed up at Wild Flower one late afternoon, out of uniform, with the
lingering crust of a rash around his neck where his stiff collar had
chafed in the tropics. Becky had turned white as a swan under the harsh
office lighting. Eleanor burst into tears. Becky sat down. Eleanor stood
up. Alden apologized for startling them. Becky flew into his arms.
Alden had been back in the States for a week. He'd made a stop in Okla-
homa, something he'd promised to do to see a friend's parents. Okla-
homa was an awful place, he said, a godawful place to have come from
and to long for.

Your friend can come visit us when we're settled, Becky said, but
Alden didn't seem to think that was likely to happen.

How abruptly, then, had Becky been willing to leave New York and
Wild Flower, Madam Tantamount, the Dellas, William. She and Alden
packed his new green Karmann Ghia convertible with cartons and they
drove up to Massachusetts, north of Boston, where Alden's grandparents on his mother's side (the Hills) lived in a big old house at the

end of a wandering driveway on the crest of a hill. Becky, who was accustomed to long Western vistas, regarded this new countryside as the land of counterpane, a child's confident and conventional concept of a world. There was the School, the Church, a square wooden House, a Tree, many Trees, a Field, a Rabbit standing in the Field, an Ice Cream Stand, all set down anyhow and colored with every stick of crayon spilled from the box. This was, after all, Alden's boyhood stomping ground. He had spoken of the happy summers he had spent here, happy summers and bright holidays. It was a wonderful place to have come from and to long to return to, when one was far away.

He had brought his grandparents an early-seventeenth-century Chinese vase painted with a dragon guarding a pearl. The old people had wondered whether the dragon's fire-breath would scorch the pearl. Grandfather and Grandmother Hill had turned rather critical. The discussion was not entirely good-natured. Dragons ought not to be allowed to get their clutches on pearls and vases ought not to encourage the practice. Nevertheless, Mrs. Hill rose and nudged aside a tall Meissen vase and an Imari bowl to make space for Alden's gift on top of a glass-fronted bookcase, and Becky had suddenly known that Alden had pictured, and that he had been sustained by the picture of, his own offering set down precisely *there* in a corner of the big cold parlor among all the other trophies of family travels and voyages and wars.

No one mentioned Vietnam, however, just as no one would mention the impending divorce of the Reverend Alomar, who was hardly the happiest choice to marry the young couple, although the Reverend was only the Almighty's Instrument on earth and one wasted one's time second-guessing the same Creator Who also saw fit to make mosquitoes in abundance and to give all the oil to the Arabs.

Becky's parentlessness put Alden's family at a disadvantage. They could not place her in their general scheme of things as surely as the Chinese vase had been shown to its spot on the bookcase top. They could not see beyond youth's masquerades: Becky's adaptations of current fads in dress and speech and outlook; the still-fresh effects of her very recent education. Becky was still up for any test, but were the correct answers inked on her hand or did she know them by heart? The family would have been certain had they been able to assess Mrs.

Carlisle's mother-of-the-bride hat and summer frock. They would have had Mr. Carlisle's number before he could count to ten taking the drinks order at the rehearsal dinner. They quizzed Becky about her early life in the West. Did they have shellfish and public libraries out there? Could she swing a lariat over her head? What exactly was a tumbleweed? In the movies, they looked like someone had emptied a vacuum cleaner bag on a windy day.

Becky found herself explaining that the Carlisles had originally come from Connecticut. They had traveled west in a Conestoga wagon in 1859, carrying the family Bible and a harmonium and six Belle de Crecy roses tied up bare root in moss and linen bundles but which had been planted alongside a riverbank in Indiana when it became plain they would not last the journey.

Where in Connecticut? Alden's mother asked.

Near Bridgeport.

I see. Olive shot a look at the ring, thinking of the pity of that ring in Bridgeport.

Where in Indiana were the rosebushes left? Alden's maiden aunt Lily asked.

I'm not sure. I don't suppose it was anyplace, back then.

So much for the Carlisle family creation myth.

Alden's sister Ginger kept straying into the small bedroom that was usually hers at her grandparents' house but had been given to Becky this time, while Ginger had been sent to a dim chamber under the hot attic roof. Ginger still kept her cigarettes in the Girls' Room desk drawer, a tangle of outworn underwire bras in the bureau, and the wedge of closet held her tennis racket, a can of tennis balls, and her bridesmaid dress, which hung in tight, plastic-wrapped proximity to Becky's wedding gown. The two dresses, limp and pale and crushed, seemed to be aware of their mutual dependencies and fates, the sole outing on a summer's day and then the nothing more required of them.

"Those awful dresses are just like one of Anne's poems, except in one of Anne's poems, the dresses would be menstruating," Ginger said. She had been carrying around a signed copy of *Live or Die* all summer.

Ginger sprawled across the bed. Becky was propped in one corner painting her nails with clear polish. She moved her knee away from

Ginger's arm. Becky didn't care for the basket-of-puppies closeness Ginger generated. She was forever hanging over the backs of chairs, thrusting that book of hers under the family's noses. "See? Signed, Anne Sexton."

"That ring," Ginger said, without rancor, watching Becky brush and swipe on polish. "Well, I never had a shot at it anyway. It only goes to the sons' wives. Mother is livid she didn't get it. Grandmother is livid on Mother's behalf. We're such a matriarchy. What about your family? May—or patriarchy?"

"I don't know. Neither I suppose. No one ever vied, at home," Becky said.

"Well, you and Alden will just drift along, like a couple of bumps on a log," Ginger predicted.

"Oh, I hope so," said Becky.

"I warn you. Don't be too complacent. Grandmother is very powerful. She's only selectively feeble so poor Lily will run and fetch for her. Aunt Lily never made the break. You can tell the year she gave up entirely by her hairstyle, those bobby-pin snail curls. It was 1952," Ginger declared. "She teaches all day and looks after old invalids all night, and then she pins up her hair the only way she knows how. It's monstrous. Mother married Father and she got away. I don't know why she kept sending us back here every summer, Alden and me. So Grandmother could have a crack at us, too," she supposed.

"I got away from where I came from and I ended up here as well, so it's all relative," Becky said.

"But you were pushed from the nest, weren't you, so to speak? It's so strange, your being an orphan, so nineteenth century. Well, Alden always liked old-fashioned girls. Daddy says at least Alden won't have in-law problems. Oh, I'm sorry, I wasn't supposed to repeat that."

Becky, who was huffing at her wet fingertips, paused and smiled mildly. She had lately resolved always to smile mildly upon her sister-in-law-to-be, which would, she acknowledged, be viewed as maddeningly meant by Ginger, so that was all right all round.

"Who is coming to the wedding from your side?" asked Ginger. "Where's your guest list? Mother said you had your own guest list. In the desk?" Ginger sprang from the bed. Becky snatched her uncapped bottle of polish before it spilled, and she caught chenille bedspread lint all across her tacky nails.

"Ciggies!" cried Ginger. "Guest list! Matches! Life is good! Let's see. Hap is your brother and he's engaged to this Rosemary Pense person? And the Dellas, they're brother and sister, you said, okay. So David Della is single and he writes? Really. What about William Baskett? He's the one in the foreign service. What interesting friends you have. You know what they say, you can choose your friends. Is David Della at all attractive, in your opinion? Don't you think that rebel army officer who just took over in Libya looks like Warren Beatty? Sort of? Something about the shape of their heads, and those hooded eyes."

Alden slept in the attic as well, in one of the dormer rooms. He slept a great deal, or tried to sleep. His light was reported to be left burning very late. Some mornings, he did not appear before ten. He was always hungry and he rattled through the kitchen cupboards, where he found unprepared root vegetables and the slow-cooking kind of oatmeal and salt. His aunt Lily remembered how he had loved Drake's Cakes and deviled-ham sandwiches when he was a boy and she went shopping and Alden encountered his old favorites when he went rummaging. He and Becky sat at the accommodating table in the middle of the bright yellow kitchen as Alden consumed sandwiches and cakes and beer, and Becky drank instant coffee crystals stirred into tonic water with an iced tea spoon. (The family rather respected her for her ability to down this stinging potion.) Becky turned to the pages she had marked in the Ethan Allen catalog she had placed on the table between Alden and herself. They needed to buy a bed—although everything else would come from her parents' estate, the nice pieces currently in storage and awaiting shipping to their new address when they had one.

"Alden, what do you think of this bed?" Becky asked.

"Whatever you say."

"It's going to be your bed too, so you should like it as much as I do."

"That's fine, that one you like."

"But I'm not sure I necessarily like this bed." Becky tapped the catalog page. "It just caught my attention, though whether in a good way or a bad way, I can't say."

"Nor do I necessarily like it."

"We could end up buying a bed neither of us likes if you don't speak up, if we both keep deferring to one another. That's the real danger here," Becky said.

Then Alden had wanted to say that he had left all the world's real dangers far away behind him, but he did not, because Becky might have thought herself rebuked when all he meant to express was his conviction that she was his safe harbor and he would strive to be her rock, and their love was like a great citadel built upon the rock beside the still waters. Details of the decor were irrelevant.

Becky and Alden had suspended intimacies during the weeks they lived in Towne beneath his grandparents' roof. Alden's manners were, of course, excellent, and he was mindful of the old people's and his maiden aunt's and his upright parents' sensibilities. For the floorboards creaked between the lightest of steps, stair treads cracked below the most considered footfalls, door hinges protested at the least push, and the old people were apt to be awake and abroad at any hour, visiting the bathroom, fumbling at the aspirin bottle. The upper hallway was a not unfrequented corridor, like a backcountry road long beyond midnight where the only car to pass in hours will, nevertheless, catch any venturing rabbit on its bumper.

But Becky had wondered why Alden and she had to exercise all the courtesy and reserve. Alden's elders, for their part, might have endeavored to turn a blind eye and a deaf ear to the young couple's activities. There was an argument to be made for incuriosity, or a semblance of such, as the elders remembered from their own experience which signs particularly not to notice. They had all been young once. Arrayed across a cloth-covered table in the big parlor was the evidence of this, their photographs in frames showing them as they had been, with uncrumpled profiles and wavy hair, so smiling or so serious, without a care in the world or profoundly caring about the universe, which range of expression ought to have reminded them how unnuanced a time was Youth.

At night, Becky lay awake as moths thudded against her window screen and some got through to flutter and thump against the ceiling. When she struck one with the heel of a hurled slipper, its eyes seared out a luminous green as it died where it dropped upon the bedspread.

She willed Alden to come to her then, to be reckless, his yearning for her too strong to resist, the steep stairs dared, the endless hallway braved, his fastidious family's feelings defied, all for his need of her. She was not even sure she would have, or could have, received him, for another picture had presented itself to her, the image of Alden's mother's avenging matron's face looming at her from above Alden's bare, straining shoulder and arching back as they were discovered in an act of love. But it would have been enough for Alden to kneel by her bedside as they tore into, then tore themselves away from, a kiss, and laughed and shuddered and burned all at once at the folly and the unfairness that prevented them. Such folly and unfairness had plagued them from the start, first Vietnam intervening and then rectitude arising. Neither was a terribly defensible reason, in 1969, in Becky's opinion, but Alden was far more romantic than she about lost causes.

Becky hoped she had not proved too easily won.

May I call you sometime, Becky? They had met at a party.

Yes, please. I'd like that.

Where shall we go?

Anywhere, anywhere at all will be nice.

Thank you. I enjoyed the evening. May I call you again?

Yes, please. I'd like that.

What shall we do?

Anything. Anything will be wonderful.

And on another night when Alden said, Thank you, I enjoyed this evening, Becky had said, Don't go, Alden. Stay. Why don't you stay? I want you to stay. She caught his sleeve and drew him toward the threefold screen behind which a divan bed had been sitting imperfectly concealed all evening.

Perhaps she had been more inclined than he. Perhaps he had stayed because she had expected him to. The divan bed had been heaped with Turkish pillows. A pillar candle and a cone of sandalwood incense balanced on a saucer bottom were set upon the shelf above the bed. Several joints rolled fat by the practiced hand of the head case in the apartment next door lay just out of sight beneath an overturned fluted tartlet tin, the last place anyone would look, beneath somebody's mother's old fluted tartlet tin. There was a box of matches because none of this would ignite without the strike and flare of a match. Becky had been too sophisticated to have left the "Theme from *A Summer Place*" on the stereo turntable. She had been too sophisticated as well for the theme of Ecstasy from *Tristan and Isolde,* sitting there at the ready but, she had reckoned, Alden was not. Perhaps Alden had not really shared her eagerness. Perhaps he would have preferred to wait.

Oh, let's get married before you have to go, she had said to Alden on a further evening spent, as all their remaining evenings were to be spent, in a close fug of candle, toke, and incense smoke, the Turkish pillows skipped across the floor like stepping stones. But Alden had told her she would mind less losing a fiancé than a husband, should it come to that (and he was sure there would be much less red tape). Becky, who had already lost so much, had pleaded the opposite case from a far greater experience than Alden (then) possessed, that one minded more being robbed of what might have been.

Then, when he came home, Becky had said, Let's elope. Why not? Instead of going to stay with your family. She had trailed her hand from Alden's knee onto the gearshift knob. She reached and tapped the steering wheel. She knew another way they could go that day.

I don't think it would be very fair to the family. And Mother has bought a hat, so be prepared for the hat, Alden had answered her.

Perhaps Alden had needed this spell of chaste contemplation of Becky. He was content to face her across the bridge table night after night as they sat hunched and holding their cards close to their breast-bones because Alden's mother had a way of stretching and endeavoring to peer at what they possessed. Olive would say, Becky, dear, I must adjust your collar. Alden, that awful old dog of Lily's has shed all over your sleeve. Here, let me. Alden's eye met Becky's and he read her thoughts, or some of them, as he bid the three of hearts and rated a smile from her. They had won the trick, but the smile reflected the course of one of Becky's other, unread thoughts. She smiled at him because she longed for him and because she could not cry out and reach for him, overturning the footed glass bowl of salted peanuts, tipping her hand for all to see.

On those bridge evenings, Olive practiced wearing her hat, which, the family allowed, did take some getting used to.

Alden played selections from *Selections of the Great Composers* for Becky on the big parlor hi-fi set. He leaped to open doors for her as she stood against walls so he could slide past her to rattle a latch. She would sit in the stuffy car, all the windows wisely rolled up lest it rain, until he bounded round to release her. Bottles of wine appeared at dinner and were appreciated by the young people, by Alden and Becky and Ginger, and, more often than not, by Ginger's particular beau that summer, the son of a fine local family (Olive *was* pleased). Grandmother Hill prodded the label lettering and remarked, We're being very French this summer, very French indeed, and someone said, Oo la la. Alden would place a rose from his aunt Lily's garden on Becky's pillow for her to find, last thing, every night, the dark and drowsy head of the flower tumbled there, and she wondered when he had stolen into her room and pulled back the coverlet and slipped the stripped-thornless stem between the sheets.

Perhaps marriage to a romantic would mean she must learn to be satisfied by a gesture rather than a caress. The courtship mattered, and less the consummation, as in a dream of love from which one is snapped awake just on the brink of falling into a finally spiraling embrace. Becky lay sleepless in her borrowed bedroom full of shorn roses and fugitive moths and perishable dresses that ought to rustle on the pages of an angry poem, and she wondered whether Alden had arranged this time here so that his knowledge of her might fade and be forgotten. Perhaps he hoped virginity could be restored and a membrane might be regrown within the hothouse confinement of the Maidens' Room.

But why had Alden wanted to forget? Had their lovemaking not been entirely successful? Becky had not been in a position to say, really, and who was there to consult? The sublime experience was, apparently, indescribable. Lesser efforts went so individually amiss that there was, perhaps, everything and nothing to be said. Becky was not prepared to say what love was, just what love was like, and she could only recall the occasion of her senior recital at the Conservatory when her accompanist had played the final note of the piece as she was still singing "Gloria." Ultimately, the blame was fixed on the accompanist, for in this case there existed the evidence of a recording which was analyzed. But if the miscue had not been Becky's fault, it was understood she might yet have salvaged the performance had she made an accommodating adjustment to her own tempo, and she might have done so were she not mindful that she and the accompanist, another degree candidate, were being assessed individually. They, Becky and Theo, the young man's name was, had been given an intermission, a cooling-off period during which they calmed down over cups of water as each privately accused the other. They returned and performed technically much better on the next piece but were adjudged to have been too cautious and insufficiently *passionato* on the day. But Becky had been loath to hear the sound of her own lone voice soaring, faltering, fading, caught out again, and she took the lesser mark—life had taught her early on that one's efforts were scored on a most impermanent record—and she had never lost much sleep over that long-ago flat B.

Still, Becky wished she could be surer, before the wedding. The question had begun to loom too large. She would rather have passed those last cloistered weeks meditating upon other aspects of married life to come, such as the difficulties of maintaining a joint checking account—would Alden understand that she always contrived to leave a little more in the bank than the balance showed, just as a nice surprise? And during the beautiful service, she would prefer to concentrate upon the solemn pledges she was about to make to Alden, promising to honor him and to obey him (she *was* an old-fashioned girl) rather than entertain anxious if pleased thoughts about the night to come which she feared would be readable across her face as the Carlisle family lace veil was, at last, lifted. Well, she was going to make sure at the reception that Alden did not drink too much, and, for her part, she was going to see to it that she drank enough.

The last week before the wedding, Alden's family noticed Becky had become listless and agitated. She paced languidly; to be stuck behind her as she traversed the upper hallway made one itch to honk her aside and zoom past. She became tearful whenever her mother was mentioned. The family was walking on eggshells just as preparations were rounding off onto the home stretch—which was going to finish in a dead heat. There had been a disaster in the fancy cake department, and as Olive observed, more eggs were going to have to be broken no mat-

ter who swayed and went pale and drifted from the room at the least
mention of the wedding.

Doesn't she know people in Maine, didn't she say? Olive remembered. We can send her off to them for a few days. She can take Lily's
old car, and remind me to remind her to go Route 1 to Portsmouth so
she'll miss the Hampton toll. I'll need her back by Friday for the studio
photographer and remind me to remind her, not too much sun. We
can't have her looking like Alden married an Ethiopian by mistake.

Why shouldn't Alden, or I, for that matter, marry an Ethiopian?
Ginger had wanted to know, but Olive refused to be dragged into that
conversation.

So Becky called Maine to say when to expect her and she packed as
Olive directed, her bathing suit and a sweater. Lily gave her a plastic
pail full of ripe red tomatoes from the garden to take to her friends,
whose own might not quite be ready to pick up there where they lived.
Lily wanted the pail back, but she left it to chance Becky would, or
would not, figure that out on her own. Grandmother Hill issued her
standard warning that FDR had gotten his polio from swimming in the
cold Maine ocean water. Grandfather Hill expelled his usual snort at
this mention of FDR, although he had not scoffed at his wife's science.
Alden told Becky to relax and enjoy herself and to watch out for jellyfish. Ginger said she wished she were going to Maine. She kept saying
she wished she were going to Maine up to the moment Becky took off
without her.

Becky hadn't minded visiting another quaint New England state.
Maine, once she hit the main part, became a meandering route with
glimpses of water given through breaks in thick stands of pine and
then sudden, windshield-wide views of a glinting universe of nothing but water for as far as the eye could see. She came upon successive clogged two-lane downtowns with packs of summer folk and
white-painted inns with mossy baskets of geraniums hanging from
the porch rafters and No Vacancy signs slung over the railings. Every
shop sold lobster, live or boiled, and beer and bait. Snug chowder-bowl
harbors supported up-and-down swells of boats and jousting masts
and intricate riggings, and Becky thought that to sail away must be
a complicated undertaking. Still, clever people were accomplishing

as much. Out, far out at sea, sailing craft scudded along going this way and that, and she wondered how the wind could blow in all directions at once. Out west, the wind had been of a single mind as it scoured down from the peaks and bent the fence posts and the trees to its will.

Becky had been told to look for the hardware store–art gallery with canvases stacked out front alongside the lawnmowers and the propane tanks and then she was to watch for the formerly red mailbox missing its front flap at which she was to turn right down the gravel road bending back through a cathedral of pines and coming into a clearing of spangled sunlight shining on a field of Queen Anne's lace where a great shingled house had been built as close as it dared be on the edge of an ocean cliff. The best view of the house was really the one from the water, as was not uncommon along the coast here. When this was explained to Becky later that evening, the practice struck her as an affected one, although she also allowed there was something to be said on behalf of being able to see as well as be seen from such a vantage. Later that evening, Becky had hovered between making automatic protest at every observation put to her and giving in to the stronger pull drawing her to the brink of capitulation.

I DID NOT SAY I WAS STAYING *with* the St. Clairs. I said, I'm staying *at* the St. Clairs'.

William had met Becky on the stone-pillared porch. They stood at the farther ends of a rag-rug runner set down against the tracking in of beach sand. Becky had stopped short of the scuffed *elcom* mat. She had set down and then picked up her weekender bag and the pail of tomatoes when no big barking dog had skidded into the screen door, howling, at her footfall. That had been her first clue. The St. Clairs went nowhere without Ludwig, and now, it seemed, they had gone off to the Berkshires for a week, taking a vacation from their vacation.

"You misled me," Becky said. "You never said on the telephone—"

"My directions were excellent, if eccentric, but that's the local ethos, which, I believe, is still genuine; however, I give them five years before it's not. You can always tell when a primitive society is about to leap forward. For starters, you can begin to receive *The New York Times* on the day, down in the village," William said.

"You know I can't stay if no one is here."

"But I'm here. As you knew I was. And you're more my friend than the St. Clairs'."

"That's not true. I've known them much longer than you and you only know them through me. I've come to visit *them*. I wanted Mimi to read the I Ching for me. And it was such a long drive. Alden's mother made me promise to go the back way. They always go the back way. They always have some private way known only to them. I keep wanting to tell them, the Donners took an alternate route, one day."

"You needed to get away. You said so in your letter."

"I said no such thing. I described events of general interest."

"You characterized certain vexatious events."

"You misread me. I never said anything of the sort."

"There's an excellent beach here." William had a way of becoming suddenly bored with a subject.

"Is there?" Becky asked. She had no wish to become suddenly boring.

"I have the run of the wine cellar."

"Do you? They trusted you with the key?"

"Trusting one with a key makes one behave."

"Does it? I'm not sure that's true. But perhaps I am not an admirable person. I'm sure I'd take advantage."

"In 1627, Cardinal Richelieu dispatched a fleet to this peninsula to fight the Puritans, who had a fort here, in his attempt to win back Acadia," William said, waving at the view.

"Maybe I can stay until four, but then I shall have to head back straightaway. I can't think what I'll tell them, when I show up out of the blue."

William picked up her weekender bag and the pailful of tomatoes, and he told her how to find the bedroom where she could change into her swimsuit.

"I'M BEING THOUGHTFUL OF THEM, ACTUALLY. Alden's people wanted me out of the way for a while so they could talk about me in their normal tones of voice. Oh, they're very nice, really. I think I just blame his mother for being alive when, well, when other people aren't. But what a wonderful beach. You'd never guess it was here, from up at the house," Becky said.

The strand curved, a crescent slice tucked into a fold of the cliffs. To anyone standing below and gazing up, the rocks seemed to soar a thousand feet into the sky. Clambering down them, the drop to earth (or sea) seemed a thousand feet as well. Becky had followed William over the side as his head plunged to the level of her knees. The path was just discernible, fortified in places with cement patches smoothing over rubble stone. An iron railing had been sunk into more of the cement, there to be clutched during a sloping slide along the ledge where the fall was sheerest. The descent ended with a sit-down scramble as baskets, towels, umbrellas, released by flying hands, scattered and tumbled too. Becky tried not to anticipate the return trip up and over the cliff face although William promised the way back was always easier.

The beach was shared by several households exercising their deeded rights. At first, she and William had been alone together, lying on striped towels beside the wreck of a sand castle—a Sky Bar wrapper threaded on a drinking straw fluttered from the top of a surviving tower. William spoke of the books he'd been reading that summer, policy tomes and local history—local, that is, to the little country for which he was headed in a few weeks' time. Becky kept her face in the shade of a tilted umbrella but let her legs bake in the sun. Olive had not laid down the law against too-brown legs, so Becky decided that her lower torso at least remained hers to do with as she wished. William was being rather thorough in his review of his reading. Indeed, William could become the littlest bit tiresome on his Subjects. Nevertheless, Becky appreciated that what he was saying was really very interesting. His voice, she decided, made a superior background noise, like the murmur of Mahler, perhaps, rather than the drone of dreaded Muzak, and she was free to let her own thoughts drift along to this accompaniment which sounded pleasing to her tutored ear.

She was thinking about William. She had never seen him undressed as he was now, wearing just his bathing trunks and a wristwatch (was he going to hold her to that four o'clock deadline?). He was neither too darkly nor too thickly covered with hair, and she was glad, for his sake, that he had not turned out to be a smooth, boiled pink man as she would have guessed—as, in fact, she had guessed when Eleanor Della once raised the question. He possessed a mountaineer's calves and thighs. She would never have said he was so fit, but he had moved swiftly and certainly descending the cliff path, and on the several occasions he had had to steady her as her feet ran away with her, his arm had tensed rock-hard and entirely reliable beneath her hand.

"Gosh." She must have spoken this aloud.

"Yes," agreed William. "The seeds of the Second Partition were sown by the First, an unfortunate but inevitable development; one wrong step leads to another, and another." He turned on an elbow to look at her. He had been watching the gulls swirling over a further disturbance in the choppy water, just below the surface.

Of course, Becky wondered then what William was thinking of her, in her bathing suit.

"Such a sad history," she said. "Such a long, sad history," she ventured.

She had never been thinner than she was that summer, a result of nerves and the ever-presence of a slender-waisted gown hanging behind a closet door and Alden's family's attitude of puzzlement and exasperation as the dinner hour snuck up on them yet again, requiring a response of some sort, usually a salad. Her bathing suit, shaped and stiffened with wires and ribbing and a lining, fit loosely on her. The material was a leaf-green poplin, glossy because the suit was new and had not yet gotten wet. Standing before the full-length mirror in the St. Clairs' guest bedroom, she had told herself she resembled nothing so much as an insect, a hard-shelled, articulated, long-limbed creature who dwelt among tender leaves. However, she had known as well that if she looked like an insect, she looked like a beautiful one, and she would not have minded had William told her she reminded him of a lovely, light, and lacy ephemeron just briefly fluttered to light there by his side. It would be, Becky felt, all right for William to tell her that.

"Where is the Iceberg?" William asked.

"An iceberg? Where?" Becky asked. Out there in the water, having floated down from the Arctic Circle?

But it seemed William had named her engagement ring.

"I was afraid it would slide from my fingers when we went in the water so I pressed it into the melted underside of the cake of soap in my bathroom because I am also afraid of burglars sneaking into the house while we're down here," Becky said.

"Tough duty, defending the Iceberg," William observed.

"Yes, well, just don't let me forget the ring."

But it was hardly fair of Becky to ask that of him.

Presently, another bathing party had braved the way down over the rocks: a mother, children, the mother's helper, a grandmother who wore a skirted bathing costume and a triple strand of pearls. She too held fears of thieves and her daughter-in-law had lost the key to the house on the first beach excursion of the season. The mother's helper understood she was there to make herself useful. She searched constantly for the key, sifting sand through her toes, raking over washed-up litters of sea wrack and sea beings, and while the loss of the key had not been her fault, blame was gradually transferring itself to her for this failure now, to find an inches-long cutout of brass.

"There is no unhappier girl in the world than I," the au pair told Becky and William when she approached them to retrieve an inflatable beach ball kicked into them by the smallest, blondest boy in her charge. (Concentrated evil, that one, William had already been moved to remark.) The girl had spun as smartly as one could spin barefooted in beach sand, and she left them at a trudge, deflating the overblown ball, working it like a bellows beneath her pumping arm.

"Do you think she enjoyed putting us on notice?" Becky asked. "I think she must have."

"Then she's not really so unhappy," William said. "If she can find even the meanest pleasure in her situation, then she is not unhappy."

"No, she can't be truly unhappy," Becky said, "because when they're truly unhappy, people don't proclaim it, because when you're really unhappy you're too ashamed . . ."

". . . you're too proud," William said.

They had spoken over one another and neither let on they had heard the other, if one had heard the other. The gulls, the wind, a child had all been crying as the surf slushed back and forth without relent.

Becky always made a show to herself of essaying to recall what had happened next, and how, and why. She approached this part of her past as if it were a historical event she knew about in a general way, much as she was aware of the Wars of the Roses, which had been, she felt, another difficult yet stirring time for those involved. She revisited those former days infrequently; the summer of 1969 was so far away and receding even further from wherever she happened to be standing at her moments of recollection, but she had found as the years wore on that she was recapturing more and more. The picture had become clearer and clearer. She remembered now how very rude the sputterings of the expiring beach ball had sounded, which, perhaps, had been another artful effect on the mother's helper's part, parading across the sand producing those awful eructations. The littlest, blondest, wickedest child had laughed so hard he sat down upon a razor clamshell and then he had cried. Becky and William, who had become practiced at feigning not to notice the evidence before their eyes, had not deigned to acknowledge the performance. How prim they had been, had had to be. The act which was to come must catch them by surprise, if not unprepared.

Becky's clearer and clearer picture of that day in Maine featured the fog that had overtaken them on the beach. The shining sea, the brilliant sky, the rise of the cliff, William beside her on his striped towel, vanished in the swirl and the sweep of the mist rolling in off the ocean, but Becky most remembered the fog's silencing qualities. To say, Here I am, was to mislead; voices could not find their way through the murk, and so she reached and caught William and held on to him. The exertion and anxiety of the blurred climb back up and over the rocks took their breath away, but any remark Becky might have spared would have been a reproachful one. This fog, of course, was all William's fault, the baffling, blinding, binding fog. By then she may have half believed him capable of ordering the elements to his bidding. Because of the power he was exerting over her she half believed this.

No one was going anywhere that night, in that fog.

Back at the St. Clairs' house, William built a fire in the library and he carried in a long evening's worth of logs from the gardener's shed. Becky began to shiver and burn from having taken too much sun on her legs. She huddled on the library sofa, opting to be unwell for a while, surprising herself by giving in rather than bearing up with her usual fortitude. William's fire crackled away, too feeble and then too fierce for her as she shivered and burned, and William prodded with a poker, endeavoring to stir or to bank the flames as she fretted. She clung to, then kicked off, a yo-yo afghan. The scent of a balsam pillow bothered her, and it had to be shut inside a cupboard. William, who had never before been called upon to attend to an afflicted fellow being, was surprised to learn he could be so tender, and he sought to add to Becky's comfort as well as springing to deal with those elements expressedly causing her discomfort. He fetched a better pillow from a living room side chair, one covered in a light, flowery fabric that clashed with the tweed upholstery of the library sofa. This mismatch had bothered Becky at the time, but she didn't say so.

She rallied at supper time as unserious invalids will sit up and display an interest in the sounds issuing from the kitchen and the prospect of the arrival of a prettily set tray. William's effectless clatters and thumps had drawn Becky to the doorway of the kitchen, where he was trying to reconcile the wrong saucepan to the wrong lid.

"Becky. What is it?" he asked. "What can I get you?"

"Oh, I'm better now," she told him.

"There's damn-all in the larder," he said.

"Haven't you been eating?" Becky asked.

"No, I must not have been," he supposed.

"Oh, William." She took the lid and saucepan from him and told him he could be in charge of the wine. It was her turn to look after him.

There were the bucket-tomatoes and a single jar of artichoke hearts packed in olive oil and an unwatered pot of basil on the windowsill (Oh, William) which could be used anyway, the desiccated leaves crumpled and tossed into the sauce. Becky found a very old box of splintery spaghetti. The water in which it was cooked turned quite cloudy, but Becky reckoned fifteen minutes of rough boiling should neutralize anything toxic that might adhere to ancient pasta. She had sloshed a measure of the wine William had selected into the sauce, which was wrong of her, they agreed, for it was a very fine wine.

They had eaten at the kitchen table. The kitchen was warmer than the big drafty dining room and more intimate for only two. Their knees touched under the square of wooden table and Becky's scorched skin flamed and perished at the contact. They talked about places they had gone together and things they done in New York.

They had not been aware when the fog lifted. The cooking of the spaghetti steamed the windows and the ongoing opacity filling the panes was now an interior phenomenon. They discovered this when they opened the back door to air out the kitchen after they turned on a stovetop burner to heat water for coffee and the spilled-on element fumed with acrid smoke. They moved to the back steps with their mugs of coffee. The moon hung low and round in the wide sky, caught on the points of a pine.

This was the first full moon to rise since the astronauts had danced upon the Sea of Tranquillity, and despite all the high-minded rhetoric hailing the landing as being an achievement to be shared by all mankind, everyone in America understood the moon was ours now, a known and owned entity, no longer mysterious and magical, but real estate. As Becky peered at the trodden-on moon, like a billion other people on earth that summer trying to spot the American flag, she wondered whether poetry would have to alter its evocations of the celestial sphere. Would yet-to-be-written works have to be different, would works already printed on the page no longer read the same? Oh yes, said William, poetry is dead, completely dead to us now.

"I should leave," Becky said. "The weather has lifted."

"No. It's too late now," William said.

She didn't know what possessed her then. Perhaps she had learned too early and too well the unending sorrow of not speaking when she had the chance and of never being given another chance to say what had cried out to be said. Perhaps she could not face another momentous church service as the words of a liturgy vied with the swell of all those unuttered words filling her head, as belatedly, briefly, she mumbled her Responses when nudged by some clearer-conscienced soul kneeling by her side. Or maybe the moon had just been up to its old tricks, after all, inducing an old madness.

"I cannot love two people at once," Becky told William.

"No. You can't," he said.

"Well, then. That's all right, then. Of course one can't, I mean to say, I was sure you hadn't mistaken any aspect of our friendship for something else." Her heart stood still and it raced, all at once.

"Because you don't love him," William said.

THE FOLLOWING DAY, THE FAMILY PARTY, the mother, children, grandmother, and au pair, made it their business to get down to the hidden crescent of beach before the entranced couple of the previous afternoon could lay claim to the smoothest patch of sand and in general behave as if they were the first and only people in the world. The family party turned a weather eye to the cliff face, alert to any rain of pebble launched from above by another descent, but by the following day, they forgot how bothered they had been by the previous couple as, instead, they resented the sudden presence of long-weekenders from New York with those loud voices of theirs and a much nicer picnic lunch packed in an ampler hamper.

Olive, presiding over the studio photograph session for which Becky had reported as ordered on the Friday afternoon, informed Becky she was too pale, she could have used a little color, and chided her for not having spent more time lying out under the sun on her old chums' lovely Maine beach. Then, Becky had crimsoned.

In the years to come, on visits back to the old house in Towne, she encountered the official wedding portrait, the chosen pose, on the family picture–crowded table in the larger parlor. Her likeness was not a featured one. She sat off to the side, near the back behind the taller frames. Clearly, she was a very minor goddess in the pantheon. She was firmly put back in her place by whoever was responsible for dusting the images and righting them when they flopped over, as they often did, for the big parlor sat above an explosive old furnace that shuddered on and off, roaring and shaking—as if they kept the Minotaur in the cellar, Alden used to say. Alden always had to have his little jokes, but Becky knew the real monster extant in their world was a frail and quiescent thing, no more than a worm coiled within a soft organ, but a thing she had to fight, nevertheless, with all her might.

Becky could only regard the girl in the photograph as a stranger. The long-ago girl must have been hypnotized into buying that dress, a lacework cage spun by dark spiders. She had been strong-armed into that hairdo. She had asked Ginger to fix her makeup because her own hands had trembled so and she had been glad then, when Ginger proved to have a heavy touch with concealer and with shadow. The girl had feared exposure and she had been granted a reprieve as she sat for her portrait beneath the cover of a mask.

On the morning of the wedding, Becky had been moved into the heretofore empty best guest bedroom (and who else had they been expecting all along? Miss Loretta Young, by the looks of the room), where she was arrayed once again, the dress belled over her head, her hair pulled and pinned, the paints and brushes plied anew. At the last, Olive arose from her knees—she'd been gluing white satin bows onto Becky's white satin shoes, making them stick with a splayed, heavy thumb. She regarded Becky's reflection framed by the full-length mirror in the closet door and she asked, "Well, well, who are *we* trying to impress?" Becky had understood the question required a clear answer. "Alden," she said. "Alden. Alden."

William had shown up at the house early. The meadow, where the service was to take place, had just been mown. A crew was at work with rakes. When the chairs were set up, he sat in the third row back on the bride's side so that Becky would touch him if he leaned forward as she walked by, a feathery stroke of floating tulle brushing his face. He would breathe her sweet heightened scent one last time with deep, drowning-man gulps. He frowned at the florist's assistant as she twined stephanotis around the chair backs. Eleanor and David Della, who probably knew more than they ever let on, took charge of William when they arrived. Eleanor held his arm, David gripped his shoulder, as the Reverend Alomar (who was in no position to cast stones) asked if anyone had any objections. For years afterward, Eleanor talked about the wedding she had attended when she had been convinced the bride was going to vow, *I don't*. But Becky kept her word and said the right things and that was that. William had uttered a groan at the climax of the ceremony. Everyone within earshot assumed he had just aggravated an old injury (those wooden folding chairs were agony) and felt he ought not to have come out that day if he was going to feel so bad.

Five

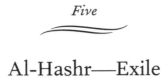

Al-Ḥashr—Exile

THEY SERVED HER MORE OF THAT SWEET TEA in a tiny glass with a sugar crust from the cup's previous outing crackling on the rim. Becky tasted mint and all the chemicals in the water heightened by hard boiling even though she was only pretending to sip. She was tasting through her nose, she supposed. She was being led by her nose here. Every entity, animal or vegetable or mineral, seemed to have been left out in the sun too long although few of the rising smells were truly unpleasant. Such dry heat preserved (it was moist heat that putrefied) but Becky was used to paler scents just as she was used to paler skins and she longed for scentlessness as she longed for silence as she longed for a cool breeze skimming off pure water to refresh her.

Somebody ought to have rinsed the tiny glass better, but they seemed to be all men here in this office as it was usually all men hereabouts she had noticed, and the Man himself, the man in charge, watched over his sovereign bit of territory from outposts on the office walls. His idealized face, stern behind aviator glasses, beatific beneath a headdress, was accompanied by iconic images both ancient and modern: a raised sword, an erect ballistic missile. But if she hadn't known where she was (the Libyan Embassy, Tunis) and who the man was (Muammar al-Gaddafi) Becky might have taken the depictions wrought in flat, poster-art strokes and colors for commercial advertisements, the product itself unspecified as if the item being put forward was unmentionable but understood by anyone in need of the product or the service. It would be some item having to do with enhancing the consumer's virility, she decided, and of dubious value; nevertheless, the purchasers would swear they had been helped, and, if not helped, they would determine that next time they needed only to apply more of the substance to a greater area of the affliction to achieve results.

Mr. Kafi was speaking on her behalf now. Mr. Kafi had accompanied her here to apply for a visa to enter Libya. He was William's agent and she was William's trust. Mr. Kafi had met the boat at Kelibia. He had met the several previous ferries, for Becky, who had let William know she was on her way to him, had only been able to give a window of when to expect her. Becky learned later how Mr. Kafi had managed to appear so miraculously out of the darkness of that first African night. She had been carried off in his stately Mercedes as Roger and Veevee, whom she had entirely forgotten, hallooed faintly from the quay and had to share a taxi into Gades with hippies who never paid their fair share, pretending not to understand the dinars whereas everyone knew hippies could work any local currency like hedge-fund managers with three mortgages and a mistress in graduate school to support.

The embassy workers were bureaucrats and, presumably, zealots of one stripe or another, and not an attractive mix, like born-again IRS agents, Becky supposed. Becky was finding it useful to understand aspects of her new circumstances in terms of her old life. *Humani nihil a me alienum puto:* she believed in that little tag of Terence, and she thought rather well of herself for not really minding the natives. Besides, in Tunis all the reasonable ones spoke French and tried to dress normally, as well, with rather endearing results.

Mr. Kafi wore pieces of several suits and a very wide tie knotted not quite right although it was hard to work out just which step he had got wrong. He was tremendously respectful of her, but Becky guessed she represented the satellite Io to the great globe of William's Jupiter in Mr. Kafi's universe and Mr. Kafi may have felt himself to have been placed in eclipse by this assignment as he reported for duty each morning at her hotel to offer to drive her wherever she needed to be driven and to shepherd her through whatever procedure had to be followed which would lead her, at last, to William. Nevertheless, Mr. Kafi was earnest and alert on her behalf. He asked her many questions about customs in the West and Becky had come to think of him as a scholarship student of culture. When she asked him about his own life, he gave cursory accounts as if to conceal certain troubles at home of which he was not ashamed; rather, he felt very protective, for they were such small, sad troubles which would recede, becoming even smaller and sadder, were they exposed to such Western eyes.

"State of marriage?" Mr. Kafi was asking her. He translated from the Arabic-only of the austere young functionary who was taking down her details for the visa application.

The state of her marriage? Surely, she was not required to go into all that now, although she had been warned that the regime was highly puritanical, and she had found that highly puritanical people could be very much ruder than those whose sense of propriety rested upon manners rather than morals. She had discovered that she did not care to stand between the doors of a mosque and the Faithful at five o'clock in the afternoon on a Friday. And was there enough space allotted on the line that the austere young functionary was prodding with his pen tip to contain the entire story of the state of her marriage? Could those worms of discharged ink he had committed thus far to the page really transmit the truth about herself, free from some inherently oriental cast (so sinuous and so lowercase)? I am a woman, she had admitted earlier in the visa application process when Mr. Kafi had put to her the question of her gender. Then, Mr. Kafi had answered in Arabic and the young man (who evidently was required to ask rather than to rely upon his own opinion, or perhaps he was not allowed to notice Becky's hair and breasts and ankles and lips) had recorded the word, whatever it was, which, surely, must mean something quite different here, etymologically. By its roots and allusions, did the syllables of Woman break down into Half a man or Other than a man or possibly, Man's delight or perhaps Man's sorrow and burden or even, A camel is a less contrary creature than a woman? Becky thought she might like to pick up a bit of Arabic, to see for herself. She had heard there were some decent poetry and interestingly revisionist versions of history written in the tongue.

"You mean marital status," Becky suddenly understood. "They want to know what my marital status is."

"Yes. Marital status," Mr. Kafi agreed.

I am a widow, Becky had been instructed to say when she and Mr. Kafi discussed what was to come. "I am a—what we said before," Becky said.

Mr. Kafi nodded and conveyed an answer to the inscribing functionary, whose impatient hand fluttered for further documentation. Mr. Kafi raised his voice in slight argument and seemed to win the point as the young man glanced from Becky then back to Mr. Kafi.

He explained to Becky, "At this point, the death certificate is usually required to be presented but I have explained that the event occurred too recently for one to have been issued before you departed on your journey here. This version has been accepted because Mr. Sassi says he can tell from the look in your eyes that lately you have experienced a loss."

ON HER LAST EVENING IN TUNIS, Becky experienced a difficulty of conscience. She sat up late in her hotel room as a ceiling fan stirred the mosquito netting, the gauzy stuff of the curtains, the light, loose cotton of the robe she wore, blurring the edges and the corners and the colors of the high-walled chamber. She sat cross-legged upon the bed, the tiny pair of sewing-kit scissors she had bought in Germany fitted awkwardly onto her fingers. A soft heap of clothing rested beside her knee. The hour was an uncharted one. The last call to prayer had long since been broadcast from the old quarter's rooftops and, as at every time the summons sounded, Becky had felt that some response was expected of her as well. The very pulse of the city quickened and then slowed again when the people hastened to their prayers and when they crouched at their prayers—just like a heart, Becky thought, thrilling at a prospect and then beating calmly at the fulfillment.

She had spent this, her last day, at a museum located in the palace of the Ottoman bey set in a garden of great if sedate late-season beauty. Mr. Kafi had driven her out to the Bardo. He had offered to drive her there, or anywhere, over the past week she had waited for her visa to come through, but she had preferred to remain in her high-walled room at the hotel, hidden behind the veiled windows, the veiled bed. She had not even cared to read. She picked up and put down the several nice novels she had brought with her as she wondered whether she would ever again be able to read gentle stories about gentlefolk who lived in leafy suburbs and went only mildly astray and somehow al-

ways found their way back home by the end of the book. A cube of
television sat atop a table but Becky had dropped a scarf over its darkened screen and tugged its plug from a low-set wall socket after the first
time she had switched it on and been shown a scene of the unedited af-
termath of violence in a wretched, shattered village somewhere in the
Arab world. An onlooker, an eyewitness had held a child's hand, all
that was left of the child, before the camera, clasped in his own hand.

All day, she lay across the wide bed. She paced the cool tile floor in
her bare feet. She soaked in a deep-sided iron tub immersed in the sul-
phurous, medicinal waters that poured from a thundering tap. She
peeled and sectioned the blood oranges a bribed bellhop bought for her
in the hivelike marketplace she could just see from her window. She listened for the calls to prayer and felt, at once, included and excluded.
She did not look backward and she did not look ahead; the way back
and the way ahead shelved off too steeply into blackness to risk taking
a step in either direction.

Always she expected Alden to appear at her door. She imagined
Alden arriving in a variety of states: Alden anguished, Alden angry,
Alden acting as if nothing at all had happened, as if Becky had just
gone on ahead to make the arrangements and he had been delayed because the way she had taken and the way he had followed her had been
dark and steep and poorly marked. He might pound upon her door and
expel the deep accusative breath he had taken in a rush of apology.
Sorry, I thought you were somebody else, he might say, when Becky
opened the door in her drifting cotton robe, in her bare feet, in the dim
veiled chamber.

When the maids arrived to dust and to clean, Becky said in French
and indicated in signed language not to pay attention to her, that she
was not really there. The maids, the pair of them, stared at her until
one nudged the other. They gathered their mops and rags and swept
and polished in circles around Becky. Becky gave them money every
day. She gave them money earlier and earlier every day because when
she paid them they went away.

Becky had, in the end, agreed to Mr. Kafi's offer of an outing if only
to let the ladies—Zahra and Wafa, she had learned their names, she
could not help becoming a little friendly after a week, *Humani nihil,*

after all—have a go at the dustiness mustering beneath the bed and along the slats of the window lattices for which negligence, Zahra and Wafa said in French and indicated in signed language, they would be blamed by the housekeeper and very likely lose their livelihoods. There was orange rind everywhere, in all the ashtrays and behind the bathtub among the pipes.

Mr. Kafi showed up at the hotel every morning as if reporting for duty and in the sun-splashed Hannibal Room Becky stood him for breakfast, which he ordered American-style with shirred eggs and lemon cookies. He went over the details of her case and predicted prompt and favorable action on her petition. He awaited her further instructions but Becky could never think of any, or, at least, of none that matched his level of dignity. (She was in need of Visine, or a Visine-like substance of artificial tears, the air was so dry here.)

Mr. Kafi suggested expeditions—to what remained of Carthage, or to Sidi Bou Said, which would perhaps make Becky think of Spain in the architecture, or they could drive down to Sousse, admittedly a trap for tourists but there was a beach and the Medina and the countryside was pleasing to be seen. You must visit the Bardo, at the very least, Mr. Kafi had insisted on behalf of the national treasure house with increasingly damaged pride, and, on the next-to-last morning, Becky had agreed, she really mustn't miss Mr. Kafi's museum.

As it happened, Mr. Kafi himself had not been to the museum since his school days, when he had wound through the exhibition rooms in a crocodile of white-shirted boys while a Museum Expert, who seemed as old as the history he told, raised his cane high in the air, commanding them to halt whenever he paused to elucidate. Mr. Kafi greeted a great scowling stone god as an old friend, though, and he remembered as well a small glass bead, sea green like a frozen drop of ocean, which had remained there all these years tucked in a corner of a display case. Becky supposed these were typical childhood memories, impressed by the greatest object and drawn to the least; children perceived the world in terms of what was larger or smaller than themselves. Beauty, antiquity, rarity, utility, history, whatever else was on offer here had to wait until one attained the stature to look them squarely in the eye, and even then, one often had to blink.

Mr. Kafi guessed correctly that Becky wished to wander on her own among the exhibits. She had outlasted his patient attendance and he finally went off to look at Ottoman glories as she lingered over an assortment of belt buckles. One had a tongue that looked like a tongue, and another took on the form of a snake devouring its own tail as the belt was cinched. The ancient world seemed to have been full of belt buckles. Possibly, ancient peoples had been very much taxed by the problem of how to keep their togas from flapping open, back before there were zippers and elastic waistbands. They must have had buttons, however. Becky could almost picture the invention of the button—by a woman, of course, who sat beside a dying fire with the mending on her lap and who toed a polished round of bone from the embers and got to thinking. Hereabouts, it must have been a problem keeping one's dignity as the desert wind shuddered through the marketplace while you hurried along toward urgent business at the Temple of Isis (Becky had moved on to another exhibition gallery), where, it seemed, women had routinely gone bearing their deepest troubles. If only you still could. Becky wouldn't have half minded receiving an earful of old-time tough pagan wisdom. Or would she just be told, what will survive of us is belt buckles?

She decided as she strolled through the palace's many cool, marvel-filled rooms that she had regressed to an adolescent state of constant self-reference. She stood before marble goddesses and could only observe that they were all very much fatter than she, and yet they still got to be goddesses. She regarded bronze gods and determined whether she would mind being married to any of them. She thought not; they seemed rigid and self-absorbed. She formed opinions of whether one mosaic, a scene of men hunting a hare, or another, a view of a vineyard, would look nicer as the kitchen floor of the entirely theoretical seaside villa she was constructing in her mind's eye from the columns and pediments she noticed in passing. She wondered just how many mosaic floors and panels the Bardo's curators expected people to admire. (Oh, there was a portrait of Virgil, so that's what he looked like, this must have been how Dante recognized him in hell.) The palace went on and on. Footsteps, voices, birdsong from some inner garden, or perhaps it was the bey's mechanical nightingale, echoed. Becky became lost, or at least all turned around, and she had neglected to look up the Arabic word for Exit though she usually made a point of learning the word in very strange foreign languages (*východ*, in Czech). She thought, Somebody really ought to manufacture wallet-size plasticined cards listing the term for Exit in all the world's dialects. *It's nice to get away but sometimes it's necessary to get out*—that could be the company's motto.

Such a pat and tidy packaging of the past, with signs printed in several languages (ours, theirs, French) explaining practices and functions and beliefs and battle plans. But history was written by those who prevailed, and lost civilizations were known only by their fragments. By then, Becky was not really seeing the vases and friezes and tablets except to register whether she had come this way before, whether she was passing through the same rooms over and over again. She could only think of all the things she had left behind, packed and stacked in boxes stored in a climate-controlled facility back in the States, and within Castle Fortune's closets and dressers and on its shelves, her books and her crepe pan and her warm winter coats and the Wedgwood bowl that held the common pins she used to pull free from Alden's new dress shirts. She had not taken her jewelry, most of which Alden had given her and which she had never thought of as her own—rather, she had always regarded those pieces as being from Alden. She thought of the car wedged into an alley between a cannery and a customs office on the rough edge of Italy and she realized she had worked her own version of the Carlisle family creation narrative of the Belle de Crecy rosebushes forsaken alongside an Indiana riverbank where, no one ever really believed, they had gone on to live and flourish. Becky was sure the roses had tumbled into the water and been swept away on some raging nineteenth-century night, although the embossed-copper label plates may have survived to attest to their aristocratic names and provenance. Then, a later eye may have spied a glint of metal in the shallows of the river, a living hand may have delved to retrieve, and a dozen different meanings may have been assigned expressing whose and why and when.

But my story will be told by the one who lost, Becky reminded herself, and she did not doubt that a loser's tale would be a far less forgiving account than a victor's. How bravely the vanquished struggled against us, the victor would choose to remember. By what unscrupulous acts did the enemy defeat us, the vanquished would insist to anyone who was left to listen to them.

"You certainly have a splendid collection here," Becky had told Mr. Kafi when at last she came upon him buying postcards in the museum shop. "There's more to see here than a person can take in," she added as she plucked postcards from a revolving carousel of postcards—a grand bed, a great urn, an oily painting, which she had, somehow, missed on her prowl through the palace, which was always the case with her and museums, so she had to play catch-up at the gift-shop postcard carousel, spinning and spinning and looking behind each stack for misplaced views, being thorough now when the experience itself had been more casually taken.

That last day had been a long day. Her room at the hotel had not received her like home when she got back late in the afternoon. It was now a shaken-out, scrubbed, and polished room, prepared for the people who would come after her. Other arrangements had been made while she was out. Those days in Tunis had dragged on forever; those days in Tunis were over before they began. Becky ate her last blood oranges in the bath and gathered the peels and dropped them, after dark, from her window because the wastebaskets were now so empty. She had remembered then, she had yet to pack.

And so she sat cross-legged upon the bed, the tiny pair of scissors from her sewing kit fitted awkwardly onto her fingers. A soft heap of clothing rested beside her knee. There was the question of markings and labels which Mr. Kafi had raised. Libya would not allow into the country any item stamped or marked as having been made in Israel. Becky couldn't recall ever having bought much of anything that came from there except for Jaffa oranges and some not very expensive pottery mugs which had surprised her when she saw where they came from. Her travel hair dryer had been manufactured in China, by slave labor, people said. Her hairbrush came from England; her handbag was Italian, and she wondered why the Libyans weren't funny about Italians as well, given their colonial misadventures in the country. Well, Becky had not been at all happy when Mr. Kafi warned her to go through her possessions to rid them of any offending tags and imprints.

"But I can't do that. I won't submit to such a dictate," Becky said as Mr. Kafi shuttered his dark eyes and his ears did not hear her. He looked, then, like a stone-carved and very non-Western artefact. Whereas my people journeyed as far west as they could go until only the mountains and the winter stopped them, Becky thought, and she resolved, once she was settled wherever she found herself, she would endeavor to teach the benighted locals by her own good example. She would start a reading group. She would establish a film series exposing them to more positive and wholesome views of the West, because she was pretty sure *Terminator 2* was playing all over Tunisia at present, if the poster art displayed outside what seemed to be cinemas was anything to go by. Although she feared the rest of the world would never flock to see *Enchanted April* even if given the opportunity. The rest of the world had declared itself to be more enchanted by loud noises and garish colors and flying body parts.

A more immediate problem faced her, however. Becky flexed the scissor blades; they rasped remindingly. As she assessed the stamps and marks affixed to her belongings, she hesitated over the Anne Klein labels sewn to the collars and waistbands of half her clothes. (Becky had always said Anne Klein must have glimpsed her on Fifth Avenue one day and said to herself, I have found my muse.) She wondered if as suspect a name as Anne Klein appeared on the list of banned entities. Had the regime gone that far? When one went as far as they seemed prepared to go, who was to say what they would consider to be too far? They should be ashamed of themselves, thought Becky, and she would tell them so at the first occasion the opportunity arose. And should the need arise, if there was going to be any removal of offending labels, let the crime be on their hands.

THE RIDE ALONG THE COAST under different circumstances would have been lovely, traveling between pine and eucalyptus groves within sight of the pale and flat and shimmering sea, traveling on through olive and citrus plantations. You could tell where the French had been because of the lacy balconies and curlicuing cornices adorning old apartment blocks fronting the esplanades in the resort towns. Newer accommodations for foreigners (Europeans flocked here) were announced by the hospitality industry's finest corporate logos branding the gates that guarded long and private approaches. But the natives didn't do so badly for themselves. They lived in stone houses and white-washed dwellings set amidst fields of flowers or at the edge of the calm, shallow sea. The people here grew grain and grapes and olives and one could manage very well on a loaf of bread, a jug of wine, and red mullet pulled from the surf, rubbed with oil, and grilled over a fire. Becky, gazing through her window, imagined what life must be like here.

Her window was cranked down. Mr. Kafi had turned the air-conditioning on high. For miles (and there were four hundred miles to go) he had resisted asking Becky to shut her window, even as he sat in a swirl of refrigerator- and oven-air—the very whirlwind, he concluded, of the chaos raised by this woman.

That morning over their final breakfast in the Hannibal Room, she had spilled coffee across her hard-won visa, blurring the critical permissions expressed on its several lines. When he exclaimed at the damage done, she had said, "But it's all such gibberish anyway." Nevertheless, Mrs. Lowe had found it necessary to unfurl her Libyan entry documents at that moment to consult them as if she didn't quite believe them. She had also regarded the Hannibal Room as if it too was not quite what it appeared to be, as if it might be something other than a sun-splashed, perfectly respectable dining room frequented by foreign businessmen with interests in phosphate and cellulose, and by foreign tourists who had come to walk among the ruins of successive civilizations on successive afternoons.

Something or somebody had startled Becky as she was making one of her slow, frowning appraisals of her surroundings. Mr. Kafi had turned his head to determine the reason for her fluster and exhalation of *Oh* (for the woman was in his charge and would continue to be until late that afternoon, and then, God willing, no longer). Mr. Kafi followed her eyes and took note of a grey-haired man, tall and thin and mildly at cross-purposes with the busboy, who was attempting to express that he was not allowed to seat the patrons; he could only replenish their beverage servings and replace their napkin should they drop one to the floor. When the tall, grey-haired man was, at last, noticed by the hostess, he was seated directly within Becky's line of sight and she had skewed in her chair to regard, instead, the hot table where the Taste of Tunisia buffet would be set out that evening. She drank her coffee sideways and forgot about the plate of sugared waffles now at her elbow. Presently, her elbow struck her saucer and jostled the cup, causing the considerable spill all over the unfolded visa, as the hovering busboy who had just withdrawn the coffee pot cried out he was not to blame.

"Yes, he is," Becky said to Mr. Kafi. "He fills the cups too full."

The backseat and the trunk of Mr. Kafi's car, parked on the street in front of the hotel, were already loaded with boxes and bundles, and Mr. Kafi had had to remove and restow what had been a painstaking arrangement in order to fit in Becky's several suitcases. Sidewalk traffic surged around them as Mr. Kafi hauled heavy cartons from the trunk. He kept his eye on passersby, any one of whom might take it in mind to snatch the case of 100-watt lightbulbs he had just set down and run off with them, disappearing into the early-morning crowd of workers on their way to their offices and shops. Mr. Kafi would have been reluctant to shout, Stop! Thief! and summon a policeman who would have been more interested in investigating the provenance of the remarkable bounty of goods heaped inside his vehicle. All of Mr. Kafi's papers were in order, anticipating any questions at the border, but the handing over of a new and excellent camera manufactured by the Swiss might have been necessary in order to verify that fact for the officer.

"What is all this?" Becky pointed at the ziggurat of boxes rising in the gutter behind Mr. Kafi's car.

"It is all for Mr. Baskett's needs. The recent sanctions have made certain items unattainable. And other items were never to be found, even under better circumstances. I am his agent in the West for procurements." Indeed, the collection of Mrs. Lowe was just another item on a list.

Becky pried apart a closed carton top. "What's in here?" she asked.

"Please, madam."

"Flour? *Farine*, that's flour. Has William taken up baking?"

"No, madam. At least not to my knowledge. There have been short-ages of certain staples."

"Cornichons and English marmalade and jars of demiglace and Pratesi bed linens. Oh dear, have there been shortages of those, as well?"

"Madam. Please."

WHEN BECKY SPOKE ON THE JOURNEY, it was to inform Mr. Kafi of a fact of local interest gleaned from the guidebook lying open on her lap. At first, Mr. Kafi had been afraid she would insist they stop—at Hammamet and Mahdia and Sfax. Then, he had been bothered as she read one page and turned to the next, concluding a detour wasn't worth the bother.

"Those are asphodels," Becky said as they drove past a gathering of roadside lilies. "They're very pretty and the people here eat them. Over there. Look." Her hand waved through her open window. She had also pointed out to him a Roman aqueduct, and an octopus drying on a wall.

Mr. Kafi was not truly uncomfortable. He neither shivered nor sweltered in the brew of frigid and desert air. He minded, he supposed, because it simply wasn't right. Mrs. Lowe should choose one temperature or the other, although in his opinion there wasn't any choice but to opt for the air-conditioning, which he was among the lucky few to possess in his vehicle. He didn't think Mrs. Lowe properly appreciated that there was a difference between those who drove the Sahel highway with their car windows wide open and those who did not have to.

"Jerba Island is over that way. Where the Lotos Eaters lived," said Becky, swiveling around to view the receding headland as if something very interesting and unusual might yet be observed going on over there.

He could not catch her eye and indicate by blameful looks that she ought to close her window. She had slipped on a pair of serious sun-glasses at the start of the trip. The frames wrapped around her temples and preter-bright mirrored lenses repelled the onlooker's glance by re-turning him his own reflection made monstrous by an acid blue distortion of skin and features. Mr. Kafi wondered if this was how Mrs. Lowe saw him, as some grotesque Punic remnant, like a child stuffed inside a jar in sacrifice to Moloch and who had not grown up straight and tall and American.

"God," said Becky, and she bared her teeth to run the side of her forefinger over their surface. Sand grit. The beach met the desert here and everywhere was sand. A carton flap, unsecured by her investigations earlier, slapped in the interior wind. Mr. Kafi kept reaching back, but he could never quite reach.

"God," said Becky again.

He decided he felt married to this woman, by some arrangement to which he had not realized he was agreeing at a ceremony whose meaning had been imperfectly explained to him at the time. He decided to slip the first of his six Om Kalsoum cassettes into his dashboard player, and the strains of Om Kalsoum's wild griefs and loves mingled with the shrilling of the wind and Becky's deep sighs for the next hundred miles.

Then, at last, still miles away from the border, they were caught up in a line of traffic, autos and buses and lorries, stalled and steaming, jerking and juddering forward in inches-long advancements. It was late afternoon. The sun had lost some of its punch but it seemed to have gained in guile. It came at one from behind and, on slanted beams, bore into the back of one's head and neck. The sun was lower in the sky, and meaner, and red.

"Why is there such a crowd trying to get into Libya?" Becky asked.

"This is the only way in now. International flights have been banned by the sanctions," Mr. Kafi said.

"Yes, yes. I know that. But the question remains, why should anyone ever want to go to Libya?" Becky wondered.

Resignation, impassivity, supper; people were dozing over their steering wheels, staring ahead at the car in front of them, eating flyblown buns and octopus sandwiches inside their crawling vehicles. Somebody else had an Om Kalsoum tape wailing on high. Within sight of the border, car and truck doors began to crack open and items were nudged out onto the asphalt; Scotch bottles and magazines from Europe and the bazaar exposing the excesses of the regime or those of female flesh.

Someone had thought twice about getting through with a TEAM USA T-shirt, which lay flat in the road, fusing with the melting surfaces as tire after tire rolled over it.

Becky was remembering, now, the last time she had seen William. That had been two and a half years ago on what must have been the coldest day in history, back in Massachusetts at Alden's family's home, the same place where she had once told Alden yes, and where, once again, she had had to tell William no. His brief winter visit was over, his mission to convince her to leave Alden and to go away with him had been a failure. Becky would not be flying off with him into exile—for this had been the very beginning of his troubles. Just lately, he had become a wanted man, he had told her, wanted by everyone but her.

She had not been very nice to him as they parted (he was going away forever and Becky had errands to run). On that frozen day, they had had to pause to scrape frost from the windshields of their cars; no one would get very far peering at the ice-domed roads through a crystal-white forest of fronds and rosette blossoms. Becky had, at last, removed the borrowed ice scraper from William's hand (his rental car had come ill-equipped). She said, "Well, then." William had said nothing. He left no final, defining words to be chiseled into the duramen of the moment. The space was to be kept a blank, in abeyance. Even on that day, he still hoped.

"Get into the car. If you're going," Becky had ordered Julie, who had been making a pest of herself, pleading to accompany Becky on her errands that day when Becky had so very much wanted to be left alone. Sucking on an icicle she had wrenched from the barn eaves, Julie dawdled, and it was William who had slid into his car at Becky's sharp command.

He had followed her down the long driveway. Julie, wrapped in a muskrat coat with sloping shoulders and flapping sleeves, wore the single red mitten she had been able to find on her two hands. She turned round and crouched on her knees in the passenger seat, facing William and waving good-bye to him with a chopping motion of her mitten-wrapped hands.

"Stop that. Stop that at once," Becky had said.

Out on the River Road, they had driven off in opposite directions,

Becky taking one way and William the other, and they had been on their ways to one another ever since, she heading one way and he the other, following the vagaries of their separate routes, urged on by the impulses of their hearts and obligations. They had, through every other season and quarter, rounded over all the curves the earth could throw at them until they promised to meet again, by design, by near miracle, at this single point.

Today could be the hottest day the world had ever known. Becky sampled the outside air by reaching her hand toward the desert—though this was not the real desert here, Mr. Kafi said, dismissing the sere reach of wasteland that seemed to stretch on forever. There was worse beyond, he said; or perhaps it only got grander out there, Becky thought.

They were nearly at the border. A line of vehicles stood halted with their trunks and doors flung open beside the fortress hulk of a corrugated warehouse. A hoarding hugely offered the image and the greetings of the Leader, and farther on, shimmering and miragelike, was the car park where William was waiting for her.

A behemoth lorry shuddered forward and then it was their turn. A border guard was peering in at them, a very young man, as everyone at the embassy had been young (Does no one grow old in this land? Becky wondered). Mr. Kafi rolled down his window (at last, the breath of a cross breeze stirred) and offered their documents to the guard, who briefly scanned them. Becky would not have been surprised to learn he could not read, or perhaps he had not had to read their papers. Mr. Kafi may have given some secret sign or slipped dollars in among the documents' pages. Whatever the reason, they were waved on. Becky almost protested that it had been too easy after her crisis of conscience over dress labels. She had expected to be required to answer one more difficult, necessary question, like the Riddle of the Sphinx, before being granted this final permission to slip out from under the yoke of a twenty-three-year-long disenchantment. She looked back over her shoulder at the receding frontier, but no one came pelting after them shouting conundrums in Arabic.

And then, there he was, sheltering beneath the late-afternoon shade flowing from a single, signal date palm. William was sitting cross-legged on the ground. He must have learned how to sit cross-legged on the ground since coming here. He was reading a book, one of the pocket-size, dark-covered, thick little volumes, Trollope or one of the Burtons, he had always, in the past, been happened upon in the act of reading. He glanced up from the page as their car approached as he had glanced up at the approach of every other car that day, and now he stood, letting his book fall to the sand.

Six

Al-Aḥqāf—The Sand Dunes

TURN RIGHT OFF THE MAIN ROAD FROM MISRATAH, just before the billboard showing the Leader standing tall among schoolchildren and pronouncing, in a crawl of Arabic, *The individual without family has no value or social life.* Pass the freestanding arch of an aqueduct, proceed between the rustle and rattle of the olive grove, and on by a burned-black wreck of an axle-over-roof intercity bus. Be alert for the marabout's tomb (which will look like what it is). Turn there. The road may seem to be lost beneath the drifting sands of the sea dunes but it is discernible as a flatter grade upon the arenaceous plane. The bright blue-painted ranch-style house with a satellite dish on its roof is unmissable. Turn here and follow an up-and-down track to its end at a pair of gateless pillars, and just beyond them stands the Villa Felix.

Romans built the villa. Other centuries and empires intervened and then the Italians returned and renovated the property in the 1930s, AD. They installed an electrical plant and sank a pump down the cistern dug two thousand years earlier. They cut and glazed window openings with a view to a view and as a cause for curtains. They laid linoleum over broken mosaic tile floors, wallpapered the flaking frescoes, and converted the early Byzantine chapel from a donkey barn to a garage and workshop. When the last of the Italian family was told to leave the country in 1970, local people moved in hot on the last of the Antuccis' heels. The new householders covered over the old linoleum with bright new linoleum and hung rugs over the flying-away wallpaper. They troweled thick plaster over the engaged columns of the loggia which had been sculpted in the naked human form. They neglected the electrical plant and dropped a bucket down the cistern, breaking a gear of the pump sunk there. A cousin's family lived in the garage. They kept the donkey in the scullery. As the windowpanes broke they were not replaced, and aluminum shutters went up eventually. Then the day came when the Nazzars bought a modern flat in a new high-rise block closer to Misratah, where three of the sons and a son-in-law had found work in the cement factory. The donkey was left in possession of the villa, which was said, anyway, to be troubled by ancient restless manes, by a woman and sometimes by a man who walked alongside her at dusk, or it may have been midnight when they walked.

William's search for someplace quiet (serene, idyllic, Old World, other world) had ended at the gateless pillars. He had long been able to visualize outside the present; what had been and what could be framed his view of things and in this instance he saw that they might be reconciled to create the entirely possible. He was not sure he had purchased the villa outright. A great deal of money for this part of the world exchanged hands as cups of sweet tea were served and papers were signed, but the double-talk translation he was shown left him unsure of his standing, although not insecure. He was here at the pleasure of the regime, but he knew that it lay within his power to assist and to please them. His willingness to do so would serve for any deed, he felt.

In the first glory of his possession, William had paced the empty villa making notes and sketches in his pocket diary, and, as his ideas and aspirations for his house became more expansive, he wrote and drew his plans upon the garage wall with a thick stick of chalk. He worked away decades', or it may have been centuries', worth of dirt and plaster and crumbling cement with the blade of his penknife, slicing through to glimpses of good design and grace of form which he had known in his bones were there to be found. He camped out for a week. He drew water from the cistern, hauling up a beaten-copper bowl. He listened for the splash when he released the rope, and his well sounded deep. He boiled the water for tea and heated cans of soup over a campfire fed with the legs and the spindles and the splintered seat of the solitary kitchen chair he had lifted over his head and hurled at the floor. His luggage was piled in an apse. His wardrobe had served for northern Europe, his tweeds and heavy twills, and on succeeding mornings he put on less and less of his clothing, forsaking first his jacket, then a tie, and on the third day he went without socks. He spread his sleeping bag across a stone bench in the atrium and he lay atop the bag every night, offering himself to stars that he had never known to be so brilliant. The moon, in her last quarter, seemed an immense absence up above, and he kept watch for her return. He knew she would come back.

William explored and he planned. He came across a shovel and whaled away at a modern wall that halved and ruined the dimensions of a great room. He burned the shattered lattice to make his evening tea and shoveled the plaster dust out the door to mingle with the dust of the landscape. One morning, for a change, he trudged over the high dune that lay between the villa and the sea. He skirted a marsh of reeds following a trail of picnickers' litter, their wrappers and bottles and bones, to a mile-long shingle washed by the merest cat lap of a tide. He stood for a while up to his ankles in the listless surf, neither the push nor the pull of it commanding him to move on. He took this for a sign. He had no one else to talk to or consult and he understood how desert mystics might come to believe themselves to be addressed by unseen beings.

But when he returned to the villa that day, William saw he was no longer alone. A line of footprints blurred across the sand, leading from the pillars to the front door, which had been left hanging open. William had been aware all along that he was being watched. He had noted the glint of the sun striking off binocular lenses trained upon him from the vantage of a not-too-distant plantation of pines. Whenever he wrenched open the door of the shack that housed the electrical plant and effectlessly tapped knobs and dials, he had felt himself under particular scrutiny. He had been waiting for an approach and he was not surprised that the move had been made while he was out. Indeed, he had absented himself to precipitate this advance, allowing an opportunity for his simple arrangements to be assessed and his blameless possession to be examined. (He had hidden his money and true valuables inside the boiler of the kitchen oil stove.) William was ready for whatever was going to happen next to happen now. Besides, he was running low on matches and soup and clean, ironed shirts.

"*Sabah-el-Khayr?*" he demanded from the threshold of the villa, which represented the alpha and omega of his Arabic. A phrase book

and the Koran, acquired to be his downtime reading, lay largely uncon-
sulted atop his bedroll. His eyes could not hold to a page when there
was so much to be taken in beyond the margins.

"Sir? Sir." A man came hurrying into the hall. "*There* you are, sir,"
he nearly accused William. "I am your neighbor. I am Adil Adib. I am
your neighbor out on the main road, that is my blue house, and I am at
your service, sir."

William could never tell these people's ages, but here was an older
rather than a younger one. Adil wore white trousers and a white polo
shirt with a pair of dark glasses hanging by an earpiece from its placket.
He had greying hair, and a black mustache covered his upper lip, curving down like a scowl above an omnipresent smile. He was tall and built
wiry and he was carrying William's paperback Penguin edition of the
Koran in his hand.

"Are you a Believer, sir?" Adil asked.

"No," William said. He did not feel any need to explain he had been
born a Methodist but now he was nothing.

"A seeker, then?" Adil asked.

"I am only curious about the local customs," William said.

"He reveals to you His signs. Which of God's signs do you deny?" Adil,
who seemed to be quoting, did not expect an answer. He gave over the
book, and William set it down upon a window ledge weighted by a
shard of red marble against the wind, which had begun to rise.

"You must close your shutters, sir," Adil said. "A ghibli is coming.
You know, a ghibli, which is a particularly strong wind."

"Yes, I know what a ghibli is. At this time of year an occurrence is to
be expected," William said, for so he had read.

"Then you are prepared, sir, for our violent weather changes, as a
knowledgeable stranger to our shores?" This was spoken leadingly.

"I am William Baskett and I shall be living here now. I intend to restore the villa to the way it was," William said, although he did not
doubt his neighbor was aware of all of this and more.

"I am at your service," Adil said again. "My sons know carpentry
and painting and electricity and plaster work and the pipes."

"This will be a specialized restoration," William said.

"And I am in contact with many specializers," Adil said.

A child scurried through the atrium archway—boy or girl? It had a headful of curls as solid as in an ancient carving, and a pair of enormous eyes. It wore a long white robe. Its feet kicked and tangled with the hem, like Sweetpea in his nightie. The child clutched William's alarm clock and held it to an ear, mesmerized by the click-click-click of the passing seconds. Adil reached for the clock and the child shouted No (presumably) and ran behind a column as Adil laughed. It must be a boy child, to be so indulged.

"My grandson, Muammar," Adil said.

William nodded at the child and extended a hand for the clock. Muammar sidled over to his grandfather to shelter behind his legs and he tucked the clock into Adil's palm. He clung to his grandfather's leg as Adil advanced to restore the clock to William. They looked like that statue in the Borghese Gallery of Aeneas and little Iulus fleeing burning Troy. This part of the world provided these visual quotations. In Tripoli, William had seen the Persian Sibyl sitting at a stall in the marketplace selling ribbons and arguing with a girl who was touching her wares.

Then Adil got down to business. He informed William that his cousin would supply him with produce and the butcheries and breads, and his daughters-in-law were the most expert of laundresses and seamstresses and workers of beads, and he would send specializers to William next week or the next week after, to put his house into repair. Further, Adil said, he knew of a Malian couple, Henry and James, who were in need of work since their English employer had departed in a hurry the previous April and who were used to Westerners' ways, the particular cleaning and cooking required by them, the polishing, the roasted beef, the importance of not disturbing books and papers spread across a desk. They were very good boys, these Malians.

All of this had given William much to think about later as he sat out the storm in a windowless storeroom. He had drained the last of his contraband Glenmorangie from a Listerine bottle, for he had promised himself he would down the last drops at some crucial instance. He tried to read by candle flicker, first his Koran and then his phrase book, but neither book seemed to have much of a plot, he complained to himself rather muzzily.

Throughout the night and the following day and night, he tried to read and he dozed and he shook himself awake to check on the course of the storm. He dunked a handkerchief in his water pail and, covering his nose and mouth, made his way through the shuddering villa to the hall. There, he grasped the latch of the outer door, which the wind snatched from his hands or pressed against with such force that he had to pull with all his might to part it from the jamb. The world beyond his doorstep had resolved into a frenzy of red particles, and the temperature had spiked from hot to hellish in the first hours. The air flew by too fast for him to catch a breath. His eyes were stung shut. He clung to the wall and blindly reached for the door as the cloth of his shirt flattened like a second skin along his arm, and then billowed up like a sail that came near to lifting him off his feet and launching him out into the void.

Yet the call to witness was irresistible. William had moved beyond assessing whether the situation had turned for the worse or the better; no measurement could be taken of such a universal fury. He was prepared, simply, to exist for the present, in a dirt-floored storeroom stocked with the least of necessities, provided with the most undiverting of reading materials. As he lay atop his pallet, he realized that this was a singularly authentic event, one that had descended down from the beginning of time in its purest form. Nothing about this phenomenon had changed: not the hot wind, not the whirling dust, not the fact of his own utter helplessness in the face of the wind and the dust. Other beings had huddled as he did now, praying the roof would hold and skimming, from the surface of a pail of water, the powdery drift of refined, invasive particles that had found a way in through solid wall. Other ancient monsters were mythical, the Gorgons and Europe's dragons, but this storm was very real and even as William shook with every shudder of the villa, he marveled. He knew himself privileged to be here in this place enduring the eternal with, he felt, his own measure of fortitude. He had never been called upon to be really brave. Any past exploits of his had required the far lesser attribute of nerve—that and his willingness to act and to move by small and secret degrees toward a never-to-be-acknowledged end. But then, men dwelt too much upon the rise and fall of empires and failed to notice the indi-

vidual riding out the storm and holding on to his own by any means left
to him.

For William could not not think of Becky now. If he were to be
killed by the collapse of a beam (instant, unfelt, he did not fear this), he
wanted his final thought to be of her. He half believed (as belief came
easier in this part of the world, where beliefs seemed to come from)
that a powerful last cry of Becky would propel him to her side. He
would be borne by this wind as it traveled on to Europe as a blown-out
squall. His cry would join the persistent woe-filled woo-ing of the
wind. His last breath would be part of the sourceless draft that stroked
her cheek. He would gaze upon her from the corners of the rooms she
frequented. He might even, with a tremendous act of will, knock a
book of verse from a table's edge and have it fall open to a resonant
passage. Becky was sensitive. She would study the shadowed corner
of a room, she would touch her cheek, she would read the verse, she
would understand. But Becky was sensible as well. He could see her
summoning some keen young priest from the Church of St. John of
the Wash House's priest's barracks who would exercise his holy oils
and holy rites over that kinetic volume of Browning (say) and send William on his way for his own good. Becky had a history of sending
William on his way for his own good.

In half a lifetime of loving her, he had wrung every change from the
experience. He had known grief and joy, ache and consolation, blame
and then forgiveness for all she had never asked and yet always required of him. He had sometimes been absurd on her behalf (just now,
fixing to haunt her, like an adolescent suicide anticipating his own fu-
neral day), but he also knew no one had ever been truer or stronger or
quieter in the service of a hopeful passion. He had held on for twenty
years and he could hold on for a while longer. Indeed, even as he
yearned not to be alone, he was glad she wasn't there with him now in
the derelict villa, helpless beneath the lash of the African night, and for
the moment, he realized, he had achieved a rare equipoise of regret and
gratitude. These were the moments he lived for—or, perhaps, lived
on. He settled back against the rough stone of a trembling outer wall as
the flame was snatched from the candlewick and there was nothing to
be done but to dream again of Becky.

Things were better the next morning, as they usually are, when William emerged from the storeroom and crunched over the sand-strewn and lifting-up linoleum, noting the damage done to his already damaged house. Although, in fact, the wind had gotten started on some desired demolition: several aluminum shutters had been wrested off and flown away, and tatters of a grape-and-vine-and-satyr-and-maiden-patterned wallpaper had been shorn from the walls of the great room. In the kitchen quarters the ancient stove's oven door, theretofore stuck shut as if welded, swung open on croaking hinges, revealing a cavelike interior of the sort William associated with excellent Old World baking.

William wandered outside and observed the enduring but not unaltered landscape. Another row of tiles was gone from the garage roof. The sea dunes rose perceptibly taller and fatter. The olive grove was ever more bent and tangled in the trunk and canopy. William saw as if with freshly scoured eyes. His small fiefdom had been threatened and had withstood the threat and he knew, then, he was going to be all right here. The cistern hatch had vanished but was not completely lost, its location indicated by the rising wave of the sand that covered it. William fetched his shovel from the garage and, satisfied to have a task to perform, began to dig.

When he next looked up, he saw a line of assorted beings passing between the gateless pillars: five adults, a small child, a smaller child, brown-skinned and black-skinned both, dressed in chinos and polo shirts, robed in tightly woven blankets cinched with woven belts. So, life still walked on earth. William paused, ready to take a break, for he was hot, and he leaned upon his shovel as Adil (who else but Adil?) and his party approached.

Introductions were made, formalities ensued. This was a civil culture on the surface. William sensed he'd been judged discourteous by his failures to salaam and to crave the indulgence of his new acquaintances with the prescribed phrases of praise and self-abasement. He had no intention of adopting local ways, and these people would be wise to remember who he was and how he had come to be there. Never the diplomat, people used to say of William.

The awful Muammar stepped forward. A filthy foot shot out from beneath the Sweetpea nightie and he kicked sand into the hole William had spent the past fifteen minutes excavating. Adil, his son, Walid, and a son-in-law, Mousa, visiting from Tripoli, laughed at this. The younger child who accompanied them aped the actions of Muammar, although he, Habib his name was, fell onto his bottom with the execution of every kick. Adil, Walid, Mousa, and Muammar laughed at him until William said, "That's enough," his tone, if not his words, apprehended by Muammar, who ceased kicking sand and began thumping Habib. The adults lost interest then, and Habib, who had long since (in terms of his brief existence) been taught the inefficacy of tears and appeals, dodged the blows as best he could.

"Here are Henry and James," Adil said, motioning to the two robed Africans to offer themselves for inspection. They rose from the abiding crouch they had assumed on the outskirts of the group and endeavored to display a wary alacrity. "These are your Malian boys I have promised to you."

One man, Henry, seized the shovel from William and started to dig out the all-but-filled-in hole as James knelt and scooped with his hands, clearing a spot for successive slices of the shovel blade. William gave them points for turning a one-man job into a two-man undertaking. They didn't question how deep, or what for. Like that sculptor in the adage about hewing at the rock until he finds the lion trapped in the stone, they would know they had finished digging when they got there, William gathered.

"Where will they live?" William asked Adil.

"We have a caravan," Henry spoke up. "We shall haul it to the strand. We think we shall enjoy life on the water's edge."

"Very well," said William. He knew he would have nothing to say about the setting of wages and the terms of their employment. He gave a nod to Adil.

"*It is He who drives the wind as harbinger of His mercy,*" Adil responded in his higher-speaking quoting voice. His son and son-in-law murmured, *Insallah,* and Muammar looked demure.

THE RESTORATION OF THE VILLA FELIX from wrecked relic to non-pareil (as envisioned) of form and function, its past recaptured, with additional water pipes and electrical conduits and perhaps an AC unit encapsulated within the walls, was nearly (but never really) completed by the time of Becky's arrival, which was to occur two years after work began, after a fashion.

Adil had, at once, demonstrated his ability to command a legion of craftsmen and day laborers. Plumbers, carpenters, plasterers, painters, and a mosaicist pulled up to the door in open trucks, on motor scooters, or driving newsreel vintage Mercedes coupes the color of silvered footage, all drawn by the prospect of steady employment bankrolled by a rich Westerner who had come to live among them at the indulgence of the regime from whom all (further) blessings flowed.

They were presented to William, whose role evidently was not to examine and then to hire or to pass on candidates. Several times he shook his head at Adil, who shook his head in reply, negating William's negative. Here, the chosen were self-appointed. Men arrived at the Villa Felix and took up hammers as if in a cause. These interviews were conducted to allow the workmen's hopes and aspirations to be expressed, and for William's taste and his ability to pay for his tastes to be praised. Ultimate success was predicted, raptures were promised, loyalty was avowed, oaths were uttered. A Mr. Mecca declared his willingness to retile William's roofs or to die in the attempt. Whereupon William wondered whether these people carried liability insurance or subscribed to some sort of workmen's compensation scheme, but Adil, whose English failed him at convenient moments as if it had suffered a power cut, smiled blandly and spoke a Yes of consummate insincerity when William asked him this.

James brewed tea. He understood the ways of the oil stove. Henry served. He stood at his full height and streamered tea from a long-spouted pot into tiny, saucered cups set on low packing-crate tables. He dispensed lumps of sugar with tongs, and he lowered sweet pastries onto plates. These people were fueled by sugar. William himself, who in the past got going on alcohol, had turned to desert dates, leathery and gritty and inspissated by the sun, for want of anything else.

"Are three electricians necessary?" William questioned Adil.

"Praise be to Allah," Adil exclaimed. *"God guides to His light whom He will."*

"Electricians are the neurologists of the building trade, you know," William said. "There will be bloodshed."

The villa was toured. The principals conferred and disputed. Assistants with clipboards attended. Sometimes they set down their clipboards and joined the conferences and disputations. William's notebook jottings and sketches were studied until all meanings were gleaned from them. The garage-wall drawings were pronounced his greatest work. William's notion of a lap pool in the atrium was so admired that one of the carpenters banged together a bench so the men could sit before the image and gaze upon it. A painter washed the waters blue when he remembered he had part of a liter of Riviera Aqua in his truck, and another painter added a surf of precise, white arabesques.

From then on, there were to be islands of order and disorder in William's life. The Libyan workmen proved to be keen dismantlers. They removed roof tiles, the window frames, the lead and copper pipes, a tin sink, a cast-iron bathtub, layers of linoleum, wrought-iron railings, the Nazzars' plastic bead curtains that had divided the villa into many zones. William's castoffs were trucked away and sold in Misratah. The crumbled plaster, shattered lath, wallpaper shreds were flung out the front door until William made the men understand they must fling such material farther away from his doorstep, out of sight.

William laid rush mattings across his newly exposed and tender mosaic floors. He secured tarps over all the window openings so the fierce sun would not further fade the now-revealed frescoes. Whenever marble was uncovered, richly colored African marble defining portals and niches, he gathered the men and told them they must not damage the stone with their hammers.

He liked the look of the stripped-down villa, which reminded him of an empty canvas or a fresh page awaiting a first, defining stroke. The villa awaited, and awaited. The men arrived each morning and convened in the garage, lounging before the lap pool, smoking villainously strong cigarettes down to the nub. The strains of their many arguments reached William. He assumed they were arguing. No discourse ever sounded cordial in Arabic.

"Adil," William said. "What are they doing? Or more to the point, why *aren't* they doing anything?"

"Materials," Adil said. "We are waiting for more materials. It is difficult these days. The sanctions of America," he reminded William.

"Isn't there a secret warehouse in the desert? Didn't you people stockpile, in anticipation? There are always ways around difficulties in a shady little country like this," William said.

Adil shrugged. "For the most powerful, perhaps there are."

"Then why can't you acquire what you need on the black market? I know there must be a thriving one, based upon all the stuff that was carted away from here with such enthusiasm to be sold," William said. "Why can't you make a trade? What we don't want for what do we want?"

But it seemed William could not avail himself of that option. His requirements were too exacting and William understood he existed upon a very specialized rung of the food chain, like a panda who could only eat bamboo shoots and here there was no bamboo.

"Am I paying these men to sit around my imaginary pool, then?" William asked.

"They work for you, sir."

"I want running water, a reliable power source, and a ghibli-proof roof over my head by the end of the week; and to close any loopholes, I don't mean an imaginary roof and some Platonic ideal of running water," William said.

"If God so wills, you shall have all that and more," Adil said.

"You people certainly know how to pass the buck," William said.

Henry and James had made an oasis of the kitchen quarters with the few elements assembled there: the oil stove, a sink, a skillet, a kettle, a pot, a rolling pin, a spoon, a paddle, a knife. Much had been accomplished with not very much. There was a sturdy square of table now, with a scrubbed surface and three three-legged stools pushed underneath. The Malians had made sure there was a place at the table for each of them.

They formed an ideal bachelor establishment, operating on the English model of the men's prior household. The archaeologist for whom they had worked had required fresh scones, and hot water to shave with, and a general condition of things humming along with no audible humming sound, as Henry had explained the terms of their last service.

"Scones and polishing," James said, as they sat around the table; William was drinking coffee, James was washing rice, and Henry was beating a piece of tin to fit the top of an old olive jar in which he meant to store more rice.

"And cataloging artefacts," Henry said. "As well as excavations on the site."

"And distillery experiments in the making of whiskey," James said.

"Also to answer to the names James and Henry as we answer to you now," Henry said.

"They are not bad names he gave us? We have wondered," James said.

"No, they are very good ones," William said. "Tell me. Just how far did you get with those distilling experiments of yours?"

The great room fresco, when uncovered at last, had revealed a man and a woman reclining upon silver couches. Propped on their elbows, they lay head to head. Their torsos sloped, their hips rose, their legs tapered, and, together, they described the lines of a pediment capping a temple. Between them, a pedestal bore a gold plate piled high with green grapes. The man and the woman had just reached for the same globe of grape and caught one another's hands instead. The expressions on their faces were not, at once, readable; as with an ancient script, the problem wanted further study. They gazed not upon one another but confronted the onlooker. Yes, confrontational, William thought; he sensed that about the pair. Or were they defiant? There was something going on with them he couldn't quite put his finger on. Was this the illustration of a myth? Was the disputed grape poisonous, or would it bestow immortality upon its possessor? Were the lovers (for William decided they were lovers) skirmishing over death or courting an everlasting life, and which did they want to give to the other and which to keep? As he studied the painting, William realized that the room depicted was the very room in which he stood. The marble inlay of the latter-day walls, though broken and lost in places, formed the same pattern as in the painting, and off to the side of the couple there was the very apse edged with an identical seashell motif, and that in the painting's day had contained a Nubian carrying a fan woven of ostrich feathers and palm fronds. But where was the corre-

sponding apse on the other side of the couple that, in the fresco, contained a fountain? Two big fish—were they dolphins? the ancients
doted on dolphins—leaped with sinuous energy from the bowl.

William considered and then he paced off a relative distance from
the existing niche to the presumed one. He rapped plaster with his
knuckles, drumming on not-the-spot, then finding the spot, hearing a
more hollow thud where he had guessed he would. He slipped a claw
hammer from a carpenter's idle toolbox, and he struck a first, satisfying
blow. Plaster crumbled and a draft of trapped air sighed from the aper-
ture, through which he peered into blackness. William bashed with the
hammer head and grabbed with the claw, shattering, yanking, kicking
away rubble. Those sporting dolphins—they looked so parched after
all those years that he fetched and flung a bucket of water over them.

A YEAR AND A HALF LATER William sat in the fresco room. He was
writing at his desk, which had been angled to give him a view of the
picture wall when he glanced up from the page he was inscribing,
whether troubled or convinced by what he had just expressed. His bed
and two reading chairs were also turned toward that wall. This chamber had certainly once been the dining room of the villa, for other revealed images showed, in further frescoes and tiles, hares and birds and
artichokes and vines. But William did not live as a Roman, not electing
as Cicero, as Ovid had, to meet and mingle with his fellow man in
large, public spaces. Rather, William sought to contain a full and very
private inner life, and, in his own way, he respected another aspect of
the ongoing history of his house, for the plan of a Roman villa, its
rooms organized around a central atrium, had inspired the designs of
both the cloister and the quadrangle of academia, those closed sanctu-
aries into which a man might retreat to contemplate and to dream upon
the object of his disaffection from the world.

William was used to getting on in foreign parts. He knew how to
shut out the sights and sounds and smells of a place, and here, too, the
villa met his needs. The modern window openings had been bricked
over and stuccoed by Adil's work crew, restoring the blank facade the
ancients had first presented to passersby, safe again, as then, from in-

vaders and sealed against the heat. Through Mousa, the son-in-law from Tripoli who seldom seemed to be in Tripoli, William had acquired furnishings in a series of tensely negotiated, no-questions-asked-as-to-provenance deals, Mousa pacing and gesturing, William, on one occasion, striking his desktop with the flat of his palm over the price of an Italian walnut chest of drawers. (Mousa often brought a photo of a piece, harshly lighted and standing alone in some infelicitous cellar or back room, looking roughly handled, like a hostage.) This dresser now held the elements of William's more suitably Saharan wardrobe, his white cotton long-sleeved shirts and cotton khaki trousers, which were laundered and ironed and kept in repair by Adil's daughters-in-law. A reed basket traveled between the villa and the Adibs' bright blue-painted ranch house out on the sand-strewn road to Misratah, conveying shirts, leeks, oranges, eggs, the in- and the outgoing mail.

William had peace now. He had a network of suppliers and obtainers. He found repose in his armchairs and upon his high, wide bed. He dined off a set of fine porcelain china painted with an armorial crest (last seen in some scuttled embassy, he supposed). He had a growing assortment of books housed in a barrister's bookcase. (" 'Law is no more,' " William had said to Adil in an intoning, quoting voice of his own the day the bookcase arrived. " 'Law has gone away.' ") The assembled volumes were a solid representative grouping of works well ensconced in the Western canon: histories, plays, poetry, nineteenth-century novels, spirited from a university library (stamped *Benghazi*) before they could be fed to a bonfire—of the humanities, as William had observed to Adil, who was helping with the boxes or, at any rate, had his hand in them. Books made Adil nervous and he shooed away Muammar, who was riffling through every volume he could grab in search of—what? some outrageous picture he could denounce?

From time to time the universities erupted into protest. From time to time a student was seized and accused—perhaps of smuggling books from some targeted library. Then, pushed into the glare of the sun, hooded, his hands lashed behind his back, and looking too slight and too trembling ever to have been a threat to anyone, the student was hanged live, and then displayed dead, on television. William had refused all the television sets Adil offered to sell him. He had seen enough of television in the hotels.

William paused in his letter writing. He glanced from the fresco to the fountain, which had been made to work again. Water flowed from the dolphins' mouths in arcing streams that collided midair and dissolved into sparkles raining down into the bowl, over and over and over again, until William flipped an Off switch. He never wearied of this water music, as he called it, but an occasional cessation only sweetened the sound upon resumption. He'd fallen into the habit of acting out these little dramas of denial and then indulgence.

Of course he was writing to Becky. He set down his pen and reached for his wineglass. Henry and James had not proved to be gifted distillers, but Adil knew a man who had been taught the art of vintnery by an old Italian and this man produced, from the vines the old Italian had planted, a rough but sturdy red. William had half convinced himself that Byron and Keats and perhaps even the Brownings, who may have had their moments, had downed something of the same sort in rustic tavernas and been none the worse for it. Samian wine, a beaker full of the warm South.

Tonight, Henry and James appeared at the door of the fresco room. "The wind is rising," Henry said. He and James were carrying pots of atrium hibiscus, which they set down inside the doorway. They retreated and returned hefting the Norfolk pine between them. This was the drill, prior to a ghibli.

"Is the car in the garage?" William asked. Mousa had found him a Land Rover, left behind by a European party of off-road enthusiasts who had suffered a fatality although the vehicle had come through all right. William had gotten it at a good price; the European party had not hung around to dicker.

"Yes. Very secure," said Henry. He loved the car very much.

They brought in fruit and bread and sustenance in tins (boneless white chicken, rice pudding, ravioli), a can opener, water in a jug, and candles and an oil lamp and matches and the kitchen shortwave radio, cutlery, a plate, a mug, the kitchen cat and its bowl for William's scraps and its cushion, the batch of scones that had been baking while all the rest was being assembled, a thermos of coffee and the jam pot and a box of sand for the cat, to be set down beneath the water-heater tank in William's adjacent bathroom.

James knotted the belt of his robe and he stood in the doorway, studying the color of the sky above the atrium.

"Two days and clamorous," he predicted.

"They are always two days and clamorous, or three days and calamitous. Well, maybe this will be the storm to carry off all the Adibs," William said. "Have you tied shut the generator shed's door? Remember last time."

"Everything has been done," Henry said. "And now we must leave."

"Are you sure you don't want to stay here?" William offered, as he always offered.

But the men preferred to ride out the storm in their beachfront caravan, and defend their home as they might, should the need arise.

"Someday you'll be blown into the drink," William said. "Or you'll be buried up to the roof. Here, you might need this to help you escape." He held up the can opener.

"You are very kind," said Henry, and he and James departed, closing the door behind them. William rose and made sure of the latch and gave the cat a look to let it know he was watching it. He returned to his desk and slid open a drawer and removed a map of the world, much folded and creased, which he laid almost flat across his desktop. He withdrew the can opener, which had made a bulge of Belgium.

The map was not so very old, published by the National Geographic Society as a magazine insert. It was a typical National Geographic production, depicting a rational, sunny world—such clean lettering, such bright coloring, such equal treatment of the nations, Angola's wretched capital city starred, just like Paris. The map had fallen from between the pages of his lately acquired copy of *Robinson Crusoe*. William supposed some student had once wished to trace the castaway's travels and travails, beginning with his two years' enslavement to a Moorish master in the North African port of Sallee (what was Sallee called, nowadays?). Perhaps the student had sought, like Crusoe, his own route of escape from subjugating forces.

"But it was out of the frying pan and into the fire, for Crusoe," William spoke aloud. This is what he would have told the student. "Better to sit tight, like us," he spoke aloud again, to the Roman lady gazing down upon him from his wall. The storm was finding its legs. The villa shook, as if kicked.

No, after half a lifetime of wandering, William wasn't going anywhere, not that evening, or any other day. He was here, in this place he had made for her. She was there, in that place she could make nothing of. His finger touched the map. He moved his finger north, in an unwavering line. *Here,* he bided, and *there,* she dallied, locked along a single line of latitude. How neatly they had arranged themselves upon the earth, this time, fixed along that singular strand that Becky need only loop round her wrist and take one first and final step into her future (or did he mean her past?) and spiral down and down like the dea ex machina she had always been to him to play out her fated part in the final momentous act of their lives, linked at last.

He must tell her this, how easy the way to him would be. He pushed aside the map and picked up his pen. *I will be there to catch you,* he wrote.

Seven

Al-Iklhāṣ—Oneness

IN A CORNER OF THE CAR PARK, on the edge of the desert, at the end of her journey, William had wrapped his arms around Becky just above and below her waist and he lifted her off her feet. Becky held him around his neck, her arms braced and propped on his shoulders. He held on to her as if she were something precious and substantial, like the statue of a saint conveyed in a procession of the faithful who bore the effigy aloft, not without effort, not thinking of the effort. Then, William began to whirl Becky around and around and she had had to close her eyes against the unreeling of the empty land and emptier sky, shutting out the passing cars and trucks, the warehouse fortress, the berobed figures looking on, so swathed and alien it did not matter what they saw. When at last William set her down, there, here, where he wanted her, she knew she stood upon an utterly new world, the one he had just spun for them out of the air and the sand and the heat.

FOUR WEEKS HAD PASSED SINCE HER ARRIVAL. They had had this entire month together; October, a golden month in the temperate zone, shone for them here as well. Indeed, Becky was dazzled. The sun struck sparks and sparkles off every surface: the sand, the sea, and glass and metal and hair and skin. Like gilt, she thought. She saw gilt everywhere, which seemed to have rubbed off on her, as she herself turned golden.

They had yet to spend an ordinary day here. Each succeeding day had seemed set aside as if every day must be a Sunday and a time for withdrawal and reflection and acts of devotion. They lay in bed late in the morning, as on a lazy Sunday, and they went to bed early as if anticipating some busy Monday morning that never arrived. Sometimes in the afternoon they retired to their bedroom and went to sleep in one another's arms. There was nothing else to do because the Sunday papers never came, full of news and editorials and word puzzles to recall them to the world and engage them in wordplay. They did not know about Sundays in a Muslim country, but Henry and James and Adil and the rest of the always-in-and-out Adib family, although constrained to talk and walk about the villa quietly, were, nevertheless, able to talk and walk about the villa freely when the Miztah and his Mizzus absented themselves.

Their bedroom, never meant to be a bedroom, was the grandest room in the villa, where the Romans had banqueted and the Byzantines had conducted business and the Antuccis had pressed olives, and which the Nazzars had divided in two to accommodate the male and female halves of their household. Their bedroom would not have been out of place as a display chamber in the Bardo, Becky had decided, with its mosaics and the fountain and the fresco and the furnishings William had collected. She felt as if she had wandered into a museum after hours, after the guards had gone away and it was all right to open the cases and walk behind the ropes. As everyone does, Becky had sometimes fancied that the exhibits stirred to life when no one was around, the people in the portraits stretching and chatting and smoothing their hair before a silvered mirror, the fragile chairs sat upon, a jeweled cup sipped from, and now it seemed as if she and William had also just come to life, stepping from some frame or breaking free of chiseled stone. She wondered how she and William had survived, and what it was about them that had been worth protecting and preserving and holding to the light as exemplars of their kind.

In the mornings, when at last Becky rose and crossed the cool tile floor, her slipperless feet adhered to, then lifted from, the always slightly salty and sweating surface with the capture and release of the lightest of kisses across her soles. For the first few moments of any day, Becky's conscious thoughts lagged behind her risen state. She perceived with sense memories, her flesh and muscles and bones informing her; the floor kissed her feet, her robe embraced her, and any interior breeze there might be caressed her cheek. She would turn and bestow a soft, blurred smile upon William as he knotted the sash of his dressing gown, and he would sweep to her side to catch her and to hold her as urgently as if they had been parted by half a world, for half a lifetime. They moved in a kind of dance, gliding round and round in slow and slower circles, coming to rest at the edge of the bed, to which, often, they returned.

William had planned all of this. He had always known this day would come, while Becky, who would never have dreamed, had not dreamed. But William had discovered this haven (a queer place in which to feel safe, tucked into a corner of an outlaw nation; then again, where would any runaway be less vulnerable to any impetuous rescuer than when guarded by such strange dragons?). He had prepared the villa and staffed the house, which ran without the interference of the entranced couple, the provisioning, the catering, the dusting, the polishing, and the laundering taken care of by silent (or if not silent, then not understandable) figures who subsided into the shadows as if their very substance was shadow. William had thought of everything and Becky was content, for now, not to think.

There was to be ceremony as well. They had missed twenty years of shared milestones and occasions, those times when an alliance, a personal domain, love, are washed in a particular glow and, more often than not, gifts are exchanged. William had amassed twenty years of untendered presents. He had, late in the autumn or early in the summer, in whatever city he happened to find himself, begun his quests, haunting shops both fine and curious (he was prepared to spend a great deal, but he could recognize the underestimated treasure, as well). Then, in those haunted shops, he was able to speak of the lady's tastes and characteristics. He was free to adjudge the potency of the gleam of a jewel against a vision of her throat, and to feel for himself the cool slide of something silk across his own skin while dreaming of hers. He limited himself only as to size in his selections. The item had to be portable, as he moved from country to country, of a dimension able to be fit inside whichever drawer was commissioned to hold an ever-growing cumulation of the uncelebrated years' unpermitted devotions.

One afternoon he dragged a covered basket from an apse and strong-armed it up onto the end of the bed where Becky was sitting upright against stacked pillows, her legs jutting out straight with her toes in the air, intent upon restoring a button to one of William's light white cotton shirts, which were no longer as new as they'd once been (and this puzzled William, for they were always to be his new shirts to him). The sight of Becky undertaking such a homely task on his behalf filled him with conflicting emotions. There was joy, of course, that the fact of Becky sewing for him had become part of the fabric of daily life. Nevertheless, he had meant for Becky never again to have to concern herself with the domestic drudgery that had been demanded of her in the past, and he blamed himself for having mentioned the missing button to Becky when he ought, instead, to have brought it to the attention of Adil to charge his laundress, and at times seamstress daughters-in-law, with the task of replacing it. But William's sense of joy predominated as Becky looked up and smiled at him. She had borrowed his reading glasses, which were the source of her amusement. The glasses kept sliding down her nose and she regarded him over the top of the dark tortoiseshell frames.

William remembered, then, among the many theretofore undisclosed and thus unopened gifts, the existence of a platinum thimble that had once belonged to Lady Emma Hamilton, its interior worn smooth by the rub of her notable finger, its tip indented where plying needles had pressed. Platinum was too soft a metal for a thimble, but then, one would not expect the possessor of the platinum thimble to work her fingers to the bone nor her thimble to the quick by incessant acts of sewing.

"What's all this?" Becky asked. She snipped off the thread with her very small pair of scissors and tossed the shirt to William as he threw parcels across the bed, hunting for one in particular. In the shops, when William at last made his choice and a box had been found to fit, someone was summoned from a back room to wrap the present in a beautiful paper secured with a beautiful bow. William had never, over the years, been tempted to unwrap any of them even as he began to forget which among the oldest packages contained what painstakingly purchased trinket. He was surprised he could forget, but he supposed this made him less pitiable. He had never brooded; he had always looked forward and kept faith and prepared for this day, which he had known would come. The presents (and there should be nineteen of them—for the first several years of Becky's marriage he had bought gifts for other women and there were several lovely watches and pearl necklaces tucked away at the back of several jewelry cases) were just fond and foolish tokens, he explained to Becky, and he had not even thought of them until now because somewhere among them was a thimble, if she insisted upon sewing buttons onto his shirts.

William borrowed Becky's scissors and he snipped off the tight ribbons whose knots had hardened with the years. He was as interested as Becky to see what each box contained. Oh, William, she said, over and over again. She had to be prompted to move on to the next gift as she lingered over the last. My darling, she said, over and over again. It was not as if she could be bought, Becky knew. She felt as if she were reaping her own ransom.

She made William recall and describe the circumstances of each purchase, where and when and why, all those bitter times revisited, but during a moment so sweet William could only remember the shop owners' marmalade cats curled beside the tile stoves and the inevitable tiny glasses of strong spirits that tasted like varnish and plums, and the groaning unlockings of safes no bigger than breadboxes which were promised to hold a prize as rare as the buyer whom they had known all along would someday walk through the door to seek and to inquire.

When she had opened the last of the gifts, when the basket from the apse was emptied at last, Becky sat back against her pillows, William's glasses propped on her nose as she leafed through her copy of *Harmonium* (first, signed) that William had found in London. She wore new ruby earrings, a ruby pendant, and a bracelet of cabochon rubies that slid up and down her wrist as she turned a page. She had draped a silk Hermés scarf around her neck and slid on a pair of soft Gucci slippers that fit like gloves. The thimble rested on her right forefinger and she tapped the back cover of her book, making some kind of metrical sense to herself. She frowned as she read. A previous reader had not known what the word *descant* meant and had penciled a definition in the margin, although further on Becky was to be not ungrateful for a note on the word *arointing.*

William gathered up the discarded ribbons and wrapping paper and stacked empty boxes. He lay down beside Becky on the spot he had cleared, catching the Faberge egg as it came near to tumbling off the edge of the bed. He picked up and put down the page culled from a miniature Book of Hours and set in an ivory frame, the colors still vibrant indigo and rose and gold, after centuries and then a further elapsing decade hidden from view in a sealed-shut box. William found himself wondering why the brilliant hues had not grown dimmer in the dark. It seemed to run against the nature of things for the blackness not to have bled into the bright colors, just as blackness had once poured into his soul.

He realized then he could categorize the gifts by era. He had gone through phases in his selection of them. There had been the earliest jewelry years when he had had conventional ideas of what to give a woman. He had decided to adorn Becky with rubies, bloodred, warm, and alive against her flesh. But after a happy discovery at the shop of a dealer in antiquities southwest of Paris—George Sand's opera glasses made of brass and ebony and with their pedigree attested to in a letter from a servant at Nohant who had been lent them (well, she stole them) to get a good look at Louis Napoleon passing through town on his way to Orlean—William had sought out further relics of remarkable women. He had, in turn, found the thimble, and Mme. de Staël's silver-and-crystal inkstand and pen, and a deck of playing cards once owned by Georgina, Duchess of Devonshire, imprinted with her noble husband's crest. He had purchased Jenny Lind's vinaigrette, although with more hope than certainty; the engraved initials *JL* might have been someone else's, he told Becky, who, just for a moment, had gone rather quiet and set the vinaigrette aside.

Then, as her children got older and Becky was distracted by their demands, her letters to William had become less frequent. As missives too eagerly anticipated, they could only disappoint him with descriptions of football games and science projects, and by her failure to respond to his own concerns, written of at length in his last, long-

unanswered letter to her. During that period, William had known himself to be tested and his devotion had not wavered. He had not loved
her less, even as he sat and reviewed every grievance he held against
her. Her power to hurt him had been immense, her least word was like
the first thoughtlessly kicked pebble that launched a landslide, and he
had resolved, then, to love her even more. Forgiveness, understanding,
tolerance, which were not qualities that leaped to mind as he reviewed
his own character, had had to be drafted into service, and, by their awk-
wardness and unwieldiness, these big concepts consolidated into a kind
of bulwark against successive onslaughts of Becky's successively let-
loose remarks. The gifts of this era had reflected William's efforts to
express his fortified feelings. He had embraced the practice of conventional high consumerism; images in magazines and anecdotal evidence
(he listened to lovely women enthuse at receptions) convinced him
love could be quantifiable in this arena. He had bought the Hermés
scarf, which he wrapped around a Vuitton clutch that contained a Montblanc pen. He had hidden a watch from Van Cleef and Arpels in the
toe of a Gucci slipper. A chased silver box from Garrads held a gold-
buckled belt from Chanel coiled within, and the Faberge egg had nested
inside another fine handbag, purchased at Dior. But one afternoon at
Cartier, he had rubbed elbows with a Saudi potentate who was shopping for his wives with such conspicuous excess and lack of warmth
that William had begun to feel a shade arriviste and he had, at once,
forsworn logos and brandings and throwing the lot on American
Express.

He had dedicated himself, then, to seeking out singular and beautiful objects that would be wrought even more precious by their association with Becky: the illuminated page, the volume of *Harmonium*
containing "Peter Quince at the Clavier" as eyes beheld. He had come
upon an eighteenth-century Spanish fan with ivory battoire sticks and
the leaf painted with an allegory of love, a Swiss orchestral music box
that played eight lilting airs, and a collection of lace lappets, Alençon,
Mechlin, and Brussels, mid to late eighteenth century, which he meant
for Becky to put to use in some Vermeer-like way, adorning herself
with them. By then she had become less obsessed with those children of
hers (wayward, willful) and her own voice came through once again in

her letters, which arrived at more regular intervals in his postbox. She addressed William's stated worries and concerns with the insight and advice he so valued, and she expressed worries and concerns of her own, to which William had responded with sympathy but no mitigating counsel. Indeed, his remarks had tended to be more inciteful than insightful as he considered the questions Becky put to him.

Becky slipped off her reading glasses and set down her book. She picked up her fan, which she snapped open and fluttered beside her face. She worked the fan to charming effect. She seemed to hold knowledge of pleasing motions within her fingertips, or perhaps the fan itself was informing them. William held up his hand to catch a bit of the breeze she was stirring. The thimble flashed on her fingertip and the rubies glowed at her ears and throat and wrist. The drift of gifts spread across the bed prevented them from turning to one another and embracing. They regarded the bounty and they regarded one another helplessly.

Much later that evening, Becky put away her new possessions. She opened and shut the drawers of her bureau, stowing her scarf, her belt, her clutch, George Sand's opera glasses, the lappets of lace, the fan. She had brought so few things with her; she had left so much behind; and she thought, It is starting all over again, as she made room among her nightgowns and stockings. She placed her new jewels and new watch inside the silver box and dropped in the thimble as well and set it atop the bureau, beside the music box, which she propped open to play, its chimed measures mingling with the water music flowing from the dolphin fountain and together sounding, somehow, like a harpsichord. She had placed her inkstand on a corner of William's desk (he was looking for a desk for her; he had shown her a starkly lit Polaroid of a rosewood davenport he thought might suit) but she wasn't sure about the Faberge egg or the framed page from the Book of Hours. William's household arrangements seemed so complete. As far as he was concerned, the only thing missing had been her.

She asked William if he was up for a game of gin rummy with the Duchess's playing cards. She dealt. Between them they remembered the rules. They passed the reading glasses back and forth as they studied their hands—like the Gorgons who had shared a single eye, William said. Oh, we're more like Darby and Joan, Becky said. But they didn't feel like monsters, nor did they see themselves as an old married couple, although the world would allege the first because of what they'd done, and their ages and their settled ways with one another might suggest the other to anyone who did not know or know of them.

"I HAD WANTED TO HAVE A POOL PUT IN, but that proved to be impossible," William was saying. Well, perhaps not impossible, for nothing was impossible if you were able to pay the price, but after running figures one day when he had, at last, pinned down Adil, William had had to draw the line through the blue-painted rectangle on the garage wall.

"All that greenery you brought in is very nice. Cool. Cool to look at, the green," Becky said. At some point in the past weeks, she had stopped saying, Oh look, a tree, every time she saw a tree in Libya. She said, instead, Oh look, a camel.

They were lying on chaises in the atrium as they did most afternoons. They held hands off and on. Sometimes William sought Becky's hand and sometimes Becky sought William's; then one or the other had to let go to brush at a fly or to turn the pages of a book. William was reading. Becky had not found much to divert her on William's shelves but she was not very interested in anything at present except William, and herself, and William and herself.

"You looked like Lawrence of Arabia, standing under that date palm, that's what I thought," she said. She was looking back, from a vantage point beyond those past weeks. She was building their history. She was, she supposed, constructing their creation myth.

"Hmmm?" William glanced up from his book. He loved lifting his eyes from the page to talk to Becky. He was leafing through Wordsworth and her voice had joined the poet's as if *A perfect woman, nobly planned, To warn, to comfort, and command* was speaking to him. "Dear?" he asked.

"I thought you looked like Lawrence of Arabia," Becky said.

"All Western men who spend time in the desert end up looking like him," William said. "They all end up looking like one another's broth-

ers. You'd think we'd all grown up in the same nice suburban bunga-
low, with the same nice suburban mum and dad, that nice Mr. and Mrs.
Ofarabia, whose boys never would stay home."

Evidently, William did not wish to resemble Lawrence of Arabia.
No doubt, he preferred to identify himself with someone who had been
less worked over, cinematically. He had spoken well of Joseph Ritchie,
explorer and scientist and friend of Keats (William said); he had mentioned James Richardson, chronicler and the enemy of slavery. William was making rather a study of the nineteenth-century gentlemen
who had once wandered through this part of the world, too restless,
too purposeful, too inspired to be contained by their own dark northern lands. William sought, Becky understood, a different context for
himself, and to provide a variant reading of his own, not always admirable, life story.

William's eyes drifted back to his Wordsworth. He had often heard
himself declare over the years that he wished he had more time to read
and now that he had all the time in the world he had found he must have
meant what he said. So often in the past he had only feigned a taste, an
attachment, desire. *Love betters what is best,* he read, a statement with
which he might have quarreled in the past.

Becky sat back and watched the teenage boy who was plying a chisel
at the far end of the atrium, chipping away at plaster to reveal aspects of
the human figures forming the engaged columns hidden beneath. The
boy was not proceeding methodically. He had, first, exposed all the female breasts; he seemed to possess an instinct for where they would be
found beneath the smooth, blank plane of the wall. The boy was Ibrahim, the son of Adil's widowed daughter.

"I'm surprised they're letting him do this," Becky said.

"Hmmm?" William looked up from his book. "Dear?" he asked.

"I'm surprised Adil is letting Ibrahim do this work. Don't these people have rules against depictions of the human form? Particularly the
nude human form?" Becky asked.

"He has to earn his keep. Ibrahim and his mother must not become
bigger burdens than they already are. Besides, I think the nudes are
blots on our heavenly copybooks, not his," William said.

Becky sighed. It was sad, Ibrahim's dad killed in Chad.

"Is that wretched Muammar dogging Ibrahim today?" William asked. The child had to be watched lest he be locked in the storeroom and fall asleep inside a sack of rice again. All that rice had had to be thrown out, or, at any rate, been given to Adil to dispose of. Doubtless, the Adibs had boiled the rice and eaten it with lentils.

"Henry has him in the kitchen. I said to keep him out of our way and to let him have those limp chocolate biscuits that got left out of the tin. Muammar is learning to tell time by the kitchen clock. If he can sit still and quiet for ten minutes he gets a biscuit, and if he can sit still for fifteen minutes more he gets another biscuit, and then, after twenty minutes, he gets another one, and so on."

"Even as the intervals lengthen, he only receives one biscuit?" William asked.

"Yes."

"Stupid child."

"Oh, I'm sure Muammar thinks he's training Henry to give him treats on demand."

"My money is on Henry to take the batteries out of the clock," William said.

"I wonder if Ibrahim would like a biscuit. I think there are some wheat digestive ones that weren't left out of the tin," Becky said. "And a glass of orange juice. He must be hot. He's been chipping away since we've been sitting here. Although he doesn't really look too hot."

"These people never do. Why is that? They must have learned over the aeons not to waste energy swiping their brows and fanning their faces. To what end? Everyone is hot here. Demonstrations are unnecessary," William said.

"I don't think they appreciate at all how uncomfortable they really are, and I suppose it would be unkind to enlighten them," Becky said. "There are any numbers of reality here it would be unkind to clue them in on."

"Why rattle their cages?" William agreed.

Becky's true complaint was with the ceaseless scrape and clip of the chisel, and she was not sure she was going to be entirely happy living with the fully exposed line of human figures holding up the rooftop with their heads, their poor heads, with missing noses and gouged eyes and dented temples. They wore tattered draperies and had lopped-off hands and battered breasts and someone had long since gelded all the men, or perhaps gravity or curious children had accomplished that. Ibrahim alternated percussive blows of his chisel with a finicky filing-away when he got down to what he obviously regarded as a good part.

"I think I shall go for a walk," Becky announced, that day.

"A walk?" William asked. Becky had not, thus far, mentioned any wish to walk. She had been content to stay in the villa after a brief tour of the immediate grounds when she had, in a dazed and delighted way, acknowledged the cistern and the power plant; water, electricity, how clever of William to think of them.

"A walk outside. Is it possible to walk outside around here?" Becky asked.

She swung her legs over the side of the chaise and reached for her shoes, which she had slipped off (for the cushions of the chaises were immaculately white, although one had always to be turned right side down after Muammar, in the early days before he had been banished to the kitchen quarters, had spilled grape juice). She held each shoe by the toe and flicked them sharply away from herself to expel any scorpion that might have scuttled inside. She motioned toward a large bowlful of hibiscus blossoms floating on water (James was very literal; when asked to pick flowers he took the blooms and never the stems). Becky's hope was that any flying scorpion would land in the bowl of water, just as in their bedroom she always aimed for the dolphin fountain. She rather thought scorpions would float, with their light and buoyant exoskeletons, but, presumably, a scorpion would need time to collect itself after being so abruptly launched from its shoe grotto, finding itself being deluged in the dolphin-fountain basin or bumping into hibiscus in the bowl, and Becky would have time to call for William, or Henry or James, or even Adil or Ibrahim, to come and kill the creature beneath the heel of her shoe, which she would offer as a weapon.

But someone, Becky thought, really ought to invent a scorpion screen to fit over the openings of idle shoes. The cover would be not unlike those weighted rounds of cloth that used to sit on the top of milk jugs to keep out the flies. Locals could weave the screens from marsh reeds and sell them to the tourists should the local tourist trade ever take off, should the political climate ever improve.

"We shall need our hats and our water bottles if we're going out," William said, "and I shall take my stick. We'll climb over the dunes and amble a way along the shore."

THERE WAS ALWAYS A BREEZE AT THE VILLA FELIX. Winds blew up from the desert and winds blew in from the sea, one strain of wind heated and the other cooled, and you could tell which breeze was which by its breath. As Becky stepped outside, she clutched her hat and unswirled her skirt from around her legs. She stood, slightly crooked, one hand on her head, the other fumbling at her knees as William harried the air around her with his stick, which seemed to help. Becky straightened and smoothed her skirt and they set off across the yard, discussing the villa's landscaping, of which, it had to be admitted, there was none.

But the grass, what grass there was, sprouted in a meaningful way if you could read the signs, where turf had taken hold against the sand, out of the wind and above a watercourse. This grass was not very green and each blade grew brittle and blade-sharp and looked poised to do battle. The grass concealed within its unclipped tangles more sharp objects: broken glass and shards of plastic. Picnickers came this way. The intercity bus let families out on the main road, who then made their way through the pine forest on foot, crying to one another, as the woods closed in on them, not to become lost forever. They reunited on the edge of the farther field, which they ran across in natural reaction, away from the forest and on toward the sea. The women ran as best they could, encumbered by the baskets and satchels they carried, and unaccustomed to the jolt and bolt of unfettered strides, they stumbled. Waiting by the gateless pillars, the children and the men who got there first chided the women for being so slow.

The picnickers did not pass between the pillars but walked on either side of them. They studied the villa openly, pointing and chattering. Perhaps they knew Westerners lived there. Word had a way of getting round; the intercity bus driver who often stopped to gossip with Adil may have mentioned to the passengers, Americans. The picnickers trespassed, nervous but puffed up, like kids who go out of their way to walk past a haunted house, and they had worn a path through what grass there was. They scrambled over the dunes, breaking down the dunes, William said, which in a more sensible country would have been protected as the natural wonders they were.

"Look at that," he said. A plastic bag trailing its handles, pale and diaphanous as a squid, luffed along the sand as if flurried along before an invisible broom. Henry and James had been instructed to chase down such trash and collect it in their spare time, but they had to be reminded. Littering: they had no idea what that meant and little feeling why anyone should mind. William might as well have asked them to pick up every loose rock in the world and place them one atop the other in a neat tower rising as high in the sky as that star they worshipped.

"But don't you remember how it used to be at home before Lady Bird Johnson started her highway beautification program? Everything used to be tossed right out the car window," Becky said. "And really, when you think about it, until very recently these people must have wrapped their sandwiches and cookies in palm leaves or acacia leaves or something, so we must give them time to come to terms with being a consumer society."

William said he'd like to give them all a swift kick.

"Perhaps a sign," suggested Becky, "bearing a polite request to pick up after themselves."

"They would throw stones at a sign," William said. "They would probably throw stones at the villa."

They were climbing over the dunes. Sand sifted away beneath each footfall. They plotted an oblique, less precipitous route, the wall of the dune rising to their left and falling off into space on their right. Becky decided any misstep would result in a soft landing below, but then one would have to begin the laborious ascent all over again. At the crest, William seized Becky's hand and motioned with that stick of his, recommending the view: the curve of the strand, the glint of the sea, the arch of the sky, the several sizable cloud constructions, although, somehow, these elements didn't really add up to very much. The strand was awash with dross, the sea itself seemed shallow, the sky hung too low overhead, the clouds were tattered at their edges, and Becky had to wonder, in this part of the world, just where the municipal sewers emptied into the bay. She thought, They can't even afford grand scenery in this country.

They made a careful descent, shelving their toes into the sand with every step. They were too dignified to fly, with windmilling arms and wheeling legs, down to the beach. Out here they were too dignified to give themselves up to an ecstasy of abandonment. Becky touched William's shoulder. He turned and he took her hand and kissed it, rather formally.

"Is that James and Henry's trailer? I've heard them speak of their trailer," Becky said. A dull grey turtle mound sat a hundred meters away, perched above the fringe of detritus defining the high-water mark. "How on earth did they ever drag it all the way out here?" she asked.

"With the sheer tenacity of their kind," William could only suppose.

They reflected upon this quality but could not picture its application, in this case.

"Perhaps they borrowed a tractor," Becky said.

"I'd have known about a tractor," William said.

They strolled down toward the water, then veered away. There had been a fish kill; pale, silvery mullet crowded the shore as if urgently seeking an exit from the sea, surging with each roll of the tide. They headed, then, for the caravan, the next point of interest along the beach, which, they saw as they approached, had sunk into the sand up to the tops of its wheels.

"The next question is, how ever will they get it out of here?" Becky wondered. "Perhaps it can be floated."

The Malians had dug a fire pit and lined it with tiles carried over the dunes from the villa; they were some of the blue tiles left over from the installation of the master bathroom shower. An aluminum pot, blackened on its bottom and up its sides, rested on a rubble of burned charcoal within the fire pit. An iron poker, also blackened along half its length, stood upright in the sand, looking useful and available. Two china mugs sat on the metal doorstep of the trailer, their dregs tried by flies. William picked up one of the mugs and sniffed. Henry and James were also buying wine from the old Italian's protégé, or they'd been helping themselves to William's stock of the stuff. Never mind if they pilfered, William thought; he was sure he wasn't paying them enough. He knew they were saving up (behind his back, Adil had warned him) to go home to open a fish restaurant on Lake Korarou and take up life again with their wives and children. William had not yet told Becky the Malians had wives and children to whom they sent money every month.

"But don't they have a nice stove inside the trailer?" Becky wondered. "I mustn't pry," she told herself, but she was a fan of tidy arrangements. Cupping a sun shield on either side of her face with her hands, she rose on her toes and stood nose to window and peered inside.

"It's adorable," she said. "It looks just like a mini Balmoral." The rug and curtains and bedspread and chair covers were woven of several tartans, and the walls and cabinet were dark-paneled wood, although, Becky narrowed her eyes, she wasn't sure the paneling wasn't faux. "Oh, there's a whistling teakettle sitting on a tiny toy Aga," she reported, "and a Chiver's jam jar, and a picture of Anne Hathaway's cottage on the wall, and another picture, torn from a magazine, of a thatched mud hut. Oh dear, that certainly looks out of place."

They wandered back the way they'd come and found the scuffle of footprints they had left on the flank of the dune. They climbed with effort and as they paused for breath at the top Becky stared off toward the horizon. William took her by the shoulders and turned her slightly, adjusting the line of her sight.

"That way is Europe. I always look, too," he said.

Walks along the shore became another part of their routine. Becky would pick up one of the luffing-along plastic bags and stuff it with other errant plastic bags, and William, instead of a walking stick, would carry a rake with which he would groom bits of the beach so they could sit on unrolled rugs and not be too uncomfortable.

ON ANOTHER DAY, BECKY TUGGED, as she had been routinely tugging, at an always unopenable cupboard door set in the thick outer wall of the hall. This time, as Becky exclaimed and the hinges groaned, the latch gave and the door fell open. She ran and fetched Henry and his twig broom from the kitchen quarters and directed him to flurry any lurking scorpions from the dark interior.

"Or big spiders, or snakes," she added, as if Henry's broom wouldn't rout them if she did not specify each creature she wished to have nothing to do with.

Henry had offered to reach his arm inside the cupboard, which ran deep, he said, to feel for the contents; his broom had struck an object. But Becky wanted to claim the thrill of first discovery for herself.

"I *knew* there was something in here," she told Henry. "You know how you get those very specific feelings, sometimes?"

"Yes, Mizzus."

She extracted from the cupboard a glass jar filled with coins, a stub of wooden pencil, and a small bound book. The jar seemed most promising but she ascertained at once that she had not come across another Misratah Horde. So much for her little shudder of anticipation. She had not found a treasure of Roman specie but rather just someone's stash of spare lire too small to be bothered with, from Mussolini's time.

"Here," she said to Henry. "These aren't anything." Which meant he could have them.

She pocketed the pencil, as it wasn't that easy to run out to buy useful little objects like pencils hereabouts, and she set aside the book for further consideration although a quick ruffle through its pages revealed an English/Latin text and small print. She then picked up the shawl that she had come into the hall to collect before she became distracted by all that cupboard business because she and William were setting off on a drive and she never ventured out without a shawl although she chafed at the need to cover herself in public. Some local women did, and some did not, wear the veil and Becky had wondered whether the veiled ones had elected to hide themselves on the days when they felt they weren't looking their best. She hoped this was the case rather than some more benighted reason. Becky's own shawl (William had bought her a very beautiful one of silk threads woven in a pattern of silver and sky-blue stripes) went up and down over her head like a sail being furled or unfurled according to a shift in the wind. When elderly men who looked like fire-breathing prophets, when young men who looked like trouble, stared at her in the street, lighting on her fair hair, her fair skin, Becky fumbled for her shawl and lifted it. Then, the muffling of sounds and reduction of her peripheral vision made her feel even more at risk, and she held on to William's elbow and lowered her covered head and walked on less surely but more rapidly, with that alarmed-creature shuffle she had always pitied in rabbits. She would rather stay at the villa; everything she wanted or needed was at the villa. Indeed, she had welcomed the occasion of a windstorm that had raged off the desert, when she and William had been obliged to retreat to the fastness of their bedroom with a picnic hamper and oil lamps and the atrium plants nodding in their pots as if the very sounds of the ghibli made them tremble. She had known, then, that for hours or for days, no one could reach them, no one could make it through the disintegrating universe to knock upon their door and make demands of them. The wind would snatch the words from their mouths and the dust would fly up to smother anyone who came to stake a claim.

But William liked to drive into the city of Misratah from time to time to try to buy the English papers or the odd American news magazine or even *La Stampa,* and there was always another place he wanted to try for lunch, some authentic café, unspoiled and genuine. Every culture had a cuisine, if only one knew what to look for, William said.

You can recognize these spots by all the policemen's camels parked out front? Becky had asked him, but it seemed William had worked out a point system involving the presence of a Hand of Fatima on the door and a butchered carcass in the window and a robe-clad waiter wearing sandals instead of Nikes, which meant he had just come up from the country bearing dried herbs and fresh spices. And when all else failed, William said, search out the blind muezzin sitting quietly in a corner.

"And what makes blind muezzins particularly good judges of restaurants?" Becky asked as she and William approached the day's destination, Kebir Zalagh, located in a storefront on a tree-lined piazza. The Italians had planted all the umbrella pines. They had made an effort with Misratah the short while they held the city between the world wars and in the midst of other, more parochial wars.

"Outside?" William asked. "Or inside?"

"Outside, please," Becky said. She preferred to be al fresco when given the option at these little cafés. There seemed to be fewer flies outside, and they were not as fat as the ones that had taken up residence within.

They lowered themselves cautiously onto wrought-iron chairs that rippled beneath their legs like waffle irons heated to the point at which one can just bear to touch the surface to test whether the element is functioning. The chairs, sole survivors of some elegant grouping, were pulled up to a plastic cube of table that allowed no space for their knees. William and Becky turned sideways, away from their natural inclination to face and to gaze upon one another.

They took in the life of the square, an old, not unpleasing colonial space, arranged with apartments above—laundry sagged across balconies—and businesses below. There was a travel agency, its windows displaying posters of oasis paradises, paradise presumably visitable in this world and not just the next one; a small-fry grocer selling things in cans stacked in tight, bright pyramids; a shop selling women's clothing—turtleneck tunics, balloon-legged trousers, dresses trussed with ruffles, all dyed a high acid aqua like someone's drugged-dream vision of the color of water in an oasis pool (vide the travel posters). Cars and trucks rattled round the square, thin-skinned old vehicles missing doors and fenders and windscreens, near-skeletal old heaps that were beginning to resemble the skeletal old donkeys they had lately replaced. Drivers reached out their windows and struck the sides of their machines as they had once beat the flanks of their animals. Old habits died hard. Everyone was in a hurry, busy being poor, working diligently to find work or to conjure work, possessing a few fish or a damaged tire to sell by the side of the road. William waved off a man offering a few strands of beads for his inspection. The man glared at Becky as an aggrieved afterthought. Her hands twitched for her shawl lying loose around her shoulders. She reached, instead, for the *Newsweek* they had scared up at the news kiosk where William sometimes had luck finding a few Western periodicals gathered in a heap and weighted down with a fragment of Roman tile.

"Local personages always know the best places to dine," William said.

"Local personages?" asked Becky, as she leafed through *Newsweek*. She was relieved when she read of no quiet tragedy in Prague involving Alden. She was not concerned that Alden would do something rash; rather, she feared some further woe would befall him, as if she had struck him the first in a series of blows.

"Like muezzins," William said. He remembered Becky's conversation and questions better than she herself did. Everything she had ever said to him had been received and considered and, it seemed, filed away within some deep and tender fold of his inner brain. "Back in the FSU, one always knew it was safe to dine wherever First Secretaries dined. One knew the places by the ZILs parked out front," William said.

"You're making that up," said Becky.

"What am I making up?" William asked.

"Everything."

"My dear," William objected. "I assure you, ZILs were the guarantee."

"Darling," Becky said. She did not really want to hear about William's time in the former Soviet Union and she did not understand how he could speak so easily about that time and place.

William sighed, and he began to read a week-old *Telegraph* above the fold and Becky turned the pages of *Newsweek*.

"Barbara Walters is getting a divorce, although I shouldn't have guessed she was married to anyone. How does she find the time? Well, maybe she doesn't, hence the divorce. And we must try to have more oat bran in our diet," she reported. "Which reminds me, where is the waiter?"

"They know we're here. I heard the scurrying and a scuffle out back," William said. "They're working out how to proceed, deciding what to make of us."

"Oh dear, how trying for them," Becky said.

"We'll say we're English should anyone raise the issue," William said.

"All right. You can be Clive, and I'm Fiona."

"Becky . . ."

"No, no, it's Fiona. The Honorable Fiona. My title is hereditary, not earned."

"Darling," William warned.

A young man had emerged, at last, from the storefront restaurant. He wore jeans, a T-shirt, and running shoes, and Becky looked askance at this inauthentic costume as William gave the merest of shrugs—no system was foolproof. The young man feigned astonishment at the presence of customers and he hustled the final few steps to their table. He carried a water pitcher but there were no glasses on the table. He turned and barked abuse at someone hiding behind the scene; fault was being found, or, at least, William and Becky were meant to think that a (quite possibly phantom) busboy had let the side down. Which had been a good sign, as William was to say later. He had forgotten to mention that there were often little dramas acted out at the really genuine places, spilling over from the kitchen quarters like the smell of burning coals and searing meat.

The waiter and William conferred at first in Arabic. William could hold his own in a conversation if everyone spoke slowly and if he already had some general idea of what was about to be discussed.

"Sir?" The waiter slipped into English. His T-shirt was in English (E.T. Phone Home) so they might have guessed.

"The mutton?" William asked, as he'd been attempting to ask all along. "How is it prepared? Cooked? To make the mutton, how?"

"How over the fire. Slow. With the fruits. Fruits? No. Fruits?" The waiter sketched a globe shape in the air. The water pitcher glinted and sloshed.

"With vegetables," Becky suggested.

The waiter agreed. "Yes, the vegetables."

"Tomatoes? Aubergines?" Becky attempted to interpret the globe shape he had made.

"What else do you have?" William asked.

"Mutton. Vegetables," the waiter said.

"And what *else* do you have?" William asked.

"Mutton. Vegetables," the waiter said.

"That sounds lovely," Becky told William. "Besides, I rather think that's all there is."

"Very well," William said. He had been in the mood for fish today. He wondered if he might not buy a string of sardines from a roadside vendor and instruct the chef here in their preparation. He peered across the square. He wondered if they might not all adjourn to the grocery establishment to purchase further ingredients to create a recipe. "We'll have the mutton dish," he said.

"Yes," the waiter said. "Yes, yes."

"Very well, then," William said. He picked up his *Telegraph* and snapped the pages into place. He began to read below the fold.

"Darling," Becky advised him. "I believe there's something else the young man wants."

The waiter stood, holding his ground, resolute yet hesitant, assuming the pose they had come to recognize and to dread here, as he worked up nerve enough and words enough to ask William for something big. Becky bent her head over her *Newsweek,* relieved, on the whole, to be left out of the picture. She supposed there had to be an upside to being a woman in this place.

Reluctantly, William set down his newspaper. He assumed a counterpose of his own, braced and full-chested, which had always worked for him in the past when dealing with the importunate.

"What is it?" he asked.

"I go with you? Home? In America?" the waiter asked.

"Certainly not," said William.

"We can't even go there ourselves," Becky explained.

THEN WILLIAM HAD TO GO AWAY FOR A FEW DAYS to Tripoli on business. He was employed, in an ad hoc way, as a headhunter for the regime, which was in sore need of technical expertise from the outside. William wasn't sure what was being taught in all the whitewashed school buildings that swarmed with students, like termite nests cracked open with a stick, he said. He speculated on the curriculum; diligent readings of the Book and the Green Book and the Big Black Book of Insults by Infidels? The study of the sciences could be problematic in Libya; so many of creation's latest miracles could not be expressed in the Arabic of the Prophet and, lately, the teaching of English had been outlawed.

In Tripoli, William was to lend his hand in landing a Polish specialist on pipeline valves. The regime was engaged in building a tremendous pipeline to carry water from ancient wells deep in the empty southern desert up to the populated, cultivated coast. The Great Man-made River, this project was called in summary boast. A much-reproduced artist's rendering of a cross section of a great vaulted tunnel running below a lush lemon grove showed how it was all going to be someday. The presence of William seated at the head of a conference table with a copy of the artist's rendering by his elbow was believed to lend plausibility to the proceedings, and William was there, as well, to console the Pole when he learned that the fluid to be carried through the pipeline was water, and not oil. Then, William would negotiate a salary, getting twice what had been proposed and half what was desired and, afterward, as Mr. Stanislav just sat there wondering what he'd gotten himself into (the others having adjourned to pray), William would quietly tell him how to avail himself of Krakus hams and sufficient alcohol in an Islamic republic, and advise him which of the less hidebound Gulf states he could most conveniently slip away to for the weekend.

"I'll miss you when you're in Tripoli," Becky said, and she and William smiled at this, at the thought of all they'd be missing.

"Are you sure you won't come?" he asked.

"You'll be busy there," Becky said, "and I'm happy here." She stood by the dolphin fountain, letting the water play over her hand as she realized that this was true.

William was packing his overnight bag. He'd slung it across his half of the bed. He selected a suit from his half of the closet. How he had enjoyed letting Becky choose which halves were to be hers—of the bed, of the closet, of the bathroom cupboard. He threw into his bag several scrolled reports tied round with black and green ribbons, the colors of the State, an old Armand Hammer trick, William said. He'd kept a drawerful of colored ribbons.

"Have I got everything?" he asked. He had never asked a woman this. He had never expected a woman to count his shirts and inventory his shaving kit, but it was part of having everything, now, getting to ask, Have I got everything?

"Socks?" Becky asked.

"My God. Socks," said William. He had lost the habit of thinking of socks.

Adil drove William to the airport with Muammar strapped in the backseat of the car, a candy stick stuck in his mouth to keep him quiet. The other children who had trailed down to the villa on the scent that something was up were left behind, but they ran after the Land Rover as it shot up the dusty track, not shouting to be included. They knew there was no hope of that. Their forlorn chase only served to abase themselves and to gratify Muammar, whose moon face floated in the car window, gazing back.

The children turned as a pack when they spotted their mothers, Emna and Noura, the wives of Adil's sons, who were coming across the field, a basket held by its handles swaying between them. They were delivering the laundry and kitchen provisions, a round of bread and leeks, again. The children danced before their mothers, darting and snatching at the basket as their mothers slapped them away with their free hands. The women wore modern dress, slacks and long blouses, but their aspects and their circumstances seemed as old as time.

Becky, who had stepped outside to wave William on his way (and who had suppressed a panicked cry of Stop, don't go! pulling herself up short), waved now at the women. They headed toward her, viewing Becky's gesture not as a friendly overture but as a command. Becky had, in her dealings with them, tried to be kind and generous and interested. She attempted to convey these intentions by smiling and offering them biscuits from a tin and ascertaining their children's names (but not necessarily who was whose); little Habib, and Habiba, Saida, and Fatima, the girls. But really, matters had not advanced very far. Becky had picked up a few words of approbation, *delicious* bread, *good* sewing, *pretty* children, which she spoke while pointing and nodding in support of her statements. Then, Emna would say, *Please*, and Noura would look pleased.

Becky had been visited just once, early on, by Sana, Adil's wife. That occasion had been as informed with the mysteries of ritual and protocol as an encounter with minor (and rather hardscrabble) royalty. Sana was arrayed in her best, a long dress embroidered with beads and mirrors and bells. (Becky wore Anne Klein.) They had ended up in the bedroom following Sana's smooth glide through the villa, that venue chosen whether from some harem instinct or because Sana wanted to see for herself the mural and the fountain and the bathroom tiles and the rich bedclothes that she must have heard about from her many informants, Becky couldn't say. After one helpless glance from Becky, James had shifted all the careful arrangements—the low table, the comfortable chairs, a bowl of hibiscus blossoms, and several rugs—from the atrium to the bedroom. The daughters-in-law and the widowed daughter, Amel, had accompanied Sana, and there had been another woman with them who was there to translate to and from English and was not there to speak for herself, which Becky had thought was a pity because she was the only woman Becky had met in Libya with whom she might have discussed books and movies and perhaps even personal feelings.

How many children do you have? Sana had wanted to know.

Four, Becky said to the translator. She had left behind four children when she came here.

Four, the translator repeated.

Have you sons? How many sons? Sana had needed to know.

Three. She had three boys scattered across the world.

Three.

The daughter and the daughters-in-law caught their breaths and their dark eyes flickered from Sana to Becky to Sana. The Adib matriarch had only two sons, her Walid and her Naji, to her credit. But Becky had not been aware it was now her turn to ask Sana for a reckoning and her opportunity to pull rank. Instead, Becky had said, I have one daughter as well, for she did not want to leave Julie out of the discussion even though she had been willing enough to leave her in Prague, racing around Prague after boys at all hours.

A daughter. Sana indicated she understood. She sighed and the little bells on her dress chimed in. Amel and Emna and Noura cast their eyes down and thought, We know, but the Mizzus does not, so the advantage remains with us.

The women had assumed, of course, that William was Becky's husband and the proud father of the three boys. Husbands and wives and, God willing, bounteous issue, this was what they knew of human experience. Although, as Becky recalled, their culture had long suffered from a tradition of bride-stealing, which, she had read, supposedly explained why they kept women hidden away, lest a beautiful maiden be spotted from afar across the wide nothingness of the desert and be run down by an enemy-stranger who, leaning low over the neck of his frothing horse, would seize her and carry her off forever to a life of sorrow and disgrace with no joy in her beauty and no happiness in her heart ever again. Indeed, the Adib women might very well believe they understood Becky's circumstances, which they would view by the light of the harsh, heedless sun that had blazed above a millennium or more of such abductions. And they might very well be made angry, or afraid, by Becky's story, for they stood only a generation away from spending lives of complete seclusion and they were, perhaps, as yet, only one wrong step away from a return to the veil. The example of Becky might very well threaten their own fragile arrangements with a more modern era and inspire them, or compel them, to drive her from their midst. Just as well, Becky decided, that she could not chat easily or carelessly with these matrons.

James had served strong coffee and the flaky, honey-laced pastries that had been sent over from the Adibs' in a provisioning basket in anticipation of the visit. A prodigious amount, Becky had thought as James pulled honey-stained paper wrappings from the sweetmeats, patiently picking away where the paper had adhered. But all of the pastries had vanished from the plates and James had been asked to brew more coffee. Becky had urged the translator to eat, to no avail. She hovered, sitting on the edge of the desk chair, rendering remarks from Arabic to English to Arabic, but she had been hired to let honeyed phrases pass between her lips, not honeyed confections.

"That picture," Sana had murmured as she gazed up at the mural. "So large. Who are they, the people?"

"An ancient Roman couple. We like to think they lived here long ago in the villa," Becky said.

"Always outsiders, in this villa," Sana said.

But Becky's guests had felt free, nevertheless, to prowl through the bedroom. Wearing sugary smiles, their best shoes kicked off unaccustomed feet, feeling free to handle strands of Becky's smooth, pale hair to test what it was really composed of, they made themselves at home. They lifted up the bedspread to see what lay beneath upon the bed, and they opened the closet door and the bureau drawers. They regarded themselves in the full-length mirror as they held Becky's dresses up to their chins and her earrings to their ears. They tottered on Becky's highest heels, clinging to one another. They discovered the bathroom. Noura, at the urging of the others, sat in the long, steep-sided bathtub and paddled her hands and flurried her feet as if swimming in the sea. The translator read the labels on all the jars and tubes in the medicine cupboard, *for the teeth, for the eye wrinkles, for the hair washing, for the hair rinsing, for the migraine, for to sleep at night, for aching, for paining.* Sana had swallowed three vitamin E gel capsules because they looked like honeyed and sweet lozenges of some medicine-candy.

The Adib ladies had been reluctant to leave that day. They had required yet another round of strong coffee and James had piled shortbread on a plate at which the visitors only picked (dry stuff, crumbly stuff, sandy stuff) until James was asked to fetch a pot of strawberry jam to spread on top of the biscuits. Becky demonstrated. The women had routed again through the closet and drawers, more deeply delving. There had been no revelations; if they learned anything at all, it was (and they already knew this from washing them) that Becky's clothes and lingerie had been sewn from the finest and softest of fabrics, silks and fine, soft cottons and fine, soft knits, and her cosmetics smelled flower-sweet and sank like magic into their skin, making the roughness vanish as the creams disappeared. Becky had wondered if she was expected to present to them as gifts those items they had most admired, and if they were not going to leave until she had done so. She asked herself what among her things she would be willing to part with. She had asked herself, Why must I always be the one who has to make such a choice?

Then, the women had gone too far. They had rummaged through Becky's winter sweaters, turning them out, setting loose their sleeves, burrowing down to the bottom of the last drawer and seizing upon a picture of the children, before Becky could prevent them: the three sons, and the girl as well, photographed together standing on a slab of stone step in front of a big white house (*the* White House? the women had consulted, not unimpressed but not unconcerned; *spies?*). They seemed handsome children, healthy children. Two of the boys were laughing, the other boy frowning at the laughing ones, the girl's mouth caught open, mid-utterance, objecting to the brotherly arm wrapped around her throat as if she had had to be pinned to the spot on the stone step for the duration of the posing and the adjusting of the lens.

Put that back, Becky said. Please.

Put that back. Please, the translator said.

I am very tired now, Becky said. They must leave.

She is very tired now, the translator said. *You must go home.*

Well, it was known that the Mizzus kept to her bed from one day to the next. The women gathered their shoes and purses and scarves, and filed out of the grand chamber, satisfied to have witnessed the phenomenon (the breakdown, the withdrawal) for themselves. Later, they speculated on the true nature of Becky's malady, but one could not really tell with those people. The Mizzus was so pale, so watery-eyed, so limp-fingered, and her appetite was so slight. Which were the symptoms and which was just Mizzus being the Mizzus? They did not know.

Becky had not paid a return visit to the Adib ranch house. She had not been asked. She may have been meant to propose herself as the Adib women had invited themselves to the villa, which seemed an excellent system, for it lay within her own power to put an end to this round of socializing.

NOW, BECKY REGRETTED HER ACT of waving to Emna and Noura as they approached, surrounded by that swarm of little ones who stuck to them like a cloud of flies above a milk jug. She did not have very much to say to the women beyond the usual Delicious (pointing to the leeks leafing up from the basket) and Good (indicating the mound of neat washing and ironing), and a new phrase she had been working on, What a fine day today is, which had startled Emna and Noura, to receive an entire sentence from Becky and one expressing a notion to which they had never given much thought—for was not one day very like another? The sun rose and shone. The wind blew in from the sea and from the desert. The earth baked. The sun set. The moon ascended. Admittedly, the moon passed through her phases, but even those changes were prescribed. Perhaps, Emna and Noura thought, Mizzus was giving thanks that a storm was not raging, nor (they consulted the sky) did one seem imminent. And, as their father-in-law would have said, *He hurls His thunderbolts at whom He pleases,* which they understood to mean that they must submit to, and indeed glory in, His onslaughts even if to afflict them gladdened Him. Mizzus was pushing her luck talking about the weather, and indeed, she seemed to be taking credit for the mysterious workings of the universe, standing there, so American, motioning toward the sky as if she owned it. The basket swayed between the sisters-in-law and the children hectored and Becky, who had used up all her scraps of conversation and received no response, wondered, What else can I do with such apathetic beings? The women bowed their heads and the children, sensing an even further diminution of spirit in their mothers, racketed more aggressively and were slapped away less energetically. Becky picked up a stick (a length of molding left over from work on the villa and left lying about). She flung the stick as far she could, throwing with an overhand release that caused it to arc and wheel through the air. The children chased the stick like a pack of feral puppies with no retrieval instinct, and Emna and Noura, finding themselves unhindered, headed for the back door of the villa.

Becky let herself in through the front door. The shock of separation from William had left her feeling strangely exhilarated. Her every thought, no longer utterly engaged by him, began to wander from a theretofore fixed point. Her day, falling empty, opened onto possibilities. Her hand, unclasped from another's, itched to do something. Still, she lingered in the hall. She heard the voices of Emna and Noura pitched in lively discourse with James, off in the kitchen. Ibrahim's chisel struck and scraped from the atrium, and Henry's carpet sweeper thumped across the rugs and tiles of the study's floor. The welling and patter of the dolphin fountain sounded cool and as if from far away. The cat, stretched in profile along a high-set hall shelf, lashed its tail, with the steady insistence of a neon arrow, pointing toward the bedroom.

Becky straightened the slight disorder left there by William's leave-taking, closing his top bureau drawer and restoring a rejected tie to its proper place on the rack, which was ordered by color and the width of stripes—Becky understood the scheme of things in William's half of the wardrobe. On her own side, as William had observed, the colors rioted; it was a chaos of beige and shades of blue.

She began to pace, then, as she would never have paced had she not been alone. Pacing was a solitary, slightly shaming pursuit, the act of a caged creature who must always believe that this time on this pass, an iron bar will have worked itself loose and free. If you want to walk, Becky told herself, you can very well go for a walk outside—later, when the sun burned less fiercely and any picnickers would have gone home and no one would stare at her and shrill at their children should they venture too close to the strange Western woman as she paced along the shore.

So, later. She had made plans for later, which was a good start, if a deferred one.

She would not have minded settling down to work on a piece of needlepoint, but she had left her ongoing project (that Mother Hen with her Chicks) at the castle. She'd left behind a stack of CDs as well. Why hadn't she shoveled them into her satchel at the last minute? But she'd been in such a flurry of renunciation; she remembered the lightness of her step as she had walked away from almost everything. She had also believed William would have his own CD collection, a similar yet different assortment from her own, which she had anticipated sampling and critiquing. But William listened exclusively to early church music and chants. She wondered why his tastes ran that way, toward the choir loft and the cloister, to low haunted sounds of praise and petition sung by heaven-bent men.

She decided she would make a list of select CDs to ask Mr. Kafi to search for in Tunis. She could not buy music here; there was nothing but Bob Marley and Oasis in the bazaar. Henry and James loved Tracy Chapman.

They had been disappointed to learn that the Mizzus did not know Tracy Chapman in America, that they had not been friends and neighbors. She sat at William's desk and positioned a sheet of writing paper and sank her pen into Mme. de Staël's inkwell and lifted it. Spherules of ink ran an impetuous dash across the blotter. Evidently, there was a knack to achieving a fine flourish of eighteenth-century scription. Becky dipped less deeply and expelled the excess ink from the nib with a stabbing motion. She had a hash of an initial *K* (for Kiri Te Kanawa), but after that she settled down and wrote twenty legible requests. With any luck, Mr. Kafi would locate at least a few of the recordings after a few days' diligent search round Tunis. He'd already been so obliging, tracking down a source for an oat-bran cereal.

And now that she had gained some expertise with an eighteenth-century writing implement, she supposed the time had come to see whether she could avail herself of the age's felicities of expression as well. She had letters to write, long-put-off letters. She was sitting at a desk with paper and pen at hand and William was not there to ask her what she was doing and to nod understandingly when she told him. She was not sure she would be able to bear any understanding nod of his, because he had no idea what he had demanded of her; if he had, he would never have asked. Yet, despite all she had given up, she was grateful every hour that William had pleaded his case in what seemed now to have been all innocence. He could not guess at the enormity of what she had done, and he must never learn how she had broken her heart even as he so tenderly sifted through the pieces.

She said nothing of this as she wrote to the boys and to Julie and to her brother Hap. She assured them she was safe and being well looked after and that she did not doubt they would all get together in the not-too-distant future. She blamed the intransigence of harsh regimes in Tripoli and in Washington for sundering them all rather than any act of her own, which was not honest but she hoped her family would prefer to blame those obdurate entities rather than herself. She described the Villa Felix (so historic) and the desert (so vast) and the sea (so serene) and she sketched lively little portraits of some of the people, detailing Adil's interference, James and Henry's plaid bolthole, the awful Muammar. She added, Wm. is well, not wishing not to mention him, but in some unlikely way she hoped no one would really notice that she had.

When she finished all her letters, Becky asked Henry to mail them from the big post office in Misratah, a clattering place where a multitude of functions were performed and where it had seemed to her that messages were indeed getting through. He could catch the intercity bus out on the main road. She gave him money for the fare, for the postage, for his dinner, for his trouble, she told him as she dealt out flimsy dinars. Henry stashed the bills into a purse which he tucked inside his robe, and he secured the small packet of letters within a fold of his sash. He seemed to understand how important they were. He flung a blanket over his shoulder before setting off, which marked him like a badge of office.

Then, although she had changed into her walking shoes and put on her wide-brimmed hat, Becky could not face the prospect of a breathless clamber over the dunes and a solitary walk along the littered strand, making her way through the picnickers' leavings: the plastic bottles that would bob out to sea and imperil the fishes, the plastic bags that the plovers would swallow and die from. She forgot why going for a walk had seemed such a good idea, and she saw no value in holding herself to an earlier promise to do so.

She passed into the atrium and sent Ibrahim home for the day, for she had grown weary of the scraping of his chisel. She gave him money in an amount that must have been more than he was owed, for he quickly pocketed the several bills she had handed him and hied off before the Mizzus could realize her mistake. The back door of the villa was still flapping in his wake as she entered the kitchen to tell James he might as well take the rest of the afternoon off; she would just want canned soup and toast for her supper, which she would prepare for herself if he would show her how to light the stove and adjust the toaster. She was also mystified by the can opener and was only slightly less puzzled after James explained its workings, so she was not confident of the soup and also realized she was quite intimidated by the toaster, which required one to reach between the glowing elements to retrieve the slice of bread; the mechanism did not now pop up, if it ever had. Nevertheless, Becky was sure she would get by, if only with biscuits from a tin and wine from the jug. All she really wanted was to be left truly alone for a spell to see, as she told herself, how she was going to be, to gauge what she had become, to test a vision of herself which was not the one refracted through William's adoring eyes, nor colored by James's and Henry's approaches to her as the lady of the villa, nor distorted by the

Adibs' sidelong glances, as if they did not quite dare look fully upon her alien face. Medusa's severed head had been buried in the sand roundabout here, Becky recalled, and the locals might yet be uneasy; old, old stories had a way of lingering on in the very air of a place.

She wandered back toward the bedroom, aware that she was now overly conscious of herself as the lady of the villa trailing through the villa's sequence of rooms in search of something to confirm her status as chatelaine. She would have been content to spot a dusty tabletop across which she might draw a pale finger in a long exclamation of reproach, but the boys saw to everything.

Yes, she and William had lately fallen into the habit of thinking and sometimes speaking of Henry and James as "the boys." Very colonial, very old Savannah, very Happy Valley of them, as William said, and he complained that he and Becky had become helplessly stereotyped: masters and servants, whites and blacks; one would have thought one had escaped from the old models. Their attitudes surely had been shaped by the late twentieth century's better understanding of everyone and everything under the sun, but perhaps they had not counted on finding themselves under such a sun as this one. The Malians didn't help their own case, if they even realized they had one to make. Lately James had been so very pleased to be given a canvas bib apron appliquéd with yellow oranges. He had never possessed such a garment, which featured, as well, a kangaroo pocket. Henry had been hinting with sighs and glances that he wanted an apron too, to wear when he undertook to sweep.

She and William had picked up the apron in Misratah in the souk. Becky doubted she could find the stall again, which had been near the street of the silversmiths. She recalled the tap-tap-tapping of the artisans' hammers. She had not known at first what the sound was. A host of insects, she had thought, who were beating their wings as a storm warning or rubbing their legs as a mating ritual. That's what had distracted her as she stood in the thick of the marketplace by the stall that sold bright flimsy dresses and shirts and aprons from Sri Lanka. Her fingers had fumbled for the hem of her scarf, at the ready to throw it over her head when the cloud of tap-tap-tapping insects swarmed, and she had, as well, selected a low, dark doorway set into a thick stone wall to shelter behind. She had kept very close to William so she would not lose him when everyone started to run. Her fingers had fumbled for the hem of his jacket as she kept an eye on the rabbit hole in the wall.

Perhaps she was wrong to cast herself as the grand lady of the villa. More and more these days, Becky was remembering her childhood. How incomplete her information had been then, as well, what gaps there had been in her knowledge of the world before a chain of references had yet to be forged. Which was why a shadow on a midnight wall could only have been a snake-headed monster and not the swaying branches of the tree just outside her old bedroom window at home, her companion in the daylight hours, that accommodating tree that held her in its abundance of arms, some rough and strong, some tender and yielding, as her mother called and called her in for lunch. Why had she always balked at being called for lunch? She had never wanted to drink her milk that grew thicker and chalkier the longer it sat in the glass. Nor had she wanted to sit across the kitchen table from her little brother, who had kicked, although not on purpose and never to hurt her; nevertheless, he did. His feet had shot out from under him as if he had been seized at the heels by the blue demons who lived under the radiator beside the kitchen sink.

But there are no blue demons in this house, her skeptic mother had told her. She had said she could not begin to understand how any daughter of hers chose to imagine that there were such creatures, and it must have been then, there, at the long ago lunchtime table, the hated glass of milk pushed to arm's length, her legs laced out of Hap's way around the struts of a straight-backed chair, that Becky had first pondered the notion of choice. She wondered why what one person could so coolly regard as a matter of volition must be, for someone else, an inescapable certainty. Becky had stood by the blue demons even as she shrank from them. She had been loyal to them and, always, angry about the milk. She detailed her demons' habits; they fell asleep curled inside teacups, their tails wrapped around the cups' handles to keep them from being swept away by the commotion of their dreams, their red rubber boots and their pitchforks stowed below in the curve of the saucer. She had, as well, locked herself into rituals of propitiation. She set out their teacups every night and hopped on one foot, chanting

Elub, Elub, Elub when any careless person spoke the evoking word, Blue. Had her mother read a few more books on child psychology instead of British crime fiction set in vicarages or among the smart set, had Mrs. Carlisle said, Drink your milk or the blue demons really will get you, Becky would have disavowed them at once and she would never have learned to become so skilled at making what she knew not to be real, real.

Becky supposed all mothers must fail their children. How could damage not be done within the confines of such an intimate arrangement? You pushed when you ought to have pulled, spoke when you ought to have remained silent, asserted yourself just at the moment when selflessness was required, and there was always a small elbow, a small ear, a small person in the way who would remember forever the occasion of these lapses.

And so Becky wondered whether her own children would not be better off without her now. She would not be there to say the wrong thing when they chose their careers or their spouses or their first houses. There would be no disagreements over wedding plans and babies' names or career volte-faces; no second guessing, no knowing better, no voice of experience interrupting happy speculations. For, as Becky had also learned lately, experience was not a teacher but a deceiver; nothing was or ever had been what she thought or meant or wished for it to be. That chain of references so assiduously forged link by link had not led in a straight shining line from ignorance to enlightenment. Rather, the chain had coiled back and around itself to hobble and to fetter her, and she had mistaken her acceptance of her life's limitations for the getting of wisdom. Next time, when she again wrote to the boys and Julie, she would tell them all this, how she would be a far better mother over distance and over time.

"Oh, don't look at me like that," Becky addressed the woman in the fresco.

Turning her back to the wall, Becky moved to the desk to clear the slight clutter she had left behind on the ink-spattered blotter; Mme. de Staël's scratchy pen, some crumpled sheets of writing paper, and her copy of *Harmonium*, from which she had copied some lines in an attempt to explain to the children, *If sex were all, then every trembling hand / Could make us squeak, like dolls, the wished-for words,* before she changed her mind, for of course you could not speak of such things to your children. She wondered to whom she might write freely and without self-censor. She had never really developed friendships outside of marriage and motherhood and William. Eleanor Della, the good friend of her youth, had died young. There was no one older and wiser to whom she could turn. Before this, she had neither needed nor missed the presence of such a person.

She stowed the pen and inkwell in a drawer of the desk and tossed the crumpled pages into the wastebasket and she stood before the bookcase slotting *Harmonium* back into its space on the shelf and she noticed then (for she had quite forgotten it) the slim little volume that she had pulled from the cupboard that day the firmly shut door had swung open.

Eight

Et Nos Cedamus Amori

BECKY WENT TO BED EARLY THAT NIGHT accompanied by the little book that had lain so long in the dark cupboard. Written on the flyleaf of the small board-and-buckram-bound volume was this inscription: *To Arturo and Florianna Antucci, An account of an earlier life lived at the Villa Felix, With the compliments of C.D.W. Wilson (translator), M.A., Oxon., June 1931.*

The hand that had written the inscription was precise. The shoulders of the *M*s were firm, the *L*s were loopless, the *O*s were squared, and the *E*s were Greek. It was the lucid hand of an old scholar or the self-conscious hand of a young one, one or the other of whom had, at the end or at the beginning of an academic vocation, undertaken a small work of translation from the Latin to the English. Presumably the inscribees, Arturo and Florianna, spoke and read only their native Italian, but perhaps they had had a go at the original text, which was printed on the left-hand page to attest to the integrity of the *rifacimento* unfolding on the right. A study of the tongue of their ancestors might well have diverted the Antuccis, taking their minds off the hard work of farming in a land even less forgiving than the one they had left behind. But then, as other matters crowded, the book had been placed in the cupboard for safekeeping, where it had been kept very safe indeed during the ensuing sixty years of revolt and war and revolution and reclamation and abandonment that overtook the villa.

Becky settled back among her pillows and turned to C.D.W. Wilson's Foreword to the Reader. The dolphin fountain splashed. The cat, whose place upon the bed pillows she had usurped, prowled the corners of the room. The electric lights flickered off, but she had an oil lamp standing by that she had lit some minutes earlier in anticipation of the generator shutting down. She adjusted the flame and she began to read.

SOMETIME IN THE MIDDLE OF THE FIRST CENTURY, *a highborn Roman matron named Polla Lucilla quit the home and hearth of her married life. She next took up residence in Oppidum Novum, a town on the coast of the African province of Syrtica located some fifty kilometres to the east of Leptis Magna. The exact date of this disencampment is not certain. Even after the closest consideration of her letters, one cannot fix the year by the light of greater events taking place within the Empire (although a "girlhood" memory of the Great Fire of* AD *64 steers us towards the eighth decade of the Christian era). This is a private account and not a public one; identifying occurrences, even if noticed by our letter writer, have not been noted. Polla Lucilla had more pressing personal concerns to express in what follows, an epistolary account of a tumultuous period in her own history when she divorced one husband and married another, forsaking her home and her family and her position in the world.*

Although divorce and remarriage had become commonplace practise in Polla Lucilla's time, the extreme prudery of the Republic having fallen hard before the, no doubt, reactive liberty and licence of the Empire, the new standards were much disapproved of and regretted amongst conservative families such as the Lucillus clan. But perhaps Polla Lucilla dreaded less the disapprobation of her tradition-bound relations than she did the collective glee of the new elements within the society at witnessing the fall of such a proud matron. Well she knew, Fama volat.

Furthermore, the Patria Potestas *was no longer in sway. Any woman in possession of her own money and her own property could now act as an independent entity availing herself of all the freedom of movement and opportunities to be found in the world at large during the Pax Romana. A woman such as Polla Lucilla had the means to make her own way. Indeed, it was to Polla herself that the villa and dependencies and olive groves and the wharf at Oppidum Novum belonged, and, as we shall see, she developed an active interest in the management of her African estate.*

Polla's letters "home" are addressed to a "Sister" whose name we never learn nor do we know her circumstances although we can, with some diffidence, attempt to imagine them. That the sisters had been close confidantes is made apparent by the frankness of Polla's expression and the fondness of her recollections of their shared "girlhood." Yet the letters stand not as a part of a dialogue between the pair. Ideas are not exchanged. Initially, questions are asked but, by all evidence, were never answered, and presently, the questions cease. Nevertheless, there is no discernible break in the "narrative" of Polla Lucilla's African experience. The letters as they have come down to us have been ordered and numbered in a contemporary first-century script, and as such they were discovered by myself when in pursuit of a different document among the archives of S. Pudentiana, the most ancient of all the Christian edifices of Rome which occupies the site of the house of Senator Pudens in which St. Peter lodged from AD *41 to 50 and from whence he led many thousands of souls to their salvation.*

One would be indulging in mere speculation to suggest that the letters were intercepted by a parent or a husband before Polla Lucilla's "Sister" was ever able to read them. Perhaps a trusted (and yet not to be trusted) household slave was bribed to steal the letters and thus guard her mistress from an association the Lucillus clan had prohibited. One might further speculate and account for the letters' numerical ordering and their surviving completeness as being the result of their value as evidence in some legal action contemplated against Polla Lucilla by interests within the clan. The Romans were famously litigious; there was as much blood sport to be had at court as at the Circus Maximus. At any rate, one may sense a tragedy here. The writing of the letters must have turned into an act of faith for Polla Lucilla as the silence between herself and the sister whom she loved only deepened. It is we who hear her now, one small voice calling to us across the centuries, and we are reminded, For a thousand years in Thy sight are but as yesterday when it is past, and as a watch in the night.

LETTER I

To My Sister, Dear Sister,

The lamp oil here is so very cheap that we have illumination in the night. Imagine, I am writing to you now at an hour which in Rome we spent in sleep and visited only in our dreaming lives. Yet I write to you tonight as if in a dream, as I must ask myself, Have I lived these last months or have I dreamt them? We accomplish such strange and wonderful deeds in our dreams and see such strange and wonderful sights, even I with my short sight. But so too in my waking life am I experiencing wonders here. The moon which wanders the night sky of Africa is larger and rougher and redder and nearer to the earth. I do not think it is the same moon that rises above Rome. It is not the pale, distant moon of Diana. I believe it must be the realm of some other, harsher goddess native to this place.

Forgive me. I dared not bid you farewell. It was better for you not to know what I planned to do. For then, when they questioned you, you could say in truth you knew nothing. You could never lie, Sister; therefore, I could not tell you the truth. But I tried, on my last visit to you, to indicate in ways which you would later recall as having had meaning, that soon I was no longer to be with you. Remember, I bid you to remember our girlhood. I asked you to remember those secrets we shared then, those things we alone can remember and now each must recall alone, you in Rome and I in Africa, remembering our house in Tibur and the coolness of the hills and the springs in the summer. Remember how we hid Judith's shuttle within the onyx vase and Grandmother chastised her because no cloth had been woven that day. Remember, too, how we complained to Mother that our lessons were harder, that we had to know more emperors and battles and provinces and poems than she had had to, and remember, Mother told us, That is so, and you also have fewer further tomorrows allotted to you. Time is running faster, time is running out, she told us. You girls were born at the wrong time. Was there ever such a Mother as ours?

We shared all our secrets and we kept no secrets from one another. You always knew how matters stood between Junius and me. The bay leaves were not brown above the lintels before I realized I should not have run into his arms but run from them. I felt in that house on the Aventine like Prosperine in Hell. I felt like Proserpine seized from the grove on that summer's day, the violets she had plucked from the spring's edge flung to the ground for her companions to find as she was snatched away to a place where there was no light, no joy, no life. Junius was so old and I so young, yet age did not draw sap from youth nor did youth ever learn the lessons which age in its wisdom can impart. Love did not grow cold; love never caught fire. I longed as Prosperine did only to return to her Mother, but our Mother did not grieve for me as the Goddess Ceres grieved for her daughter. Our Mother told me we are not like the Gods, and she chastised me for believing we might think and feel and act as they do. We are but Mortals, she reminded me. Why then, Mother, if I am Mortal, must I dwell in the House of the Dead, I asked her, but she gave me no answer.

Secundus came to the banquet in the company of his uncle, Marcus Sullus, the senator and hero of the German campaign. Secundus was on a visit from Syracuse. He had come to Rome on business. The Sulli have vineyards and they manufacture musical instruments, lutes and cytharas, they make them. Syracuse is the most beautiful city in the world, Cicero said, and Secundus said as well. Most beautiful, he said again as he looked at me.

What? asked Junius, cupping his ear. What did you say, boy?

So very beautiful, Secundus said, as he took my arm, for Junius had stumbled and fallen against me.

We were to dine that day upon a dove who had died in her cage. Junius thought this a great joke and all of his cronies and clients laughed with him but Secundus did not, nor did I. We shared another glance, one which was sad amidst the laughter. Then, as always, Junius's guests began to speak of commerce and politics and of their day in court and of the strategies they had employed in their old Wars. At that house on the Aventine, we were never to have civilised discussions as they do in the most cultured of homes. But that day Secundus lifted his strong voice above the chatter of the others and he posed a question, one which lately had been raised by the poet Martial in the company of Parthenius, the Emperor's freedman.

Secundus asked, Why does lost love when enacted on the stage give us enjoyment, but does not do so in real life?

Junius's stupid guests paused for a moment but having no thoughts they returned to their own matters. Only Secundus and I had something to say on the subject of lost love.

I said, There is great virtue to be found in suffering and we admire seeing examples of virtue being acted out for our enlightenment.

Secundus said, But we do not enjoy virtue.

I agreed, No, no, we do not enjoy virtue. We do not enjoy virtue at all.

I said, Perhaps we enjoy learning from the mistakes in love that others have made so we ourselves can endeavour to avoid them.

Secundus said, No, no person is ever wise when it comes to love. We have the example of a thousand tales of love and no person has ever learnt from a single one of them.

I agreed, We do not profit from the mistakes of others. We only learn from the mistakes we ourselves have made, and then it is too late.

Secundus said, But it is never too late. There is always another scene to be written, another act to perform, another play to mount. That is why we enjoy tales of lost love in the theatre. We know that after the play is over, the actors will kiss and revel and drink wine and be heaped with praise for their success. The actor who is slain today as Actaeon will rise again tomorrow as Leander. We know this even as we weep for Actaeon, that we will cheer Leander on another day.

I said, I enjoy anything that is not real life. I enjoy the most terrible tragedy, the cruellest story, the most pitiful story enacted on the stage because for a while it makes me forget.

Sister, I did not say what I wished to forget. I did not have to tell him.

Junius had fallen asleep on his couch. The wine glass was overturned in his senseless hand, bleeding red liquid, drop by drop, slowly now, as if some hours since he had scored his wrist with a blade.

Secundus said, Come with me to the theatre to-morrow.

And so it began. I met Secundus at the theatre and at the circus and at the baths and in the houses of friends where we listened to singers and to players. Secundus knows so much about music. He plays the cythara he brought from Syracuse, a pearl-encrusted instrument of his own manufacture from which he draws the sweetest of sounds. And he sang to me, Sister, as Orpheus sang when he entered the realm of the Dead to reclaim his Beloved.

Secundus said, We must not look back. We must only look forward together to to-morrow.

But where shall we go? Secundus wondered, then.

I said, We shall go to Syracuse the beautiful. I long to see the harbour and the temple.

Secundus said, Syracuse is not far enough away from Rome. They will find us.

I said, I have a farm in Africa. We shall go there.

September the first was the day we set to run away, the day when all of Rome is on the move and the streets pulse with the bundles and household goods and carts of those moving from one abode to the other. Our own activities would be swallowed up among them like an egg downed by a snake. I bundled together my jewels and my robes and blouses, my image of the Goddess carved in ivory, and my special amulet whose message *Isis Victrix* will charm away all evils that shall seek us on our way. I took the mirror in which I appear most pleasing and thin, my twenty silver cups and plates and spoons, and Miriam, whom I know I can trust with my life—with the life that has been returned to me. But remember well, Sister, I bid you not to trust your Rachel. Do not let her see this letter I have written to you.

I loved the voyage across the pathless sea. She sighed and swayed beneath us like a loving Mother. The mariners read the stars. They set their course by the glimmering heavens. Secundus and I sat upon the deck beneath a tent of fine cloth. Secundus played his cythara, which was the cause of the calm sea that the music charmed, the mariners said. On the second day of the voyage, a boy pulled a great mullet from the sea. It died, gasping, on the deck and its colour changed from red to blue before our eyes. The Captain said, This is an omen of great changes ahead for all of us.

LETTER II

To My Sister, Dear Sister,

Are you well? I have not heard from you. I entrusted my last letter to the master of a corn barge setting off from Oea. He was on his way to Rome and I told him where to find you. Did he find you? Are you well, Sister? Is the family angry with me? How very angry are they? Do not let them be angry with you. I should feel so sad to know that you are in trouble when now I am so happy.

I think back often, Sister, to our young days when we walked from our house in Tibur through the chestnut grove and down the hill to the beginning of the road to Rome. The road to Rome was made glorious by the fact of its being the way to Rome. Do you remember—every house, every shrine, every tree, every stone was touched as if with glory by the association? We wished never to live in any other place, neither in Rome nor some place within Rome's orbit.

How do I find myself here, then, in Oppidum Novum? How did my feet carry me so far? But it was not my feet that so willed this. It was my heart that flew from my body which I had to chase, to run after, to sail after, in order to retrieve my heart so I could go on living. This is a small place. One road goes one way, the other road the other way. There is only one of each thing here   one bath, one workshop owned by a freedman of coarse appearance making marble statues in that strange coloured stone they have here. There is only one archway celebrating the Triumphs of the God Augustus. The amphitheatre is very small and built into the side of a hill so that to enter it is like falling down a hole. Yet Oppidum Novum seems more like Rome than Rome to me. The old virtues are in practise. The good people of Oppidum Novum are very good. The men are strong. The matrons are modest. The children play quiet games of soldiers and of mothers nursing their golden-haired dolls. The Latin they speak is very correct although I miss the sound and subtleties of Greek.

I did not know what to expect of my property here. I remember

Grandmother's stories of her visit to her African estate. How I loved those stories. When I arrived, I first looked for the mosaic floor showing Semele binding the wounds of Cupid, which was an allegory, remember, Grandmother told us, and you said, But I thought it was a floor, which is why I think Grandmother left the estate to me, because I understood what she was telling us. But my sleeping chamber here is scarcely fit for a moth.

We live two miles (*trans. note—mille passuum, a Roman mile*) from the town. To travel to the villa we passed through the olive plantation. They are more grey in colour here, and more gnarled. We are next to the sea and the sea winds twist the branches like the painful limbs of an old, old man. There is a wharf which is mine, jutting out to meet the sea. A lighthouse sits high upon a rock and at night the harbour is as bright as the day. The birds hover and wheel in its vicinity all the night long, crying and calling to one another.

Curius Quintus, my foreman, did not know of our imminent arrival. He was living in the villa like the Master. Secundus routed him and in the past weeks we have learnt many things about him which do not please me. He has not been honest and he has indulged the slaves, who are fat and lazy. He has been conducting a secret business, as well, in the animal-export trade, sending them from my wharf to Rome and to all points of the Empire for service in the circuses—lions, bears, ostrich, apes, every creature that walks the earth here. Although we cannot accommodate elephants. They sail from Oea on larger vessels than can sail into our harbour. I do not like these animals. They roar and they wail and they stink and they die in their cages. But their skins are valuable too. We have a Moor here who is very skilful with his knife and can achieve an entire pelt in one piece, emptied of the flesh and blood and bones of the creature. We fetch good prices for our peltry.

Secundus is now in charge of the estate and the olive press and the animals. How brief was our idyll, Sister, those days when I alone existed for him and he for me. But Secundus is securing our fortune. He says we are as orphans and must make our own way now, the two of us alone.

But you should see Africa. How I pray that someday, when the heat of anger has cooled, you will be allowed to visit me. Come for a year,

Sister. We shall have such fun. I walk every day through the groves and into the town. My feet will become broad and splayed like a peasant's, and I must not let myself turn brown like the people here. I shop in the market. Such wonders are there which we never knew in Rome. Miriam follows me with a basket, which I fill with fruits and figures carved from ebony and perfumes I have never known before. They are so strong and sweet. But as we enter the town, Miriam will never walk beneath the Arch commemorating the God Augustus. She says her God will not allow her to do so. She says he rules alone with no other Gods beside him. I tell Miriam that he must not be a very powerful God because look at the fate he has allowed to befall her and her people. And one day a week, Miriam's God will not permit her to work or to cook or to serve me no matter how I chastise her. I asked her, What if we all obeyed your God? No work would be done. Nor will Miriam travel on the day of the new moon although in this matter her God is being solicitous of his people, for no traveller wishes to be overtaken by night at her darkest hours.

But I shall pray to any God who is listening that this letter will find you, Sister, and that you are well and happy and do not feel too alone without me.

LETTER III

My Dear Sister,

I do not hear from you, nevertheless as I write to you I feel that you are with me. I hold my stylus and form my words and think of the day you will read this. I want you to see and to hear and to know about all that surrounds me here. It has all been such an adventure.

I am alone today. Secundus has travelled to Leptis Magna to conduct business having to do with our olives. He says I cannot understand the business, how men trade amongst themselves. He tells me my task is to petition the Gods for a bountiful harvest here and a poor one in Baetica or his scheme will come to nothing. How I long to see Leptis Magna for myself but Secundus says he must go there on his own to determine if the place is suitable for me to visit. He must make certain that the inns are not too rough and the people are not too uncouth, although that is not the reputation of the place. But Secundus says he has heard of other aspects of Leptis Magna from which I must be shielded. Indeed, I must cling to the tatters of my honour. I stand very close to the edge of the cliff, for that is where I have situated myself.

The wind blows strong to-day. I cannot go outside wrapped in a cloak for the wind will snatch me and carry me off. I shall fly away like a bird. I can only wander through the villa. I have not told you of the portraits Secundus had painted on the walls of the triclinium. He wished to surprize me. For seven days I was not permitted to enter the room. For seven days the artist, who is a young fellow with no manners but a pretty smile, ran back and forth between the triclinium and the atrium where I sat at my loom to look at me and carry the memory of the look of me back to his masterpiece. My expression was not always pleasant. This African wool is harsh to the touch and it creases my fingers with welts and the cloth I weave is not fine, as we are used to. Thus, I feared my picture would not be pretty. There would be something of the African cloth in it, I feared.

Miriam, who has the gift of invisibility of all her kind, stole glimpses and she said our images appeared like magic, mine and Secundus's. He reclined on his couch posing and advising the young artist to darken his hair and to make his mouth less soft and red. As for me, I do not think my arms are as long as the portrait would have them, nor are my eyes so widely set. They look like those of the leopards who switch back and forth in their cages below the wharf. But all those who have come to the villa to dine say the likeness is true. And they say the painted dolphin fountain beckons them with waters as cool and as sweet as that of the real dolphin fountain spouting and burbling in the apse. One day Secundus advanced to the painted fountain holding out his cup, but he was very drunk.

We have many guests, Sister. Secundus has made many friends here. Although Oppidum is but a provincial town, it sits along the great road which unwinds from Tingi to Carthage to Alexandria. The road is fast and good. Those most sweet-smelling of violets plucked from the hills of Cyrene arrive in Oppidum smelling as sweet as when they were snatched from their springside bowers. The town is much frequented by touring players and athletes and poets who will sing for their supper and we are visited by world travellers who have journeyed far and wide to behold the ancient wonders of creation. Even consumptives come here, sent by sea, to greedily gulp the curative air of Africa before they die.

Yesterday a troupe of Greek rope dancers and conjurers performed for us as we dined on grapes preserved in smoke and a lion who had died in his cage. We were entertaining the retinue of Decius Mundus, a knight of princely means from Thrace who has undertaken to visit every corner of the Empire. He has lately come from Memphis, where there can be seen a lock of the hair Isis tore out in agony after the death of Osiris. Decius Mundus said she had fair hair, as I knew she must. And, Decius Mundus said, in Thebes he saw the fallen colossi of Amenophis the King. At sunrise, the fallen colossi will sound a note like that of a broken lyre string. Decius Mundus and his retinue commemorated their witnessing of this marvel by cutting their names into the statue's legs. It is the custom there.

I spoke to Demaratus, a Greek and a philosopher whose salary Decius Mundus pays. As Decius and Secundus discussed the next day's races, Demaratus and I discussed this topic between us—Is the setting sun extinguished every night and is a new sun rekindled every morning? Demaratus said, Yes, the sun is extinguished, and I believe this must be so. How I long to travel to the place where that occurs, to see with my own dim eyes such a sight. Perhaps my sight will become less dim after the experience. I long to travel, Sister, or shall I say, I long to travel further, for have I not already travelled a very long way to get here? But even Miriam has witnessed more wonders than I. She has been to the place in Joppa where Perseus found his Andromeda and released her from her chains. To this day, evidence of the shackles is to be seen in the rock where she was kept. And now Miriam longs to travel to Egypt, for she believes her husband is there, toiling amongst the other men sent to the mines when Jerusalem fell.

But Secundus says we must stay where we are for a while. We must keep quiet and to ourselves lest more scandal whirl around us like the sand and wind. We must even avoid certain visitors from Rome who will carry back false tales of us. To that end, we have been obliged to kill a bear who wore bells and danced, brought to us by traders from Numidea. Too many people came to watch it perform, people of whom we cannot be sure. The Moor skinned the bear and the pelt will fetch a good price by our agent in Rome so the loss will not be as great.

Most of all, I long to see Rome again and to feel the black basalt pavement beneath my feet as I walk with you, Sister, alongside the yellow-running river beneath the green shadows of the laurels and the bays.

LETTER IV

So much time has passed, and so swiftly. How busy we have been here on the estate. The olive harvest was bounteous, more bounteous than those accounted for in years past. We learn more and more of Curius Quintus's duplicity. I have heard he has moved to Sabrata and purchased a tavern there with his ill-gotten gains. May he hang himself.

The press toiled without cease, day and night, extracting the oil. I warned Secundus he overworks the slaves. We must consider them for we have far fewer of them to choose from now that the world is at peace and we cannot acquire men so easily as spoils of war. But Secundus said that is why we have slaves, to toil for us. He said, when the harvest has been gathered and the press has been idled, they too will be idle and it will become work for him to find work for them when all they care to do is eat and sleep and make trouble amongst themselves. The Germans turn pugnacious and the Gauls become very disagreeable when they are idle. Secundus is going to put them all to work building an aedicula on the small hill at the edge of the olive grove. To please me, he says the temple will be dedicated to the Goddess. It will be open on all sides to the cooling breezes and we shall linger there and be refreshed in the evenings as I offer my prayers, which will be received with favour, I believe. The floor will depict the rising of the Nile occasioned by the Goddess's tears, that great flood of tears which takes and gives so much, for her grief nurtures her people. She suffers for them. The work progresses. Secundus has ordered a statue of the Goddess from the freedman who owns the sculpture workshop in Oppidum. An architect has drawn plans. Secundus has ordered the best Luna marble to face the pediment because he knows I do not like the dark stone of Numidea and do not consider its colour to be suitable for the Queen of Heaven, the Lady of Mercy.

I am sitting on the hilltop where the temple will stand. A canopy has been raised against the sun. A table and chair have been carried out. The air is still today but the Nubian wields his fan skillfully. I tell him, Do not ruffle the pages of my letter to my sister in Rome. Some tame gazelle have just approached me. Fetch dates from the house, I tell Miriam as they nuzzle my empty hand. I shall feed them.

The gazelle have wandered up from the wharf. Curius Quintus could not steal the animals or the cages or the warehouse when he absconded. Legally, the business he began is mine. His forgeries in my name will stand if I do not challenge them. My barrister here says the case is a very elegant one and that it pleases him.

But this business is not an elegant one. We must deal with the roughest of types, for such are the men who venture to the wildest ends of creation in search of beasts. These men must live and think and act like beasts as they engage in the pursuit of them. These men seem scarcely human to me. Their beards are thick and tangled and they wear the ragged skins of the very beasts they seek. They have battled the beasts in their lairs, one against one. Their cheeks and brows are scored by scars and they have lost eyes and fingers and hands and arms. A Moor from beyond the mountains has no feet. He never leaves the back of the strong little pony who carries him everywhere. He entered the warehouse on his pony and at first I believed he was a centaur and my heart leapt. How our fortune would be made were we to find such a marvel of nature. We seek the white panther, the giant crocodile, and Secundus has read in ancient books of a race of African men who have the heads of dogs. We should pay a bounty for them, Sister.

At present we have here awaiting a ship a cargo comprised of a lioness and two cubs, a rhinoceros, five giraffes, some hyenas, and nine ostrich. They eat so much. We must keep a pack of boys who chase down hares and kill them with stones hurled from slings or catch them alive in nets for some beasts will only eat live flesh. Other creatures will not eat flesh at all and must be provided with the grain or the grass they require. We have a Greek here who has made a study of the diet of every animal on earth and who oversees the feeding of our inventory. He himself resembles a house cat and eats black bread and snails for that is all he is given.

The hunters linger after we have paid them and tell such tales of their exploits. Their voices are harsh and their language is shameful yet their tales are as exciting as any great story of heroes and battles and magic. They use sorcery. They know many secrets, many charms and beguilements. A lion will lie down before a virgin, they say, and fire will transfix a serpent. As they follow their quarry across the desert and into the forests and on towards the mountains, racing up on their ponies or running by foot more swiftly than hares, they pause to read signs only they can discern of the passage of a buffalo or a bear. The men will crouch. They will crawl with their ears pressed to the Earth and She will tell them what hooves have torn, what clawed extremities have lately shattered her breast. The hunters will seek the impress of the tracks and the broken ground and the scattered stones, and they will pick up those stones and strike at the footprint, so hobbling the beast they seek. The beast will slow and stumble and drag to a stop and then the hunters will strike with their nets and their ropes and their clubs, falling upon the magicked creature and securing it.

There is such a thirst for these animals. We despatch them to every corner of the Empire. They are carried onto the ships, pacing and howling in their cages as if they cannot wait to set sail and to arrive and so to stride into the bright bowl of an amphitheatre to meet their glorious fates. Although you will laugh, Sister, when you read this, because you know I do not really know of what I am writing. My shortsightedness never allowed me to see what was unfolding in the arena for we had to sit so high up and so far away in the stands in the place reserved for women. The figures below appeared to me as no more than impressions of colour and shadow and motion. Do you remember how often I said to you, Tell me what is happening? Tell me what is happening now.

You said, The elephants are carrying torches in a procession. A lion is holding a living dog in its great jaw. The lion is not devouring the dog. He has spat out the dog and the dog has wandered away, addled.

He is squatting and scratching himself, making sure that his haunches have not been eaten. That is why everyone is laughing now, you said.

I asked again, What is happening, Sister, as far below on the field, more impressions of colour and shadow and motion converged. The people began to stir. They exclaimed and they cheered. They shouted and they stood and they swayed and they roared. I tugged at your arm. What is happening, Sister? You turned to me without recognizing me and knocked away my hand. Your face shone alight, transformed by the tears and the blood of what was happening below. I studied you then, Sister, and tried to see in you what had moved and thrilled all the people of Rome present in the stadium, except for me.

Perhaps if I pray to the Goddess with all my heart, perhaps if she is truly pleased with the temple that we shall build her, she will bestow blessings upon my eyes and I will be given the gift of seeing the bird upon the branch and the contest in the arena. Perhaps I shall be able to see so far away that I shall know what the next day, and the next, will bring to me.

LETTER V

Sister, such disaster has befallen me since I last wrote to you, many months having elapsed. My hand trembles as I write and the words tumble and crowd one upon another there is so much to tell. How swiftly Fortune has altered her expression, her face exchanging its smile for the most horrible of grimaces turned against me.

We have had a fire. The warehouse and its contents have consumed themselves. *Etiam periere ruinae.* The ashes smoulder still, and the reek of the smoke returns me to our girlhood and the days after the Great Fire when we were taken to Rome to witness for ourselves what devastation can be wrought when men are heedless and the Gods are forgotten. Only the iron bars of the cages survive, twisted by the heat of the fire so that they rise from the ruins like skeletal remains. The beasts have perished. I heard their dying screams. We have lost, as well, a cargo of thuja wood worth many thousands of sesterces, and a great quantity of oil which had yet to be sent to Rome.

We were awakened by the cries of the watchman. The night turned as bright as day as the fire took command. The slaves ran with buckets filled with water from the well and water from the sea. Secundus directed them until the cause was lost. Then we could only stand and watch as the flames formed a wall no man could penetrate. The roof fell in one piece with a sound as soft as a sigh as it settled. It smothered the flames which then crept up from underneath the roof and grew bolder again as they beheld what destruction they had wrought. They leapt to complete their work. They flew across the yard and ignited the oil-press building. This structure went up like a torch, its wood impregnated by the splash and spill of oil for so many years.

Early in the morning we returned to the villa. My skin was as black as a Moor's with soot. We drank quantities of water and wept for all that had been lost. It was then, weeping and falling to his knees, that Secundus confessed to me that his factory in Syracuse had also burned, not long before he came to Rome. His means are thus strictly reduced. There is no reserve we can draw upon to pay for rebuilding the warehouse and the olive press. Further, Secundus had debts and his debts have grown greater in the past year. His speculations have not paid off and he has accrued gambling debts as well. Two broken-down nags cannot pass him by on the road that he will not wager that one can outpace the other. He will bet upon the landing of a fly, whether within or without the rim of a cup of wine.

But we still have the wharf and the groves, and the huntsmen will provide us with more animals. Parts of the press are salvageable, the stone and the great iron screw. I have told Secundus, All is not lost. It will be difficult but we can rebuild. We have set free half the slaves, those for whom there is no work left. They left us reluctantly. They asked, What shall we do? Where shall we go? We are a long way from home. But such is their lot in life. I have told Secundus he must work harder and the slaves who remain must work harder. I too shall work harder. I have taken over the accounts. I have told Secundus he should regret that his codex was not lost in the fire because of the story it has told me. I had no idea of the extent of his gambling debts.

Secundus is melancholy. His former merriment has abandoned him, that merriment which in the past he has always been able to rediscover in wine. Now, wine makes him ever more dolorous. With each cup swallowed, a new grief occurs to him. No one comes to the villa now. He invites no one, nor do I think anyone would seek to come to such a luckless place. They fear ill fortune will attach itself to them like fleas. Instead, Secundus spends more and more time in Oppidum at the tavern playing dice. I fear that for Secundus I have become yesterday's intoxication and yesterday's game of chance whose winnings have been pocketed and spent.

Do you remember, Sister, how when we were girls we complained to Mother because we had to learn more lessons than ever she had had to? We had to memorize more emperors, more battles, more provinces, more poetry, more songs. How unfair it was to have to know so much, we said. We asked, Can we not just forget some of the more distant dates and people? I thought of you, Sister, and of Mother and the schoolroom today as I sat at my loom. As my hands performed the familiar motions and my mind roved freely, I asked myself, Why am I still obliged to learn too much?

Nevertheless, I have not lost all hope. I have found a new recipe for a cosmetic which will make my face shine brighter than my mirror. It is made of African barley and vetch and eggs mixed with the pounded horn of a stag crushed into a powder to which is added narcissus bulbs and gum and spelt and honey. I have sent Miriam to the marketplace to collect the ingredients. I twisted a silver bracelet from my arm to pay for them. Also, I must remember to speak gently to Secundus and to oversee the preparations of his favorite foods. He has a taste for the simple dishes of childhood. He favors soft porridges and sweets and milky puddings. I bid the slaves to be gentle when they carry him home from the tavern at night. They do not show proper respect and I will not tolerate insolence from slaves.

Oh, Sister, has Secundus bewitched me? Did he magick me away? Has he hobbled my feet to bind me to him here in this place? Why did I love him? Why do I love him still? Must I go on and on and on loving him forever? I have consulted my heart and I am afraid my heart has told me, Yes.

Now, I must tell you this last thing. It is the most curious story I have ever heard. Before the fire, we had with us a troupe of clever apes.

They had been taught to act in a play, just a silly farce in mime, a tale of improbable lovers and the usual misunderstandings with all made right and happy in the end. The apes played their roles remarkably well. The heroine, who wore a fair wig and carried an ivory mirror, was almost affecting. The hero seemed almost handsome, for an ape, as he strutted across the stage. I believed they had all perished in the fire, our hero and our heroine, and the apes who played the old miser and the comic servant and the fortune-teller and the judge, all dead, I feared. But their clever fingers which are so like our own must have worked loose the bolt of their cage and they fled from their infernal fate that night.

For they have been seen since the fire. I have been told they have been spotted down on the strand and out beyond the grove and on the wasteland behind the baths. According to the reports they are seen acting their play over and over again for I suppose it is all they know how to do. The heroine ape wears straw on her head and her precious mirror is but a bit of broken pottery. The hero ape was burned in the fire. He has no fur on his chest and arms now and it is said he sometimes forgets his part and must be supported by the others until he remembers where he is and what he is doing. They wait in motionless postures as if on a frieze. But they scatter when anyone approaches and will not allow themselves to be captured again. Nevertheless I am told they are a marvel to behold from afar.

Finis

WHEN WILLIAM RETURNED from his business in Tripoli, Becky had not at first shown him the book of letters. She had not known why she had hesitated. She had slipped the volume beneath the nightgowns in her dresser drawer. But then, she possessed all the time in the world these days in which to consult her thoughts and discover her reasons. As she lay in bed later and later each morning, as she passed the hours doing the nothing much in particular which, nevertheless, so fully occupied her, she fell into a brooding state which William had not really recognized for what it was. Perhaps he had always envisioned her like this, lingering in bed, so languidly reaching for a fallen pillow, effectlessly delving with a blind-seeking hand, trailing the silky sleeve of the dressing gown she had taken to wearing for most of the day. (Let me, said William, bending and restoring the pillow.) Nor had Becky sighed at him and then denied she had sighed as she sighed some more. Nor had she gone so far as to weep, which would have stricken William to his very soul while still failing to express precisely what she meant, which was this: Polla's story and her own story and a thousand thousand other stories like them were as old and as enduring as the earth itself, and Becky felt, at present, simply too tired to pick up and sort through any more pieces of a life.

Then again, William may have noticed more than he let on. He was aware that the pre-trip-to-Tripoli idyll had become the post-trip-to-Tripoli next chapter that he had known all along must be turned to. Indeed, he had had enough of the dream life and he looked forward to taking the next big step toward a real life, which he and Becky had never really known together. They had only shared hopes that had dissolved into memories of hope and then they had fallen into this deep enchantment of the past months, from which, it seemed, the dedicated spell had just lately lifted. Now, William felt himself to be a most privileged observer of this new mood of Becky's. When she ignored him as he entered a room, he understood that his presence was no longer remarkable but, rather, a part of their ordinary life. When, one evening, Becky had finally let him know he could not make coffee to save his life, he had so far forgotten himself to suggest, You do it then, and so she had, raising her eyebrows but rising and disappearing in the direction of the kitchen, where she had slammed a cupboard door and rattled a pot. She had lowered her eyebrows at him when she returned, and watched him take his first sip (hot, he had burned his tongue on her behalf), saying, You see? (Well, not really. Becky's coffee was no better than his own, and William believed the beans were at fault and not anyone's brewing methodology; he would ask Mr. Kafi to procure a better brand, next time, a French roast from France.) And sometimes, of late, at night, Becky would turn from him instead of toward him, but she did so as naturally as she would turn away from the too-bright sun even as she was content to lie within its warmth, and William, although unembraced, felt neither cold nor alone.

He knew as well that during his recent absence, Becky had entertained thoughts of her left-behind family. He knew that she had written
to them at long last, for she had used up his stock of envelopes and spattered his blotter with ink from Mme. de Staël's pen (and he was touched
that she had availed herself of his gift to her, taking so much trouble,
for truly the pen was unworkable and he wondered why she hadn't
used the Montblanc pen; perhaps she'd forgotten about it, for somehow
it had found its way to his lower desk drawer where he kept paper clips
and rubber bands and batteries about which he wasn't sure, a new supply and an old cache of discarded batteries having somehow become
intermingled, and the fitting and refitting of dead and live batteries into
the power cavity of his shortwave radio had turned into an ongoing
test of his logic and intelligence).

William did not mind that she had turned to her family. He had no
right to mind, and besides, he knew he stood first in her world. Becky
had proved that to him; she had, at last, chosen. They, her children and
her brother, the happy rancher (William guessed), had been admitted
to her forward thoughts only in his absence, and William prayed they
would respond to Becky with messages of their continuing affection
and their new understanding of her. Then, although Becky might miss
them all very dearly, she would not miss them acutely, not if she could
be sure of them. Otherwise, the work of repair, reforging the broken
links of trust and love, would command her time and attention and
there would always be weak spots that remained and places where the
mend showed to which she would return and return. So much depended on those letters from her family, which did not and did not come.

During this time in which all those letters at last sent and those letters not yet received (and those letters still to be revealed) occupied
Becky's thoughts, William decided they needed to go out and about
and attempt some serious sightseeing. Perhaps he meant for a series of
postcard moments to distract her, in the offing. There were still a few
English-language bookstores hanging on in Tripoli and on his recent
visit he had picked up, along with a paperback trove of Henry Greens
and Iris Murdochs, a travel guide titled *Libya, Sandcastle by the Sea,
From Barbary to the Bedu, A Handbook for the Pilgrim-Traveller*. It was
an old book, although not a secondhand one; the volume had been sit-

ting on its original shelf for more than thirty years, a fact that spoke to a condition of stasis endemic countrywide. So, presumably, the land-marks, the mosques, the tombs, the vistas, the dunes, the frondy oases, the Greek and Roman remains, the Byzantine bric-a-brac, even the camel photographed standing so quaintly and picturesquely in the middle of the coastal road, had not gone anywhere in the meanwhile, and William was confident *Sandcastle by the Sea* could be relied upon at least as far as it went. If certain later-appearing realities of the local scene were not featured, in William's view those omissions were not to be missed anyway.

"We are fortunate to have such interesting sites in our own vicinity," William said. "Places seldom visited and, indeed, not easily visitable by outsiders these days. We should take advantage of our unusual oppor-tunities."

"Oh, all right," said Becky, setting down her book, *The Nice and the Good*. She could sit in the car and brood as well as she could droop about the villa, less comfortably so, but perhaps glimpses of the passing scene would spike her reveries (which had been spinning round and round themselves of late) with sharp little reminders of where she was and what she had done. She was, she thought, in danger of becoming too fond of her dolors, and as a person from whom selflessness and helpfulness had so often been asked, she had responded with sympathy to every adverse emotional state except that of self-pity. (You are al-ready sorry for yourself, so why must I be as well? she had asked her children when they sniveled, and oh, the remorse that had brought on, as the kids felt bad about feeling bad—Becky supposed, at that very moment, they were complaining about her to their therapists and a smile crimped her lips as she realized she was now pitying her children's therapists.)

Over the following days, they embarked upon set expeditions. Prepa-rations stirred the otherwise becalmed household. Henry filled the Land Rover's tank with fresh petrol and he lined up auxiliary tins of fuel and a drum of water and several spare tires in the cargo section; he provided an extra fan belt that Becky tucked into her satchel. She was familiar with the ways of fan belts, she said, because Alden was never very good at mechanical things, she nearly said. James assembled a picnic hamper, packed in layers of fresh fruit and sandwiches on top, with additional tinned and bottled supplies weighing the bottom down to the Vienna franks and the guava juice and the Polo mints, which was, as William said, a preview of what they planned to serve at the Apocalypse (for which event they would have excellent seats here in Libya, he felt). Adil, who was always in on everything, produced several sticks of signal flares, and he lent them the rolling-about sections of a fit-together metal pole along with a folded square of army-colored canvas which, he promised, would form a tent should the sudden need for shelter against the night or the day arise. He gave them a red banner attached to a flexible bamboo pole with which they were to mark the location of their tent should they be buried by a sandstorm.

For the sight of William and Becky—he fetching his wide-brimmed hat, and she just remembering her shawl, as they were about to drive off on one or another of their journeys—moved something in the Africans' hearts. They, Adil and Henry and James, were made uneasy by the recently hatched look of Westerners, by their pale smoothness and this impulse that compelled them to advance in curiosity toward the unknown. Any flash or movement or bright color drew them onward, which was how fledglings got themselves killed and eaten in the wild. One must learn to be afraid at an early age, but so often the first lesson was the last, in this sere and dangerous country.

"Do not stray from the macadam," Henry said.

"There is hot soup in the plaid thermos," James said.

"Make it home before dark," Adil advised.

"We'll be fine," William said, in the manner, he felt, of James Richardson. Westerners, William believed, were far better at this than the natives, and always had been.

William and Becky followed washboard roads over which *Sandcastles* counseled them to drive swiftly even though it seemed to fly against nature to do so. They passed steel mills, inspirational billboards featuring the words and the image of the Leader, entirely new towns of high-rise apartment blocks, police barracks, and municipal edifices, and troupes of schoolchildren planting tree seedlings on the encroaching desert dunes. The locals could not drive. Single cars on the untraveled roads inevitably veered into the trunk of the only palm tree in sight, just as in all the old *New Yorker* cartoons, Becky said. Forgetting Henry's words, they took off across the desert when the road curved away and they could see where they wanted to be, just ahead. They aimed for the watchman's hut. Then the watchman had to be raised by rapping on his door and tapping on his window, interrupting him in the act of brewing tea, for he had seen them coming from a long way off, eyeing the dust cloud until he could make out just what it contained. Glasses of tea were offered and could not be refused. Becky had memorized several elegant phrases of acceptance and appreciation, and she recited them.

Then, they made their further way toward a cluster of columns rising above a fallen pediment. (After they had been chased from an ancient mosque by an elderly mufti, William had decided to make a study of the classical; no one presided at the temples now and no one minded ignorance of a dress code or the hours of worship, and one could speak in one's normal tone of voice, or even raise one's voice above the press of the wind or against the sheer emptiness of the landscape.) They found the gathering of horizontal statues they had come to see. William said he was developing housemaid's neck from craning sideways to get a look at so many objects left lying about on the ground, but Becky found them restful to contemplate. The sand blew up and over and across the sleeping figures like a blanket alternately tugged on or kicked off. When her day had come and gone, Becky said, as the days of these former personages had passed away, she would rather like to go to sleep forever undisturbed. She almost laid herself down to see how it would feel, the sand sifting away to fit beneath her contours, soft yet firm like a superior mattress, but trying out a potential final resting place for size struck her as self-dramatizing and William would worry about her and sand would infiltrate her clothing, working its way down between her bra cups and her skin for the rest of the day to remind her that she was still composed of flesh and feelings.

" 'Temple of Mars,' " William read. Sometimes there were signs at these sites. Sometimes the writing was so faded that William tossed cupfuls of water at them to make the letters stand out darker against the bleached wood.

" 'House of Tibellus Naso,' " William read. " 'Foundation of.' It's much smaller than our place. Perhaps he had a bigger country house as well."

They were walking along a roadway of great slabs of stone set down one after another, the beginning and end of which they could take in at a glance, a road rising from and heading toward nowhere now.

"You can't get there from here," William said, using a Down East accent. "Anymore." Maine, they thought of Maine then. Evidently this truncated road could still carry them as far away and as long ago as that.

Some olive trees, surviving or sown since the day, rattled as the wind stirred and leaned closer as the people passed, as if they were pleased to see a bit of life. Ancient stones described the ancient spaces. Although all stones must be as old as the earth, as Becky observed, so why are we particularly interested in these stones?

"We're interested in man's arrangements of them," William said.

"So we look at stones and see ourselves?" Becky asked. "We are so arrogant."

"No," William said. "We are in need of reassurance that what we do matters and lasts."

"They are such a burden," Becky said.

"They anchor us," William said.

Their car shone at them from far off in the car park, an unsolid shimmer of accumulated heat. It would be hell to put themselves back into that, they thought. They were in no hurry to leave. Smoke smudged from the chimney pipe of the watchman's hut. He would be preparing their farewell glass of tea; the welcoming tea had lodged bitter shreds of mint in their back teeth, at which they worked with their tongues.

"Telephone?" William leaned forward and read another marker. "Surely not." He unscrewed the top of his water bottle and doused the sign. "Oh. Tepidarium. This was the tepidarium. And over there should be a floor. Yes." He consulted *Sandcastles*. "Thought to have been part of a theater. Vide, the mosaic tile design with the masks of Thalia and Melpomene central to the motif." They had crossed the road (funny how they each looked left and right before crossing) and they paused outside the theater, as if some distinction could yet be made between being within and without its vanished walls, as if some sort of ticket was even now required for entry.

"But how can they tell all this?" Becky wanted to know. She gestured up and down the desert road, no dwelling place, no public space rising higher than her knees; the occasional column remained upright, but only because they had long since shed the original entablature they had been charged to carry, only then had they been able to stand up to the passing of the ages on their own; not a soul in sight, neither the living nor the dead walking here. "The Temple of *Mars?* The House of Whoever-He-Was? Anyway, why a tepidarium? Why not the calidarium? How can they be so sure from these scraps?" Becky asked.

"They can tell by the pipes," William supposed. "And by accompanying artefacts. By patterns repeating themselves. Patterns are always repeating themselves."

"But this all seems so haphazard. Look at that shovel over there that someone forgot. I'm sure you could sink a shovel down anywhere around here and hit marble or a mosaic or a coin with a face on it, and then make up stories about all of them," Becky said.

"I should like to do that," William said. "I'd like to organize a dig of my own and to discover another Troy, perhaps, who knows, some scene of a great battle buried by the sand and the ages. There's an entire Persian army gone missing somewhere around here. Well, somewhere out there in the real desert. But you can't just dig anywhere. You have to know where to look."

"Back in Colorado we could always find arrowheads," Becky remembered. "There was a spot alongside our creek where you could tell people had been. Even after a hundred years it was still inviting. There were overhanging shade trees and an easy slope down to the water and a nice stretch of beach and a deep, cold pool carved out of the rock for swimming in. You just knew other people had chosen to spend time there. There was this human patina present. Though God knows why anyone ever chose to stop here in the middle of all this nowhere. Maybe Allah knows. He seems to have a different take on most matters."

But, as William allowed, this had been someplace once, and he could see the town as it must have been. He could raise the broken walls and reset the fallen pediments and assist the toppled statues to their feet. And, he said, he could see Tibellus Naso, that local worthy, threading a path through the morning market crowd as he made his way to the— restored to its old Roman eminence—courthouse, intent upon bringing an action against the stonesmith artisan from whom he had ordered an image of Amor. For upon delivery, the image had not pleased him. Amor's wings were crooked, and he was flexing his bow in an incorrect manner. But then, all but a lucky few men are disappointed by love, William said, as he caught Becky's hand and kissed the back of her wrist. Becky wondered when last a couple had kissed here, in the middle of this broken road.

"You can resurrect all that?" she asked. "From this?"

BECKY HAD GIVEN WILLIAM the letters of Polla Lucilla when they returned from their outing. She had watched him as he read the slender volume. He sat at his desk, the place to which he retreated to deal with matters calling for his full attention, and Becky had promised him, This is interesting. He reached for his pen; he never read anything without a pen at hand to underline a part he liked or to cross out a passage he quarreled with. The book lay flat across his blotter; he'd subdued its springing pages by cracking its spine. Becky had pulled over a chair to face the desk and William, who looked up from time to time to smile at her over some aspect of the narrative.

"Which part?" Becky asked.

"That Secundus was smooth," William said.

"What now?" Becky had asked again.

"Andromeda's chains. I wish I had seen them."

"Tell me," Becky said, then.

"Polla and her centaur."

William had closed the book with a sigh of complete satisfaction. Becky had heard the sigh before, occasioned by great art, great wine, herself. They turned toward the wall painting.

"So that's who you are," William said. "Well, you've lasted. I'll grant you that."

"I think Polla was tough," Becky said. "And Secundus was rather a sorry fellow."

"Yes," William agreed. "He was a cad, but perhaps adversity stiffened his spine. Let's hope that going through the fire steeled him."

"As for Junius," Becky said. "Well, that was a mistake on everyone's part. He probably had his version of events. We only have Polla's word for what happened."

"There are always three sides to every story: yours, mine, and the truth. That's an old Estonian proverb, or so an old Estonian always used to tell me," William said.

They wandered outside then, drawn to walk through the setting of the long-ago story. The human patina Becky had spoken of—William said he had always sensed something alive about the villa and its environs. It was night but the moon was bright and the land was touched with a sheen of memory. Details had receded into shadows and they saw, plainly illuminated, what had only ever really mattered. The wind had worn itself out blowing hard all day and the air was still and slightly chill. Becky had not thought to bring a shawl and so William wrapped his arms around her.

"The sea is there," he said, and they listened to the rise and retreat of the surf, the rush of sound ceaselessly hushing itself. "So, the wharf should be over there. And the press will be near the olive grove, which would place the warehouse midway between the wharf and the press, surely." Already, he could make sense of this world. "The Romans were very like us," William said. "They thought like us and did things like us."

"I think I'd have wanted the press farther away from the house, actually," Becky said. "But I wonder, did they ever build the temple, with its pediment of the best Luna marble? On a hilltop, Polla said. That's where they meant to put it. I don't really see any hills around here, though; what has happened to them? Have they all been worn away, the hills?" She gazed all around (a good long look undazzled by the sun) and she thought she detected a slight elevation above the flatness beyond the dark outline of the electric shed where the land just might have been swelling with something.

"I suppose I'm going to have to get used to buckets of sand and holes in the lawn," Becky said.

"What lawn?" William asked. "Now is the time to be thankful we don't have one."

OVER THE FOLLOWING WEEKS, William visited classicists at Benghazi and Tripoli Universities, and he met with the archaeologists at Leptis Magna. William was received in offices where shabby, lovely rugs covered the floors and couches, and dusty, precious vases and urns and amphorae and sculpted heads and gesturing hands and furls of drapery were left lying about. This clutter of the ages was scooped from chair seats so William could sit, and drifts of antiquities were swept from desktops so he could set down his briefcase and pop the latches, for he always brought with him maps and the Wilson book, and other books besides, and rolling about in his briefcase pocket was a representative glass bead he had unearthed in the villa's dooryard (first-century, someone who knew how to tell had told him), which William produced in proof, a small green thing placed upon the table.

Always, a portrait of the leader, depicted in one of his more sedate poses and costumes, watched from the dark wall where he had been hung by the back of his neck. Other walls bore framed diplomas displaying the seals and calligraphic flourishes of Old World institutions of higher learning: universities from their world and his world, as William noted, where he liked to think charism possessed monks and blind and visionary imams still taught student bodies still garbed in gowns and stoles who gathered in torch-lit halls where arcane knowledge flickered and then leapt ablaze. Then again, as William discovered, Professor Amama at Benghazi had come to the subject of Roman aqueducts with degrees in structural engineering and hydrology from the University of Michigan, and William had to remind himself not to become too carried away, even as he rubbed elbows with Jupiter's foot, recently unearthed near Sirt. He made notes on hinge fractures and the bulb of percussion, some things he was told he would need to know about flints, if indeed he was going to need to know about flints. His people were rather beyond striking and shaping flints, William thought.

The scholars and William dipped sugared almonds into glasses of tea. Conversation flowed in learned and courteous streams in the direction of the subject that had brought William to them. The past seemed such a presence to all those in attendance that the claim of a deep familiarity with the affairs of Septimus Severus, say, seemed almost a social boast and, indeed, Africans had played their role in ruling the Roman world. They had distinguished themselves early on, William was reminded; Africa had fed the empire with grain and men and ideas and emperors.

Great books were hauled out and thumped open, and fragile lucubrations were slipped from cupboard drawers and a page was rustled to in support or refutation of a theory. A scholarly male Arab assertiveness began to thicken an atmosphere already heady with histories. They were all aware of the existence, or once existence, of Oppidum Novum. Dr. Sherif of Tripoli produced a map of modern-day Libya upon which he positioned a see-through acetate overlay marking the hundreds of Roman towns and outposts and roads that covered the emptiness of the present-day land with former glories, although Dr. Sherif did not speak of lost glories. He referred to this time as the first Roman occupation as he glanced at the portrait watching from the corner.

"There you are, or, rather, there they were," said Dr. Sherif, tapping the spot with his pen. But, he pointed out, the good deep harbor had long since silted over, which had been the case up and down the coast. Sponge divers had reported seeing something that could have been the lighthouse that shone at the harbor's entrance; sponge divers were often the most informed reporters of antiquities submerged in the sea. The dunes had risen a hundred feet higher with the centuries, even more profoundly burying what lay beneath. Oea had been the main port for handling the animal-export trade; the small operation described in the Wilson book had not been at all significant. Yes, Dr. Sherif knew the letters of Polla Lucilla. On his trip to Libya in 1931, Mr. Wilson had inscribed copies to anyone who had been anyone, and the book was not so much a rarity as an oddity of its kind. Nevertheless, in an ideal world, all known sites of historical significance would be excavated, the artefacts cataloged, the record made complete. But the last several decades, for which Dr. Sherif might have been said to hold some measure of responsibility, had been busy ones in this part of the world. He counted off the intervening wars and revolutions on his fingers—the latest and the last revolution being a glorious one, of course, he hastened to add, and subsequently, the State had been too much preoccupied with forging a glorious future to look backward.

But no one seemed to know any reason why William could not mount an enthusiastically amateur expedition in his own backyard. No one would mind, providing no national treasure left the country (even now the government was negotiating for the return of a magnificent Venus the Italians had spirited away and then brazenly put on display in the Capitoline Museum, yet another stolen bride causing trouble for everyone because she was so very beautiful; Dr. Sherif smiled). Someone from some ministry would probably decide there were fees that must be paid and licenses which must be purchased, William was told, and an inspector might call from time to time to declare an interest and to keep an eye on things and his hand in—or more likely out, as William understood.

He began a course of study on archaeological method, reading through a stack of books and tracts recommended and lent to him by his new near-colleagues. He dispatched Mr. Kafi, well primed with lists and addresses, to search out instruments and implements necessary for the practice of archaeology. Never until now gadget minded (William had never taken up a hobby of any stripe; his only outside interest had ever been Becky), he brought to his current project a novice and naive belief in the power and efficacy of items that arrived in unpriably sealed boxes whose contents, when released from the molded foam contours that contained them, rolled and scattered across the floor, requiring assemblage. Who wrote these things? he asked of the accompanying instruction manuals, Louis Zukofsky? (You were never in my house on a Christmas morning, Becky thought but did not say.)

Mousa, who had stopped by one day to drop off a television set he had acquired at a price too good not to pass on to the Miztah and Mizzus ("Very well, but put it in the kitchen," William had conceded), said he knew where he could pick up a differential fluxgate gradiometer for use in the field. Henry and James, who were tuning in the new kitchen

TV (they set the color bar high in the green-tone area), said they knew how to work a gradiometer. They had been trained by their previous employer, the English archaeologist, although he, Sir David (had they not mentioned their previous employer's title?), preferred a different machine and methodology, that of resistivity surveying, the application of which was rather an art but James had the gift of knowing whether he had detected a natural or a manmade object buried below the surface, which had saved Henry a great deal of fruitless digging. Mousa said he'd look for one of those, then, and a satellite dish, of course. There was no point having a television without a dish.

William had also begun a correspondence with the director of the Italian National Library, who thought it was a pity Mr. Baskett could not present himself in person in Rome and so meander the archives at will, for, frankly, every nugget in the Biblioteca's possession had not been fully considered and made note of, and who knew what a motivated amateur seeker would find? William's bedside lamp burned late as he read Roman histories and polished his rusty Latin with the help of a grammar and a dictionary. He had forgotten how he had loved Latin, hearing those direct, rational voices of people from the past who spoke and thought much as we do, and William began to form theories about the similarities between the Pax Romana and what the world just lately seemed to have entered into, the Pax Americana. But William did not believe the Americans would be able to keep the lid on for two hundred years as the Romans had done.

Most nights, now, Becky fell asleep beneath a satin eyeshade she had bought in the bazaar, selecting the plainest one the stall offered, worked in white, setting aside the pair with long-lashed and sidelong-glancing eyes appliquéd above the sockets, although William had confessed he found the goo-goo eyes strangely compelling; some art had gone into their execution. But the shade pressed too hot across her brow; the satin and the padding of its construction could not breathe, and elastic ruching tugged at her skin and Becky awoke often, only to puzzle at the ruffle of a turning page and the scrape of a pencil upon a block of paper. Where was she? Who was she with? Why was she blindfolded? Those few seconds of uncertainty that filled the space between sleep and a return to her senses caused her to wonder where she went when she dreamed, and on those nights Becky sought sleep only to awaken again to see if she could catch herself there, where she had gone on her own. At last, however, because she could not bear its too-fevered feel against her forehead, she pulled off the eyeshade and flung it away as she also cast off the attempt to track the course of her wanderings. There was no point in knowing, anyway, for she was not going anywhere now.

She turned and watched William reading by lamplight, like Psyche first glimpsing Amor by lamplight, Becky thought, and like Psyche, she saw that the man she lay beside was not and never had been the monster people said he was. (Becky too had been reading the old Roman writers.) William smiled at her rather absently. He reached as absently to smooth a few damp strands of hair that snaked across her brow and cheek, not liking the look of them there.

"How much longer?" Becky asked. She wanted him to join her in sleep.

"Just to the end of this chapter," William said.

"I NOW KNOW WHY PEOPLE ARE always shown meeting at wells in the Old Testament, like Jacob and Rachel, those two," Becky said. "Look over there at the cistern, Noura and Emna chatting it up with James. This really could be five thousand years ago, except their buckets are made of plastic and oh, there's a jet plane overhead." Her eyes followed the straight white streak of a vapor trail across the otherwise empty sky. Aircraft in the sky were not all that common here and cause, if not for concern, for curiosity. She was aware that when the leader flew all planes were grounded, although she pictured his flight as that of a solitary bat on the wing, proceeding with a skittish swooping and a swirl of black cape. Such extravagant thoughts and speculations about the leader had worked their way into her mind; he packaged himself very effectively, with all those billboards and his face on the one-dinar bills, and one could not help oneself, embroidering bits about him.

"Is there something the matter with their own well?" William asked as he frowned at the trio, who seemed to have been lingering there since ancient times idly chatting and, by the evidence of all that surrounded him in this vast, vacant landscape, not getting much work done. They lifted glimmering handfuls of water from their buckets to their lips, spilling more than they swallowed in silvery rivulets that vanished in the air before reaching the ground as if disappearing down the gullets of invisible creatures who crawled across the sands and haunted the water holes. William was not sure if he had once heard tales of such beings or if he had just made them up on the spot.

"The water up at their house isn't potable," Becky said.

"Is ours?"

"Well, not for us, but it's all right for them, apparently."

"I don't know how they survive," William said. "Hi, there," he called. "No." He waved a pointed trowel at Muammar, who was pawing through a tray of shards set down in the wedge of shade struck off a corner of the electrical shed.

"They're already broken," Becky said.

"He will break them even more," William said, "which seems a pity."

"Muammar," Becky called, "help your Mothers with the bucket."

"Which one is his mother? I didn't know we knew that," William said.

"Well, I assume one or the other must be, although they've both been cagey about claiming him. That's why I employed that generally respectful term for a female relative which may or may not denote mother." Becky had been making progress with her language studies over the past months. Twice a week, she studied with Miss Haddad, the translator who had accompanied the Adib women to the tea party at the villa. Twice a week, Miss Haddad came from Misratah on the intercity bus and then Henry drove her up and down the dirt track, to and from the bus shelter out on the main road. Miss Haddad, sitting in the backseat of the big English car, felt treacherously like Fatima, the old queen; she had, as a child, been raised onto a traffic cone so she could snatch a glimpse of majesty riding past in a limousine. She had seen a hand waving, such a very white hand. Gloved, Miss Haddad realized later, as she had not realized at the time.

"Though I wonder whether it will ever be any good," Becky said.

"What? What, dear? What will never be any good?" asked William, concerned.

"My Arabic. Will it ever be really good? There's supposed to be such wonderful poetry I'd like to be able to appreciate. Like Antara Ibn Shaddad, Miss Haddad says he's the Walter Savage Landor of the desert, which I gather she means as a good thing, but I can't quite seem to find myself lost in his verse."

"Hi!" William called to Muammar, who had sidled away from the box of shards at William's first cry and then calculated his return as the Miztah and Mizzus no longer attended to him. Muammar lifted a sharp-sided curve of bright aureolin yellow and snapped it in half between determined fingers to see what could be contained inside so much yellow.

"Hi!" William called out again as the set of Muammar's shoulders hitched with his brief act of destruction. William chucked his trowel at the child. He scaled it, scoop flashing in the sun, aimed in a direct shot at Muammar and failing by just a meter to hit him. Muammar, who had turned at the shout, had stared at the flying trowel. He had blinked his remarkable eyes at the near miss and fled then, his robes aswirl around his bare feet as he made for the kitchen door, which, these days, with the household spending so much time outside, had been outfitted with an exterior latch set high enough above Muammar's best efforts to reach it.

"James," Becky called. "Give Muammar a biscuit and then send him on his way with the women. And tell him he'll never have any more biscuits if he doesn't help his mothers with the buckets. Let him learn to be a little gentleman," she remarked to William.

"Hereabouts, a gentleman is someone who doesn't make his women carry laundry on their heads while they're lugging the water buckets and hauling the donkey home," William said.

"I think of this as my missionary work," Becky said. "Although, to be fair, that bucket is bigger than Muammar. Still, I want to see him struggle a bit."

She watched Muammar undertake to lift the water bucket. He planted his legs, his knees jutting out the stuff of his robe, and he grasped the handle with his two hands. He lifted, straining like a little bulldog, although Becky doubted Muammar had ever seen a bulldog. She supposed he was more like a donkey, although donkeys always seemed to labor hardest when they were determined not to do something. The bucket rose as high as Muammar's chest. The boy tottered forward, then back, with a few near-dancing steps. He lost his grip on the handle but caught the bucket with both arms as a wave of water swelled over the rim and doused him all down his front. His robe clung; his big-bellied body stood out in relief to the great diminution of his dignity. Becky wondered if the distended stomach was evidence he suffered from some parasitic worm, and she thought she ought to mention to his mothers that perhaps they really ought not to trust the water from the villa's well.

"*Stupid,*" cried Emna.

"*Oaf,*" said Noura.

They walked off, each woman carrying a jerry can on her shoulder. Muammar set down his bucket and sat in the sand, his legs straddling the bucket as he stared down into it. The women did not look back; they could not do so very easily, for the weight of the canisters seemed to have locked their necks into place, and they would have to come to a full stop even as the slosh and heft of the water impelled them onward and cumbrously turn themselves round like barges in order to see that the boy was now lying down, curled up against the bucket's cool, sweating side.

Becky lost interest in Muammar then, as Ibrahim, who had been crouched in an excavation trench working with a trowel and a brush as he had been taught to do, called out that he had found something.

Ecce, Ibrahim had exclaimed, which had been William's idea. His working team was a polyglot one, consisting of several of Ibrahim's school friends (from the tech high, not the madrassa), some very raw Malians just up from the country, and a hydraulic engineer from Seoul who showed up when he had time off from his job on the Great Man-made River project and who believed the most ancient of Romans (the admittedly most mysterious Etruscans) had had their origins on the Korean Peninsula, his theory based upon a perceived sameness be-tween the Romans' favorite condiment, garum, and Korea's own kim-chi. William said his crew needed to have a few vital words in common to facilitate matters. Using Latin meant not playing favorites, Wil-liam said.

"Yes, Ibrahim?" William asked as he hopped into the trench. Ibrahim had already made a few significant finds: a pair of ivory dice, perhaps Secundus's own, perhaps with a little bit of luck still left in them; a small crocodile carved in stone, perhaps the fetish of a crocodile hunter; a handful of glass beads, less their strand of string or wire, perhaps Polla's own ornament—or perhaps the necklace of one of the Antucci women, Becky thought, for who was to say Signora Antucci had not been a collector of antique jewelry and that the clasp of her favorite ancient glass-bead necklace had not finally given out one day as she was walking from the house to the olive grove with a pitcher of fruit juice and a plate of biscotti for her husband. And indeed, Becky thought, the day would come when she and William and the villa and its dependencies were themselves but dust and some futuristic Ibrahim would come along (an Ibrahim living in happier circumstances of liberty and enlightenment, Becky hoped, although she still saw him wearing a pair of big-seated jeans and a University of Spring Break T-shirt in her mind's eye). He would sift shovelfuls of sand through a screen of mesh and uncover Lady Hamilton's thimble and Jenny Lind's vinaigrette, and an unusual object only identifiable after further research as George Sand's opera glasses sans the lenses. Perhaps, the members of the dig would say, perhaps, they would speculate, perhaps all of these remarkable women had once convened upon the site; perhaps they had had a very good reason for doing so, and the expedition would search further for proof of that reason. Perhaps these articles could be understood as votive offerings left at the altar of an object of adoration, and they would then seek the altar.

Becky had not mentioned these further possibilities to William, though she was quite sure she would have pointed them out to Alden, undermining his certainty and questioning his conclusions, upsetting whatever careful arrangement he had made of his shards and pieces. Alden. She found she could bear to think of him, these days, admitting a random thought of him now and then if the recollection was of some manner by which she had done badly or might have done better by him. She hoped these accruing instances of her earlier failings had already occurred to him and that, perhaps, he was leagues ahead of her along the way to deconstructing their past.

"Cave," William was saying, handing Becky down over the edge of the trench. She sat on the rim and swung her legs over and slid to the excavation floor, not very gracefully. The trench had grown long, cutting a good thirty feet across the presumed site of the warehouse, a place where the gradiometer had indicated there might be a foundation.

The sun seemed to burn harder and hotter down in the trench, and the sand and dust stirred and flew even grittier and dirtier, as if to descend those several feet below the surface was to return to a long-ago day that had been preserved there, all of its elements sealed off and fermenting in the dark, growing stronger. Becky understood now how the opening of tombs inspired tales of curses wished upon the discoverers. She felt they were being warned off here by the blast of heat and the sting of the sand and the dust. Still, she did not believe in ancient malisons; she only saw how one might come to be susceptible to the idea and so unsettle oneself into making grave missteps and costly errors for which one might then blame someone else.

Ibrahim, Henry, James, the Malian worker who was called Alpha, all stood around as William photographed the latest artefact in situ, and he made a note of the depth and where upon the grid of the excavation the item had been found. Then, Ibrahim was allowed to proceed. He knelt in the dust and working with his brush alone slowly exposed what seemed to be a length of very white bone and the darker links of a chain.

"This was a cat," said James, as he leaned in for a closer look. "That is its femur." He and Henry had been given training in animal anatomy by Sir David and they knew something of the subject on their own; they had come from a harsh land littered with the skeletal remains of creatures overtaken by hunger or thirst or predators.

"That was a very big cat," Henry said.

"Was it a lion?" asked William.

Henry and James were not sure. A lion? they asked Alpha, but he was not certain about a lion from the time of the forefathers, when he had heard the land was green and generous and beasts and man, as well, had been greater beings than we know now, and also more wondrous; there had been winged snakes and antelope as big as oxen, Henry said Alpha had said.

"Perhaps this was a lion," James said.

"Is that a chain still attached to the leg?" Becky asked.

"Vinculum," William came up with the Romans' word. He recalled, as well, that *femur* was the Latin for femur.

"Poor creature," said Becky. She knelt beside Ibrahim and flicked aside a few grains of sand.

"Very good chain," Ibrahim said. He was paid a bonus for each significant find that he made. "Very good chain now." He prodded a link with his brush.

"Cave," James said.

"Do you think the lion perished in the fire?" Becky asked.

"In the fire. Yes. We are finding ash at this level," William said. "Our findings are consistent with the letters' information."

"Someone ought to have set him free," Becky said. "Someone at least ought to have tried."

"Perhaps someone did try," William said. "I cannot imagine not trying."

"But Polla didn't say so," Becky said.

"Polla wouldn't have concerned herself with that. But the slaves may have made an effort. That Greek who fed them, I don't doubt some fellow feeling for their mutual captivity must have existed. He'd have done what he could, I'm quite sure," William told her.

"Yes. We can only hope so," Becky said. "But can't you at least remove the chain from the poor creature's leg, now, at long last?" she asked.

But William thought the relic was a far more interesting artefact as it had survived and that it must stand as a true representation of the way things had been for all of those displaced creatures trapped on the rough edge of Africa beside the silted-over harbor waiting for the ship that was never going to come for them now.

SO THIS WAS HOW IT WAS GOING TO BE. Becky required nothing more of the world than William, and for William Becky had always been the world. That they were no longer at liberty to travel in the greater world did not dismay them. They were as fixed as stars now, above and beyond the earth. What Becky was, eventually, to speak of as their common crimes, their separate acts of perfidy and utter selfishness, could not have been true crimes, she was to argue. They had not, in the end, been punished for what they had done, and we define crimes by the punishments they earn, she said. Besides, no judgments mattered but their own and each guessed what one had risked and dared for the other and neither saw the need to forgive the other as, quietly, they forgave themselves.

Any way of life will assume a routine and a rhythm of its own as even the extraordinary circumstance becomes ordinary. Every morning, William rose early to spend a few of the cooler hours on the excavation site. He knelt in the trench and worked with a trowel and a brush, filling a bucket with sand, which he then sifted through with every hope; the occurrence of the occasional shard or bead or bone kept him going. He returned to the villa to shower and breakfasted in the atrium with Becky on tea and compotes of fruit and flatbread freshly baked by James. Then William worked at his desk, cataloging finds. He was corresponding, as well, with an attorney in Washington he had retained, for William had concluded that the case against him must not be such an open-and-shut one (no charges had been filed). William sought not vindication for himself (*that* case would be unwise for him to press); rather, he was after the release of his frozen pension assets (a very nice point of law was involved, the attorney said). Sometimes, William had to go to Tripoli on business. He assembled a suit and tie and dress shirts. He remembered to pack socks and he threw a handful of green and black ribbons into his grip, although he was no longer sure whether the comments that greeted his scrolled and beribboned documents were pleased or ironic ones. Sometimes, now, Becky went with him. They stayed in an icily echoing suite in an icily echoing hotel and Becky would visit the ophthalmologist, a lovely man, a Lebanese who had trained in Germany and was much better than any doctor in Misratah. As Becky said, These people can admire a woman's eyes—she had made a little progress with their poetry—but they cannot prescribe glasses.

Later in the afternoon on an ordinary day, William oversaw whatever might be happening on the site. He conferred with Henry (James would be preparing dinner), or upon occasion with Mr. Park, who would show up and pitch a tent in the shadow of a dune. Mr. Park spent long hours bent over the sifting tray, scrutinizing the least bit of pottery for a Korean character or image. He was not very friendly; he was, most likely, well sunk in a sort of madness, although one could never be entirely certain whether he was truly crazy or just being Oriental about things, William said. The Africans respected him, whatever his state was; they left food and water at the door of his tent like temple offerings which were, gratifyingly, accepted and consumed. To Mr. Park fell the credit for unearthing a most lovely amphora, almost intact, which was donated to the museum in Leptis Magna, and was put on display in the permanent collection with a small sign attesting to its origins at Oppidum Novum.

Becky was to say that the empty and changeless and timeless landscape held hours she had never known existed. After she breakfasted with William, she spent several of those hours at her toilette. She lay in a deep bath as oil-swirled waters cooled around her to a degree at which she would be seized by a small, satisfactory shiver, a respite from the heat of the day. She was now very much concerned about the condition of her skin. The sun, the wind, the dryness of the desert all sought to ruin her fair complexion; she felt the burn and strain and collapse of tissue. She had realized she could not bear not to be beautiful for William, or at least, she wanted to be able to glimpse in her dressing-table mirror some semblance of the woman William believed he saw when he beheld her with his dear, dazzled eyes. Age was enemy enough, and Becky imagined she could count a line etched on her face for each lost year (a grimace revealed them). She made cosmetics purchases at the bazaar. She sought out the stalls where jars and bottles of emollients were sold, oils and creams and capsules which were to be broken open and a trickle of elixir expelled to be applied to the eye or the brow or the throat (Miss Haddad had translated the mystifying directions for use; no, one did not swallow these capsules). The products were scented with almond and honey and mint, and sometimes with something that reminded Becky of milk which sat just this side of being clabbered, so unlike the faint synthetic sweetness embuing the products of Elizabeth Arden or Prague-Matics. These must be the secret fragrances of the harem, Becky thought, as she leaned back from her mirror (those inches of withdrawal were themselves ameliorative; the facing image smiled back at her in spontaneous tribute to that). She rubbed onto her hands a lotion that promised to bleach away some lately appearing freckles.

The next hour she devoted to the study of Arabic. She learned best aurally and she played and replayed a series of conversational tapes in which Mr. Salam discussed the Weather and History and Business with Mr. Kilani, and there was Miss Awdi who soliloquized about her neighborhood and her neighbors and her busy household in which her exact status was not given, although whoever she was, she got around. Miss Awdi's great subject was Health (Miss Awdi's neighborhood's air must have been most insalubrious) although Becky concluded every ailment sounded fatal in Arabic. Then James brought Becky luncheon on a tray (grilled peppers, yogurt; steamed zucchini, hummus) and he and Becky discussed what James would prepare for dinner. They shared recipes and it was during one of these conversations that Becky learned of James and Henry's ambition to return to Mali and to their families (of whom James had no pictures, for, of course, Becky had asked to see some). They were going to open their restaurant. Well, the place was going to be just a stall in the marketplace, but they would also have a table for their patrons set English style with a tartan cloth and a cruet of Chef Sauce. James and Henry had already labored for five years abroad, and they had calculated they must work and save for another seven. Becky had asked William why they could not pay the men more so they could return home sooner. Indeed, the sum the men sought to save was heartbreakingly small; a gift could be made and be scarcely felt by us, Becky said. But William told her they could not upset the local economic system. Henry and James would suffer the resentment of their peers, and he and Becky were themselves more bound than most to observe the customs of the country that had received them. Besides, William was in no hurry to lose such excellent servants, and a pair who had been English trained, by a lord, to boot. Thereafter, Becky could never decide whether it was kinder to ask or not to ask about the Malians' so-long-to-be-deferred plans.

Becky spent other hours of her days brooding about her neighborhood, perhaps following Miss Awdi's model of inquisitiveness. Becky's interest advanced to the Adib establishment and from time to time she resolved anew to attempt to reach out to the child Muammar, or at least to attempt to steer him from the path he seemed so set upon, although Becky could not really characterize where that path would lead here. At home, she might predict poor grades, a minor drug problem, and the millstone of an unsuitable girlfriend wrapped around his neck, all combining to cause him to fail to reach his potential. Perhaps that was her difficulty in assessing the likes of Muammar, for Becky had no idea what that potential might be in his case and so no notion of what missteps must be guarded against. She may have hoped to turn him into a Western boy; he liked to take things apart (or, at any rate, to smash them to pieces), and Becky wondered whether he might not possess the potential to become a mechanical engineer—were they the ones who knew all about the inner workings of machines? Perhaps some schooling could be arranged for Muammar in Europe or the States in the years to come.

She would have made an effort with the other children of the household but they ran away when she called to them (while William said their first mistake had been in feeding Muammar and it was just as well not to repeat the error with the other ones). Only Muammar came when he was summoned, although he always approached as if granting a favor, ceding the gift of his presence. He seemed to drift to Becky's side as if at the whim of the desert wind, his short steps concealed by his long robe, and by the time he reached her, Becky was already reminding herself she did not have to like the child in order to help him. Indeed, she meant to help him by eradicating his old identity and shaping an altogether new one for him—for his own good, she told herself.

Becky would place the child on a bench in the atrium, one made from two Doric column tops supporting a slab of dark red marble between them, and she would sit upon the end of one of the chaises. She never offered Muammar her lap; they were both too formal for that. Becky undertook, then, to read to the child. There were no children's books at the villa; those on sale in the bazaar were charmless at best, and vicious at worst, Becky felt, and so she held up illustrated guides to

African birds or Mediterranean fish or Greek and Roman ruins, and she invented stories about the pictures. *This beautiful swallow will fly day and night over the jungle and the mountains and the desert and the sea and the mountains again, to visit her summer home in Europe. She will build a nest for her babies high in the branches of a beautiful green tree or atop a cathedral spire or above a castle tower, and a lonely girl who sits in the castle tower will hear the song of the bird and she will think to herself, How far this pretty bird has flown to sing so sweetly for me.*

Muammar would slide from the marble bench before the story's end. He may have realized that the Mizzus's stories had no end. *This beautiful temple was consecrated to the great god Neptune. He was the Allah of the Oceans. He carried a fork and he ruled the seas.* When the Mizzus was caught up in one of her tales, they would go on and on. *This beautiful fish was very adventurous and so one day she decided to follow a pleasure yacht as it set off on a ride from Ibiza to Capri to Venice. The Venetian fish were very proud yet very nice. Some day Venice will be ours, when the city sinks into the sea, they said, and then we shall swim through the palaces and the museums and the Basilica.*

Yes, Muammar, what is it? Becky would ask as he floated to her side. No, Muammar, no, she would say as his hand snatched to tear the page from the book and she would snap the volume shut upon his hand as if it were an insect.

Late in the afternoons, Adil made an appearance bearing the day's post and some item he had been commissioned to procure, or he might come with a report on the status of his hunt for alkaline batteries or a replacement fender for the Land Rover after William sideswiped a roadside marabout's tomb in one of those *New Yorker* cartoon accidents he and Becky had thought so amusing and so inexplicable when they happened to others. A note was dispatched to Mr. Kafi to procure the fender in Tunis. William had returned from the dig site by then and was to be found in the atrium freshly showered and enjoying a cocktail with Becky; one day gin and vermouth had suddenly become available in the souk and, as William said, God knew they could always lay their hands on olives. He was inclined to chat with Adil. Adil, who always hesitated and then always refused a drink from the sweat-sided silver pitcher, would accept a tonic water and bitters, which he sipped as he smoked several Camel cigarettes (as William and Becky's eyes met in amusement over that detail, Camels).

William and Adil would discuss the shortages of consumer goods (lately, Becky had decided she needed a stationary bicycle) and they blamed the United States and the sanctions for every incident of un-availability, even, occasionally, for the intermittent scarcity of oil to run the villa's generating plant.

"Oh, now really," Becky said. "You people have more oil than you know what to do with."

But the United States denied Libya the machinery parts necessary to extract the oil from the earth, William and Adil reminded her. How very powerful an enemy was America, both William and Adil agreed, and how very forcefully one must stand up to her, as William had done and Adil would do, if ever given the chance.

Just get rid of You-Know-Who and put someone sensible in charge of your country, and America won't be able to do enough for you, Becky thought but did not say.

Sometimes Adil registered further complaints. He would make him-self comfortable to do this, propping himself against a column, one foot braced, one knee locked, wielding his glass and his cigarette like a socialite. "The West tells such lies about us," Adil would say. "I go to see a Hollywood movie and every time the terrorist, every time the villain is an Arab man. It is prejudice, it is racialism. *Why do their rabbis and divines not forbid them to blaspheme . . . Evil indeed are their doings . . . They spread evil in the land, but God does not love the evil-doers,*" he spoke in his higher-pitched quoting voice.

"Oh, come off it," Becky told him. "Haven't you ever noticed how movie Nazis always have blond hair and blue eyes? I've had to put up with that annoying stereotype my entire life," she complained back at him.

If Adil had brought mail that day, Becky would toss through the envelopes. She would go over them again after her too-swift and too-anxious initial pass. She sorted more calmly when she knew that nothing was there for her, when relief attended her disappointment. For if there was to be no word from the boys and Julie, she need not yet suffer their words of reproach, which, as the weeks went by, Becky began to believe would have arrived betimes, their anger flying from their pens and hurled at her. But never had Becky expected too ready an acceptance of what she had done. She had been such an excellent wife and mother; she had been loved (or, as she sometimes thought, valued) for her constancy and capabilities; and for her children to forgive her now, when they had been forsaken and replaced, would strike them, and herself, as a repudiation of the time when they had thought themselves to be safe and satisfied and had believed the same of her. Such a conundrum for them; the kids would have no idea what to do or say, and Becky, to whom they had always turned for guidance, was not there to tell them how to proceed. They would have to find the path back to her on their own, and more for their sakes than for herself, Becky prayed they would happen or chance or light upon the way. To Becky, their silence had come to seem as unquiet as that of an empty house where a clock pulsed and boards creaked and the pipes hissed and sighed waiting for someone to come home, and this became the construction she had raised around her hopes and where she would have to live, this lengthening while.

In the evenings, William and Becky would retreat to a small sitting room where two chintz-covered chairs faced an ottoman. They settled foot to foot, the ottoman pulled by Becky's heel and pushed by William's toe through a deep-piled, deep-colored carpet closer to her. A pair of long, forest-green velvet curtains were kept drawn across a blank wall as if shutting out a winter's night in a northern city, and, as Becky said, one might almost experience the hot, fusty air as having risen from the most excellent of heating systems, the thermostat nudged up several notches by the brush of a passing elbow. Becky would select a CD to place inside the player, although many of the new selections Mr. Kafi had purchased for her had turned out to be bootleg copies; Sir Neville Marriner and Miss Iona Brown, in a madcap moment, turned their talents toward a performance of "The Lark Descending"; Aida died in the arms of Radamès and then recovered sufficiently to sing "O cieli azurri." How can she tell what color the sky is, William pointed out, if she is stuck in that vault? But Becky said it must be a hopeful sign if criminals had found that counterfeiting the classics to this part of the world was worth their while.

They would read in the evening, as well. William had his English poets over whom he drowsed and his Roman histories over which he dreamed. Becky selected something from among her accumulation of novels, for there was occasionally a book or two to be found in a marketplace. Becky wondered how a copy of *Elders and Betters* had come to rest in a stall in the Benghazi bazaar. She supposed there must be a practical explanation; cleaning women carried off the volumes left behind in hotel rooms and in airport lounges and made a few dirhams passing them on to the trader in such goods. Then again, Becky liked to think that some of the books had taken off on their own, hitching rides in briefcases and shopping bags, shedding their bright and telling dust jackets and moving anonymously around the globe, turning to face a wall or laying themselves down flat upon a table to escape detection, for, Becky felt, there was rather a subversive element to this phenomenon of Western novels disseminating themselves to all the corners of the earth and she thought, Perhaps this is how we shall prevail, through human stories of imperfect people trying and all too often failing to do what was right.

Presently, on those quiet evenings, William would startle himself awake, his chin dropping onto his chest, his glasses pitching down his nose to lodge on his lower lip, and he would, for an instant, feel as if he had been seized from behind in a headlock by some pursuer. He would snatch his glasses from his face and stare at them, the earpieces twisted, in his hand.

"Well, darling?" Becky would ask, to which William's response was to rise and to lift his oil lamp, and he would pass through the rooms of the villa holding his lamp aloft and swinging its light into the shadows. He tried the door locks; he touched the kitchen stovetop to make sure all the surfaces were cold; he gathered the cushions from the atrium chaises and stacked them on a bench in the hall, for sometimes even here rain would fall and William was afflicted with an entirely suburban conviction that the one night he forgot to move the cushions would be the one night the local heavens opened up. He inspected the bathroom for scorpions, next. He flurried the towels and turned over the bath mat and peered into the tank and he stamped his feet to send any adventuring creature back to its crevice. Becky, a few steps behind him, wrapped in a robe and with her hair swirled inside a turban, thanked him for being so brave (and she said this with no hint of mockery for him or for herself) as she retired to the bathroom to perform the further rituals of her nighttime toilette.

William would lift the cat from the foot of the bed, where it had trod a hollow in the covers, and he expelled it from the bedroom. Then he lay upon the bed and listened to Becky's balneal sounds of running water and aerosol hisses and the scrape of jar lids being opened and shut, which were endlessly pleasing to him; this further, final wait for Becky to complete her bath and to come to him struck him, then, as an echo of all (of the few) grace notes that had attended the grander, graver theme of half a lifetime of separation. William could not bear for that time to have meant nothing and so he decided that it must have meant this, all along; that presently the door would open and Becky would emerge from a mist of steam and of scent and tell him she was sorry she had taken so long.

THE LOCALS WERE TO BECOME USED TO the fact of Westerners in residence at the villa (she was said to be American, and kind, although he seemed English). The couple was seen in passing and in the vicinity, their big English car cleaving the shimmer of heat rising off the asphalt, materializing and then vanishing in the usual, unremarkable mirage. They were observed shopping in the marketplace, where they would dicker over the price of fish and fruit, although never too fiercely, and they did not offend by appearance or action. They gave alms; they interested themselves in the polytechnic college, to which they sent technical books and gifts of money. Their faith, if faith they possessed, was observed quietly and at home.

The Westerners were welcome to the old villa situated so far from town and set at such a distance from the main road, beyond the dark pine forest, beside the dusty olive grove, beneath the mutable dunes that receded and advanced at the bidding whim of the wind and the sea. And everyone had heard of the Roman ghosts who walked the grounds at midnight, spirits denied rest, denied Paradise, who had lived and died before God sent his Signs and Revelations to man and who had had no Guardians to watch over them and to carry their souls to Heaven at the last. Well, let them wander, if not in peace then at least undisturbed out there. The strangers in the villa had never mattered to anyone except themselves.

Nine

Maritus et Uxor; Hâc Mortuâ Ille Fit Viduus

(from *Orbis Pictis* by Johan Comenius)

AFTER THE BETTER PART OF A WEEK HAD GONE BY, Svatopluk was persuaded to drive out to the castle to see what had become of Alden. The office had been scraping along well enough without him, a testament to himself and to his staff, Alden would have said, although all was not entirely in order. On Monday afternoon, Jaroslav had indulged himself in a long-nursed desire to shout at a certain supplicant, Alden having previously declared it was never "useful" to remind a stupid peasant he was a stupid peasant; to do so only made him more mulish. On Tuesday, Michal cooked a lunchtime sausage on a hot plate balanced atop a filing cupboard he had shoved in front of an open window to let the cooking smells drift outside rather than trap the scent of old fat and hard frying in the office, but Franca felt and Tilla agreed and Svatopluk thought so too, that this public release of cooking odors into the leafy professional air of the Hradčany district was the worse offense. Passersby on the avenue below had looked up and sniffed inquiringly. On Wednesday, Tilla brought in a basket of sewing, being obliged, once again, to let out the waistbands of her husband's trousers, an operation that now necessitated harvesting fabric from an interior seam in order to fashion a gusset. Then, on Thursday, there arose the question of paychecks which, while neither issued nor signed by Mr. Lowe, nevertheless needed to be signed off on by him, when he would verify names and amounts against a list as, he had once confessed to Svatopluk, he wondered how people could get by on so little. On Thursday afternoons, he would move from desk to desk, laying flimsy scrips facedown upon blotters and the staff, who theretofore believed they had secured highly satisfactory positions within the highly challenging new order, experienced the slight chill of their Boss's passing shadow and his evident view that tactfulness was called for in reference to the matter of their weekly wages.

"Aside from our own need to be paid," Jaroslav said, "we should inquire after Alden's well-being. We have not heard from him since his return from Bratislava. Presumably, he returned. We know he was there, for they have faxed us for further urgent clarifications regarding the business that brought him."

"Perhaps he became ill upon his return from Bratislava." This had been Franca's worry for the past several days. "Perhaps he is too ill to send us word from his sickbed."

"The wife will attend to him then," Michal said. "If he is fever ridden, she will cure him with the chill of her presence. If he coughs, she will quell him with a look."

"Oh, but *she* is missing from work as well," Tilla said. "I know, because I met her assistant, her Maria, on the Nerudastrasse, although Maria did not seem very concerned. She is conducting an important new romance and she has been coming in to work late and leaving early, so Mrs. Lowe's absence has only been a convenience to her."

"Is Julie ill too, then? Have they all been struck by the same contagion?" Franca asked. "Has anyone seen Julie?"

"Where should any of us see young Julie?" Jaroslav asked. "Gallivanting until dawn at the Club Disco? But perhaps they have all gone off to observe one of their national holidays. Americans have so much to celebrate. Let's see. What could it be, what blessing is it now they must pause to give thanks for? When was the baseball invented?" he wondered.

"Thelonius Monk's birthday is coming up," Michal said. "He is a true Libra."

"No, stop," Franca said. "I am afraid this situation may be serious, and shame on Maria for taking such advantage."

"But Maria's new man is very prominent," Tilla said, "and Mrs. Lowe approves of him. Indeed, Maria consulted her on strategies to captivate a lover, and Mrs. Lowe counseled her. Do not be too elusive, she said. If you want him, go after him, she said. Maria took her advice because it was what she intended to do anyway, but *I* told Maria to make very certain what she wants."

"Perhaps Mrs. Lowe has gone off after this fellow for herself," Michal said, which everyone was to remember afterward. Prescient, Tilla said. No, Michal said, just the result of a decades-long tutelage in the American blues.

"Well, you would know this man's name," Tilla promised. "Maria met him at the party."

"That party." Jaroslav shook his head. "At my home, we still speak of that party."

"Svatopluk, what can you tell us?" Franca asked. "Have you not called Mr. Lowe at the castle?"

Svatopluk, who had remained aloof from the conversation, his head bowed over a ledger just lately wrested from the possession of a former Party official, looked up and said, "I have not been able to elicit any information from anyone there."

Not able to elicit any information, the staff mouthed at one another. What did that mean?

"What does that mean?" asked Jaroslav.

Svatopluk had been ringing the castle all week. Julie was not to be found at any of the usual places at the usual times. The International Youth, a pack of whom he had tracked down at a favored Kovárna, reported Julie had not been at school—not a mystifying absence as such, but she had missed a much-anticipated excursion to the National Gallery, for Julie had been heard to remark that she kind of liked looking at old stuff. Indeed, she had been known, of her own volition, to duck into a pretty church or a house with a plaque by the front door and very courteously stand before a picture of a saint or a roped-off room in which someone who had once notably lived had then as notably died.

When Svatopluk had, at last, telephoned the castle, Julie had snatched up the receiver on the instant. She was breathless, as if she had run from the Great Hall to the library to answer the telephone, but she can't have come on the run; she had to have been sitting with her hand upon the receiver, feeling, before hearing, the vibration of the ring.

"Yes? Yes? Yes?" she had said, and then on a falling note uttered, "Oh, it's you."

"My little flower," Svatopluk had spoken the endearment, almost in protest.

"It's no one," Julie said to whoever was with her, not taking care to muffle the mouthpiece. "I can't talk now," she told Svatopluk, her voice trailing off to a whisper as if, in fact, the power of speech was forsaking her at that moment.

He had tried to get through a second and a third and a fourth time, but the line had been ever engaged; early in the morning and late at night he had made the attempt, and Svatopluk guessed the household was in wide communication with places in the world where the hour was neither early nor late, or perhaps where the hour tolled very early and very late indeed. That there was a crisis at the castle was clear, and Svatopluk, for whom the personal loomed rather large at present, had convinced himself that he must figure in no small way in the emergency. He had been assured that the elder Lowes had possessed incomplete information regarding Julie's activities, and his own part in them, but he now feared that those least noticing of parents had, at last, noticed something, and that Julie's assertion, I can't talk to him, had arisen from a hard-held position of I won't talk to them, for which she must be commended but from which after all, in decency, she must now be released.

"I think the time has come to investigate," Svatopluk announced to the office. "I shall drive out there and see what is going on."

"Don't forget about our paychecks," Michal said. "If Alden is in no position to dispense them, then we shall elect you Boss. Oh, don't be sentimental, Franca," he told her, for she had uttered a little cry of protest.

SVATOPLUK HAD PULLED UP BEFORE Castle Fortune's great western door, the massive and iron-studded occasional portal through which the exalted guests and the fire-breathing conquerors of other days had passed, necessitating, for the admittance of the exalted guests, the sliding of a reluctant bolt and the lifting of a stiff latch, and a two-fisted, full-body haul open; while the invaders had battered with a ram until the hinges splintered from the frame and the door slammed itself open, pitching backward onto the stone floor. There was now, as then, neither bell pull nor knocker for a visitor to twist or to thump demanding entry; the exalted guests would have been watched for and met by a golden overspill of interior lamplight as they pulled up in their carriages—and the invaders would have long since announced themselves by other means.

Svatopluk had paused to muse upon his own approach to the castle. The Tower, he reflected, rose too high and too smooth-sided to scale without mountaineering equipment, with which he had not supplied himself and, anyway, did not own, carabiners and such. He could, he supposed, scrabble his way by handhold and toehold up and onto the belvedere and enter through the French doors which were never locked, were he not wearing his better suit and his best shoes and a favorite shirt. Then again, as he knew perfectly well, the Lowes and their visitors commonly came and went through a modest, modern side door where an eternally aglow button was positioned which, when depressed, caused a peal of bell notes to din through the castle, making the elder Lowes start and spill their cocktails over their hands. No, Svatopluk had decided, if he did not want to announce himself, neither did he wish to imperil himself; he would just rather see for himself before he engaged with the family.

He drove on and parked on the farther side of the woodcut stand of trees and set off across the parkland toward his objective, for he now had something in mind. He crossed and recrossed the meandering gravel path, like someone who has at last become fed up negotiating a maze. He did not worry that he would be observed from the castle, for in his experience, its denizens only took in large, distant views from the castle's high windows. Besides, certain draperies, notably fraying and fragile, were always kept drawn, and he recalled earlier telephone conversations with Julie during which she had inquired after the current weather with as little clue to local conditions as if she were speaking to him from the States. Thick stone walls and lofty roofs combined to create a constant interior climate of coolness and rising drafts and shreds of mists which were dismissed by Julie as ghosts. She had explained to

Svatopluk how very easy it was to forget about Out there when In
here, and the thought briefly occurred to him (before it vanished) that
the castle inmates had simply not remembered they had work and
school to go to that week and were, at present, sitting around in soft
armchairs reading and dozing and only rousing themselves to throw
pillows at the ghost mists, then rising to collect the pillows when they
found they had thrown them all away, and the contours of their armchairs and sofas required recushioning and replumping. Svatopluk
pictured this; he preferred to picture this, but he believed nothing of
the sort.

He skirted the garages, then, and clopped across the cobblestone stable yard and hurriedly passed beneath the archway of moss-clad stones,
dripping sumpish water onto his better suit and his best shoes. He
emerged on the southern aspect of the castle to which was appended
the conservatory, which he approached, hurried along by the downward slope of the lawn. He knew precisely where there was a large,
loose pane of glass, for Alden had, just before leaving on the Bratislava
trip, asked him to arrange for a glazier, which Svatopluk had done. The
man had agreed to come a week from Tuesday, reluctantly, this far out
from the city.

Svatopluk popped out the sheet of glass, pushing at then catching
the pane by its sides as it swooned backward. He stepped over the low
sill. Such a pity, he thought, to let the big lemon tree die—and the other
plants in their pots, ferny things and twining things and glossy-leafed
things and sharp-edged things, were struggling, more grey than green,
the dirt they lived in gone dry as dust and as hard as asphalt beneath the
late-September sun. The conservatory was Mrs. Lowe's domain; she
wandered its ways wearing a pair of red-and-white-striped gauntlet
gloves and trailing a low flowing hose from pot to pot. Always the hostess, Svatopluk thought, pausing to offer plant after plant a "drink." He
had followed her on her rounds one day, sipping from his own drink
which had been offered and accepted. He had come to see Julie (well,
to possess her and be possessed by her, up in her Tower, up in the
clouds). The parents were supposed to have concert tickets but Alden
had come down with a sore throat and Svatopluk had had to feign an
interest in Mrs. Lowe's botany projects as he invented a message for

Alden which he claimed was important. Alden is gargling with saltwater and honey, Mrs. Lowe had explained. He may be a while.

And to add to the confusion of that occasion, Svatopluk had gone away convinced Mrs. Lowe believed him to be a homosexual. (You showed up pale and nervous and very well dressed and you reeked of that cologne of yours, Julie said. I was completely emasculated, I was cut off at the knees, Svatopluk agreed. I endeavored to suppress my libido as I discussed with your mother with a light, eager voice, what the Czech word for the snapdragon flower is, once we had established what snapdragons are. But what did Ma say to make you think she thought you were gay? Julie asked. She started to ask me the word for pansies and then she blushed and changed the subject, Svatopluk said. Gosh, your English is good, Julie told him.)

What I have endured for that girl, Svatopluk thought, all this breaking into of castles and risking my career; she steals my shirts; she fills my waking and working and dreaming hours with reveries of her. Oh, but if something has happened, I believe now, it must have happened to the mother, thank God (and may God forgive me for thanking him for that). Those sere and ruined plants are my clue; they are a sign.

He had entered the castle proper. He prowled a long corridor and climbed a strange (to him) stairway. He found himself in the Great Hall—one always came back to the Great Hall here—and he set off on forays from there, seeking with method, opening doors, inquiring, and collecting echoes in reply. He came upon them, at last, in the library.

Julie, lying across the leather sofa, an arm flung across her brow, her ears plugged into a Walkman that lay upon her stomach, sensed and then saw Svatopluk standing uncertainly in the threshold.

"Dad? Dad, look," she said.

Alden was seated at the long, beast-legged table, bent over a mess of papers and the creased and billowing expanse of a map. He slowly turned toward Svatopluk. Julie sat up and then she rose to her feet. The Walkman dangled from her ears and thudded to the floor, pulling off the headset as the faintly loud strains of the Cars played on. She made a helpless gesture toward Svatopluk, a shrug and a shake of her head, and she held up a hand to warn him away from herself as if she were too terrible to be approached.

"Look, Dad, Svatopluk," she said softly. "Svatopluk," she said again, more softly.

"Sir," said Svatopluk. "Sir, pardon my intrusion. I did not mean to disturb you."

"Why have you then? Well, what do you want?" asked Alden.

"It's the paychecks. They require your authorization."

"Right. Let's have them," Alden said. He cleared a portion of the table, sweeping away papers which fluttered and flew anyhow.

"Dad," Julie protested, stooping and gathering fallen pages. "You be careful. This is one of Ma's letters." She held out a sheet of writing paper covered with dark-inked words and Alden took it from her. He pushed back his chair and swayed to his feet and carried the letter from the library. He bumped past Svatopluk, who had remained in the doorway, that forbidding gesture of Julie's having caught him there, loath to advance and longing to retreat. "Sir?" Svatopluk called after Alden. "Your signature."

"Damn," said Julie. "I shouldn't have said, about Ma. I mean, mentioned her. God, it's been awful around here. I have honestly had to start smoking over this." She reached into a back pocket of her jeans, which she had paired with a black turtleneck. She was in dull plumage today although her face was fiercely made up in an effort to mask the red eyes and pinkened nostrils of long-term tears. She extracted a sat-upon pack of Spartas.

"Damn," she addressed the pack, extracting a bent cigarette. She flared a match and very conscientiously applied flame to the tip as if she thought tobacco was a difficult substance to set alight.

"My new foul habit is entirely Miss Mopsy's fault," Julie said. "Only she's been so nice. Well, actually, I think she's enjoying herself. No one's made her clean anything all week. She can't. Dad's told her not to touch anything. Like, we're living in a, in a crime scene—either that, or a shrine, maybe. I'm not sure which it feels like. So then, Miss Mopsy, her and Mrs. Cook hanging out in the kitchen, told me smoking would calm me down because, believe me, I am not calm."

She sat again, slumped, subsided, upon the leather sofa, which she had made into a sort of nest; she had a blanket, a water bottle, a sliding-about cache of CDs, a tumble of books, a stack of plates with most of a sandwich on the top one and other old sandwiches squeezed between the layers of the stack. There was a box of self-serve Kleenex, the next tissue rising unfurled and on offer. (Yes, certainly there had been tears here.) She scraped a covered stein out from beneath the sofa and flipped open its clapper top to tap in ash. "Oh, thanks. Yeah, watch the batteries," she said.

Svatopluk had retrieved the Walkman, left lying as if wounded and crying out upon the floor. After a moment, after Alden did not reappear, he sat down beside Julie.

"What are you doing?" she asked him.

"Attempting to embrace you and to comfort you." He had wrapped an arm around her shoulders and tucked an arm around her waist and pulled her toward him. She offered her mouth for a kiss, a smudged and nicotine-flavored kiss, also breath-minted and waxy deep-red-lipstick tasting—and salty. Svatopluk listened to the kitten burr of her novice smoker's lungs.

"Wait. Don't let me burn you," Julie said, breaking away as her cigarette grazed the hair on his head. "What are you supposed to do with these things during, you know—" She pitched it into the stein.

"They're not for during, they're for after, my pet, my sweet, my innocent. Why wouldn't you speak to me? I have been so mystified. What has happened? What has become of your mother? I can sense her absence everywhere," Svatopluk said.

"I know. I know. You miss her too and you're not even us," Julie said. She swiped a handful of Kleenex from the box and ground them deep into her eyes as if to force the spill of tears back down into their ducts, and she fought against the eruption of sobs welling up from her throat, a flood of sorrow determined to break out somehow. "This is *so* stupid," she said.

"You must breathe into a paper bag," Svatopluk said as she gasped after breaths. Where was a paper bag to be found within all of this great castle? He half raised himself from the sofa, than sat as Julie tugged at his suit-jacket sleeve.

"I'm not going to breathe into any bag," she said.

"It will help."

"Nothing will help. Not ever."

"Yes, I see. I understand that, but the benefit of bag breathing is physiological. I do not pretend it will address your emotional state."

"Just don't go on telling me what will help. We are way beyond help here."

"Tell me what happened, Julie," Svatopluk said again. "Has your mother passed off?"

"Passed off? Oh, you mean away, has Ma passed away? 'Passed off'—I think you're thinking of 'pissed off,' which, actually, is more the case if you want to know the actual truth of the matter," Julie said. "And I can't blame her for leaving us, the way I've been acting." She swiped the Kleenex across her eyes.

"Leaving you? Is that all? Has your mother gone back to America, then? I'm sure she'll return, all in good time, after a little rest at a spa. Have you spas in America? We have all thought at the office that Mrs. Lowe needed a stay at a spa."

"No, no, no. Ma's in flipping Libya, or that's where she was headed, and no one would stop her. The embassy acted all ooh-ick about it when Dad asked them to do something, I don't know what—whatever embassies do about missing Americans. And Interpol was all like, 'Get a life, guy,' on the phone. But then Dad's uncle has this congressman pal who's been using the CIA to look for Ma because they want to find Mr. Baskett too."

"Who is this Mr.—"

"Baskett. Ma knew him ages ago in New York and he's been pining after her ever since. We all thought he was a big joke."

"We?"

"Me and my brothers. I mean, we knew. He used to send Ma kind of inappropriate letters and was way too attentive whenever he came to visit. You know, talking to Ma and listening to Ma and leaping to his feet and not letting Ma carry keys. But Dad always said, Of course Mr. Baskett loves your mother. Who doesn't love your mother? Dad always said."

"Indeed?" asked Svatopluk.

"I mean, at first we didn't think anything. Ma left a note saying she was going away for a while and she'd let us know when she got there. Dad and I figured maybe she'd *said* where she was going only we weren't paying attention. It's been like that lately. We figured maybe she'd gone to Salzburg for the festival and Dad even looked up when it was, only it was over. Then, he started to notice Ma had packed a lot of her clothes, and there were pictures of us kids missing. Then Dad found her ring, and a lot of other jewelry she usually wears, but her *ring*—that big engagement ring that never came off. And by then we hadn't heard from her all weekend and Dad started looking every-where for I don't know what he thought he was going to find and he discovered all these other letters Ma had written to him thrown out in the trash—drafts of letters explaining where she was going and why and stuff, pushed way down in the trash. I mean, she'd thrown them away so I don't think she really meant what she said. That's what I said to Dad, Look, she's thrown them away so don't pay attention to what she said. Don't you think?"

"Possibly," Svatopluk said.

"Yeah, I don't think so either but somebody's got to stick up for Ma now that Dad's sicced the CIA on her," Julie said.

"But what interest has the CIA in a minor domestic matter? And why Libya? Americans can't go to Libya now, can they?" Svatopluk asked. "America is very angry at Libya. I have seen the paperwork at the office, who can trade with whom, like decreeing who could play with whom when we were children."

"Mr. Baskett's in hiding there. He ran away because he did some-thing spy-y or something. He worked for the government so he knew stuff. He's a very horrible person. Maybe Ma just feels sorry for him."

"I'd say your mother must feel more than sorrow for the man," Svatopluk said.

"Well, now I think Ma was just waiting for us all to grow up before she could take off. I was the last one. I guess she must have decided I can look after myself now. Well, I kept telling her to butt out of my life so I guess this is my fault. If I'd've known I'd've let her buy me dumb sweaters and make me appointments at her hairdresser's, like she begged to, and last week she really tried to talk to me about applying to college next year. She was being nice. She wanted to know what *I* wanted, except when she didn't get sarcastic when I said I wanted to go to medical school I thought she was being sarcastic by pretending to take me seriously. Because *I* was being sarcastic. I mean, maybe I could be a psychiatrist, I don't know. Do you need science for that, just to talk to people? Only who wants to talk to crazy people? And anyway, what about Dad? How could she have left *him*? Someone's got to do something about him because I have to go back to school sometime."

"Surely, your father will recover from this. He has many responsibilities. He has been missed at the office. Indeed, he has yet to sign off on the paychecks, which is very urgent," Svatopluk said. "Where can I find him so he can do so?"

"I don't know. He's either still trying to write to my brothers about what's happened, or he's on the phone to all these countries he thinks Ma may have gone through, and he's probably—what time is it?—no, he's definitely drinking. I wouldn't disturb him, if I were you. You won't get anywhere. Mrs. Cook keeps trying soup but she's not getting anywhere either. You'd better let me sign whatever it is you want signed. It'll be all right. Don't think I haven't done this before. Even when people have reason to be suspicious, I get away with it. Dad's writing is easy, like all block letters. Ma's was always harder to do. Her signature just sort of trails off into this flat line. You know, like writing her last name bored her or depressed her or something."

"Very well," said Svatopluk. "The staff need to be paid, and I must get back to the office with these. But when can I see you again? I have missed you very much. I will be very discreet. I have discovered an alternate way into the castle—"

"Actually, I don't think it's all that hard to get into or to get out of here. Much easier than you'd think, either way," Julie said.

"IT SNOWED AGAIN LAST NIGHT. The trees are dusted and glistening and they do not look real from my window," Franca said. But then, all views from the castle windows seemed dreamlike.

"How shall we get down the Avenue?" Michal asked.

"We shan't. But need we go anywhere? I have no need to go anywhere." Franca leaned back in her chair and reached for a piece of toast. The dining room table had been set at one end with six places. Someone was keeping track of how many (and whom) to expect for breakfast these days—the greater expanse of the table stretched, polished and empty and reserved. There was coffee in a thermal carafe on the sideboard, and milk and orange juice still in their waxy cartons. A shiny toaster was plugged by a relay of cords into a wall socket and a sleeve spilled out slices of bread. There was butter, and honey and marmalade in jars, and fried eggs on a platter. There were big boxes of American cereals, Wheaties and Fiddle Faddle and Kix. Sometimes, but not this morning, there were sausages steeping in a shallow water bath.

"I have a meeting this afternoon at the Ministry," Michal said. He had slung his tie over his shoulder as a precaution against yolk stains.

"You will be able to get out by then. The men will have come with the truck and the plow."

"Yes, of course. There are such excellent arrangements here at the castle."

Franca smiled. Lately, ensuring the excellence of the castle's arrangements had fallen to her. She said, "I love the look of that dark ribbon of the Avenue unwinding through the parkland in the snow. It is like a road in a vision, I think."

"Did Tilla and Pavel argue very loudly last night, or was that also a dream?" Michal asked.

"Hush. Here they come. I must brave Mrs. Cook to ask for fresh coffee for them."

"And that new jam from America, the blueberry preserves. I do not see it today."

"All right. But I'll tell her I'm asking for *you*."

"No, the castle's walls are not as thick as Tilla and Pavel believe them to be," Michal said. "I am certain I would not have dreamed of Tilla calling me a useless layabout; she does not know me well enough to have discerned those qualities in me. I shall move my room away from theirs. I have had my eye on the Peacock Suite."

"*Hush.* Good morning, a lovely morning. You see, we have been given snow," Franca greeted the couple.

"At least we need not go out in it," Tilla said.

"Michal has a meeting at the Ministry."

"But Franca has arranged for the men with the plow."

"Pavel, you must clear the belvedere of all this snow," Tilla said.

"Why must I?"

"Alden likes to pace there and you have nothing better to do."

"Alden paces the Long Gallery in this weather," Franca said. "He and Tommy."

"Ah, then. Is there any coffee?" Pavel asked. His hand hovered above the carafe. He preferred to avoid the disappointment of having nothing pour into his cup, nothing or not enough. He would want to crawl back into bed, dragging the pillow beneath the covers with him down to the foot of the bed where darkness lingered.

"I was just going to ask for more," Franca said. "And I must take up Alden's tray now. I must make sure he is awake. We were up very late, last night. Working," she added.

Tilla caught Michal's eye as she shook her head and he shrugged.

"Besides, I have no snow boots," Pavel said. "They were lost along with everything else."

TILLA AND PAVEL HAD BEEN THE FIRST to move into the castle. A crisis had visited their lives; their beautiful mansion apartment house in the Malá Strana district, where they lived in a beautiful flat, the sole privilege remaining from Pavel's former position within the old order, had been sold to Marriott Corp. and they had to be out by the end of the week. Pavel had been informed of the impending sale some months earlier and he had been notified again when he was observed carrying lengths of lumber and a bag of nails across the building's elegant foyer, gouging the plaster with aftward flailings of six-foot planks as he negotiated his way onto the lift. He had spun a fantasy for himself that if he refused to budge they would build their new hotel around and about him, where he would then abide entombed like a pharaoh. Pavel had had to be sedated and carried off on a stretcher to a bed in a hospital ward. Tilla had been called at work.

This had happened not long after Alden had returned to the office. He did not care; he might as well be there as anywhere when no place at all seemed right. A cord of misery drew him on, dragging him from day to day along routes crowded with sorrows. Everywhere he looked he saw mourners following coffins into graveyards and Gypsy women with ailing babies begging by the river and dumb alcoholics huddled in doorways. He vowed that when Becky returned to him he would not add to the world's store of human failures. He would forgive her and try to understand why she had left him and to address the faults and insufficiencies within himself that had driven her from his side during this testing time in their marriage.

"There is room enough at the castle. You and Pavel must go there," he had told Tilla, bitterly owning to the empty, echoing rooms and banishing the vision that had come to him of Tilla and her husband sitting by the side of the road surrounded by all their earthly possessions; he saw upended tables, an Old World blanket chest, and a pianola exposed to the hard, grey rain of Prague.

"Bless you," Tilla had said. "But only until we find another place, I promise you." She fetched Pavel from the hospital. He wore blue pajamas beneath his duffle coat and paper slippers. We are going to the castle, he told his ward mates, who knew he was a mental case. During his stay, Pavel had acquired a large yellow dog with a thumping tail named Tommy—won from the night porter over a hand of faro, Pavel claimed, although Tilla was quite certain the animal had been a gift to his mistress from whom, lately, there had been a final break and she (her name was Marta, she was a journalist) no longer had to pretend to care for the beast.

Then, Michal had needed a place to stay when the staircase leading to his attic apartment collapsed. "Pavel has some boards and nails he won't be using," Jaroslav had said, and Tilla, bristling at his cruelty, had said, "Michal, you must come to the castle. Alden will not mind. He probably will not even notice."

For by then the cord had frayed and snapped, leaving Alden drifting and directionless and indifferent. He no longer noticed the beggars and he did not now envy the dead. His patience had not been rewarded; he had given Becky six weeks to come to her senses and come home. The mercy he meant to display had not been met with contrition. He could not believe Becky did not know she could return to him, and it seemed, then, that she had elected not just once but once again to refuse all that he offered her. He would still forgive her (he knew that) but he would do so less easily and less quietly and he was not disinclined to hope (or to admit to himself now what that he had been hoping this all along) that she was and would continue for some time to be unhappy until she learned the lessons that suffering imparted.

Michal had retrieved his few belongings as best he could. The municipal authorities summoned a forklift and Michal was raised, feeling like a passion-play Christ as he floated upward to the level of his door. He assembled his clothes, his books, his papers, his albums, his trumpet, and a carton of canned goods from his larder: spiced beets and chopped kale and sliced peaches which he begrudged his shiftless neighbors who would undoubtedly hijack a forklift of their own and loot what remained in his forsaken flat. He lived in such a slum, a lingering mark of his disfavor within the old order. But the castle beckoned, and the magnificent hi-fi in the library with the soaring ceiling, and the parkland where he could play his trumpet without eliciting complaints, not that he could really play. He could not produce what he deemed to be music but sometimes he had a great desire to set loose and free all the loud wild sounds he could muster from his instrument.

Finding himself driving half his staff into the city every morning, with Pavel tagging along (he was temporarily selling men's furnishings in a department store), Alden had, one day, questioned why they needed to go into the office at all. He had been conducting most of his business from the castle, anyway, working later and later into the night, for he could not sleep and he dreaded making the attempt. Less and less did he care to venture out. Winter had settled in, the old stones of Prague exuding a damp cold that seeped into his bones to meet the ice in his heart. Acquaintances met on the street continued to ask after Becky. Still visiting in the States? they inquired, repeating the official line that had first explained Becky's absence. Besides, the dog could not be left on his own all day at the uncertain mercy of the female servants (Miss Mopsy shooed him with her dustpan and brush, and Mrs. Cook hit his nose with a spatula, warning him away from her larder). Tommy was noticeably cowed by women (his and Pavel's mistress had been harsh) but he brightened in the presence of men, thumping his tail and tenderly taking their hands into his mouth as if to say, Please, stay.

Julie had asked, "How am I supposed to get to school if you don't drive me? I'm not taking two buses and that smelly tram just to get to school." So it had only made sense to ask Svatopluk to stay at the castle during the week in order to drive Julie into the city and then to stop by the office to collect the day's post and to meet with scheduled clients until the time came to retrieve Julie. His position was not correct, effectively serving as chauffeur, assuming the mantle of the disgraced Josef as Julie teased him to wear the jacket and the cap, but, certainly, the arrangement facilitated his courtship of Julie, which had hit a rough patch. She had turned skittish. A harsh life lesson on the subject of un-everlasting love had just been served to her and she devoted many hours, locked in her Tower, to writing speculatively in her diary. She recorded what Svatopluk said and did, and dissected how he had said and done it. Sometimes she read to him these passages from her diary. You sit there and I'll stand here, she told him, pacing off ten feet between them when she admitted him to the Tower, but only to talk. Svatopluk rather enjoyed hearing about himself. He came off well enough, he thought; at least she quoted him accurately as he quoted lines of Neruda and Pavel Josef Šafařik he had rendered into English. He was interested, as well, in Julie's reconsiderations of her childhood, which she was re-remembering by the light of recent events. He laughed at the funny parts, which startled Julie, who had not realized that her memories could still seem to be such happy ones. And when they laughed, she let him kiss her.

Presently, Jaroslav, who had been grumbling about these new arrangements, resigned to assume a new position within the Department of Tourism. He had been given Silesia, but only because no one else was fool enough to accept it, Michal said. Of her own volition, Franca began to commute to the castle, taking the tram and two buses and walking up the Avenue, the frozen gravel crunching painfully beneath the thin soles of her fashionable pumps; she believed gravel must become harder as it froze, or, at any rate, the castle gravel did. She brought her luncheon sandwich and fruit and a split of white wine in a satchel, and a fresh pastry for Alden's coffee break. She was sure he wasn't eating well these days. There were hollows in his temples and shadows under his eyes and his beautiful suits bunched in the back. She always had an extra apple to offer him, and half her sandwich, if he wished. He had only to ask, if tempted by what she had brought.

They settled into a routine working in the library. Franca organized papers and typed reports and telephoned Svatopluk, who sat alone, now, at the office, to ask him questions or to tell him things. She made a workspace for herself at one end of the long central table; she had an IBM Selectric, a good lamp to see by, a steno pad, pencils, a powerful stapler with which she crunched together the pages of final reports. The dog, that new yellow dog, lived underneath the library table in a lair of its own, curled on a square of silk carpet. He thumped his tail whenever Alden spoke, as if, Franca thought, the dog meant to mock the quickening that occurred in her own heart whenever Alden looked up from his papers and said, Franca.

One evening she stayed late until she was sure she had missed the last bus back to the city. What shall I do now? she asked not very anxiously, for she knew perfectly well she would have to spend the night. Tilla lent her a nightgown (Terylene, green) and Franca improvised a toothbrush from bundled Q-Tips. Since no one seemed to care where she was to sleep, she selected the next but one bedroom down from Alden's door. All the others had chosen bedrooms in a distant wing. Her chamber was hung with dark draperies and crowded with heavy carved furnishings including, beside the bed, a prie-dieu—as if, Franca thought, some noblewoman had been immured here on the eve of her wedding, or, perhaps, her execution. Either that, or the lady in question had merely been expected to be good. Franca had rinsed out her underthings and draped them over the prie dieu, where they failed to dry thoroughly by morning.

After that, Franca made a habit of missing the bus, and it only made sense for her to keep a few things at the castle for those occasions, an accumulation of things: a nice new robe and matching nightgown and pony-skin mules from a lovely little shop, very French, very expensive; the better elements of her winter wardrobe; a loofah and hair dryer and her magnifying mirror (for sometimes a hair grew on her chin); a softer pillow; several new novels about contemporary life and love in Prague and environs to occupy her mind as she sat up late with her light on.

Some months elapsed. The holidays had been gotten through, some-how, at the castle. All invitations were refused, no lights were strung, no fir boughs hung, and no one got what they wanted. Then, with the New Year, the country split in two. Franca swore she could feel the quake and shudder of the dissolution as the hour struck. The work of the office increased as the framework they had built for the new economy was suddenly seen to need propping and stabilization when put into use. Alden had had to remind the staff as they clung to their parts and pieces of the framework that the marketplace ruled now and not the State, and word from on high (he gestured vaguely upward) in-sisting there was no unemployment, no debt, no economic disparity within society, no longer made it true. Let's all quit insisting how good things used to look on paper, Alden advised them.

"HAS JULIE GONE TO SCHOOL?" Alden asked when he appeared in the library where Michal and Tilla and Franca were already at work. He had carried down his breakfast tray. He had established that he was ca-pable of doing this, so that Franca would not linger in his bedroom waiting, and chatting as she waited, while he sipped at hot coffee and scraped carbon from his toast and peeled back the skin of an orange. For Franca to linger in his bedroom seemed very odd to him, and it was odd enough to be awakened by her tap upon his door. He did not understand why she had taken it upon herself to "let" him sleep until eight, but no later. Sometimes he remembered to set his alarm for ten to the hour so that he would be standing beneath his noisy shower with his eyes closed and the spray drumming into his scalp and back as Franca came and went, setting the tray down upon the foot of his bed, made nervous by the thought of Alden's nudity and nearness. She would drop the tray upon the first flat surface she encountered and withdraw.

But on the mornings she found him still in bed, Franca had a way of pulling open his window drapes with a strong and graceful sweep of her arms; the flung draperies parted, their rings spinning along the rod. On dull mornings, as Franca stood at the window, her skin seemed to glow from within like a pearl, and on sunny days as she stood taking pleasure in the sun her skin seemed touched with honey. The effect was beguiling, but Alden never was to realize how much he looked forward to seeing whether a day dawned pale or golden upon Franca's skin. And had she known that Alden looked and that he noticed, Franca would have flushed a deep mottled red instead.

"Yes. Julie has gone to school," Franca said. "She has even finished her history paper on the Rise of the Czech Movement for Independence in the Nineteenth Century. Svatopluk helped her with a few insights."

"How did they make it out through the snow?" Alden asked.

"They took the Range Rover instead of Svatopluk's little Opel," Franca said.

"They had trouble on the hill. Svatopluk spread sand and pushed. Julie got behind the wheel then," said Michal, which had been amusing to observe from a warm perch in the castle.

"But I have arranged for the plow to come," Franca said. "Also, here are your telephone messages and a prospectus you must read, and the minister has a pressing query which you must attend to first."

"I have a meeting in town this afternoon to discuss the Brno matter, and I need to know our final position," Michal said.

"These figures make no sense to me," Tilla said. "Do they make sense to you?" She pushed a page across the table toward Alden, who frowned at the run of numbers and pushed them back to Tilla.

"Boy, here boy," he called out. "Tommy, here Tommy." He slapped his thigh as the dog, who had come on the double at the sound of Alden's voice, skidded over the flagstone floor. "Hasn't anyone walked you, boy? Do you want me to walk you? Do you, Tommy, do you?" Alden asked. "Nobody remembered to take you out? Well, I remembered, boy." Alden left the library, the dog frisking in circles around his heels. "Has anyone fed you, Tommy? Has anyone remembered to give you your breakfast?"

"I let the creature out at six a.m.," Franca said. "I let him out, and unfortunately, he came back. And he eats in the evening. Mrs. Cook gives him what she gives us, in a cracked mixing bowl."

"Alden loves that dog," Tilla said.

"It is a classic case of transference," Michal said.

"Yes, yes, we know," the women said.

"But he must move on," Franca said.

"He *has* moved on. To Tommy," Michal said.

"I had a spitz who ran away right before I married Pavel. I often wish I'd just gotten another spitz puppy," Tilla said.

"Yes. You see. You should always replace what you had with what it was in the first place you loved," Franca said. "Only nicer and younger."

"And not inclined to wander off," supposed Michal. "But how I miss the old Alden, and nodding my head and snapping my fingers to his jazz-riff lectures. I have been thinking, lately, of the time he attempted to convince us that prosperity is not a zero-sum game. Perhaps not, but we have all since learned that love triangles certainly ensure there must be someone who comes up short."

ALDEN LET TOMMY AND HIMSELF OUT THE SIDE DOOR. Tommy took the lead, knowing Alden would follow him as he made his way along the track Julie and Svatopluk had stamped in the snow earlier that morning. His nose dropped, his tail rose erect and waving. When Svatopluk's furrowed boot prints and Julie's smooth-soled steps turned toward the stable yard, Tommy picked up the scent of the path he and Alden took on their usual morning walk around the castle. The trail they had broken through the old snow unwound as a distinct groove below the fresher fall.

The path meandered. They revisited the spots where treasured smells had settled for Tommy to rediscover as he plunged his muzzle into the snow. As they came round the sharp corner beneath the thrust of the belvedere, Tommy raised his hackles and barked at the figures standing about in the sculpture park, whose appearance always surprised him because he received no warning olfactory signals of their presence, Alden supposed. Tommy was an inveterate groin sniffer; he was just the right height.

Alden brushed a stone bench clear of snow and sat down facing the figures: the female forms of a Diana and a Daphne and a kneeling Echo, half buried in the snow; the Hussar on a tall, fine horse; the modern piece, a cube with a hole cut through it, which, presumably, was making some kind of comment on the interdependence between square-ness and roundness, though mostly Alden wondered how someone had reamed such a precise cut from the center of a solid block of granite without shattering the stone. Here was a piece of modern art that did not make him want to say, I could do that.

Tommy raised his leg against the robes of a bronze monk who bore an ellipse of birdbath, icebound now, and then he returned to Alden's side. He squatted on his haunches and stuck a foot in his mouth, chewing at the bobbles of ice dangling from the fur sprouting between the pads.

"Poor guy, poor fella," Alden said, as Tommy's ears flattened and his tail swept snow from side to side. Franca had told him Tommy didn't speak English, and Alden had reminded her that Tommy didn't speak. Nevertheless, he seemed to understand.

Alden lit a cigarette, cradling his ungloved hand in the gloved one as he struck a match. He lifted his scarf against the bitter cold. He was in no hurry to return to the castle and the demands of the office. He needed some time alone to think about what had heretofore been un-thinkable. He had delayed and deferred and distracted himself from the subject long enough with a mix of unreasonable hope and willful blindness. But he had scheduled a teleconference with an attorney in New York that evening whom he intended to ask to regularize the situation. Alden did not know what he meant by that phrase, "regular-ize the situation," but he supposed he would be told.

For recent events had caused Alden to take steps at last. Becky's name had found its way onto a list of local missing persons when an in-quiry had been made on the first day of her disappearance, and a week ago Alden had been called upon by a policeman who described the body of a woman just pulled from the ice-clogged Moldau: a middle-aged woman wearing a dark raincoat and plastic boots, a paisley-print dress, and a brooch of a knotted design. No, no, that cannot possibly be my wife, Alden said, and the officer whose time had been wasted and whose English had been taxed informed Alden he ought to have in-formed the authorities that Mrs. Lowe's whereabouts could now be ac-counted for. Well, you can't have been searching for her very hard, Alden answered back. He'd been shaken by the conversation; even though he had known the body could not possibly be Becky's, he had for a few panicked seconds not been sure.

Then, as if a dam had burst, immediately in the wake of the news of the drowned woman, had come word of word from Becky. She had written at last to the boys and to her brother, and the boys and her brother had sent Alden copies of Becky's letters and copies of their own replies to Becky. By this, the boys and Hap meant to be humane and fair. They knew Alden would be relieved to hear that Becky seemed well and happy enough even as such information pained him, and by this honorable policy of full disclosure from one camp to the other the boys and Hap meant for both sides to understand they were not choosing sides. Alden, who surely was more sinned against than sinning in all of this, reflected that everyone had to be more than fair to Becky and less than fair to himself to achieve such evenhandedness. But it was odd how the boys and their uncle had acted alike in this. He knew there had been no collusion. He had always been aware that while Hap liked and approved of his sister's husband, he had never cared for his sister's children, and he now seemed to prefer to believe she had left them rather than Alden. Hap said as much in his letter to Alden, a copy of which, he said, he would also send to Becky. Alden wondered how Hap and the boys were keeping all their documents in order (and he wondered as well whether Julie had heard from her mother—he had not asked and she had not said). Further, both Hap and the boys had written that they were delaying the sending of their replies to Becky pending the addenda of any message from Alden, as if Alden could not write to Becky on his own now that he knew her address. But they seemed to be offering the shield of their sponsorship. They would stand between Alden and Becky, absorbing or deflecting any arrows, any blows one might aim at the other. The letters had already taken many weeks to arrive at their scattered destinations and, no doubt, the eventual answers would need many weeks more to find the Omar al Mukhtar Road, as if all of this were happening a thousand years ago when time and distance stretched equally long between any two points on the map. Although Alden wished the date was a thousand years hence, that centuries had passed since all of this transpired and that they, the participants in this muddle, were all far beyond caring who had never loved—or had always loved—whom.

Hap's reply to his sister was practical and supportive. He had written, mainly, of financial matters. For years he had been keeping track of Becky's share of the ranch's profits, which he had invested or applied to improvements of the stock and land. He suggested, now, that some income be sent to her, and he mentioned a sum that surprised Alden. He had thought that Hap presided over a hobby farm, that the horses and the cattle and, lately, the llamas had been props of some sort, just filling in the background and chewing up the scenery. There was a fine front porch at the ranch house where they had all sat one afternoon naming the llamas Fernando and Dolly and Red Hot.

Alden supposed this financial information would be useful to relay to the attorney when he spoke to him that evening and, most likely, not in Becky's best interest for him to know.

" 'Cry "Havoc" and let slip the dogs of war,' " Alden addressed Tommy with the calm, kind voice he always used when speaking to him. Tommy shot Alden a charming smile over his shoulder and then went back to worrying an ice ball from his foot.

Becky had written individually to the boys, although her message had not varied and certain descriptive phrases were repeated: the walls of the villa were honey colored; the dunes were vast; the sea seemed such a living presence; and she missed her children. There were camels in the road; the moon and the stars hung low and large and illuminated in the African night sky; and she could only hope they would understand why she had done what she had done although she herself scarcely understood. She was spooked by the local scorpions but she was learning to deal with them. She had then made some charming fun of elements of the local population and, at the last, she mentioned William. *Wm.*, she had written, as if he were something in a footnote at the bottom of a page which might or might not be consulted: op. cit., s.v., n.b., in re Wm.

Alden had the boys' letter to Becky with him, folded in his shirt pocket, transferred from yesterday's shirt pocket, and the day's before. He could not have said whether keeping the letter just there caused him to feel closer to his sons or to his wife (for he had slowly become aware where the letter sat in relation to his heart, and he was rather dismayed by the theatricality of the gesture, but he could not remove the letter to a trouser pocket without invoking further characterization and farce). He was proud of his boys, and he believed Becky would be proud too, and he thought of how their eyes might have met above the pages of the letter, Becky's eyes going a bit swimmy, and Alden would have had to say something like, One of the boys must be dating a psych major, just to leaven the moment. He reached inside his coat and retrieved the folded square of paper and he read again,

Dear Ma, I have been elected to write to you. I was in California on a course when your letters found us, and Brooks and Rollins and I met to discuss what to say to you, which will now be conveyed to you by a single voice, my own.

First, you asked how we are. We are fine. My promotion came through and I am on my way to Kansas for another course. Brooks and Rollins want you to know they have decided to concentrate on Applied Technologies because that is where the opportunities are and the money is. This does not mean they have entirely abandoned the Theoretical. However, they feel if you can think it you should be able to do it if you have the practical skills and know-how. And as nothing is unthinkable these days, it should be interesting to see what they achieve.

This is what we want to say to you:

1.) You are our mother and always will be.

2.) You are also a person in your own right.

3.) Our father is a good and excellent man.

4.) We do not think he will get on very well without you. He is the worst loser in all this at the moment, but we believe you will be the worst loser in the end.

5.) We will not choose between you and Dad, which, to be fair, you didn't ask us to.

6.) We were not great kids but we think we are turning out all right now and will be ok in the future.

7.) But what about our sister?

8.) We do not know when we will see you. As a member of the

Armed Forces, I cannot travel to Libya. Nor will Brooks and Rollins, at present, because to do so might compromise any security clearances they may need to get—the government is all over the tech sector. But you can come to any of us at any time, at any place. Just appear and we will be so happy. We will keep you supplied with our addresses as they change. It is terrible not to know where someone is.

9.) We want to know if you know what it was Wm. did that led to his current necessity to reside in a place like Libya. Has he told you? We do not believe so because we do not think you would remain in this man's company if he had come clean with you. I am enclosing the complete report, which Brooks and Rollins accessed through means of their own and which is classified at the highest level. Witness all the NATO intelligence he traded in. Perhaps he will argue that no real harm was ever done, but you cannot know where the first wrong step will take you in the end.

Well, that's it for now. I don't have anything else to say. What did you expect us to say? This is not a rhetorical question. What do you want from us, Ma? What are we supposed to do? Tell us, and we'll try. Love, Glover (and Brooks and Rollins too)

"Okay, Tommy," Alden said. He chucked his cigarette over the Hussar's helmeted head. "Let's go, boy." The dog took off, racing ahead and then doubling back in repeated maneuvers of advance and return to see what was keeping Alden, who was in no hurry to get back to the castle and the demands of the day ahead.

IN THE EARLY SPRING, ALDEN'S SISTER, GINGER, arrived in Prague primed to assist. She would have been there sooner but her first grand-child, a little girl, had lately been born and Ginger had been occupied by shopping for the event and telephoning California daily as yet an-other thought occurred to her regarding prenatal care or preschool registration. After the birth, she had gone out to Santa Barbara for a week to help and advise her daughter until the other grandmother showed up with a suitcase full of exquisite but impractical things she had been knitting for months. Ginger's turn at visiting had gone rather well. Betsy, if she had to choose between mother and mother-in-law, decided she preferred her own mother, and when she told Ginger this, Ginger had come to the conclusion that Sally, the baby (ill-advised as everyone had thought her conception to be—Betsy was too young and still in school and Andy was just making his mark in the world), seemed to be working out.

"Alden, let me look at you. Alden, how are you?" Ginger cried. "My word, would you look at this place. Hello. How do you do. Whose dog is this? Here fella, I won't bite."

Ginger had made her own way from the airport and out to the castle and into the library where Alden and his staff were working. They all looked up and saw a commanding woman with wonderful hair (Franca's description of the newcomer as they were talking it over later) surrounded by luggage and duty-free carrier bags.

"Where's Julie? I have some things for her," Ginger said, picking up and putting down one of the shopping bags.

"She's at school," Alden said, rising and approaching his sister. He hefted her garment bag and looped the handles of her carry-on satchel over his arm. Michal advanced and introduced himself and relieved Alden of his burden.

"Oh, yes," Alden remembered. "And here are Franca and Tilla and Tommy." Ginger received little waves from the women, and Tommy, watchful, emitted a whiny yawn.

"Where shall I put these?" Michal asked.

"We have prepared the Empress Suite for Mrs. Tuckerman," Franca said.

"Oh my, the Empress Suite," said Ginger. "What fun this is going to be."

"AREN'T YOU EXHAUSTED?" Alden asked Ginger much later that first evening. Ginger had explored the castle from the cellars to the Tower. Julie had returned from school and been exclaimed over. She endured and then succumbed to her aunt's embrace and she approved of the perfume and CDs and magazines and almost all of the outfits Ginger had brought her. They had all dined on several courses served with some ceremony upon the best emblazoned china by Miss Mopsy and by Mrs. Cook as well, who had wanted to see for herself this new American lady. The staff, swelled by the additions of Svatopluk and Pavel, had set about getting to know their Boss's sister by telling her about themselves. Ginger had sat at the far end of the long Dining Hall table from Alden, who sat at the head. She took Becky's theretofore left empty old place without thinking of what she was doing, and Michal was to say later that he hoped Mrs. Tuckerman had sat upon and flattened for good that shimmering and persistent ghost.

"Oh, I'm miles beyond tired," Ginger said. She had wandered down to the library where Alden was still at work at his desk. "I'm not sure I can find my way back to my room, anyway."

"Up the grand staircase, past the presentation clock."

"No, no, I know where my room is," Ginger said. "I just thought you might like a moment alone with me to talk—well, to talk about that matter no one is speaking of."

"It is all being handled. I consulted someone a while back."

"Oh dear, has it come to that? Are you going to divorce her?"

"No. I thought I would but I found I didn't have the appetite for going after her, although I was informed I had quite the case against her—a cache of letters admitting she's with William. 'Admitting'— that's a legal term for ceasing to pretend, I think. But Becky is to be told that, if she wishes, she may institute proceedings. I'm not sure that would be wise, however. At present, in some odd way, she is still under my protection, or within reach, at any rate, should she need to be reached."

"But what are you going to do?" Ginger asked.

"Do? I'll do what I'm doing."

"For the rest of your life, what are you going to do?"

"Must I decide that this very evening?"

"Of course not. But you know what I'm saying. You can't just drift along indefinitely. Is there anything practical I can do for you, now that I'm here? That's why I've come, to be useful. What about her things? I noticed them all over your bedroom when I was having my snoop round the castle (what a charming suite of rooms, by the way). Let me pack them up for you."

"I don't know."

"She's not coming back."

"You did, that time you left."

"When Louis came and got me. Besides, I ran away *to* home, back to Aunt Lily, and not off with some man. I think this is very different from my little escapade."

"Yes, I know it is. There's nothing to be done."

"Oh, don't say that. Perhaps I'm wrong. Perhaps she'll come to her senses. I don't want to be right about this, I truly don't. Why don't you go to see her? Don't you think you owe it to yourself and her to do that? Just go and see for yourself. I'll come with you, if that will help. Oh, don't look at me like that."

"Do *you* want to see something?" Alden asked.

"I don't know. Do I? What?"

There was a television set in a corner of the library. Alden slipped a videocassette from a desk drawer and inserted it into the attached VCR. He pushed buttons. The screen pulsed and glowed as a mechanism whirred. Tommy stretched out in front of the TV as if he thought they were going to watch him.

"You know we saw Arthur when he was filming here?"

"Yes. How was Arthur?"

"He's turned into an utter ass, but he wangled us parts in his movie. Just as extras in a crowd scene, which I'm not even sure has made the final cut. But some weeks later, Arthur sent this cassette—I think they call them dailies—of the scene we were in. I'll tell you, moviemaking is the most tedious process imaginable. You do the same thing over and over and over again and nothing ever goes right and you do it over again and something else goes wrong. Here, the tape's cued up, you'll see. It's an establishing shot, that's the entrance of a theater. The gentry are alighting from carriages and the riffraff are milling about, as we were directed to do."

On the morning of the shoot, they had presented chits at the entrance to the downtown Prague location. Becky had been shown into one trailer and Alden into another. Alden had been outfitted with a beggar's rags. Smooth holes and crisp tatters had been scissored into a pair of trews, a shirt, a coat, stockings. A cloth cap was pulled over his head. He was told to grin, and several of his teeth were blackened with a paste that had taken days to dissolve from the enamel. A makeup person shaded his face and neck and the backs of his hands with a grime-colored substance that he wasn't sure wasn't real grime, and some fellow who seemed to have the final say had sent him back to the trailer to have a gold hoop attached to his earlobe, clamped there by the pull of magnets. Then, he had been given another chit to present at a breakfast buffet table. Arthur had waved at him from a distance—the principal actors were kept in a kind of gilded corral—and Alden had been dismayed to find that he was still recognizable.

Becky's transformation had taken much longer. Alden swiped a muffin for her as the food began to disappear from the buffet table and he felt that the presence of a stolen muffin crumbling in his pocket helped him to understand his character; his was a loving but luckless soul, and Alden wondered how someone could come to such a state, ragged and toothless and caught up in a Parisian mob.

Becky emerged at last from her trailer. Her chit had gained her access to the world of the gentry. Her hair had been piled on her head, and swags and braids were attached. Makeup had been applied heavily, her skin made whiter, red circles rubbed into her cheeks. She'd been given bee-stung lips and a beauty mark. She wore a wonderful gown of real silk and lace—fabrics could not be cheated on film. She had been laced in so tightly that each breath she took rubbed against corset bone. She had been rather stunned by the expanse and rise of décolletage the costumer had achieved by a near-architectural cantilevering of flesh. She had asked for a shawl, for she was chilly, but she was given jewels instead, a necklace of immense yellow diamonds which were not real, for precious stones *could* be cheated on film.

She had not wanted the muffin Alden had saved for her. She was far too elegant to eat—a sip of champagne and a strawberry was all she might manage, she had said. That was all she could fit between her bee-stung lips and beneath the press of corsetry. Then, she and Alden had been pulled aside. As a favor to Arthur they were going to be given a little something to play. A coach was going to pass into the frame and stop in front of the theater and Becky would alight, as Alden emerged from the throng of passersby. Charmed by the presence of such beauty, he was to snatch off his cap and execute a low bow as Becky swept past him.

Aspects of the actual filming had been quite interesting, Alden told Ginger. Technicians had blown in some sort of cinematic smoke to give the scene the shadows and depth of early evening, and the day had also turned grey on its own. The sound effects were to be added later: the clap of the horse's hooves and the rumble of wheels across cobblestones; the low babble of the crowd; the incidental music produced by some strolling players who had just been taught how to hold their instruments and shown where to place their fingers. In the dailies, it was odd how the ambient sounds of the director's growled-out orders and modern traffic noise had given the scene the air of a documentary; the actors seemed more real rather than less so, without the gloss of whatever art was to be applied later.

Becky had been led to a carriage that resembled a wobbly armoire on wheels. She had stroked the nose of the horse, a chestnut mare with a gentle nature who had given Becky a rather blameful look as she and her billowing skirts were fitted inside the carriage. Becky had leaned from the window and asked an assistant director whether a lady would have ventured out alone to the theater in that era. He had not known (it was not his business to know) but had felt that she might have a point and suggested that hers was, perhaps, an unsanctioned excursion. Becky had asked, then, wouldn't the lady have made some attempt at concealment—perhaps she ought to wear a veil? But the assistant director had been distracted by several members of a troupe of acrobatic monkeys who were climbing the facade of the theater after being frightened by a fire-breathing man, and Becky was left to decide on her own that her character would descend from her calèche cloaked only in froideur.

They had played the scene. The pretty horse was urged forward and the carriage swayed into the shot. Becky decended from the carriage, her foot, which seemed very remote within its swirl of skirts and petticoats, placed upon an unsteady rundle step which sagged and then sprang back, launching her from the vehicle. Her bosom heaved as she just caught herself. Alden broke free of the crowd. He snatched off his cap and held it to his heart as he made a low bow before the grand lady.

Becky shot him a look of alarm and twitched her skirts away from him. The scene had not gone satisfactorily; the riffraff had all been staring and grinning into the camera. They were told not to do so, and the worst offenders were turned around to face away from the lens. Becky was assisted back into her carriage. Alden's cap was restored to his head and more of the grime was applied to his nose and brow and the backs of his hands. The pretty mare was urged forward again. Becky exited the carriage, more carefully taking that treacherous rundle step, the effect of the heaving bosom lost now, to caution. Alden emerged from the mass of merrymaking common folk and he snatched off his cap and made his low bow. The surging crowd toppled him forward onto his knees. Becky shrank from him, apprehension flooding her face. But that shot had been spoiled, as the pumped-in smoke billowed along a breath of errant breeze. They tried yet again; the carriage rolled forward, Becky emerged, Alden bowed, Becky shunned him coldly. A banner detached from the facade of the theater and entangled with the strolling musicians. Over and over the scene had had to be played. There was no end to the ways in which the shot could go wrong, and no end to the ways in which Becky could reject Alden.

"You see how she feels about me," Alden said as the tape ended.

"She was acting. She had all that training in performance when she was a music student," Ginger said. "She's almost a professional."

"She gave all that up years ago—for my sake, no doubt, although I never asked her to. I was proud of her music. No, what we have here is a uniquely late-twentieth-century phenomenon, actual film footage of the nuances of antipathy that had accrued over the decades of a marriage. It unreels like a time-play, twenty-four years elapsing in thirty minutes. The worst look, I've decided, was the pitying gaze she gave me at the very end. I'm certain she had already made up her mind to leave—she was gone the following week. Indeed, I recall the evening before she asked me whether a leather passport holder was hers or mine, not that it had ever mattered, what was hers or mine."

"Is this what you do, Alden, sit here late at night and replay the tape?" Ginger asked. "Please, don't. It breaks my heart to think of you watching it over and over. Really, I cannot bear it."

"Then there's that look where she seems to be rather fascinated by me. She stares at me as if I were some strange and curious insect she is about to swat. Let me show you again. That was take number nine, which was ruined by that bird flying at the horse's head. Nice horse, by the way."

"Please, don't. It's not necessary. I saw."

"Whereas I believe I achieved a remarkable consistency in my performance. I found my mark. I snatched off my cap. I essayed that courtly bow for all I am just a beggar. But perhaps what Becky desired all along was variety."

"Well, maybe a change is what you need too."

"Oh, don't start, Ginger."

"You need someone young and uncritical who will adore you," Ginger said.

"I have Tommy now."

"Oh God, Alden, I've changed my mind. I withdraw my previous remark," Ginger said. "What you really need, Alden, is someone older and wiser and experienced and sensible who will know what to do with you."

AFTER THE WORKING DAY, AFTER DINNER, the inmates of the castle scattered to the corners where they had made their niches. Michal had moved the hi-fi from the library into a vaulted dungeon chamber with superb acoustics, and he played Coltrane and Brubeck as he slumped in an easy chair wearing dark glasses and a pork-pie hipster hat of recent purchase. Pavel retired to the morning room, where he sat in a deep armchair and undertook to complete Becky's forgotten needlepoint canvas, endeavoring to match the tension of the stitches already worked by Becky; she had tugged the wool into a tighter weave than felt quite right to him. He sipped *Borovicka* from a pale green rummer, his stitches becoming looser as the evening wore on. They would have to be picked out and redone the following evening. Tilla could be found in the Armaments Chamber running on the treadmill she had bought herself. She measured her times against a stopwatch and took long swallows from a bottle of an electrolyte-fortified sports drink. She was training for a marathon and had penciled in Boston for 1995. Julie now frequented her mother's little bandbox salon in the evenings. She lay upon the pillow-heaped sofa, the headset of her Walkman clamped over her ears as she plugged away at her homework and read her assignments for the next day. She had become, she realized, a serious girl. She memorized lines of Czech vocabulary, and her recitation of the verb *to be* could bring a tear to the eye, Svatopluk said. *What might have been, what should have been, what will never be,* Julie would intone. *To lose, to lack, to mourn,* she had learned those as well; even the IY, fidgeting through their hour with Herr Wolfe, would fall silent and listen and did not mock when Julie spoke Czech. Svatopluk sought out Julie in the bandbox salon, and he sat at an end of the sofa reading some book of his own on policy or history with Julie's stocking feet in his lap, which he would caress absentmindedly as, as absentmindedly, she let him until they heard someone approach (the castle was an echoing place of footfalls on stone floors and the cracks and creaks of great, hinged doors). Then, Julie would tuck her knees to her chin and Svatopluk would frown down at his heavy book.

Franca was most often to be encountered in the conservatory at the close of day. She tended to the plants. The office foliage had been moved there and she had set out dozens of coffee cans sprouting with the slips and seeds of things she had sown. The old plants, which she had not thought were her place to throw away, stood jammed beneath the potting bench, turning browner and more brittle as if bound now to grow ever deader. The glass house had collected the sun's heat and when Franca switched on the main, she felt as if she were standing in a space of warmth and light carved from the pressing blackness and chill of night. Her own image was reflected and re-reflected on the windowpanes, and the seedlings in their containers had multiplied into a forest of coffee cans and green questing shoots. She was very aware, in the conservatory, of the boundary, of the wilderness beyond the boundary, and of the place in between where she shimmered and shone and her garden thrived. She thought, If I could just push the boundary gently and become neither caught within nor cast without but to exist *with,* on that delicate, shining plane that would shatter so easily at the first wrong move, *there* is where I would wish to be.

She watched herself in the window for a while. She raised her arms and she swayed in a sort of dance. She twisted her hair into a knot on her head and slipped her sweater sleeve and a bra strap from her shoulder. She sighed and shook her head and her hair fell back into place. She began to move capably among her charges.

She had sent all the way to her grandfather's farm outside Klatovy for jars of manure tea, which made the best fertilizer in the world but was such unlovely stuff. Every time she unscrewed a jar top she conducted an argument with herself whether to draw on the red-and-white-striped gloves with long cuffs that Becky had left behind on the potting-bench shelf. The gloves, stiffened by dried-on dirt, were molded to the shape of Becky's hands; the fingers curved in a final attitude as if around the handle of a trowel, or, at any rate, they still held on to something with a lasting grasp. The absent Becky always won the argument, and Franca's fingers grew rough and her nails always needed tending.

That evening, Franca was watering the tomatoes. She had a dozen plants started. They were eight inches high and beginning to form crowns, if that was the proper word. Franca was not entirely confident of what she was doing, but she was fond of pottering here. She had decided that plants appreciated small, consistent attentions. She watered the tomatoes daily, and other plants were placed on other schedules. She gave the ex–office plants a good soaking once a week, and a forced morning glory vine demanded twice-daily visits. It was a very thirsty little rover.

"Franca. There you are. I've been looking all over," Ginger said, entering the greenhouse. "I need your expertise. I am negotiating to buy a pair of lovely old teardrop diamond earrings I've found at a fascinating shop near the Cathedral and I want you to help me."

"But I know nothing of jewels," Franca said.

"That's all right. I know all about them. I just need you to translate for me, accurately. There's a question of provenance. Mr. Pancner keeps going on about, well, it sounds like 'Czarina.' Come sort things out for me tomorrow and I'll buy you lunch afterward."

"Perhaps he was saying *zářiti,* which means to shine."

"Yes, that could be it. You see how I need you. Although I'll be desperately disappointed if there's no Imperial Russian connection. What's that odor?"

"Fertilizer," Franca said.

"Pah," Ginger said. "Well, what are you growing here? I adore flowers."

"Tomatoes."

"I adore tomatoes." Ginger was most encouraging.

"And this will be a lemon tree I started from a seed."

"How sweet. How ambitious. And how clever of you to use those old tin cans for pots, although, I'll tell you what, let's look for some pretty clay pots tomorrow after we get my earrings."

"And this is a peach I started from a big seed, and an apple, from a very delicious apple I ate one day, and here are gooseberries and raspberries I am also trying to cultivate."

"Why, this is just like a little pie nursery. I'll have to come back in ten years when this greenhouse has turned into an orchard and then we can bake ourselves silly in that fabulous French oven," Ginger declared.

"Oh! Does Alden intend to stay in Prague that long? I have wondered about his plans," Franca said. "Ten years, you say?"

Ginger was rubbing a peach leaf to see if it smelled like peach. The lemon leaf smelled like lemon, and the apple leaf smelled green, she thought. She was not a fan of gooseberries, although she was not sure she had ever been exposed to a really good gooseberry tart. She had seen recipes for them in magazines, however, which had always looked like too much effort for something she wasn't entirely sure of.

"Ten years, you say?" Franca asked again.

"Oh no, I shouldn't think so. Actually, part of my reason for being here is to convince Alden to go home and then see."

"See what? What must Alden look for in America?" Franca asked.

"Oh, well, isn't that the big question? Why are we here, where are we going, what does it all mean, who am I? Who are you? for that matter. It's so unfortunate when our comfortable arrangements get upset and we have to ask ourselves the basic questions all over again. Believe me, the fun in life is in the accessorizing, so to speak, after you've finally decided, shall I wear the diamond earrings or the sapphire ones when I go out with my husband." Ginger smiled. "Anyway, don't forget our date tomorrow. Svatopluk will drive us into town early and we'll make a day of it. Alden tells me you never seem to leave the castle lately. He says you always seem to be here, and, you know, we really can't have that."

ALDEN WAS SITTING UP LATE, AS ALWAYS, in the library. Julie had come in to say good night. She leaned to kiss his brow and she patted his head in a kindly but helpless way and she knelt and did the same to Tommy, who thumped his tail even as he slumbered on. Don't work too hard, she told Tommy. Svatopluk had appeared to ask, Is there anything else, sir? to which Alden replied, as usual, No, you've done quite enough.

Surely not, sir, Svatopluk answered.

Ginger looked in and sighed at Alden and mentioned cocoa. She was, as she was fond of saying, a great brewer of hot chocolate, but Alden did not rise to her suggestion. I'll tilt some schnapps into your mug, Ginger offered, but Alden thought not. Well, don't sit up too late, Ginger told Tommy. You're so crabby in the morning when you do. Then Michal padded softly up to bed, snapping his fingers and muttering hep-hep-hep as Tommy stirred at the sound of the snaps. Tilla and Pavel passed by the library door bickering in Czech as Tommy raised his head and growled deep in his throat.

The castle slept. Alden could tell from the quality of the silence and the stillness that enveloped him at this hour: such peace, although his days were placid enough, he had arranged for them to be so. He supposed this sense of release was a remnant of other, more crowded days. He remembered back when the kids were all very little, how Becky had said what an accomplishment it had seemed to have the four children tucked into bed and at last asleep. They have survived my mothering another day, she would say, and I have survived them. They had been fed (the kids had been impossible eaters; they had fixated on pizza and french fries early). They had been bathed (the kids had been such hydrophobes; he and Becky had always been chasing naked children, slick and slippery as seals, through the apartment). They have said their prayers, Becky would report, although Alden asked why they couldn't just skip that step. The boys and Little Becky had piped through Now I lay me without doing much damage, but they tacked on endless addenda items, highly specific requests for Go-Bot action figures and *Star Wars* weaponry, and they described the terrible punishments they wanted God to visit upon their enemies—upon their teachers, and a man in the park who had shouted at them. What if we pray on the children's behalf? Alden wondered. After all, they had not let the children play on the balcony or light matches or clean up after broken glass.

Alden started. He had been asleep and dreaming scenes from the past, or dreaming up scenes. He was quite certain he had never suggested the children not be allowed to pray. He was sure he had explained to them at the time what was and what was not proper to take up with the Lord. One could pray for the recovery and comfort of sick and suffering people, and world peace, and always, ask God to make you a better person, although now Alden wondered whether it would be interfering to ask Him to make someone else a better person, to make her see the light and come to her senses and return to the fold.

"Is someone there?" Alden asked. Tommy thumped his tail, reached among his own dreams by his master's voice.

Franca stepped forward. She had not wished to startle Alden, but she had been willing him to awaken on his own, which he had seemed likely to do. He was sitting upright in his desk chair with his head sagging ever lower onto his shoulder as his breaths rasped and caught on the crick in his throat.

"What are you doing up?" Alden asked her. Briefly he thought of fetching her a glass of water and leading her by the hand back to bed.

"I am too aroused to sleep," Franca declared. "Your sister has told me something."

"Pay no attention to Ginger. We never do," Alden advised.

"Your sister told me she wants you to return to the States and she has come to Prague to convince you to do this. Alden, is this so?" Franca stood before his desk. She was wearing her dressing gown; she had plaited her hair and brushed her teeth. There was a fleck of foam of which she was unaware drying at the corner of her lips and her late, ineffective effort to sleep had creased and reddened the cheek she had crushed into her pillow.

"As I said, we never listen to Ginger, but yes, and besides there is something else." He indicated the drift of papers across his desk top. "The Field Marshal's heirs have filed a claim for the castle and they may have a good case. I've been wanting to get out of my lease here but I'll make disgruntled noises and force them to scramble a bit to accommodate me. They sound like high-handed types to come waltzing back after sitting out the last fifty years in Canada, where I'm sure they were utter bores on the subject of their lost glory."

"People should accept their losses," Franca declared. "And move on."

"Ah, well. But I suppose we can't really appreciate everything they've been through." Alden had suddenly swerved to the side of the von Holbeins.

"Then what will happen after the castle has been claimed?" Franca had to ask because Alden had not thought to tell her.

"Oh," said Alden, not understanding even when she asked him, "you'll have ample time to relocate. I'll give you the telephone number they give Americans to call to find housing here."

"I cannot afford a castle or a mansion. Besides, I have kept my flat."

"That was very wise."

"I mean, where will you go?"

"Oh, don't worry about me."

"I mean, where are you going?"

Alden could not suppress a yawn. "Forgive me," he said. "It's been a long day. It's been a long haul. I'll be returning to the States in a few months. I've done what I was asked to do here, and I hope Svatopluk will take over at the office and that all of you will stay on. You'll be absorbed into the Ministry, most likely. They'll need you—you know where the bodies are all buried," he assured Franca.

"I want to go to America," Franca said.

"I'm sure you'll get there someday. Everybody seems to eventually. Tommy is coming to America, aren't you, boy? Aren't you, boy? See how happy that makes him?"

The dog had risen. He stretched and sniffed Franca's dressing gown and recalled she was no one of interest to him.

"I was happy *here*. I was happy working for you, Alden," Franca said. "The past three years have been the happiest time of my life. I shall never again be so happy."

"You don't mean that. It's very young of you to say that sort of thing. You should never attempt to predict what the past will turn out to have been. You can never know until later what was really going on at the time. Believe me," said Alden.

Franca shook her head.

"Well, I have to take Mr. T out before we turn in. That's one of the many things I'll least miss about this place, all the long walks just to get to a place where Tommy can walk."

"Don't go," Franca said.

"Tommy hasn't been out for hours. See how his ears perk when I say the word *out*? Don't tell me he can't speak English."

"Please let me come with you," Franca said.

"Not in your dressing gown and those light slippers. You'll catch a cold. It's a chilly night. You run off to bed, there's a good girl."

A FEW EVENINGS AFTER THIS, Ginger climbed the Tower stairs. She breathed hard; her new earrings swung and struck against her jaw. She was wearing the diamonds for practice; their swinging and striking the jaw aspect took some getting used to. Her ascent of the obliquely treaded, curving, and night-black stairway was made more difficult by the tray that she carried and held carefully level in front of herself which bore two rattling cups and saucers and two trembling spoons and an unsteady porcelain pot containing hot cocoa.

That motherless girl, Ginger was thinking. I must make an effort.

She had been packing up Becky's belongings. She had worked around Alden's schedule. He did not want to know anything; he did not wish to be consulted. Ginger, who in different circumstances would have most cheerfully rummaged among her sister-in-law's lovely things—her folded, lavender-scented linens and lingerie and scarves, her organized closets full of dresses and suits and shoes—was not really enjoying the job. She had slipped on a jacket or two and held skirts to her waist less to see how they looked than in an attempt to try on Becky's persona. Ginger had experienced a moment of pure panic extricating herself from the anaconda grasp of a long, dark jersey gown. She had thrown away all of Becky's half-used cosmetics: her dipped-into jars of creams, her partially dispensed atomizers of cologne and perfumes. Nothing was more haunting than a left-behind scent. Michal had been most helpful, hefting cartons out to the stable loft. He had uncomplainingly lifted the heavy boxes of books and had appreciated that he must not drop the collection of crystal Becky had purchased during their early days in Prague and had never used.

Alden had not wished to discuss the matter of Becky's left-behind jewelry other than to point out Becky had not taken anything he had given her. Why not? he had wondered; they were hers. Ginger said she probably meant for them to be distributed among the children, among Julie and the boys' wives when the time came—when Julie could be trusted not to have the sapphires reset for her nose and navel piercings, and, Ginger warned, any one of the boys was capable of making a disastrously inappropriate first marriage, so she would take a wait-and-see attitude initially and in the case of Grandmother Lowe's big diamond, there really should be something in writing to make clear that Glover would want his ring back. Oh, just see to it, Alden had said. I know, I'll send everything to Aunt Lily for safekeeping, shall I? Ginger said. Lily will hide them somewhere splendid until the time comes.

Ginger had mailed two shoeboxes packed with bracelets and rings and watches and necklaces and brooches, the shoeboxes heavily taped and very legibly addressed and numbered 1 of 2 and 2 of 2. She had not been able to do the math or summon the Czech in order to negotiate insurance on the packages, so she could only hope they would be all right as the parcels were tossed into a wire basket behind the counter of the main post office. Franca (who had been no fun at all on the earring-buying expedition, translating Mr. Pancner's long sentences with a few terse words) had been nowhere to be found prior to the post-office trek. Pavel, who sat at his needlework as if at the center of a web and who was Ginger's best informant on castle doings, said Franca had moved back to her flat that morning and would be working from the office now, putting herself back in the swim of things, he believed, and networking for a new position once her old Boss left.

Ginger labored on up the Tower stairway. She thought what an excellent idea to keep a teenager so remotely situated beyond eye- and earshot. She had lately been thinking of where Julie would next be placed. Lord knew where Alden was going to land. He was being quite impossible, talking about starting a fishing camp in the Yukon, but Julie had to be considered as well and Ginger was beginning to think she might very well have to take her. This late-night, impromptu cocoa party using the pretty chocolate pot and cups and the silver spoons had been laid on to let the girl see What Fun an aunt could be.

Light spilled from below the sill of Julie's door. Ginger eased one hand out from under the tray and brushed a knock and reached and released the latch. The tray shivered and her hand shot back to steady it as she nearly stumbled across the threshold, announcing, "It's the Cocoa Lady."

Julie and Svatopluk were in bed together. Julie pulled the sheet up to her chin and attempted to cover Svatopluk, but the bedclothes were disordered and had slithered off the side of the mattress and, somehow, had become anchored below a leg of the bed. There was a long tearing sound and a sudden release of the duvet as feathers flew up.

"Oh," said Ginger. "Just shut your eyes, Svatopluk, and pretend you're invisible. I have to sit down at once. Those stairs." She set her tray upon the floor, wondering by what miracle she had not dropped it. She tossed aside a drift of discarded clothes (exuberantly discarded, they looked to her not-inexperienced eye) from a chair seat and sank into it. She was sorry she had worn her new earrings for this. "Do I smell cigarette smoke?" she asked severely. "For shame, Julie. Such a filthy habit."

"Dad smokes," Julie spoke up. She rather welcomed the opportunity to change the subject. She brushed off Svatopluk's hand as it crept beneath the blanket and tapped out Careful against her thigh. He dragged a corner of the sheet back over himself.

"Not when he was your age," Ginger said. "Your dad started smoking in the army."

Svatopluk could not suppress a groan.

"Yes, your tender age," Ginger repeated. "Is your friend Sputnik aware of your age?"

"Don't call him my *friend* like that," Julie said. "*Or* Sputnik."

"I'll call him whatever I please. But that's neither here nor there. I must think. What, what, are we going to do about you, young lady?" Ginger settled back and crossed her legs, flinging off a flimsy silk scarf that had caught on her raised toe.

"I'll write to Ma. She wrote to me, you know. She'll say I can come to her when I write to her and tell her. I've been thinking of what to say to her, now that I'm not quite so mad at her. I don't know why I'm not quite so mad, but I'm not. Now I'm mostly sad. About everything."

"You will not join your mother."

"Yes, I so too will."

"They put young females like you to death in that part of the world," Ginger said. "Your mother cannot help you. No, Becky has most effectively removed herself from the parental equation."

"But you can't tell Dad. You'll get Svatopluk fired from his job and we're over here to help these poor people get back on their feet, Dad said."

"Svatopluk ought to be out on his ear," Ginger said.

"And Dad will be terribly upset and disappointed in me and he'll only blame himself and he's already so depressed. You can't do that to him," Julie said.

"Alden's in no position to deal with you," Ginger agreed. "What a pair of parents you have, Julie. But that's a subject for another day. All right. My heart has stopped racing. I don't know which was worse, those stairs or the shock of seeing you two. I'm not a young woman anymore." She regarded them with dislike for having made this clear to her. "I'm giving you five minutes to clear out, Svatopluk. I'll be waiting for you at the bottom of the Tower," she warned as she rose and took her leave. Her footsteps scuffed cautiously over the stone treads, feeling for each one; she was not about to give the pair of them the satisfaction of plunging to her death this particular evening.

"That was not very dignified," Svatopluk said. He motioned and Julie curled into his arms, her chin on his chest and her heart in his hand.

"And really bad timing," she said, for they had been about to bestir themselves and get dressed and wander down to the kitchen to fetch mugs of cocoa. They glanced, then, toward the prettily set tray abandoned on the floor, but neither made a move toward it now.

"I shan't forgive that woman," Svatopluk said.

"Well, it was inevitable that somebody would find us out. Somebody always does, in the end," Julie said.

"Tchah," said Svatopluk. He wondered where that woman had flung his trousers.

"Undignified, ill-timed, unforgiveable, inevitable," Julie repeated slowly, tapping out each syllable across Svatopluk's skin. "You know," she said, "I think we have just come up with an excellent working definition of Love." For she had been asking herself lately, whatever does it really mean, To love?

Summer, 1993

GINGER AND JULIE, AUNT AND NIECE, *were driving north in a small rental car along the west coast of Ireland. Ginger kept saying she could not get over how green everything was. Julie, feeling curiously peaceful now that everything had been decided, did not react to the repetition of this observation, as if she could not see for herself what a lush little country they had just landed in. According to Ginger, there would be several sights to see along the way: some windy cliffs, a low-lying blur of islands, and a funny little city where they would stop for lunch. They had had a nice enough lunch, and Ginger mentioned there was a cathedral, but Julie was keen to press on and she'd already seen enough of cathedrals elsewhere.*

Ginger told Julie the secret of driving on the wrong side of the road in places like Ireland. "Don't think in terms of left and right. Just think of where you, the driver, are relative to the middle of the road, and keep yourself centered," she said.

Julie said she understood what Ginger meant and so Ginger let her drive once they turned off what was purported to be the main road. Ginger leaned back to play passenger and she began to note the sheep wandering loose among all the loose stones. She wondered how much it would cost to buy one of the roofless cottages left behind by the edge of the ocean. Next stop, America, she kept saying.

"Look at that lake. They call them 'loughs' here. Maybe you'll pick up some Gaelic," Ginger said.

"Maybe."

"Pick it up and put it down again, I mean. Who speaks Gaelic these days? Crones and cranks, I don't doubt. Look, our turn is coming up. I just saw the sign."

They drove along an avenue of famous rhododendrons. Justly famous,
Ginger declared them, although the blossoms had already come and gone.

"Oh, it's just like a castle," Ginger said, as the abbey rose into view
above the fold of a vale.

"Sort of," Julie said. She was wise to the ways of castles.

"Pull over," Ginger ordered Julie, then.

"Why?"

"Before we get there."

"We are there."

"Not quite."

"Oh, all right." Julie eased onto a verge of velvet lawn.

"Listen to me," Ginger said. "Sending you away to Convent Board-
ing Summer School in Ireland was never meant to be a serious option. I
just wanted to make you think about the error of your ways. I only knew
about this place from research I conducted when Betsy first threatened to
marry Andy."

"Which she did."

"Well, yes, it was only an empty threat to let her know how I felt."

"So, can I marry Svatopluk?"

"Certainly not. Besides, has he even asked you?"

"No."

"Well, I give him credit for showing that much sense, at least. I hope you
weren't expecting him to ask."

"Uh-uh. I liked things just the way they were," Julie said. Then again,
she had liked the way things were before that, and before that.

"You're going through with this just to punish us all. Come home to
Kansas with me where you can be awful to me in more comfortable and fa-
miliar surroundings. Turn the car around," Ginger ordered. "Mind the rose
hedge, though."

"But I'm enrolled. And I've bought all that stuff."

They had sent away for crested blazers and plaid skirts and cotton-poly
blouses and the Prague shops had been full of stolid, flat-heeled shoes. Tilla
had sewn name tags onto Julie's knickers and knee socks and nightgowns,
and Julie had been intrigued by the sparseness and specificity of the posses-
sions she was to be permitted: a toothbrush and a Holy Bible and a hairbrush
and a tennis racket. Alden had asked her whether she hadn't signed up for

white-collar-prison summer school by mistake but Julie felt as if she were setting out to raise a new civilization from the simple ash siftings of an old one. They had even rationed the people she could know. She had had to submit the names and addresses of approved correspondents: her dad, soon to be back in New York; her mother, still in Libya; her brothers; her uncle Hap and aunts Lily and Ginger; and S. Palacky in Prague and someone named B. Hewson, there in Ireland. Ginger, proofing the list, hadn't asked questions or exercised her veto power. She had only been encouraged to find she had made the cut.

"Well, at least they know you're not a Roman Catholic. I'm not sure if they'll look upon you as a challenge or a lost cause. Just be polite when they mention religion, as they probably will."

"I'm very interested in religion."

"No you're not."

Julie drove on as Ginger wondered what had possessed her to let the child take the wheel. Julie parked neatly at the end of a straggling, angling line of cars and tossed her aunt the keys. Ginger understood, then, that she would be leaving alone.

But how nice the nuns were. They had laid on a tea for the arriving students in a small and rather underfurnished parlor; the Grand Family had left the Order the house but not the contents. However, the nuns were dressed in full sail. Ginger was glad to see they had not forsaken the veil. You never knew where you were with those business-suited nuns who wore wedding rings because they were the Brides of Christ. Ginger was never quite sure what was going on there and, uncharacteristically, she had never dared to ask.

The nuns called Julie their dear child and bade her to sign a book opened to a page of signatures which straggled and angled like the cars parked outside. Then, as if sure of her now, they sent her off to her dormitory room to wash her face and change into her uniform, shepherded by a freckled girl who seemed to believe she had drawn the long straw by being asked to show the American girl the ropes.

"Ought she not to have showed up in mufti?" Ginger asked. "But she reckoned it was her last chance for a while to wear her cowboy boots and her Lurex teddy."

"Oh no, we like to see the styles," said a sister.

"These girls nowadays take matters rather to the extreme," Ginger said,

feeling someone ought to speak up for fashion. "Indeed, I forget what my niece looks like beneath those kohl-lined eyes and the black lipstick, though I daresay she's a pretty little thing."

"Juliet is a lovely young creature," said the sister.

"Juliet?" asked Ginger. "Oh no, my niece is called Julie. Actually, her name is Becky but it's just as well she dropped that."

"Your niece wrote Juliet *in the book."*

Ginger had to see this for herself. She moved across the room, smiling at parents, pupils, nuns. She acquired a cucumber sandwich en route, crustless, crisp; there was nothing wrong with the catering here, although the standard might slip when no one was keeping an eye on them, she thought. Then again, a Jesus or a Mary seemed to be watching from every wall.

Ginger flipped the volume open to the last written-upon page and ran a figure down a trail of signatures (so many Bridgets and Tiffanys) and she found her, Juliet Lowe. The Julie *had been scrawled fluently; then the pen had paused as the big idea suddenly bloomed. The small, firm cross of a* t *had been appended, and so Juliet had been born of a union between martyrdom and romance.*

"Lord, what next?" Ginger asked, as she snapped the book shut.

About the Author

Nancy Clark lives in West Wilton, New Hampshire, where she is at work on a third and final novel about the Hill family, *July and August.*

A Note About the Type

Pierre Simon Fournier *le jeune,* who designed the type used in this book, was both an originator and collector of types. His services to the art of printing were his design of letters, his creation of ornaments and initials, and his standardization of type sizes. His types are old style in character and sharply cut. In 1764 and 1766 he published his *Manuel typographique,* a treatise on the history of French types and printing, on typefounding in all its details, and on what many consider his most important contribution to typography—the measurement of type by the point system.

Composed by Creative Graphics, Allentown, Pennsylvania
Printed and bound by Berryville Graphics, Berryville, Virginia
Book design by M. Kristen Bearse